LOVE'S SWEET REVENGE

ROSANNE BITTNER

sourcebooks
casablanca

Published by Sourcebooks Casablanca, an imprint of Sourcebooks,
Inc.
P.O. Box 4410, Naperville, Illinois 60567-4410
(630) 961-3900
Fax: (630) 961-2168
www.sourcebooks.com

Printed and bound in the United States of America.
LSC 10 9 8 7 6 5 4 3 2

This book is dedicated to all my faithful fans who wanted another story following Jake Harkner and his family. I am so grateful to everyone who loves these stories as much as I do. My devoted readers are what keep me going back to the computer to tell more stories. When I finished the second book of this saga (Do Not Forsake Me) and the Harkners were headed for Colorado, I knew I had to go with them, and I knew my fans would want to continue Jake's story and learn what happens after they settle into a new life there. Love's Sweet Revenge is that story… but it won't end there. I already know I need to write a fourth book. I have already titled it The Last Outlaw.

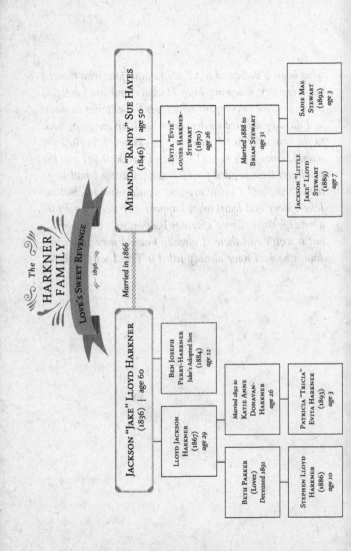

The
HARKNER FAMILY

Love's Sweet Revenge

1896

JACKSON "JAKE" LLOYD HARKNER (1836) | age 60

Married in 1866

MIRANDA "RANDY" SUE HAYES (1846) | age 50

BEN JOSEPH PERRY-HARKNER
Jake's Adopted Son
(1884)
age 12

LLOYD JACKSON HARKNER
(1867)
age 29

Married 1892 to KATIE ANNE DONAVAN-HARKNER
age 26

BETH PARKER
(Lover)
Deceased 1891

STEPHEN LLOYD HARKNER
(1886)
age 10

PATRICIA "TRICIA" EVITA HARKNER
(1893)
age 3

EVITA "EVIE" LOUISE HARKNER-STEWART
(1870)
age 26

Married 1888 to BRIAN STEWART
age 31

JACKSON "LITTLE JAKE" LLOYD STEWART
(1889)
age 7

SADIE MAE STEWART
(1892)
age 3

Foreword

Love's Sweet Revenge is the continuing saga of outlaw Jake Harkner, a ruthless man who walks on the edge of darkness, and the woman (Miranda) who taught him his true worth—and the meaning of love. For those who might not have read the first two books in this series, following is a short review of what has brought Jake and his family to events in this third book.

Book one, *Outlaw Hearts*, brings Jake out of his lost and lonely world into one of hope when, as a young wanted man with a brutal past, he meets the woman who completely changes his life. The story covers twenty-six years of Jake and Randy's struggle for peace and a normal life together as they raise a son and a daughter. Book two, *Do Not Forsake Me*, finds Jake living the dangerous life of a U.S. Marshal in "No Man's Land"—Oklahoma. Through both books, Jake and Randy's incredibly strong relationship spawns a solid and fiercely loyal family that will capture your heart and whose story of devotion and faith holds them together through the challenges that confront them because of Jake's outlaw past.

Love's Sweet Revenge finds Jake and his growing family finally settled into ranch life in the spectacular foothills of the Rocky Mountains of Colorado, but Jake's past reputation and his famous Colt .44s lead to a devastating shooting that takes Jake right back into the darkness that always threatens to consume him. This book is a gritty, hard-hitting story that brings to life the "real" American West and tells an unforgettable love story.

PART ONE

One

April 1896

JAKE LEANED AGAINST A ROUGH-HEWN SUPPORT POST on the sagging front porch of a line shack, taking in the magnificent scenery before him. It was so quiet this morning that even striking a match seemed loud. He lit a cigarette and inhaled deeply.

Since leaving a lawless Oklahoma Territory and his job as a U.S. Marshal, he still couldn't quite get over the fact that he shared a fifty-thousand-acre cattle ranch here in Colorado with his son. It took that much land and more to support enough cattle for a man to make a living, and the J&L had grown fast. Thank God Lloyd was finally fulfilling his own dream instead of riding with him in the dangerous job of hunting down criminals and murderers in No Man's Land. Oklahoma and the devastating events there were behind them now.

He shivered a little, wearing only his long johns against the chilly morning. He slowly exhaled, watching the cigarette smoke drift lazily into the yellow-blue sky. Behind him the purple, snowcapped Rocky Mountains rose like bastions of the West, and before him the foot-hills sloped downward to sparkling Horse Creek, which ran right through the middle of a vast green valley. They called it Evie's Garden, after Jake's beloved daughter. And far across that valley, he could see dark slopes of pine mixed with the white trunks of aspen, all spilling from purple heights like a waterfall. To the south end of the ranch lay a spectacular bowl of grass called Fire Valley because of how the sun could oftentimes light up the yellow grass.

Lloyd had bought most of this land from a widowed rancher's wife who could no longer take care of it. He'd added several thousand more acres by procuring adjacent government land in a special sale. With money inherited from his first wife, Lloyd paid the greater share for the J&L, and that was fine with Jake, because it would all be Lloyd's someday anyway. Jake was happy for him—damn happy. Lloyd was a loyal and steadfast son who'd given up too much for his father. He deserved happiness and success.

A few horses grazed in the valley below, mingled with some Durhams and a couple of Herefords. Both were meaty stock, and as the herd grew every year, so did profits. If Lloyd could manage to buy some government land to the south, where an abandoned fort now stood, the J&L would grow by another ten thousand acres.

He watched the valley begin to light up from the rising eastern sun, and a tiny lark landed on a thin branch that didn't look strong enough to hold even one feather. It tweeted sweetly, greeting the morning. Jake still had trouble trusting the peace and quiet he'd known here. At sixty years old, he was bone weary, and some days he hurt everywhere. Years of horrible abuse as a child, followed by an outlaw's life on the run that led to prison, and then the rugged life of a U.S. Marshal had taken a toll on his bullet-scarred body, let alone the inner scars and the brand of having murdered his own father.

Inside this dilapidated little line shack lay the woman who was responsible for pretty much one hundred percent of the peace he enjoyed now—the woman who'd taught him it was possible to forgive, both himself and others, the woman who'd taught him the meaning of love and who'd dragged him from the pits of hell to a new world, where a man could enjoy family, and hope.

Ten years younger than he and looking much younger than that, Miranda Harkner was still beautiful and slender and gentle and soft and loving, after all he'd put her through over the years. A bit to the south lay the lovely, sprawling log home he'd built for her. He'd bought her all the most modern appliances, including a huge coal cooking stove with two ovens, plenty of cooktop room for big meals, and a warming rack above that. She had two big iceboxes, kept cold by straw-packed ice brought down from the mountains by some of the ranch hands.

Randy loved to cook, but cleaning the coal heater and the ovens was a lot of work, so he'd hired a Mexican woman for that and to help with other housework. As far as he was concerned, his wife had been through enough hard work, and some of it without him. He'd made sure she had whatever furniture she wanted—fine china and hutches to store it in, her choice of rugs and antiques—and any lovely dresses she desired. She was still beautiful, and she complemented any dress she wore.

He closed his eyes and shook his head at how undeserving he was to be loved by such a woman. He wanted her to have everything good and beautiful he could give her. His heart ached at the thought that she still suffered anxiety whenever he was gone for long periods of time. This resulted from his absences when running from the law and the years he spent in prison—then having to ride away for days or weeks at a time as a marshal.

That anxiety was part of the reason she'd come with him this time to check the southern and western borders of the ranch. Early spring meant looking for broken fences or signs of rustling or squatters, and for cattle that might have been ravished by wolves or those that had not survived the cold and snows of winter.

This moment had to be the best he'd ever known in his long and battered life, right here, standing in a little weatherworn cabin in western Colorado, his wife asleep in a homemade pine bed inside, nestled into its feather mattress. More birds joined the little lark and flittered here and there, chirping their songs to spring. Soon the aspen leaves would open up and glitter in the wind, but he didn't doubt another fierce snowstorm would swoop down from the mountains across the foothills one more time before winter was truly done with its violent wrath. That was expected in the Rockies, but today smelled of real spring.

He jumped when he heard a rustling sound, his hand going to his hip in a reflex he couldn't quite get over, but this morning his gun wasn't there. A deer jumped out from behind a limber pine.

A deer.

Not an outlaw. Not a lawman. Not a drunk. Not an Indian. Not a cattle rustler. Not a prostitute. Not someone out to claim he'd killed Jake Harkner.

Just a deer.

"Jake?"

He straightened, taking a last drag on the cigarette and tossing it into the dirt beyond the cabin. He went inside to see Randy huddled under the quilts.

"What are you doing outside in your underwear?" she asked. "You'll catch your death. Come over here and warm yourself up beside me."

Jake grinned as he shut the door. "You might regret it."

"And why would I? I have never regretted inviting you to bed."

Jake laughed lightly and walked closer. "I've already taken care of a few things and cleaned up. I was out there enjoying the peace and the view, waiting for my love-starved wife to call me to her bed." He lifted the covers and crawled in beside her.

"Well, far be it for any wife of yours to be love-starved," Randy quipped. "I wonder sometimes if all men your age still enjoy sex as much as you do, or if it's just because you romped with too many wild women in your younger years and can't quite get away from the enjoyment."

"It could be the latter," he answered, pulling her into his arms, "or it could be because my wife is still a beautiful woman who makes me want her every time I look at her." He kissed her lightly. "And who can get pretty wild herself."

"Speaking of wild women, don't go hanging out with any when you make those trips to Denver. I know your penchant for befriending ladies of the night."

"If I did, you'd know it. You always do." He kissed her eyes.

"Mmm-hmm." Randy smiled softly as she traced a finger over his dark eyebrows, the thin scar down the side of his face. "The fact remains that you are still an extremely handsome, well-built man who could have any woman he wants," she answered, leaning up to kiss him again. "And a lot of women want you because you are famous and mysterious and notorious."

Jake frowned. "I'm mysterious and notorious?"

Randy fingered his still-thick, dark hair, now streaked with hints of gray. "You know darn well that's how some women see you."

Jake moved on top of her. "The only woman I want is right where she belongs—underneath me." He grinned as he ran a hand over her bare bottom. "And you're naked."

"Well, I was lying here thinking what a quiet morning it is and how nice it would be to have morning sex under these quilts with the man I have loved for going on thirty years, and knowing that no one and nothing can take him away from me ever again." She kissed the hairs of his chest where they peeked out from his partially buttoned long johns. "Where is the peppermint we always share in the morning?"

Jake reached past her to a nightstand and picked up a

stick of red-and-white peppermint, always part of their ritual when they had morning sex. He put one end in his mouth, and she took the other end. They sucked and licked at the candy until their lips met, ending in a deep kiss. Jake ran his hands into her golden hair. "I love the way this hair is all messy in the morning," he whispered near her ear, "love how warm you are."

He kissed her again, running his tongue suggestively deep and tasting more peppermint as he grasped her wrists and moved her arms over her head, pinning her there as he left her mouth and trailed to her neck, down to taste her breasts, moaning as though tasting something sweet and delicious. Every move he made was done gently, carefully, always with the realization that he could easily hurt her because of his big frame and how she sometimes seemed lost under him.

He moved his hands down her arms as he traced his kisses down her belly and to the inside of her thigh. He knew exactly how to bring out the woman in her, exactly how she liked to be touched…and tasted. He worked his magic in gentle circular motions until he felt her totally relax, then continued the magic touches that helped her bend to his will before they would become one. He kissed the scars that reminded him she'd nearly died from childbirth and the newer scars from four years ago when he thought he was losing her to cancer.

Not his Randy! He couldn't live without her. He couldn't take one more breath without this woman who'd saved his life, both physically and emotionally. She deserved his love and attention, deserved to be made love to in all the ways that pleased her.

He moved fingers inside her, feeling the moistness that meant she wanted more. He kept touching and tasting her, deliberately drawing her to him until he felt the pulsations of her climax. He quickly unbuttoned the front of his long johns to satisfy his own needs, moving inside of her while grasping her bottom and pleasuring her with every touch and every thrust of the mating ritual.

He groaned in his own aching need, still enjoying this woman who had given him so much and still wanting to give back. He always felt he couldn't get quite enough of her.

"Who do you belong to?" he whispered near her ear.

She arched upward rhythmically as she whimpered her reply. "Jake Harkner."

He gently pinned her to him. "Every inch of your beautiful body, *mi querida*."

For several minutes he pushed deep in sweet rhythm, needing this, aching with love and with feelings he'd never quite gotten used to after all these years. He still couldn't get over how good it felt to love and *be* loved. No longer cold, he perspired from their lovemaking. He felt her pull him in with another climax while calling out his name in sweet satisfaction. Finally, Jake could no longer hold back his own relief, glad he could still please her this way. Making love never got old for them, both of them eternally grateful to still be alive and together.

They lay there quietly, Jake moving to her side and letting her snuggle against him under the quilts. He'd once said he wanted the peace of being allowed to lie in bed with his wife until noon if he wanted. He'd found that peace. He could only pray that this time it would last.

"Let's not get up for a while," Randy told him. "Take today off. We have enough supplies to stay here for a day or two."

"Whatever my woman wants."

"How long before we get home once we do leave?"

"We are actually only about a day's ride away."

"I feel guilty staying longer. I miss the grandchildren, even though I know they're surely fine."

"Then quit worrying like a mother hen. It's your turn to enjoy the moment, so don't feel guilty. We're staying at least one more night."

"Katie and Evie can certainly handle things."

At the remark, Jake rolled onto his back, sighing deeply. "Do you think Evie is really okay now? I still worry about her."

"Jake, no woman who went through what she did could have a better husband than Brian to help her get over it. You've seen how happy they are now. Brian is a good and patient man. He could have a lucrative doctor's practice in a city somewhere, but he came here because he knew it would be good for Evie to be close to her family. And you don't know it, but Evie is carrying again. I think that's a pretty good sign they are doing all right."

"That's great news! Why didn't you tell me sooner?"

"Evie wanted to spring the news herself at Sunday dinner, so be sure to act surprised." Randy moved an arm across his chest. "She's a very, very strong woman, a survivor, just like you. You need to think only about your blessings, Jake Harkner, and blessing number five will be here in about six months."

He smiled sadly. "When those two little girls put their arms around my neck and give me kisses, I wonder sometimes what they will think of me when they find out the truth about Grandpa's past."

"They will always know and remember you the way you are now. Your past won't make a bit of difference, because they never knew the old Jake." Randy leaned up to meet his gaze. "And you *are* going to keep your promise that *all* the grandchildren will know *everything* when they get old enough to understand. We aren't going to hide anything from them like you did with Lloyd, Jake. We both know how that turned out."

Jake reached up to toy with her hair. "I can't very well avoid it, now that Jeff's book about me is in stores. According to Jeff's last letter, the *Evening Journal* is even serializing the story in weekly segments." He sighed. "I just worry that the past isn't through with me."

Randy rested her head on his chest. "Jake, that book needed to be written so people would understand, and we can set the money aside for the grandchildren. It's something you can leave them."

"Oh, I'm leaving them with something, all right. A legacy they have to live down."

"Nonsense. No trouble has come from any of it. If anything, it's made people in Longmont and Boulder and Denver and anyplace else we go look at you like some famous character they want to get to know."

He caressed her ash-blond tresses. "Yeah, well, maybe for all the wrong reasons."

Randy kissed his chest. "The Holmses and the Larsons are good neighbors, and a lot of people we've met since coming to Colorado truly want to be your friend, Jake."

"I find that questionable. My only real friends are my family, and maybe the men who work for me and Lloyd. Some of them might seem like worthless drifters to someone on the outside, but I know a good man when I see one, and Cole and Pepper and the rest of them are good men."

"I suppose, but that cattle buyer's wife who flirted shamefully with you when they visited the ranch a few weeks ago *also* wanted to be a *real* friend."

Jake frowned as he rolled her onto her back, then moved on top of her again. "You jealous of that cattle buyer's wife?"

"Maybe."

"Hell, you know I'm a good boy. There isn't a woman in all of Colorado who can hold a candle to you."

"And there isn't a woman in all of Colorado who can resist your gloriously fetching smile." Her eyes teared. "It's so nice to see you smile more often, Jake."

"Well, for once I have plenty to smile about."

Randy traced a finger over his lips. "I so love lying here in your arms, everything so quiet, me so safe right here with you." She wrapped her arms around his neck. "Make love to me again."

He kissed behind her ear. "That an order?"

"Yes. You're a hard man to give orders to, but you're so obedient when I get you in bed."

"I aim to please."

"And you please me just fine."

There was no foreplay this time, just a slower buildup of kissing and touching that led to the ecstasy of mating again. Jake took her with a little more deliberateness, his way of making sure she knew she was the only woman in his life, his only reason for existing. He loved this new peace they'd found, prayed it would not end this time and that nothing could separate them ever again. He still had trouble with blaming himself for the hell his son went through after learning about Jake's past and losing him for the four years he spent in prison—or the guilt over what Evie suffered at the hands of his enemies back in Oklahoma.

But that was all behind them now. Surely the worst was finally over.

Two

PETER BROWN SET HIS PIPE ASIDE WHEN HE HEARD THE jangle of the doorbell. As he rose from the mahogany-colored leather chair behind the desk in his den, his wife walked past the doorway. The several slips under the taffeta skirt of her deep blue dress rustled with each step.

"I'll get it," she told Peter.

"We have servants for that," he reminded her.

"I am perfectly capable of answering a door, Peter," she answered.

Peter smiled sadly. After losing his first wife, and then falling in love with the wrong woman back in Oklahoma—a woman who would never belong to anyone but Jake Harkner—he felt protective and possessive of Treena, a woman in her forties who was quite beautiful and who understood lost love. She'd been widowed for two years when he married her within a year after returning to Chicago—a move he'd made in an effort to forget Randy Harkner.

"Peter, it's Jeff," his wife called to him.

Peter walked into the hallway, over the oriental rugs that decorated the hardwood floor of the mansion he'd purchased on the north side of the city, wanting to afford Treena every luxury he could. She came from wealth, and his law business was thriving. Treena was sweet and understanding and just as lonely as he when they first realized they were both ready to love again.

Peter grinned and put out his hand to greet Jeff Trubridge, also now a married man since coming back to Chicago. Their friendship was a strange one indeed, created by the very wild adventure of being brought together because of their association with U.S. Marshal Jake Harkner back in Guthrie, Oklahoma—an experience neither of them would ever forget.

"Jeff!"

Jeff grasped his hand, smiling but also looking oddly concerned. "Peter, it's good to see you. It's been a year since we got together for dinner after I won that writing award."

"And a well-deserved award it was. What brings you clear up here today? Aren't you usually running around the city, digging up stories for the *Evening Journal*? And, by the way, I read your column every Sunday. Your articles about politics are very well written."

"Thank you." Jeff turned and hung his hat on a rack beside the door.

"Don't tell me you're here to ask me about *my* political viewpoints," Peter joked. "I'm a lawyer, which means I can't afford to take sides. I never know when a wealthy democrat, or a notorious councilman who is getting paid under the table, or some republican senator who is actually honest will need my services."

Jeff adjusted his wire-rimmed spectacles, laughing lightly at the remark. "An *honest* politician? There aren't many of those, either in Illinois or in Washington."

Both men laughed, and Jeff thanked Treena as she took his hat. "Nice to see you again, Treena."

"And you," Treena replied as she hung Jeff's hat on a rack beside the door.

Peter led the young writer down the hallway.

"Actually, I wish I *were* here about politics, Peter," Jeff said as he walked beside him, "but it's something—I don't know—kind of personal in a way. Just something I wanted to share and see what you think."

Peter noticed Jeff held a rolled-up piece of paper in his hand. "Don't tell me you're serving me an eviction notice."

Jeff grinned. "From what I see here, you can well afford your home," he answered. "This is all really beautiful, Peter. And you look happy."

"I am." Peter turned to put an arm around Treena. "My wife saw this place and said *I want it*, so I bought it for her." He leaned over and kissed her cheek. "Have Helen bring us some brandy, will you, dear?"

"Of course." Treena nodded to Jeff and left them.

Peter watched her walk away, admiring her still-slim waist and her auburn hair. She had lovely skin and green eyes. But her hair wasn't golden, and her green eyes didn't sometimes look gray. She wasn't Randy Harkner.

He led Jeff into his office and closed the door. "Have a seat, Jeff. You're looking very good…very happy."

"I *am* happy. Anna is going to have a baby."

"Well! Congratulations! When is she due?"

"In about five months. After she delivers and she's well, I'd like to have you and your wife to dinner and let you see the baby."

"I'd like that very much. Children are something I've never been blessed with. My first wife couldn't have children, and, of course, Treena won't be having more. I guess I will have to be a father vicariously through my good friends."

Jeff took a seat. "And I thank you for that." He sighed as he sat down, sobering. "I, uh…I guess maybe it wasn't necessary to come all the way up here and bother you with this. It's just that…well, you and I share a certain closeness with Jake and Randy Harkner that few people—actually almost *no* other people besides Jake's family share. After all, you're the one responsible for getting Jake's sentence reduced, and you're handling his trust, and the book I wrote about him is doing pretty well."

Peter frowned. "This is about *Jake*? Has something happened to him? Is Randy all right?"

Jeff met his gaze, and Peter realized he'd given himself away. Jeff was the only person out of all of Peter's friends who knew how much Peter had loved Randy Harkner. That love still showed itself sometimes, and Peter felt angry with himself for allowing it. He had a wife now, and he truly loved her.

"Nothing like that," Jeff told him. "As far as I know, Jake and the family are all fine. I'm just a little worried about something, and I thought maybe you could advise me whether I should wire Jake. I hate like hell to worry him or Randy. I think they're finally happy and at peace, but a man like Jake will probably never be able to completely rid himself of the past."

Someone knocked on the door.

"Come in, Helen."

A heavy-set serving maid came inside, carrying a silver tray with a crystal bottle of liquor and two small glasses. "Your wife said to bring this for you, Mr. Brown," she told Peter.

"Thanks, Helen. I'll pour the drinks."

The maid nodded and left, closing the door behind her. Peter uncorked the liquor and poured some into each glass, then handed one to Jeff. He walked behind his desk and sat down in the leather chair, taking his glass of brandy and holding it up as though in a toast. "I take it we both need a drink before you tell me why you are here."

Jeff held up his own glass. "It wouldn't hurt."

"Well then, here's to your new baby to come, and to Jake and Randy's new life in Colorado."

Both men sipped their brandy, and Peter leaned back in his chair. "So, what is the news?"

Jeff sighed, taking another sip and then leaning forward to set the glass on the edge of Peter's desk. He unrolled the paper still in his hand. "This came across my desk yesterday. Since I'm the one who became close to Jake and was at that shoot-out when he rescued his daughter from those bastards who'd abducted her, my boss gave me the assignment to write the article about this." He handed the paper to Peter.

Frowning, Peter unrolled the paper and read it.

Lansing, Michigan. Mike Holt, a survivor of the infamous eighteen and ninety-two gun battle with Marshals Jake and Lloyd Harkner at Dune Hollow in Oklahoma, was freed from federal prison April first, eighteen and ninety-six, after winning an appeal. A judge has ruled that there is no real proof that Holt himself brought any physical harm to Harkner's daughter, Evita Stewart. His conviction was changed to aiding and abetting an abduction, and it was determined that Holt's three years in prison constituted enough time served.

Peter closed his eyes. "Jesus," he muttered.

"Yeah." Jeff reached out and grasped the glass of brandy, leaning back and taking another sip. "Of course, being Jewish, I wouldn't use that term. For me, it's more like Holy Moses." He smiled sadly, staring at the glass of brandy in his hand. "I was there, Peter. I can't say Holt ever raped Jake's daughter, but he sure as hell didn't try to stop the others from doing so. What bothers me is that I remember the man threatening Lloyd. The day of the incident, Lloyd shot down his brother, because he was trying to run. Lloyd shot him in the back. None of the men there that day will testify to it. They were all so furious over what happened to Jake's daughter that they didn't care, but Holt isn't going to forget. I remember the look in his eyes when he said he'd get Lloyd for what happened. He meant every word of it." He shook his head. "I can't blame Lloyd for it. He saw what they did to his sister, and he was crazy with a need for revenge. And as a deputy marshal, he had a right to shoot down a culprit trying to run from the law."

Peter nodded. "And now you're afraid Holt will head for Colorado."

Jeff rested his elbows on his knees. "Jake is pretty

famous now because of my book—not that he wasn't already pretty well known all over the country. The man is a legend, and everybody in Guthrie knows he moved back to Colorado. That kind of notoriety will make it easy for Mike Holt to find him…and father and son are stuck together like glue. All Holt has to do is find Jake, and he'll find Lloyd. I really, really hate the thought of the past rearing its ugly head again for either one of them."

Peter rubbed at his eyes. "Or for Randy."

"Yeah. Not many women would put up with or survive what that woman has."

Peter took another swallow of brandy himself. "Jake thinks Holt went to prison for a good twenty years. He probably figured he wouldn't live long enough to see the man get out."

"Well, even at twenty years, *Lloyd* would likely still be alive, but maybe after that long, Holt wouldn't care anymore. The fact remains it's been only four years since everything that happened, and it's all still pretty fresh. I just wanted to know if you think I should warn Jake."

Peter closed his eyes. He could see her as though she were standing right in front of him: Randy Harkner, small, beautiful, elegant, gentle, totally devoted to one man. He could see Jake: tall, broad, rugged, dark, dangerous—a total contrast to his wife. And he could see Lloyd: built just like his father, sometimes getting that same look of danger in his eyes, his hair long like an Indian's, his smile handsome and bright, just like Jake's.

"What a pair father and son are," he said aloud. "And what a pair Jake and Randy make. I wonder what life out there in the foothills of the Rockies is like for them. God knows men like Jake and Lloyd fit that country. And then there's that bit of a woman they call wife and mother, living in wild country where there are wolves and grizzlies and…" He glanced at Jeff, realizing he'd given himself away again. "A woman like Randy belongs in a house like this one, going to teas and concerts and the best restaurants in the better parts of a big city. In spite of the life she's lived as an outlaw's wife and then a lawman's wife, sometimes poor, sometimes on the run, sometimes completely alone while her husband would leave her, and those four years he was in prison... in spite of all that, she can be as gracious as the finest, highborn woman of society. She'd fit right in with the upper class, yet there she is, living in a log home in the Rocky Mountains with a man as far from high class as they get."

Jeff stared at the glass of brandy in his hand. "And he loves her like no other man could. I've been to the J&L, Peter. I've seen their huge log home. Randy has the most modern conveniences a woman can have on a remote ranch. The whole house is wrapped with a broad veranda, wicker chairs, rockers, porch swings. The porch is in turn surrounded with rosebushes. You probably remember how much Randy loved roses. Jake has made sure she has plenty of them to fuss over. And he hired a Mexican woman to do all the heavy chores."

Peter nodded. "Good. That's good."

Jeff sighed. "Randy is very comfortable, Peter. Their home is the finest house she's ever lived in, and it's truly a home of their own. The J&L is magnificent. Randy and Jake's house has several bedrooms to accommodate guests, and there are almost always one or two kids staying overnight there. The great room has a vaulted ceiling and a huge stone fireplace at each end. Randy has lovely furniture and a beautiful oak hutch filled with Queen Anne and Hepplewhite antiques. She has two Tiffany lamps, and two of her front windows are stained glass at the top. The polished wood floor is decorated with a beautiful Aubusson carpet in shades of green. Jake sits in a big, red stuffed chair near that fireplace, and he just... fits the big room. You know how he is."

"Oh, yes, I know very well how he can take over a room when he walks into it."

"Well, you'll get a kick out of this. He sits in that chair with his two little granddaughters on his lap, and he tells them stories."

"Stories?"

"Reads them fairy tales."

Peter had just started to swallow some brandy, and he nearly spit it out when he broke into all-out laughter. "*Jake?*"

"Jake."

Both men laughed hardily. "Oh, Lord help us!" Peter continued laughing as he spoke. "God knows the kind of stories he *could* tell them! They sure wouldn't be fairy tales! I'm surprised he hasn't sent them screaming to their mothers." He poured them each another drink. "I *have* to visit them, because that is something I want to see!" He sobered a little. "Randy writes us occasionally and asks us to come and visit. She wants to meet Treena." He slugged down the second drink, then just stared at the glass. "Is she really all right, Jeff?"

"You know Jake. As much as you love her, Peter, he loves her more. She is his whole reason for existing, and he is in turn her whole world. She's protected and loved. Jake has her right up there on that pedestal he's always set her on. She wouldn't be happy living any other way, and you know it."

Peter absently twirled the glass between his fingers. "Of course I know it." Peter sighed deeply, running a hand through his hair. "Old memories can really sting sometimes, Jeff."

"I know. I have some of my own. Half living with them for so long left its mark."

Peter met his gaze. "I think you should tell Jake about Mike Holt. He and Lloyd have a right to know so they can at least be on the lookout."

Jeff nodded. "I think so, too. Of course, a man like

Jake is always on the lookout anyway. He'll never quite get over wondering if someone is out there ready to make a name for himself."

Peter grunted a laugh. "God help the man who thinks he can take down Jake Harkner."

Jeff smiled and nodded. "I've held those guns, and I've ridden with the man. He's the best friend anyone could ask for when you're sincere and honest…but you sure as hell don't want to be his enemy." He rose. "I'd better get back. I have a cab waiting for me. You can keep that paper if you want. I'll get more details." He sighed. "In the meantime, I'll send a wire to Denver. A courier rides out to Jake's ranch once a week with news. I'll be sure the wire says someone should go out there right away. If I wait till it hits the papers, it might be two weeks or more before Jake would know. He gets the *Denver Post* in bunches every couple of weeks. He lets Randy read them and pick out anything he might care about. Jake isn't a man with the patience to sit and read for hours."

Peter also rose. "No doubt about that. There isn't much of *anything* Jake Harkner has patience for, except for his wife and those grandchildren." He walked around the desk and shook Jeff's hand again. "We had quite a time back in Guthrie, didn't we?"

"We sure did. You don't run with a man like Jake Harkner without it leaving some pretty vivid memories." He squeezed Peter's hand. "And you don't meet up with a woman like Randy without her leaving one hell of an impression."

Peter didn't reply. He felt as though someone was physically squeezing his heart. He released Jeff's hand and headed for the door. "Thanks for the information, Jeff. And if you need me for anything—anything at all—let me know. I'm glad you told me about this. Please keep me updated on anything you find out, will you?"

"You know I will."

Peter opened the door and walked out with Jeff, who first took his hat from the stand at the door. The two men looked at each other once more, vivid memories swimming between them. "You let me know about that baby," Peter said.

"I will." Jeff turned and left.

Peter watched him climb into the carriage that had brought him there, and the driver snapped a small whip, urging the horse into a trot. The horse's hooves echoed on the brick driveway as they drove off, reminding Peter of another horse—a big, black horse that held a big, well-armed man back in Guthrie, Oklahoma. In some ways, it seemed a lifetime ago.

"Peter? Are you all right?"

He turned to see his wife standing there, watching him. "What did Jeff want? You look upset."

Peter smiled sadly and reached out to embrace her. "He just wanted some advice on something," he told her. "Nothing to worry about. Why don't you go start changing for that benefit we're attending later? I'll be up in a minute."

Treena leaned up and kissed him lightly. "All right. But you are clearly upset. When you're ready, you tell me what's going on, Peter Brown."

He kissed her cheek. "I will. I promise. Go on with you." He watched her turn and go up the wide, winding staircase to the bedrooms, then walked back to his office, going over to a bookcase. He took out a hardbound book, staring at the title.

Jake Harkner: The Legend and the Myth.

Legend for sure, but no myth. The man was very real, and Peter had no doubt he could still be very dangerous—and ruthless. If Mike Holt had any intentions of finding revenge for the shoot-out at Dune Hollow, he'd be wise not to act on them. Jake Harkner might be a little older, but a man like that never got softer, and he sure as hell still knew how to use those guns.

Three

LLOYD LED HIS HORSE INTO ONE OF SEVERAL whitewashed board-and-batt barns on the J&L, weary from a long day of herding cattle into pens and sorting cows and their calves from the breeding bulls. Among the male calves, some would be castrated and fattened up for slaughter. Grown steers ready for market were separated into their own holding pens in preparation for the new herd that would be coming in after spring roundup. They'd already found one bull they called Gus, the meanest of them all. The ornery animal had nearly managed to gore Lloyd's horse earlier in the day.

"Ole Gus is one mad bastard, Sammy," Lloyd told his horse, patting the animal's flank. "Good thing you're so good at what you do. Things will get a lot livelier once we head out for roundup and bring in more cows and their calves. There's a lot of hard work ahead for you and me both."

Cattle splintered into every direction through the winter, and finding all of them on fifty thousand acres was a daunting task every spring. Lloyd thanked God that he'd found several new calves already, all healthy and alive. It always hurt to find those who'd not survived the wolves and the deep snows. Every time he came across a dead bull or steer it made him feel lonely. It brought back memories of Beth, buried back in Guthrie after bleeding to death from a miscarriage. At least he had Stephen, a part of Beth he could keep forever. Sometimes he had to fight the old urge to blame Jake for all the years he lost with Beth, but it was really his own fault for running off in anger when he learned the truth about his father's past. If he'd stayed…

Lloyd forced his mind away from that old pain. He wondered at his own ability to feel sorry for a dead animal when he could shoot a man down with no remorse. Routing out the scum of the earth day in and day out as a U.S. Marshal did that to a man. It was even easier for Jake, who long before becoming a marshal had lost count of how many men had met the wrong end of his gun. Yet there was so much goodness in him, and a kid couldn't ask for a better father. When he feared he was losing Jake to death after the shoot-out back in Guthrie, that's when he knew more than ever how much the man meant to him. He'd not leave him again—ever.

"Live and learn, Sammy," he mumbled, wondering why he was talking to a horse that didn't understand a word he said. "Some of us are slower at it than others." If only Jake had told him the truth about his childhood and what led him down the wrong path in his early years, it might all have been different. But as a father himself now, he was beginning to understand how hard it would be to tell his own son he'd killed his own father and lived the first thirty years of his life as a wanted man.

He threw his saddle over the sidewall of the stall, then removed the blanket. "I'll give Stephen the chore of rubbing you down, boy," he told the gelding, proceeding to remove the animal's bridle. "Time to teach the younger ones how to run a ranch, since it will be theirs someday."

Life was good here. He was more than happy that his days of riding beside Jake as a marshal were over. So was Katie. And Evie. He sobered at the thought of what had happened to his sister back in Oklahoma. She was damn strong, strong deep inside like their mother, and tough like Jake. They didn't come any stronger than his parents. But Katie—she was growing stronger every day, too.

God knew a woman had to be strong and determined to put up with the likes of him and his father. It felt good to know that his marriage to Katie became more solid every day since coming here to Colorado, their love becoming deeper and more devoted. He was finally able to see Katie for who she was—a sweet, caring woman who knew how to please a man and who was a good mother to his son, Stephen, and to the baby girl they'd had together. He was finally able to stop comparing her to Beth.

He walked over to take a bag of feed from a shelf on the opposite side of the stall. "I'll give you a few oats, Sammy, but not too much." He hoisted the sack to his shoulder and carried it back to the horse, grunting a little as he set it down and untied the bag. "I don't want you getting the colic," he muttered. He lifted it again, pouring some into a trough.

"I like watching those muscles at work," a female voice spoke up as he lowered the bag of oats to retie it. The voice startled him a little. He whirled to see his wife standing outside the stall.

"*Katie?* Where in hell did you come from?"

"Cole Decker rode in earlier and said you were on your way back. I know this is the barn where you always put Sammy up." She put her hands on her hips and swayed a bit seductively. "I took our little Tricia over to Evie's so we could be alone. Stephen and Ben are out in the south pasture helping Terrel Adams corral a few breeding cows. I've been watching you from the loft."

Lloyd grinned. "You little vamp. You sure were awful quiet climbing down that ladder." He carried the bag of oats out of the stall and stopped to close the stall gate, then set the oats aside and grabbed her close, whirling her around and planting a long kiss on her. He moved his lips to her neck. "Honey, I need a bath and a shave and—"

"I don't care. You can do all that when you come to

the house. I have a couple of blankets laid out in the loft. All you have to do is put that board over by the door through the handles so no one can get in and then come join me."

Surprised, Lloyd set her on her feet. "Are you serious?"

Katie darted away. "I most certainly am." She ran over to the ladder, lifting her skirt to show most of one leg before she scurried up the narrow wooden steps.

"Sweet Jesus," Lloyd muttered. He hurried over to the barn door and closed it, picking up the board used to slip through the handles to keep it secured. He practically ran to the ladder, climbing three rungs at a time up to the loft to see Katie's dress was already off. He stood there a moment just looking at her soft, white skin and the way her bright-red hair spilled over her shoulders. Her blue eyes glittered with love as she unlaced her camisole. He loved her colorful glow—all white and red and blue, and in the most pleasing places...pink.

"You sure, baby? I really do need a bath, and—"

She opened the camisole to reveal full breasts, pink nipples peaked from desire. She proceeded to drop her underpants. "I'm sure." She sat down on a blanket spread out over the straw and lay back. "Come here, Lloyd Harkner."

It didn't take Lloyd long to undo his gun belt, throw it aside, and get his clothes off. He knelt down and drank in the sight of her as he ran his hands up her legs, over her belly. He plied her breasts, scooting his knees between her legs and bending close to taste her taut nipples. He kissed her neck, licked her behind the ear, moved to her mouth, and she opened her lips to greet his tongue. Lloyd kissed her hungrily, apologizing then for wanting to just get inside her without foreplay.

"I'll allow it this time," she told him with a sexy smile, "but when you're through, I demand that we do it again—and you have to pleasure me first."

He kissed her over and over. "God, Katie, this is so sweet of you," he groaned. "I'm so sick of nothing but cows and horses and men who smell worse than the animals. I hope I don't smell that bad."

"You always smell good. Right now you smell like a fresh stream of water."

"Yeah, well, I bathed in a creek the best I could just yesterday, so I wouldn't be too hard to be around when I got back."

Katie smiled. "You're never hard to be around." She gasped when he rammed himself inside of her with pent-up need. She arched to him in response, leaning up and capturing his mouth with her own.

They moved in wild rhythm, and it wasn't long before Lloyd's life spilled into her, life he hoped would again take hold, and they would have their second baby together, another brother or sister for his Stephen, another baby for his precious Katie, who'd lost a baby girl and a husband before they met and married.

They both needed this. They'd both lost one love and found another. And they'd both come to understand that that was okay.

"I'm sorry, Katie. I just couldn't hold it in. It's been too long." He raised up on his elbows. "And you're so damn beautiful."

Katie pulled at the leather tie that held his waist-length black hair at his neck. She let his hair fall down and surround her. "Lloyd Harkner, your skin is so dark next to mine." She fanned his hair out even more. "Are you sure you don't have Indian blood?"

"Not that I know of, unless some Indian stole my mother away one night, and she never told Pa."

Katie laughed. "I'd like to see any man steal Randy Harkner away from Jake."

Lloyd grinned. "Yeah, any man who made off with my mother would be one sorry sonofabitch." He kissed her eyes. "It would be the same if some man dared to touch my Katie."

She smiled, leaning up to kiss his chest. "For the rest of my life, you'll be the only man touching me."

"You bet." He kissed her, groaning with renewed want. "I can't believe you did this, you brazen little hussy," he told her, kissing her throat again.

She ran her hands over his arms and shoulders. "Why, Mr. Harkner, I declare, you are the most handsome man in all of Colorado," she told him with a teasing fake southern accent. "You make me feel like a tiny little flower lying under a big oak tree, or perhaps a shivering, helpless captive of a wild Indian, with all that hair and that skin tanned dark. I suppose you intend to ravish me now."

Lloyd laughed. "Oh, I intend to do just that." He met her mouth again, moving a hand to secret places. "How much time do we have?" he asked between kisses.

"Evie said she'd keep Tricia—"

A kiss.

"—as long as necessary," Katie answered.

Another kiss.

"You mean she knows what we're up to?" he asked, kissing her breasts.

"Of course she does."

"Good Lord, she's going to tease me something awful when Mom has us all over for Sunday dinner."

"No more than we'll tease your parents about riding the line alone all this time."

Lloyd leaned down and kissed her hungrily again, grasping her face in big, strong hands that could so easily break her, yet gently adored her instead. "You're one wild woman, Katie Harkner."

"And I love a wild man," she answered.

Before they could act on their desire to make love a second time, someone yelled to Lloyd from outside the barn.

"Lloyd! You in there cavorting? Your parents might need you!"

Lloyd wilted a little and sighed. "Now what?" He moved off Katie and leaned down to give her one more quick kiss. "I'm sorry, honey."

They both sat up. "Go see what he wants," Katie told him. "Here." She handed him a towel she'd brought with her, and he cleaned himself as best he could.

"Lloyd!" one of the men shouted again.

"Just a minute!" Lloyd yelled, frowning with irritation. He stood up and pulled on his long johns. "Sounds like Pepper," he told Katie. He buttoned his long johns and hurried over to the loft door, swinging it open to see three ranch hands on horseback waiting below. He directed his words to the one called Pepper. "What the hell do you want?"

Pepper grinned. "What're you doin' in your underwear, boy?"

"None of your goddamn business, you dirty-minded old sonofabitch. What's going on?"

Pepper looked over at Cole Decker and Vance Kelly, and all three men chuckled. Pepper, whose real name no one knew, looked back up at Lloyd. "Well now, I hate to interrupt, but Vance here has a message some special courier from Denver brought out and gave to your sister a few minutes ago. She looked kind of upset when she read it—said to give it to you. And that ain't all. The courier—that fella called Jason Hawk from Denver—he said he's pretty sure some rustlers might be headed toward the western edge of the J&L. Your pa is in that area. Anybody knows Jake Harkner can handle a few rustlers, but your mother is with him, so between that and whatever is in this message, we didn't have much choice but to come and get you."

"Shit," Lloyd grumbled. "Wait up!" he yelled down to them. He turned to Katie. "I'm sorry, but I'd better go see about this. And here you had things all set up for us to spend some time together."

"It's okay."

Lloyd saw the anxious look on her face, like the one she used to get when he had to ride away for days or weeks at a time as a marshal, never knowing if he'd make it back. "This is different, baby. It's just a few rustlers, and we have extra men. If my mother wasn't out there—"

"I understand. We'll pick up where we left off when you get back and the kids are sleeping." She gave him a weak smile.

"Sure we will." Lloyd hurriedly dressed, then strapped on his gun belt. Katie sat there wrapped in a blanket, and he leaned down to give her a quick kiss. "I love you, Katie-girl. I should have said it sooner."

"And I love you. Be careful, Lloyd."

"Hey, it's me and Pepper and Cole. I'll tell Vance to stay here and keep a lookout. We'll be fine. If there are rustlers out there, they will definitely regret trying to steal from us." He put on his wide-brimmed hat. "And if Jake gets to them first, they won't live long enough to regret *anything*."

He scurried down the ladder and, needing a fresh horse, quickly saddled a roan gelding in a nearby stall. He led the horse to the door and removed the board that kept it closed, then mounted up and ducked his head as he rode out of the barn.

Katie stood up and hurried over to the loft door, staying to the side and out of sight.

"Did Jason say how many there were?" Lloyd was asking.

"Quite a few, maybe six or eight," Cole answered. "Jason has rode all over this country, and he knows what looks right and what doesn't. He said this particular thing didn't look right, because he knows this time of year we'd never be herding cattle to Denver yet. Lord knows Jake can handle six or eight men on his own, but when your ma is with him, that might put a kink in things."

"Where did you say he spotted them?"

"He noticed them when he was up on Echo Ridge near the place you call Evie's Garden. The rustlers were south of there, camped like they belonged there and weren't afraid of bein' caught."

"Damn," Lloyd swore. "That's hours away. We'll have to ride hard and fast."

"Yes, sir," Vance answered. "I'll bet them men have no idea they might run into Jake Harkner. They'll get one big surprise if they do." He handed out an envelope. "And here's the message the courier left with your sister. She said you should see it right away."

Lloyd's horse skittered sideways as he took the envelope. He quickly opened it. From the loft, Katie watched his whole demeanor change. She could feel it. He removed his hat and shook his long hair behind his back. He'd not retied it. "Did my sister seem okay? Was she real upset?" he asked.

Katie's heart pounded with wonder at what was in the note.

"She seemed shook up," Vance told him, "but her husband came home from helpin' that neighbor kid who broke his arm. She seemed calmer once he got there. What's in the note?"

Lloyd shoved the note into a pocket inside his denim jacket. "One of the bastards who was at Dune Hollow is out of prison, and he'll be after my ass for sure."

"Oh no!" Katie groaned.

"First things first," Lloyd continued. "Let's go catch us some rustlers."

"Jason said it looked like they were headed south toward Denver," Vance told him.

"And by now Pa is headed south, too. He'll come around the south border and head on up to the house.

Hard to say if he's ahead of them or behind them."
He studied the very weatherworn and life-worn Vance
Kelly, who was about Jake's age and who Jake suspected
had a very colored past but judged him to be a depend-
able man. "You stay here, Vance, and keep a watch on
things. I'm not sure what this sonofabitch who just got
released might do. I killed his brother, and he swore to
get revenge, so you stay close to my wife and my sister."

Katie's heart pounded with dread at the words.

"You can count on me," Vance answered. "I've
handled my share of men like that."

"My wife is up in that loft. You wait for her to come
down and follow her back to the house; and don't you
make any jokes about us being up there, understand?
You be respectful."

"Jesus, Lloyd, you don't have to tell me that."

Lloyd looked at the other two. "We'll ride all goddamn night if we have to—try to cut them off before
they run across my father. They'll be going a lot slower
than us and will stop somewhere tonight, so we might be
able to catch up with them by tomorrow." He kicked his
horse into a hard run, and the other two men followed.

Katie watched them ride off. Pepper and Cole were
good men, older like Jake but solid and able. Jake
suspected Pepper and Vance were former outlaws, but
then, so was Jake Harkner, so he knew men like that
better than any other kind. He read men pretty good
and seemed to sense which ones could be trusted. So
did Lloyd.

"Take care of him," she whispered in a quick prayer.
She hurriedly dressed. She felt embarrassed at having to
walk out there and face Vance Kelly, but there was no
getting around it.

It seemed they would never be able to totally relax and
enjoy the new life they'd found out here. She supposed
she would just have to get used to the fact that where

there was a Harkner man, there was almost always some kind of danger, even without wearing a badge. All they needed was the name, and guns were required. But she loved Lloyd, and she'd learned to live with the danger.

Besides, this was nothing compared to what happened back in Oklahoma. At least not yet.

Four

"YOU GETTING SORE IN ALL THE WRONG PLACES FROM too much riding?" Jake turned his horse to face his wife.

"It's not the *riding* that's got me sore in all the wrong places," Randy teased, taking up the reins of their packhorse.

Jake laughed in the teasing way he had of making her feel embarrassed.

"On a trip like this, a man your age should be too tired for frivolity, Mr. Harkner."

"Don't underestimate what a man my age is capable of, Mrs. Harkner." Jake winked at her as he lit a cigarette.

"In your case, I don't underestimate *anything*," Randy shot back.

"You're the one who kept offering herself to me," Jake teased. He grinned and turned his horse, heading down a pathway toward the valley below.

Randy followed behind him, pulling the packhorse along. "Just don't be underestimating *me*, dear husband. I've been just fine on this trip. I'd rather put up with the hard ground and lack of comforts than be home worrying about what's happening when you're gone for too long at a time. We went through enough of that back in Oklahoma."

"Well, being a marshal back there proved more dangerous than all the grizzlies and bobcats and rustlers here, but even so, I'm not bringing you along every time I do this. We needed the time together, but these trips are too dangerous for you."

"Are you giving me orders?" she called out.

Jake kept the cigarette at the corner of his mouth when he glanced back at her. "You mean by saying you can't come with me next time?"

"I mean exactly that."

He turned away. "Then I am giving you orders. What if something goes wrong? You're a distraction. I might not be as alert as I should be."

Randy smiled. "I *like* being a distraction. That means you're still attracted to me. A woman my age needs to know that."

"Hell, you're ten years younger than I am. Maybe I'm the one who needs to know he's still wanted."

"Half the women in Colorado want you."

"Easy, Midnight." Jake pulled up on the reins to the black gelding he favored over the other horses he owned. The path had suddenly banked steeper, and small rocks tumbled as Midnight whinnied and stepped lightly to his master's command. "Stay there!" he told Randy.

Randy slowed her horse, a gentle gray gelding called Shortbread. She watched with concern as Jake led Midnight down the steep path that had become more of a washout after a short but hard rain last night. Rocks and dirt tumbled as Midnight half slid down the bank to a flatter pathway. Jake dismounted and tied the horse, then grasped at trees and rocks and anything else he could to keep from slipping as he climbed back up to where Randy waited. She noticed how worn-looking his black leather boots were in spite of being fairly new. The silver Mexican conchae and extra-fancy stitching made them sturdy enough for the wear and tear of ranching, but they were already scratched and dirty.

She wore leather boots herself, and a split riding skirt. She shivered under the extra sheepskin jacket Jake had made her bring along, and she was glad for his advice.

Mountain mornings could be very cold, even when the weather was warming in the valleys.

Jake reached her and took a last drag on his cigarette, then threw it down and stepped it out extra hard, as he always did when in the pine forest. "Get off Shortbread. We'll walk down using the trees to keep our balance. Let Shortbread and the packhorse make their own way. The last thing I need is for you and that horse to take a fall out here where there's no help." He reached up and grasped her about the waist, helping her down.

"I do have help," she teased. "*You're* here."

"Yeah, well, I'm no damn doctor." He leaned down and gave her a quick kiss. "And why on earth would you think I'm not still attracted to you, after the three days we spent up in that cabin?"

Randy smiled, wrapping her arms around his waist. "I just like hearing you say it, that's all."

He yanked her wide-brimmed hat farther down on her head when she looked up at him again. "See?" he told her. "You're distracting me again. And there's Shortbread and the packhorse, already headed to the bottom. Come on." He kept hold of her arm as they made their way down the escarpment, Randy voicing little squeals at a few precarious slips on wet needles. Jake kept a firm grip on her arm as they made their way over and around fallen logs and broken limbs, skinny pine branches snapping under their feet.

"What a relief!" Randy exclaimed when they reached the flatter pathway.

"Must have rained harder than we thought last night." Jake helped her remount and handed her the reins to the packhorse again. He untied and mounted Midnight, and they headed farther along, ever downward, until they reached the vast expanse of green valley below the cabin.

Randy glanced up at the line shack, feeling a little sad wondering if and when they would go back again. Their last three days there were the sweetest, most peaceful, most satisfying days they had ever spent together. It was as though all the bad things they'd ever faced together never happened, as though he was thirty again and she was twenty and they were starting over. "Jake?"

"Yeah?" He kept riding ahead of her, heading even farther into the valley, where they would turn south and head closer to home.

"I really enjoyed our time at the line shack. We can go back again sometime, can't we? Maybe after roundup?"

"Sure we can. It's just that I can't take you with me every time I leave the house. I have my ranch work, and you have work to share with Evie and Katie—and the grandkids would have a fit if Grandma was gone all the time. They are probably already asking about you."

"Oh, I know that. I wouldn't *want* to be gone all the time. It's just that this time together seemed so special. I'm glad I came along."

Jake slowed his horse and let her catch up. He looked her over lovingly. "I'm glad, too. But I love you, and I want you to be safe."

"I'm always safe when I'm with you."

He smiled and shook his head. "Well, out here it's the unexpected things that even *I* can't stop that worry me. And I like you at home because, after days of mending fence and herding and branding cattle and seeing nothing but the ass end of cows and horses, I look forward to coming home to something that looks a lot better."

Randy laughed. "It's nice to know you think I look better than a cow's hind end."

"Woman, your own hind end is the prettiest thing I've ever seen." He rode off again. "And if we don't stop this kind of talk, I'll end up dragging you back up to that cabin."

I wouldn't mind, she thought. She remembered another time he'd ridden away, back in Kansas a lifetime ago after she'd nursed him back to health from a gunshot wound—when he was a wanted man and thought it was best that he leave her before things became too serious between them. She remembered wanting to beg him to stay because she'd fallen in love with him. She knew even then that Jake Harkner had lost his heart, too—that for the first time in his life, he'd begun to understand what love felt like. Back then it scared him to death.

"If you don't stay home next time I leave, how can I come home to you all warm and comfortable and rested and baking that great homemade bread?" he called out, interrupting her thoughts.

He rode a little faster, and Randy nudged Shortbread into a faster trot to keep up. What a contrast he was to the angry, mean, unhappy, wanted outlaw he was when they met. It had been a long time since she'd seen that dark, brooding side of her husband, the look that came into his eyes when something happened to threaten anyone he loved, or something came along to wake up ugly memories. He was a man capable of extreme gentleness for his size and demeanor—but also capable of extreme violence against anyone who threatened those he cared about.

"Have I told you how you fit this land?" she told him, urging Shortbread up beside him. "When I watch you from behind, I see a big, tall man on a big horse, handling a big ranch in big, big country. You fit this land, Jake. It's like Jeff said in his book."

Randy loved Jeff's description of Jake, saying that he had a way of filling up a room with his bold presence—that sometimes it seemed he filled up the whole land.

Jake turned and bridled closer, then reached out and pulled her off her horse and onto his own horse in front of him. "Ma'am, if you don't quit your flirting, we'll never make it home. I'll end up making camp early, and we'll be cavorting right out in the open. Some of my men could show up any time and catch us in a very compromising position."

Randy laughed and sat sideways, removing her hat and resting her head on his chest as he kept his horse at a slow walk. Jake reached over and grasped Shortbread's bridle, pulling the horse close enough to grab the reins. "Here."

Randy wrapped the strings of her hat around Shortbread's saddle horn, then took the horse's reins. Jake urged Midnight around so he could grab hold of the packhorse. "Hell, between hanging on to the packhorse and handling my own reins, I can't put my arms around you."

Randy wrapped her own arms around his waist, still clinging to Shortbread's reins. "I'll just hang on. I know we can't ride like this for long, but I like it."

Jake kissed her hair. "So do I."

"I love you, Jake."

He didn't answer right away. Finally, he said, "To this day, after almost thirty years, I still have trouble figuring out *why* you love me. I've put you through so much."

"You've loved me as deeply as any man can love a woman, and that's all that matters. After all these years, I feel like we're not just husband and wife, but lovers. Does that make any sense?"

He laughed lightly. "You are determined to make this ride difficult for me, aren't you?"

She leaned up and kissed him. "You're fun to be with when you're like this, all relaxed and happy. And you didn't answer when I said I love you."

He kissed her hair again. "That's because *I love you* isn't good enough for the likes of you. I was trying to think of something better than that."

She threw her head back and looked up at him. "Worship? Adore?"

"Something like that."

They both laughed, and she hugged him again. But

even without looking at him, she felt the sudden change. He halted his horse, and she felt his whole body stiffen. She leaned back again and saw the darker look of the old, defensive Jake Harkner, the wanted man always on the alert. He was looking past her.

"Jake?"

"Rustlers. They've seen us. Hang on to Shortbread." He turned Midnight toward the foothills. "We're heading for those rocks to the west!" He urged the horses into a faster lope toward an outcropping of rocks that looked as though they'd tumbled there from nowhere. "Get down!" he told her when they reached cover. He hung on to her arm as she slid off his horse. Jake dismounted. "Tie the horses farther into the trees." He yanked his rifle from its boot.

Randy pulled the horses into the trees, her heart pounding. In moments like this, she trusted her husband to know what to do. She obeyed every order.

Jake ducked behind a huge boulder. "Get the shotgun and my leather pack with the extra cartridges and buckshot," he told her, cocking his repeating rifle.

Randy took the shotgun and ammunition from the packhorse and carried them over to him.

Jake set both rifle and shotgun against the rock while he checked his Colt .44s, the guns that had brought him so much notoriety…and often too much heartache. "You stay down, and I mean *down*," he told her.

Randy knelt beside him and peeked through an opening between the boulder and another rock. In the distance a good six or seven men were herding a fair number of cattle south.

"How do you know it's not Pepper and some of the other men?"

"None of my men would be riding in bunches like that this time of year. They're spread out—a couple here, a couple there. And we aren't rounding up yet, at least not in this area. They wouldn't be out there with that many cattle." He rested on one knee, picking up the Winchester and positioning it in the same opening to watch. "They're still a little too far away, damn it!"

"Jake, please don't take them on by yourself."

"I don't think I'll have any choice. Take the shotgun and keep it handy. If anything happens to me, *use* it!" He handed her one of his six-guns. "And then shoot the rest of them with this if you have to."

Shoot the rest of them? "Jake, why not just let them ride on?"

"Because it's *my* cattle they're stealing, and besides that, they're already coming this way. Don't touch the trigger on my .44 till you have to. They have a feather pull, and you'll end up shooting me or yourself. Just set it aside for now, but be ready to use that shotgun."

Randy carefully laid the six-gun on a flat rock, closing her eyes and praying she wouldn't have to use it, worried that all the sweet and wonderful things she and Jake had shared the last few days could end in disaster here and now. Crouched on her knees, she peeked around the other side of the second boulder to see five men drawing closer, all very well armed. Two more were making their way around either side of the boulders where she and Jake were holed up. Her only consolation was that if any one man could take on seven or more against him, it was Jake Harkner.

Five

"JAKE, TWO OF THEM ARE TRYING TO WORK THEIR WAY behind us."

"I know. You just stay low, understand? Keep an eye behind us, but you let me do the shooting unless something happens that I can't."

The whole time Jake spoke, he kept a keen eye on the five men cautiously approaching. Randy jumped when he suddenly fired his Winchester, then cocked and fired again before the crack of the first shot even finished echoing through the valley.

"Jesus Christ!" someone yelled.

Jake fired again. A man cried out. "My leg! I'm shot!"

"The other three are sneaking through the tall grass," Jake told Randy. "Keep watching our backs."

Randy struggled against tears, remembering another gunfight back in Guthrie, when she almost lost her husband to nearly unstoppable bleeding. Another gunfight, back in California years ago, when he took a bullet to the hip. Another huge gunfight when they both saved Lloyd from a gang of outlaws out to kill him. And when he rescued their daughter Evie from hell itself, he and Lloyd were both wounded.

"Who's there?" one of the rustlers called out.

"Jake Harkner! And those are my cattle you're stealing, you sonofabitch!"

Things got quiet for a moment.

"Shit!" someone swore. "*The* Jake Harkner?"

"I've never come across another man by the same name!"

"Goddamn it, Harkner, we didn't know it was *your* cattle we were stealin'."

"You do now!"

"You did your share of rustling once yourself, you damned outlaw!"

"Long time ago—and a different man!" Jake shouted. "I'll give you one chance to ride off, long as you head north and you leave my cattle behind. Nobody has ever gotten away with rustling off the J&L, and I intend to keep it that way!"

"Jake, behind you!" Randy gasped.

Jake whirled, his six-gun out, and fired in the blink of an eye. It boomed much louder than the Winchester, and the man sneaking up on them flew into the air with a scream, a huge hole in his chest.

"Billy, there's a woman with him!" a second man somewhere behind them called out.

"Lie down flat!" Jake ordered Miranda.

Randy did as he told her, just as a bullet pinged against the rock right where she'd been sitting. She felt Jake's weight on her then when he laid himself over her. Randy squinted and covered her ears when he fired his .44 five more times.

Randy heard a man screaming. It sounded like he was running toward them. "That was my father, you bastard!" he was yelling. She felt Jake move, realized he was reaching for the six-gun she'd left lying on the flat rock. More shots rang out, pinging against the rocks and ricocheting in all directions.

She felt Jake's body jerk. "Jesus!" he grunted. He fired the second .44 twice. Another man cried out.

"Jake, are you hit?" Randy screamed from under him.

"Just grazed. I think it was a bullet that ricocheted off a rock."

"Come on out, Harkner!" one of the men in the grass yelled. "You can't stay there forever. The minute you up and run, we've got you, on account of we'll take your woman down first. If you don't want her to suffer, you ought to come on out of there."

"You two are all that's left," Jake shouted. He remained on top of Randy. "Do you really think I can't take you both down, even out in the open? Let's make it a fair gunfight! You two against me!"

"Jake, no! You're hurt, aren't you? You're hurt!"

He moved off her, staying low. "Load my other six-gun, quick!" he told her. "And stay low like I told you."

Staying on her belly, Randy reached out with a shaking hand and grabbed the empty gun he'd left near her. She grabbed the bag of cartridges nearby and dumped them on the ground, picking out the right ones for his .44s. She nervously began loading the gun while the man Jake had shot in the leg lay groaning and crying. "My leg! My leg!" he kept hollering. Suddenly, he raised up and pointed his gun at Jake.

Jake fired again.

"You bastard!" one of the others swore. "He was wounded!"

"So am I! He should have stayed down!"

"The poor guy was confused from pain, you murderin' sonofabitch!" the first man answered.

"I've been called worse!" Jake turned to Randy, still keeping his head down. "Keep your fingers away from that trigger," he reminded her.

"I know." Randy noticed the back of his jacket was soaked with blood. "Jake, you're bleeding!"

"Doesn't matter. I can't let them get to you. Finish loading that thing and give it to me."

Randy slammed the cylinder closed and handed him the gun, keeping the barrel pointed down and her fingers away from the trigger. One of the men behind them groaned.

"Jake, one of those men back there is still alive."

"I doubt he's in any shape to do us harm," Jake answered, shoving his six-gun into its holster. "How about it, mister!" Jake yelled louder. "An even gunfight, me against the both of you!"

Randy realized he was using his only option at flushing them out once and for all.

"You'll lose, Harkner, and then your woman will be all ours, or at least at the mercy of which one of us is left!"

"Hank, that's Jake Harkner you're talkin' to," the other man yelled. "You shouldn't have threatened his wife. He's taken on a lot more than just two men on his own. Let's just get out of here!"

"I'm not leaving without taking that sonofabitch down," the first man growled. "He killed Cal, and Cal was already wounded!"

"That's the whole point! He don't miss! You know his reputation! Let's just go!"

"Too late, boys!" Jake shouted. "You get up on those horses, and you're dead! I said you could ride off, but I've changed my mind. You shouldn't have threatened my wife! Your only chance now is to face me down fair and square."

There came a long silence. Randy noticed Jake grimace with pain, and perspiration began to bathe his face. "Jake, don't do it! You're hurt!"

"Not bad enough to let either one of those bastards get to you. Remember what I said about that shotgun!" He shimmied up to the crack in the rock to keep an eye on the men lying beyond in the grass. "Make up your minds!" he yelled. "Sure death—or a tiny chance at living!"

"This ain't fair! You're Jake Harkner."

"And you made the decision to steal my cattle!"

"We didn't know this was your spread."

"Hank!" the second man shouted. "Somebody is riding toward us from the north. Let's get out of here!"

"Harkner ain't gonna let us leave." The one called Hank dared to stand up, his hands in the air but six-gun still in hand. "I'm callin' you, Harkner! Fair fight, but Billy here gets to be part of it, just like you said."

"I ain't drawin' on no Jake Harkner!" Billy answered.

"We have no choice, Billy! Put your gun in its holster. Let's get this over with!"

Jake slowly rose, holstering the gun Randy had loaded for him.

"Jake, don't!" Randy begged.

"Stay put," he told her. He walked from behind the boulder, noticing riders in the distance. He could tell it was Lloyd because of how his long hair flew out behind him in the wind.

The one called Billy slowly got to his feet. He carefully holstered his gun, as did Hank. They held their hands away from their holsters.

Jake staggered slightly.

"He's hurt!" Hank sneered. "I *told* you. We've got a chance, Billy."

"Then let's get this over with. More men are comin'!" Billy answered. He went for his gun. Hank went for his at the same time, but before either of them could clear their holsters, Jake's gun was blazing, and they both went down.

Randy started to rise, not noticing until then that the man left alive behind them had gotten to his feet. She grabbed up the shotgun and fired.

Jake whirled at the boom. Randy was sitting on the ground, still clinging to the shotgun.

"Jesus!" Jake holstered his guns and knelt beside her. "Randy?"

"I'm okay. The shotgun knocked me down."

Jake helped her to her feet, pulling her close. He wrapped his arms around her. "You sure you're okay?"

"I'm fine." She glanced toward the man she'd shot at. "I think I missed. The shotgun kicked up when I fired it."

Jake kissed her hair. "Stay put." He walked over to check out the man. "He's dead," he called out, "but not from any buckshot."

Randy closed her eyes with relief, unable to accept killing a man as easily as her husband did.

Jake came back and pulled her close again, hugging her so tightly she could barely breathe. "That's it. You're not coming with me again."

"Jake, you can't judge by this." Randy hated realizing the spell was broken. The trip had been so beautiful, until now.

"I mean it, Randy."

Still shaking, Randy broke into tears. "I don't want the morning to be spoiled. You promised me we'd go back to that line shack. It's so beautiful and peaceful there."

"We'll figure out a way. You're just upset right now. All I know is that I can't bring you with me this time of year, when the men are so spread out. You're safer at home when I have to go this far."

"I hate it when you're gone." Randy clung to him.

"Well, I'm here right now." He sighed, keeping her close. The far riders came closer. "Lloyd is coming, and he has more men with him." He rubbed her back. "It's okay, Randy."

Randy pulled away, wiping at tears with a shaking hand. "Lloyd's coming? How did he know there might be trouble?"

Jake kept an arm around her shoulders. "I don't know. I'm just glad he's here."

Randy kept her arms around his waist as the riders drew nearer. Lloyd charged up the hill to where they waited, dismounting before his horse even came to a complete stop. "Pa! We heard there might be rustlers in this area. You okay?"

"We're all right," Jake told him. "A bullet ricocheted off the rocks and ripped across my back, but there's no bullet in me that I can tell. I think it's just a gash."

Lloyd touched Randy's shoulder. "You all right, Mom?"

She closed her eyes and pulled away from Jake. "I'm just a little shaken up. I shot at one behind us, and the shotgun slammed pretty hard against my shoulder. I have a feeling I'll be bruised by morning." She began to cry then. "It's just that I never know when I'll lose your father to something like this."

Lloyd pulled her into his arms. "Mom, you know that mean sonofabitch doesn't go down easy." He leaned down and kissed her hair and turned to Jake, keeping an arm around his mother.

"Thanks for the kind names you call me," Jake quipped.

"Just saying it like it is," Lloyd told him, loving to trade barbs with his father, who never spared words himself when voicing exactly what he was thinking. He gave his mother a gentle squeeze. "You've turned this woman into a nervous wreck over the years."

"Lloyd, I'm fine," Randy objected. She pulled away. "Take care of your father."

Lloyd frowned, walking around to see that the back of Jake's sheepskin jacket was soaked with blood. "Take off your jacket and let me look at that wound."

"I'm fine."

"Damn it, Pa, you're bleeding worse than you think! I saw enough blood after that gunfight back in Guthrie. I don't need to see you nearly bleed to death again. For all you know, you need stitches."

"And who will do that? *You?*"

"Hell yes. I would take great pleasure in yanking a needle through that wound and hearing you yell."

Jake scowled at him as he removed the jacket. "I'll just bet you would."

"Turn around, old man. Let me at least put some whiskey on it."

Jake sighed. "Thanks for coming," he told Lloyd, sincerity moving into his eyes. "If something had gone

wrong, they would have gotten ahold of your mother."
He winced when Lloyd tore open the back of his shirt.
"Go through those men's gear and see if you can find
some identification," Jake called out to Pepper and Cole.

"The bleeding is slowing. I'll put whiskey on it
anyway, just for safekeeping." Lloyd walked over to his
horse and took a flask from his saddlebag, along with a
roll of gauze.

Jake glanced at a shaken Randy. "You really all right?
You're not hurt anywhere?"

She walked up to him and leaned against his chest as
he moved an arm around her. "I'm fine."

Lloyd returned with the supplies, and Randy felt Jake
jerk when Lloyd doused the deep cut with whiskey,
then pressed the gauze against the wound and held it
there a moment.

"I'd rather *drink* some of that whiskey," Jake told him.

"I expect you would."

"I suppose I've added another scar to my back,"
Jake grumbled.

Lloyd glanced at his mother. Randy saw the pain in his
eyes at knowing the scars on his father's back were nearly
all put there by Jake's own father when Jake was just a
little boy—by the buckle end of a belt. "I suppose so,"
he answered quietly, "but I don't think it will have to be
stitched up. We'll let Brian look at it when we get back."

"God knows it's a good thing your sister married a
doctor," Jake tried to joke. "He doesn't need a practice
of his own. His family keeps him busy enough."

Lloyd smiled sadly. "Yeah, well, if you'd learn to stay
out of trouble, we wouldn't need him so much."

"Hey, Jake!" Cole called out as he rummaged through
the clothing on one of the bodies. "Do you ever leave a
man alive when you get into something like this?"

"Sometimes," Jake answered, taking a Lone Jack cigarette from a pocket on the front of his shirt and lighting it.

"Remind me to stay on your good side," Cole answered sarcastically.

"Just don't try rustling any of my cattle," Jake joked, taking a deep drag on his cigarette. "When I start shooting, I generally figure it's best to plant the bullet where I can be sure the man shooting at me can't shoot back anymore."

Lloyd made ready to wrap some gauze around the wound.

"Leave it," Jake told him. "I'm more concerned about your mother. Just give me my jacket and one swallow of that whiskey."

"I'm just fine, Jake," Randy reminded him.

"No, you aren't. You might have messed up that shoulder, and I know what something like this does to you emotionally."

Lloyd handed his father the jacket and the flask. Jake took a deep swallow of the whiskey, which told Randy he was in pain, because he never drank otherwise, at least not around her. He had too many bad memories of his cruel, drunken father beating his mother. She glanced at Lloyd and knew he realized the same.

Jake handed Lloyd the flask and grimaced as he tugged on his jacket. He pulled Randy close again. "I'm goddamn sorry, Randy. We had such a nice morning."

"You didn't ask for this."

Jake kept Randy close as he watched Cole and Pepper rifle through the pockets and saddlebags of the dead men. "How in hell did you know there might be trouble?" he asked Lloyd.

"That courier from Denver, Jason Hawk, saw them from Echo Ridge. He was on his way to us with some news, and he knew we wouldn't likely be herding cattle to Denver this early in the season. When we heard there might be rustlers out here, we rode half the night trying to catch up with them, or with you—whichever came first. I was hoping you'd miss them altogether, but no such luck." .

"Jason never comes out in the middle of the week like this," Jake commented. "What did he want?"

Lloyd seemed hesitant. He sighed before answering. "It's not exactly good news. Jeff Trubridge wired us about something he thought we should know right away. Trouble is, Jason gave the note to Evie, and it upset her. Brian is home now, though, so she'll be all right. He always knows how to reassure her."

Jake came instantly alert, and Randy felt a sick alarm as they both faced Lloyd. "What's wrong?" Jake asked.

"Lloyd, is Evie okay?" Randy pressed. "She's going to have another baby and shouldn't get upset."

"*Baby?* Sis is pregnant again?"

"Yes, and don't let on that you know. She's going to tell us at Sunday dinner. I already told your father to act surprised."

"What the hell is wrong?" Jake asked, raising his voice more. "Why is Evie upset?"

Lloyd rubbed at his eyes. "Shit. I didn't know she was pregnant again. That just makes things worse."

"Makes *what* worse?" Jake asked.

Lloyd pulled the note from his pocket and handed it to Jake, then looked at his mother. "Mike Holt is out of prison—won some kind of appeal. He'll come after me as sure as the sun shines every day." He turned to Jake. "The past just keeps on rearing its ugly head, doesn't it?"

Jake closed his eyes and ran a hand through his hair. "Thanks to me."

"I didn't mean it that way, Pa. This one is my fault, too, for shooting Holt's brother in the back. But after what happened to Evie—"

Randy saw it then—that little flame of Jake Harkner that lived in her son. The dark, vengeful side. She always hated seeing it, because Lloyd was raised in love. He never knew the horrific childhood his father grew up with, and he was far more forgiving than Jake, but he had the ability to wreak revenge if warranted, the ability to shoot a man with no regrets if that man dared to harm one of his own.

"I just don't want that man to suddenly show his face to Evie," Lloyd told Jake. "I don't think she could handle it if she saw even one of those men again."

"We should have killed every last one of them when we had the chance," Jake grumbled.

"We couldn't just execute the ones left alive, Pa, much as we would have liked to. You would have ended up back in prison, and Evie would have never lived that down. We couldn't let her see her father and brother deliberately murder those men. And maybe she was able to forgive them, but having to face any of them again... who knows what that would do to her? She's happy now, and thank God she has the best husband a woman like her could ask for. If she's having another baby, that's a damn good sign their marriage is healed. I'm just trying to figure out if we should discuss this with her or just leave it alone and hope the bastard doesn't show up."

"I'll decide when the time is right to talk to her about it," Randy told them. "She might even bring it up herself."

"Let me talk to Brian first," Jake told her.

"Katie will be none too happy about this either," Lloyd told them. "This will scare her to death after all that happened back in Guthrie. I left her in the barn and took off without even explaining anything, but she'll find out before I get back, and she'll be upset."

"You probably should have stayed with her and let the other men come out here," Jake told him.

"When my parents could both be in trouble?" Lloyd tried to make light of the situation as he gave his mother a teasing grin. "I figured I'd better try to keep this old man from getting himself into more trouble. Sometimes I'm the only one who can do that."

Jake scowled at him. "I could make you sorry for calling me an old man, but I wouldn't want to mess up that pretty face for Katie."

Lloyd grinned. "That'll be the day."

Jake held his gaze, the look in his eyes softening. "It'll be okay, Son. We have good men working for us. We just have to be extra alert for a while. For all we know, Holt will want to stay out of trouble, and he won't show up at all."

"Yeah, and fish don't need water." Lloyd glanced at the other men as they continued rifling through the belongings of the rustlers. "Stay here with Mom. The other men and I will get these men buried." He frowned at Jake again. "You go wielding a shovel, and you'll start that cut bleeding all over again."

"Be sure to save all their trap," Jake answered. "We'll have one of the men take them to Denver and report this." He saw the worry in Lloyd's eyes at the remark. Lloyd and pretty much everyone else in the family always feared something could happen to land Jake back in prison. "I was in the right, Lloyd. They were rustling cattle. If I hadn't shot them, they would have been hung. There won't be any trouble over this."

Lloyd nodded. "I know. It's just—"

"The name. I know."

Lloyd smiled sadly. "I'm glad we found you and Mom okay. I sure as hell know this was something you could handle, Pa, but there's always that little worry that something could go wrong this time, and I didn't like thinking Mom could be left out here alone."

"So, you came back because of *her*, not me."

"Of course I did. I knew damn well you'd be okay on your own." Lloyd grinned, and Jake couldn't help his own smile.

"Well, you did right," he told his son. "Let's get these men buried and get home. There's a lot of rounding up and branding to do." Jake called out to the other men. "Any of you recognize any of those men? Did you find something with their names on it?"

"Got names off of five of them," Cole answered, "but I don't know any of them. Pepper doesn't either."

"Any of them carry the name Mike Holt?" Jake called back.

"Nope." Jake watched Cole limp over to his horse. The man had an old leg wound from the war, and that was all Jake knew about his background. Cole Decker was of slender build but strong as a horse, and he tended to drink too much, but he was a happy drinker, not a mean one, so that was okay with Jake. He suspected some pretty shady doings in the man's past, not much different from Jake himself.

"You'd better go check out the one they couldn't identify," Jake told Lloyd. "Maybe we'll get lucky and find out it's Mike Holt."

"Yeah, sure."

Lloyd left to take a look at the bodies, and Jake turned to Randy, keeping her close. "Okay, woman, you're right. I don't just love you. I *adore* you. I *worship* you." He hugged her even tighter. "And I'm glad as hell you're all right."

Randy breathed deeply of his familiar scent, then looked up at him. "Let's go home to the grandchildren. Suddenly, I want very much to see them and get back to a normal routine. It helps me handle things like this."

Jake leaned down to kiss her. Randy thought how few women could have a moment like this with their husbands while surrounded by seven men he'd just shot dead. She hugged him tighter. "Oh, Jake, don't let go for a while."

"I never let go of you, even when we aren't together."

Jake watched the other men start digging graves closer to the trees. "I suppose you'll want to pray over those no-goods," he told Randy.

"It's the right thing to do."

"If it was up to me, I'd strip them down and leave them for the buzzards."

Randy laughed through her tears, needing the relief from the tense drama of what had just happened. His remark was so typical of Jake Harkner. "Oh, Jake, God is going to have a time with you when you get to heaven," she teased, her ears still ringing from the boom of her husband's guns.

"Yeah, well, I think He and I will have a whole lot to talk about. Let's just hope that conversation takes place a good ten or twenty years from now."

Randy hugged him tighter, unable to begin to imagine life without this man. Always there was the worry that the next gunfight would be his last. "I love you, Jake."

He sighed, rocking her slightly in his arms. "We'll go back to that cabin again before summer is out. I promise."

"Can we stay even longer next time?"

"Sure we can."

"Jake, I'm scared for Lloyd."

"Nothing will happen to Lloyd or anybody else in this family. I won't let it."

That's what worries me even more. Randy looked up at him, felt his lips on hers in an oh-so-familiar kiss.

Lloyd glanced their way, then returned to digging a grave—more men dead from his father's famous guns, and now Mike Holt was on the loose. He hated to face it, but had a sick feeling this was just the beginning of new troubles for him and his father.

Six

RED ST. JAMES SWALLOWED ANOTHER SHOT OF WHISKEY, studying the man who'd just come into the Okie Saloon. He wasn't a regular. For the most part, a man could pretty much figure who'd show up which nights and where he'd sit, which ones played cards, and which ones always sat at the bar and gabbed. Guthrie had its share of saloons, and most men had their favorites.

"I won't be in here much after this." The words came from Red's friend, Fenton Wales. "You know how it is for a farmer come spring."

Red nodded, still watching the stranger. There was something familiar about him.

Fenton removed a rather soiled hat and ran a hand through his thinning hair. "What the hell are you looking at, Red?"

"That stranger that just walked in. He looks familiar."

Fenton turned to look. The man sat at the bar, his back to both of them. "I can't tell without seeing his face."

"Can I get you boys anything more?" A well-known prostitute-turned-barmaid sauntered close, her buxom figure pleasantly filling out a deep purple taffeta dress that showed just a hint of cleavage. It was obvious to any man that there was much more bosom billowing beneath her fitted bodice.

"Dixie, the law doesn't allow us to order what you have to offer."

Dixie grinned. "Now, you boys know I shut down my place months ago. I'm getting too old for that, and things weren't the same after Jake Harkner left town with that gorgeous son of his. I am working an honest job here, boys, and just wanting to know if you want more drinks." She looked both men over seductively. "Now, Red, you've got a wife at home. So even if I was still in business, and in spite of those big, strong arms and that barrel of a torso and handsome grin, I wouldn't do business with you." She jerked on his red beard, then glanced at Fenton. "But you, you big ole rugged farmer, if I was still in business, you'd be welcome…with open, uh, arms, if you get my meaning."

"I get it all right," Fenton joked. Laughter filled the room.

"Is it true Jake Harkner never monkeyed around them times he visited your place?" Red asked with a wink.

"And risk losing that wife he worships?" Dixie grinned. "Honey, I'd have liked nothing better than to have that man in my bed, but no, we were just good friends."

"Well, a man…or woman…couldn't ask for a better friend than Jake," Fenton told her.

Red noticed that mentioning Jake's name caused the stranger at the bar to turn and look.

"You've got that right," Dixie answered Fenton. "I hope Jake and his family have found some peace in Colorado. I have to say, though, I miss that handsome outlaw something awful, just awful. And that son of his…" She shook her head. "I never knew God could make men that good-looking. And then he had to up and get married. Life just isn't fair."

"Half the town misses all of them, especially Jake's wife and that beautiful daughter," Fenton mused.

Red grasped Dixie's wrist and signaled for her to lean closer. "Hey, Dixie, go ahead and bring me and Fenton a beer," he said, lowering his voice. "And I want you to go up to the bar and cozy up to that stranger that just walked in. See if you can get him to tell you his name. And tell him to come over here."

Dixie glanced the stranger's way. He'd turned away again. "Sure, honey."

She sauntered away, and Fenton shook his head. "She's something, that Dixie."

Red nodded as he watched the stranger. "Fenton, I know that man. I just can't pinpoint it, but I know him, and something about him smells."

Dixie ordered their beers, then spoke with the stranger as she waited for the bartender. She glanced at Red and Fenton, and the stranger turned, eyeing them closely. A look of arrogance showed itself as he straightened and cast Red what seemed almost like a warning glare. Dixie brought over the beers and set them on the table, and the stranger followed her over.

"You two askin' about me?" His eyes were a steely blue, and he needed a shave. A tan, wide-brimmed hat covered wavy, mousy-brown hair.

Red felt a deep dread. It was all coming back to him now—the medium build and a belly that pooched out more than it should for a man who otherwise was not that much overweight, plus…the odd Z-shaped scar on his chin. He remembered that scar. "I'll be goddamned," he growled. He jumped up so fast that his chair fell over. "You're Mike Holt!"

Everyone in the saloon turned to stare, and Dixie stepped back. "My God," she muttered. "You filthy rapist! What are you doing in Guthrie!"

Holt took a defensive stance, stepping back from Fenton and Red. "I was cleared of them charges, and I'm just moving on through—headed west. I ain't from here, and I don't intend to stay."

"You came here to see if it was true that Jake Harkner doesn't live here anymore!" Red roared. "And if you're headed west, you're out to *find* him!"

Fenton also rose, folding his powerful arms.

"Where I go is nobody's business!" Holt sneered.

"How dare you come to Guthrie!" Red bellowed. "What the hell were you thinking?"

"I told you they cleared me of all charges!"

"Not *all* charges! Far as I'm concerned, any man who stands by and lets other men abuse a beautiful, innocent woman is just as guilty of rape as the ones doing it to her! Get the hell out of Guthrie while you're still able to walk, Holt! A lot of people in this town were right fond of Evie and her husband—fond of the whole Harkner family! Me and Fenton were at that shoot-out. We know what happened, and you're just as goddamn guilty as the rest of them! I don't care *what* that judge decreed!"

Practically everyone in the bar began moving toward Holt, who backed toward the door.

"I think we ought to teach him a lesson," one of the other patrons spoke up, "in case he's got plans to go make trouble for Jake or Lloyd. He ought to know he'd better not try it, and he should know how we feel about what he did back at Dune Hollow."

"I'd like to shoot you myself," Dixie sneered at Holt.

Holt looked her over scathingly, his upper lip curling when he spoke. "You that whore Jake Harkner used to fuck when he was off pretendin' to be a lawman?"

"You bastard!" Red roared. He landed into Holt, shoving him out the door and into the now-bricked street. A man known around town for his fighting skills, he pelted Holt over and over while the rest of the men urged him on. Even Dixie screamed for Red to "beat him to a pulp!"

Holt was no match. It took only a few punches for Red to land him flat on his back, helpless against more blows. Finally, Fenton pulled Red away.

"You'll kill him and go to jail!" he warned Red.

Red stood there panting, looking down at a bloodied

Mike Holt. "That was for Jake—and for his angel of a daughter!" he growled, his hands still clenched into fists.

Hearing the ruckus, Sheriff Herbert Sparks was already on the scene. "What's going on here?"

"Sparky, that man on the ground there is Mike Holt," Fenton told him. "One of them that was at Dune Hollow—that one that got released."

"Arrest that sonofabitch!" Holt told the sheriff, pointing to Red.

"For beating the hell out of a filthy rapist?" the sheriff answered. "I don't care if he kills you, mister, so I suggest you get out of Guthrie just as fast as you can, or I'll come up with some kind of charge that warrants a hanging." He stuck his thumbs into his gun belt, which was half hidden by his big belly. "Everybody in this town was real fond of Harkner's daughter, Holt, so you picked the wrong place to hang your hat!"

"I was new to Hash Bryant and his gang." Holt put a shaking hand over his bloody nose. "I never came to Guthrie before what happened out at Dune Hollow. I didn't figure anybody here would know who I was, 'cause I ain't never been here before."

"Well, you figured wrong!" Red stormed, inching closer again.

Holt scooted away. "I have no intention of hanging my hat here, as your sheriff puts it. Like I said, I was just on my way through."

"It makes no sense you'd stop here, of all places," Red answered, "unless you were trying to find out about Jake. You can bet we'll wire him that we've seen you, so he'll be on the lookout. If you have the tiniest thought of looking that man up—or anybody in his family—you'd better think twice. That's Jake and Lloyd Harkner you're fixin' to make trouble for, and there ain't a man still livin' who ever went up against either one of them!"

"*I'm* living!"

"Only because Jake promised his daughter he'd not murder you in cold blood! He was a lawman then, but not anymore. If he gets you alone, you'll never live to tell about it. Now get out of Guthrie! Go back east, or north or south or wherever you choose. Just get out of Oklahoma and stay away from the Harkners! They've finally found some peace, and they *deserve* it!"

Holt got to his knees, then staggered to his feet. "You've got no right telling me where I can and can't go," he grumbled, looking around at all of them. He ran a hand through his hair, then found his hat and shoved it back on his head. He pushed his way through the crowd and walked up to his horse, untying it and heading up the street.

"Sparky, make note of that bay he's riding. Make sure it's not tied anywhere in town come morning," Red told the sheriff.

"I intend to do just that."

Red looked down at a couple of swollen knuckles. "By God, I'm getting too old for this," he told Fenton. "But I just couldn't help it. Soon as I realized who he was—"

"I know." Fenton put a hand on his arm. "Come on back inside and have another drink. We can wire Denver in the morning and warn Jake we've seen Mike Holt snooping around Guthrie."

Red nodded, glancing in the direction Holt had gone. He couldn't see him. "I wish there wasn't so much law and order these days," he complained. "There was a time when the town could have hung that sonofabitch, and nobody would have cared."

❧

Brad Buckley watched from the shadows. He'd walked out of a saloon across the street from the Okie when he heard the commotion outside—heard everything that was said. He stayed out of sight as he walked up the street, following Mike Holt. He waited until he was sure no one was watching, then hurried to catch up with Holt.

"Mike! Mike Holt!" he called in a rough whisper.

Holt stopped and turned, quickly pulling a rifle from its boot on his horse. "Who is it?" he asked.

"Name's Brad Buckley. I don't mean any harm." Brad stepped closer. "Is it really you—one of them that was at Dune Hollow?"

Holt kept the rifle ready as he studied the big, strapping, barrel-chested young man. "What's it to you?"

Brad put out his hand. "I want to shake the hand of a man who was in on fucking Jake Harkner's daughter."

Holt cautiously shook his hand. "And why would that be?"

Brad shook his hand vigorously. "Mister, Jake Harkner killed my pa *and* two brothers four years back when he was a U.S. Marshal. And he just about killed *me* once— slammed his rifle butt into my chest and nearly broke my breastbone in two. I was months recovering. I hate the sonofabitch, and, well, I heard what was said back there. *Are* you thinking of looking up Harkner?"

"It's his *son* I'm after. Me and my brother joined up with the Bryants on that thing in Dune Hollow. My brother gave himself up, but Lloyd Harkner shot him in the back *after* he had his hands in the air and had put down his guns. He started to run off, and Lloyd shot him down like a damn jackrabbit. After it was all over, I told that kid I'd get him for what he done to my brother, and I intend to do just that."

"Can I ride with you? I have my own score to settle. I'm sick of Guthrie. My ma died last year, and I've got nothing left here. All I do is think about how I can get back at Jake Harkner for killing my father and causing me ungodly pain for months. I know for a fact he headed for Colorado. A man as notorious as Jake Harkner shouldn't be hard to find just by asking around, and where Jake is, you'll find Lloyd, too. They're inseparable."

"You know how to use a gun?"

"'Course I do."

"All right. I'm camped outside of town. You can join me if you want."

"Hell, I have a farm, such as it is, just northwest of here. You're welcome to come there with me and sleep in a real bed under a real roof."

Holt nodded. "That's right friendly of you, Buckley. I'm hurtin' pretty bad from that damn red-bearded man's fists."

"I bet. Red St. James is the town gunsmith, and he's known for his fighting skills. He's never been beat arm wrestling."

They started walking together.

"Hey," Brad said, "if you don't mind my asking... I saw it in the news. They said you were released because there was no proof you actually raped Jake's daughter."

"And you want to know if I did."

Brad shrugged. "Can't help wondering. I sure would have liked to have been there and had my own turn."

Holt stopped walking. "Well, son, I had my turn at her, and it was sweet. The best part is, she was blindfolded."

"*Blindfolded?*"

"Yup. Some of us decided to blindfold her when we took our turn. It was pretty entertaining. And now I could walk right up to her, and she wouldn't recognize me. When I was done with her, I went back to a barn where me and some of the other men slept, and she never really saw me. When the shooting was over, her husband had already taken her behind the cabin so's she wouldn't have to see those of us left alive."

"Yeah, but Jake and Lloyd saw you. They won't forget. So whatever you have planned, you'd better make sure you truly have the drop on them, or you'll be pushing up daisies."

"I don't really know for sure what I'll do, but I'll damn well pay back Lloyd Harkner. You can bet on it."

Brad grinned. "Well then, we *both* have scores to settle. Maybe between the two of us we can find a way."

"Maybe so."

Holt started walking again. "Lead me to your farm, my boy. I'm hurtin' pretty bad."

"Sure. My horse is back at the saloon where I was when I heard the commotion. You stay here and wait. I don't want anyone in town to know we've been talking. I'll be right back."

Brad hurried back down the street, wanting to laugh out loud at his luck. He'd been wanting to get out of Guthrie for a long time. Because of Jake Harkner, his whole family was gone, and nobody around Guthrie wanted what was left of the Buckleys or their outlaw friends the Bryants. The possibility of getting his revenge against Jake Harkner was the best reason of all to leave Guthrie, and he'd damn well never come back.

Seven

RANDY FOLDED A QUILT AND LAID IT ACROSS THE FOOT of the bed, smiling at how big the bed was—specially built from black walnut for Jake's tall frame. Jake had ordered the wood shipped from Michigan and hired a carpenter from Boulder to build the bed and a matching six-drawer dresser. The set was quite grand, but also quite heavy. Getting all of it up to her and Jake's loft bedroom had been quite a project.

She turned and headed downstairs, still a bit overwhelmed by her lovely home and thanking God for what she and Jake finally had here together. Only a hundred yards away on either side of their home were equally lovely log houses belonging to Lloyd and Katie and to Brian and Evie.

She untied her apron and tossed it over a chair, then stepped out onto the wide veranda where she could hear laughter and guitar music coming from the bunkhouse. It was Sunday, and the ranch hands were enjoying a day off. Teresa, the Mexican woman who helped with housework and the children, was at the cabin she shared with her husband, Rodriguez de Jesus. Dinner with the entire family, a Sunday ritual that Jake insisted they keep, was over, and in the absence of church, Evie had read from the Bible and had sung a hymn before the meal.

Randy breathed deeply of the fresh mountain air and glanced over at Jake, who sat leaning back in a chair, one foot up on the porch railing. He smoked quietly, watching the usual bedlam of the whole family together. She smiled, knowing that Jake still couldn't get over the fact that he had such a big family. Tricia and Sadie sat near him, playing with dolls. Tricia called Jake Poppy, and to Sadie, Jake was Gamps. Sadie had her mother's long, straight black hair and big, dark eyes. She was going to be as beautiful as Evie someday, the Mexican blood from Jake's mother showing through. Tricia had her mother's very red hair but Lloyd's dark eyes.

In the distance, grandson Stephen rode horses with adopted son Ben, who could be spotted anywhere because of his very blond, almost white hair. Seven-year-old Little Jake was chasing after Stephen and Ben, asking Stephen to saddle a horse for him, too. Ben and Stephen were good riders already, and it was obvious that Stephen, tall for his age, was going to be a big man like his father and grandfather.

Evie sat on a blanket with Brian under a huge pine tree that had its branches cut off at the bottom so people could use it for shade. Randy thanked God for Brian Stewart every night in her prayers. He'd been a godsend for their family, not only as a good doctor who'd literally saved Jake's life more than once, but also as the perfect man for Evie—attentive, caring, steady, and solid. What happened back in Oklahoma might have destroyed some marriages, but not theirs. Evie was so good-hearted and trusting that she needed a man who had a delicate but sure way of handling her. Helping her through her ordeal was something few men could have managed.

Randy walked closer to Jake and put a hand on his shoulder. "It's nice to watch our growing family, isn't it?"

Jake smoked quietly for several long seconds before answering. "Do all those beautiful children and grand-children really belong to us?"

"All from your seed, Jake Harkner."

He looked her over suggestively. "I believe you had a little bit to do with it," he told her with a sly grin.

She squeezed his shoulder. "If you hadn't forced me to submit to you in the back of that wagon all those years ago, we wouldn't have all this."

"*Forced* you?" He reached up and grasped her wrist. "Woman, you all but said, *take me—take me!*"

Randy pulled her hand away. "Oh, you can be so cocky sometimes!" They both grinned, and Randy sat down in a rocking chair nearby. She studied the man beside her. How he'd survived everything he'd been through in life she'd never understand, but here he sat, still tough and strong and sure and able. Only she knew how hard he struggled with physical pain he never talked about. His emotional pain was worse. A preacher back in Oklahoma had helped him deal with his inner demons, but it would never all go away.

Her thoughts were interrupted when Lloyd and Katie rode up to the porch, both sitting on a big roan gelding with only a blanket on its back. Lloyd kept an arm around Katie, who was perched in front of him and sitting sideways, a towel over her arm. "Can you two watch after Stephen and Tricia for a couple of hours?" he asked.

"While you and that beautiful woman sitting in front of you do what?" Jake asked teasingly. He loved to make Katie blush. She smiled and looked away.

"Nothing you and Mom haven't done a hundred and twenty-five thousand times," Lloyd shot back.

Jake broke into hearty laughter. "You underestimate us, son. I think it's probably been more than that."

"Yeah, well, you need to keep yourself out of trouble, or Katie and I will never catch up on more important things. Now that we know Evie is carrying, we have to keep this little contest going and have the next babies within a couple of months of each other, like Tricia and Sadie were. I can't let Brian outdo me."

"I have a feeling that will never happen," Jake said

with a wide grin. "And you know you don't need to ask us to keep an eye on Button here." He looked at Tricia and winked. She shot Jake a bright smile that showed the dimples in her cheeks Jake liked to kiss. "Now get going. We have a lot of work ahead of us starting tomorrow, but you'll probably be too damn tired from the fun stuff."

"That will be the day." Lloyd turned the horse. "We're going swimming down by the pond," he called back as he rode off.

Jake watched after them. "He looks like a damn Indian," he remarked.

Randy smiled. "You're always saying that. He has beautiful hair, and Katie likes it long. They're so happy now, Jake."

"I'm glad." Jake tossed his cigarette stub and rubbed at his eyes. "That thing with Beth—"

"It's over, Jake."

He rested his elbows on his knees. "Do you think he really has forgiven me for all of that?"

"Jake, that young man would die for you. So would Evie. And I love that he's turning out to be so much like you—his sense of humor, his thoughtfulness, his ability to love."

"Yeah, well, I have plenty of other traits I'd just as soon he didn't take after."

"He's a good father and a good husband, and so are you."

He grinned and shook his head. "Woman, you just won't admit to the other Jake Harkner, will you?"

"Why should I? I know the *real* Jake, and he's a good man."

Jake glanced at his granddaughters, who were hugging their dolls. "I just hope being related to me doesn't bring disaster to these precious little girls, or to Stephen or Little Jake."

"It won't. The past is past, Jake."

"Is it?" He glanced at Evie and Brian. "Did you talk to Evie about that telegram?"

He'd asked the dreaded question. Jake practically worshipped their daughter, considered her an angel sent from God. What had happened to Evie just about killed him, spiritually and physically. "You said you'd talk to Brian and that I should wait," she told him.

"Randy, I know how close you two are, and I can tell you've been holding back on me. When Evie announced at dinner that she was carrying, there was plenty of joy around the table, but I saw something in her eyes that reminded me of the terror I saw there that day at Dune Hollow. And I saw how you looked at each other. What are you keeping from me?"

Just then, Tricia got up and climbed onto Jake's lap, interrupting their conversation when she threw chubby arms around his neck and gave him kisses. Not to be outdone, Sadie did the same, both girls giggling as Jake growled and tickled them. They lavished him with more kisses, Tricia shouting "Poppy" and Sadie squealing "Gamps." Considering the fact that Jake had shot seven men just three days ago, Randy thought the sight of him doting on his little granddaughters extremely comical.

Jake grabbed both girls about the waist and carried them down the steps, setting them on their feet. "Go find Grandma some flowers," he told them, "and take some to Evie, too, but don't pick any of Grandma's roses. The thorns will poke you." He ran a hand through his hair to straighten what four small hands had made a mess of and came back up the steps.

"Jake, when we go to Denver, I want to find that place where they sell rosebushes. I want to plant more roses around the porch...yellow ones, of course. The ones we bought last year look beautiful, don't they?" She studied her roses, proud of her green thumb.

"You're avoiding the subject we need to discuss," Jake answered as he walked over to his chair and sat down again, his smile fading as the girls ran off. "Let's hear it," he told Randy.

Oh, how she hated having to reopen old wounds. She stared at the blooms on a nearby rosebush as she spoke. "I asked if there was anything Evie wanted to tell me. At first she said she didn't want to because she was scared how you would react. Jake, she's so afraid of you going back to prison."

Jake took yet another cigarette and match from his shirt pocket. "I'm not going anywhere. I just need to know what's got her so upset. It's more than the fact that Holt is out of jail." He struck the match and lit his cigarette; his smoking was almost constant when he was upset. He glanced sidelong at her as he inhaled. "Just tell me, Randy."

She closed her eyes. "It isn't the news itself that upset her, Jake. I mean, she's healed from the horror of what she went through, and things are good now between her and Brian. Thank God for that man."

Jake stood up with a deep sigh and leaned against the railing, facing Randy. "And?"

Randy hesitated, hating to tell him anything that could bring back the old Jake, the dark and ruthless Jake…the Jake who still had to remember that if he stepped too far out of line, he could be arrested again. He had to remember he was no longer a U.S. Marshal. He was Jake Harkner the citizen, a man whose reputation could be used against him.

"Randy, talk to me."

She sighed. "What's bothering her is…something she never told any of us. Brian knows, but she didn't tell us because… Well, mainly because she's embarrassed about it, and because she's worried how you'll take it, but she thinks you need to know because it could be important."

Jake folded his arms. "I promise not to do anything crazy. Just tell me what I'm dealing with."

Randy rose and stood beside him, watching Evie sweep little Sadie into her arms when the child ran up to her. "They, uh...they blindfolded her, Jake." She didn't have to touch him or look at him to know his whole body had stiffened with an oncoming rage.

"They what?"

"When some of the other men with Marty and Hash came to take their turns, they blindfolded her so she wouldn't know who was...raping her...and they told her that any minute they would...bring her terrible pain and...they would kill her and she wouldn't see it coming. They said that so she'd be even more terrified."

"Jesus God Almighty," Jake muttered under his breath, seething.

Randy reached over and grasped his arm without looking at him. His bicep was as hard as a rock. "Please stay calm, Jake. It will break her heart if she sees you explode." She squeezed hard, thinking how silly it was to think she could physically stop this man from anything he might decide to do. "Jake, she only told me because she thinks we need to be aware that she doesn't even know what Mike Holt looks like. He could walk right up to her, and she wouldn't even realize he was...one of them. That's what scares her."

He pulled away.

"Jake, don't say a word to her about it. She'd be devastated. She hated for you to know, because she understands how easily you blame yourself for all of it. Remember that she forgave them. That's how she lives with it. And she needs her father to stay calm."

"I should have killed the sonofabitch when I had the chance!" The words were spoken in a gruff but lowered voice. Randy knew the vision of his daughter being so brutalized was torture for him.

"That would have broken Evie's heart, Jake. She doesn't want her father to be the man he was the first thirty years of his life. There are laws now, Jake, even more so than when you were a marshal—and a judge sentenced you to serve that duty as part of a reprieve from prison, allowing you to use your knowledge of outlaws to *help* the law rather than ride against it. But you're still Jake Harkner, and now that you're no longer wearing a badge, the law will be watching you. The book Jeff wrote has made you even more famous, which makes you even more noticeable." She turned and looked up at him, almost gasping at the look in his eyes. There it was—the ruthless outlaw.

"He needs to die, and you know it!"

She grasped his arms. "Jake, do you love Evie?"

"You know you don't need to ask that!"

"And do you love *me*? And those beautiful little granddaughters out there? And Stevie and Ben and Little Jake and the new grandchild on the way?"

He pulled away and turned. Before he'd even finished the cigarette, he threw it out into a puddle left from a soft rain the night before. He grasped the railing so tightly his knuckles turned white. His breathing quickened as he shook his head, and Randy knew he was struggling with a rage that wanted to explode out of him. She could almost hear a rumbling sound. "My God, how can she forgive something like that?" he said, his voice husky with fury.

"Because she's full of God's grace, Jake, and she knows that's the only way to stay sane. She loves Brian and wants to be a good wife and a good mother, so she has to go on with her life and be a woman for Brian and leave the past behind her." She deftly moved an arm around his waist, realizing she was probably the only person who could touch Jake Harkner when he was like this and not worry about him roaring at her and shoving her away. "Jake, please look at me."

He just shook his head and stared at the puddle of water. "Some say I should have let her testify, but I damn well wasn't going to put her through that. It was better that every man there was presumed guilty."

Randy watched his jaw twitch in repressed fury. Finally, he turned to look at her, and she leaned up and kissed his cheek, kissed the thin scar from when he got into a wild fight with their adopted son's abusive father. "Jake, you can't let this eat at you. Mike Holt might never show up, and even if he does and tries to make trouble, you have to let the *law* handle it. The *law*, Jake." Her eyes teared. "After all we've been through making sure you're a free man, I don't want to spend my old age sitting alone on this porch while you die in prison. I'm already scared of what might happen from the shoot-out with those rustlers the other day. Everything you do gets extra scrutiny."

"A man has a right to protect what's his. Those *rustlers* broke that law you're talking about. I didn't! And they would have come after *you* if I hadn't made sure they couldn't."

She moved both arms around him. He was rigid with anger. "You can't save the whole world, Jake. You can defend us, but you can't go looking for someone who *might* do something to one of us. It just doesn't work that way anymore." She pressed the side of her face against his chest and felt his mother's crucifix against her cheek. He'd worn it under his shirt his whole life…ever since he'd witnessed his father murder his mother and little brother and then was forced to help bury them. Those ugly memories that visited him deep in the night were what kept the battle between good and evil raging deep inside his soul. It was only the love he'd found with Randy and their family that kept him from going over the edge. "Just promise me you'll be careful. It would destroy us all to see you go back to the dark hatred and maybe even go back to prison." She breathed in his familiar scent. "I've grown used to finally having these arms around me every night, Jake."

She felt some of the tension leaving him. He finally softened a little, embraced her, and kissed the top of her head. "Believe me, woman, I don't want to do something that means I *can't* have you with me in bed every night, but a man should have the right to avenge the abuse of his own loved ones."

"If there is good cause, yes. But I know you, and you'd like to kill that man on sight even if he doesn't do one thing to provoke you."

"He's *already* provoked me, just by existing! Randy, I can't promise what I'll do if I see him."

"Then you have to prepare yourself, and you have to hope it never happens."

Jake gently pushed her away. "Go sit with Evie and ask Brian to come over here. I need to talk to him for a minute."

Randy leaned up and kissed him. "Evie will get through this. She has Brian, and she's a strong, tough young woman. She gets that toughness from you." She detected tears in his eyes.

"Maybe she's like me in toughness and strength, but in no other way is that angel anything like her father, thank God. Inside, she's much stronger than I've ever been or ever will be." He kissed her forehead. "Go get Brian like I asked." He stepped back, and Randy reached out and squeezed his hand before walking off the veranda and out to where Evie and Brian played with the girls.

Jake watched Evie, her beautiful smile, her long, dark hair, the way she hugged the girls. She was genuine goodness, and the thought of what she'd suffered made him feel physically ill. He lit yet another cigarette, wondering how he was going to deal with the fact that a man like Mike Holt had been freed from prison instead of hung. He contemplated all the ways he might be able to kill the man and get away with it.

Brian left the women and walked up to the house. The medium-built, good-looking, and always-dapper Dr. Brian Stewart was as different from Jake and Lloyd as a man could get, and that was fine with Jake. He was a soft-spoken man of incredible patience and kindness, and he barely knew how to use a gun. He'd never even gone hunting.

"Randy said you wanted to talk," Brian told Jake as he came up the steps. "I take it it's about Mike Holt."

Jake took a drag on his cigarette and met Brian's gaze. "What do you want me to do?" he asked Brian.

"*Do?*"

"If the man shows his face anywhere near Evie or anybody else in this family, I can make him disappear, if you want me to," Jake told him.

Brian studied the darkness in his father-in-law's eyes. He'd seen that look before. "Simple as that?"

"You bet. Just don't tell Randy or Evie what I said."

Brian sighed as he moved beside Jake and joined him at the railing. "Jake, you never cease to amaze me with your candid admissions. You said that like it was as easy for you as shooting a rattler."

"No difference, as far as I'm concerned."

Brian shook his head. "The last thing Evie needs is for her father to go back to prison, Jake. Nothing is worth that. If that man shows his face, you'd better have a damn good *reason* to kill him."

"I already do."

"You know what I mean. It would just bring it all back for her. And I doubt he's crazy enough to come anywhere near this place. The trouble is, Evie wouldn't know it if he stood right next to her."

"Someone should have told me all of it a long time ago."

"We figured he'd be in prison too long for it to matter, and Evie knew what it would do to you if you knew everything. Her biggest fear, Jake, is you or Lloyd going off the deep end over it. That's why she forgave them and wanted you to know it." Brian rested his elbows on the railing and watched Evie and their tiny daughter Sadie. "This isn't any easier on me than it is on you. Even *I* wouldn't recognize the man. That day…there was so much confusion…and after I took her behind the cabin to tend to her, I never looked at any of those who were left alive. I couldn't." His hands moved into fists. "That's the only time in my life I wanted to kill men rather than save them, so don't think I don't understand this time how easy it is for you to consider doing so yourself. Part of me wants to tell you to do it, but we live in different times now, Jake, and all the healing Evie has done would be for nothing if something happened to you. She adores you, and your well-being is far more important to her than any kind of revenge. Just keep that in mind."

Jake kept his cigarette at the corner of his mouth as he spoke. "She really all right now?"

"Most of the time." Brian cleared his throat. "I have to tell her sometimes to just…look at me and think about how much I love her and treasure her. Look at *me* and know who she belongs to."

"Shit," Jake muttered. He closed his eyes and turned to lean against a support post. "I'm worried about Lloyd, too. Mike Holt vowed that if he was ever free, he'd get Lloyd for shooting his brother."

"That worries Evie, too. You know how much Lloyd means to her."

The women were walking toward them now, Evie holding Sadie and Randy holding Tricia. The younger boys came charging up to the house on horseback, Little Jake sitting behind Stephen with his arms wrapped around his cousin's waist. The boy clamored down and ran up the porch steps to Jake. "Grampa, go riding with us and let me ride my own horse, will you?"

Jake tousled Little Jake's hair and glanced at Evie. "You care?"

Evie set Sadie on her feet. "Daddy, if not for you being around to keep Little Jake busy, I'd be a worn-out old woman already. I think the two of you share the same restless soul, so yes, take him riding. Brian and I have trouble making him sit still for his lessons. You need to talk to him about that."

"I'll do my best."

Little Jake tugged at Jake's hand. "Come on, Grampa."

Jake took his hand and walked down the porch steps and close to Evie. He put a hand to the side of her face and kissed her forehead. "Everything will work out, baby girl. Don't be worrying about me or your brother, understand?"

Evie gave him a hug. "I didn't want you to know all of it."

Jake hugged her close with one arm while still holding Little Jake's hand. "You just concentrate on that good man you're married to and on having another healthy baby. I'll take care of anything that comes up, and I won't be careless about it."

"But Lloyd gets as angry as you sometimes. I'm scared for him."

"I'll talk to Lloyd. He has a son and a daughter to think about, let alone a wife. You just take it easy for now. We have a lot of work ahead of us that will keep us right here on the ranch, so there's nothing to worry about for now, all right? No stranger gets onto the J&L without somebody knowing it."

Evie pulled away, wiping at tears.

"Mommy cry," little Sadie said, looking at Evie with lips pouted.

"Mommy's fine, sweetness," Randy answered, kneeling in front of her granddaughter. "Come inside and have some cookies, Tricia."

Evie took a deep breath and put her hand on Little

Jake's shoulder. "You be a good boy and do what your grandfather tells you, understand?"

"Can we go, too?" Stephen spoke up when he and Ben rode closer.

"Yeah, Pa, let's all go riding," Ben declared, his face already sunburned from riding most of the afternoon.

"And as far as I'm concerned, Daddy, you can take Little Jake on roundups and let him help with branding and feeding the cattle and anything else that keeps him busy," Evie told him. "He needs a way to get rid of all that pent-up energy."

Jake smiled. "Okay, boys, let's go saddle up Midnight. Maybe Little Jake can ride Shortbread. She's a pretty gentle horse." Jake headed toward the barn, hoisting seven-year-old Little Jake under one arm like a sack of potatoes. "And we can't ride near the pond. Your uncle Lloyd is there with Katie, and they want to be alone, so let's ride in the other direction."

"Awww, they're kissin', aren't they?" Little Jake spoke the words in a singsong tease.

"You'll never find out, you little troublemaker," Jake answered, hiking Little Jake over his shoulder. The boy laughed all the way into the barn.

Evie watched after them. "Is Daddy really okay with all this?" she asked her mother.

Randy sighed. "No one really knows what's going on inside that man's head," she answered. "But he knows the rules have changed, Evie, and he'll keep that in mind. I'm more worried about those boys wearing him out. He has aches and pains the kids know nothing about. At their age, they wouldn't even understand that kind of pain."

Brian came down the steps and moved an arm around his wife. "Let's go inside and help the girls with those cookies." He urged her up the steps, glancing back at Jake as he headed for a barn with two grandsons and an adopted son in tow.

"I'll be back before dark," Jake shouted at them without turning around.

Brian smiled. "The wild bunch," he dubbed them.

"And Jake is wildest of all," Randy added. "Lloyd said once that when Jake is with those boys, it's hard to tell sometimes which one is the man and which one is the child." She turned to Evie. "Let's go inside and have those cookies."

Evie and Brian walked through the screened door, and Randy watched Jake out in the corral with the boys. She remembered when she first had Lloyd, how terrified Jake was of being a father. Now there he was out romping around with grandsons.

So far. He'd come so far. Inside she was both furious and terrified over the situation with Mike Holt. The man's release could end up destroying all of this. Jake Harkner was not going to rest easy until he knew where the man was and what he was up to...and he'd rest even easier if Mike Holt was dead. That was what terrified her.

Eight

"LLOYD HARKNER, I AM SO EMBARRASSED THAT YOUR parents know why we came here."

Lloyd grinned, helping Katie down from his horse. "What makes you think they wouldn't have known anyway?" Lloyd jumped down and grabbed the blanket from the horse, handing it to Katie while he led his horse to a small tree and tied it. The day was warm, and he removed his shirt as he headed back to where Katie was spreading the blanket on the grass. She laid a towel beside it. "Get undressed, woman. We're going for a swim."

"*Naked?*"

"Of *course* naked."

"What if one of the hired hands comes around?"

Lloyd unbuckled his gun belt. "I told them not to."

"You mean *they* know, too?"

"Sure they do. What's wrong with that? We're married, aren't we?"

"*Lloyd!*"

"Sweetheart, we don't get enough chances to do this at home, what with Stephen being old enough to know what we're doing when he hears all those sounds coming from the bedroom"—he tossed his shirt and dropped his gun belt onto the blanket—"and Tricia crawling out of bed in the middle of the night to come and sleep with us." He bent down and removed his boots and socks.

"Oh, Lloyd, I can't strip naked right out here in the daylight."

Lloyd began unbuttoning the front of her dress. "Sure

you can. You stripped naked up in the loft a few days ago. What's the difference?"

Katie smiled, her cheeks growing red. "The difference is a *roof* and *walls*! A *little* privacy is better than none at all."

Lloyd pulled the dress down over her shoulders. "*No* privacy just makes it more exciting." Still, he paused. When she gave a shy nod, he continued pulling the dress down over her slips, until she could step out of it. He pulled off her slips and moved up to unlace her camisole. "Have I told you lately how beautiful you are in the sunlight, all white and pink and blushing red mixed with those blue eyes? You're like a flower garden, Katie."

She laughed lightly, moving her hands over his solid stomach and chest, up to his powerful shoulders and down his arms. "You tell me that all the time." She kissed his chest. "And here you are looking like an Indian." She reached up and pulled some of his long, dark hair over his shoulders. "Am I your captive?"

"You bet you are." Lloyd met her mouth, tasting her lips eagerly as he pulled the camisole all the way off and threw it aside. He moved his lips to her breasts, kneeling in front of her as he gently massaged her breasts and continued kissing down her belly. He pulled her underwear down, kissing at the place he thought the sweetest he'd ever enjoyed. He felt Katie's fingers dig into his hair as he moved his tongue between her legs to kindle the hot juices of desire he loved bringing forth from her.

"Step out," he told her, his voice husky with desire.

Katie moved her feet to step out of the underwear, and Lloyd pulled off her shoes and stockings. He worked his way back up to her lips as he unbuckled his belt, then deftly removed his denim pants, pulling his underwear off with them.

"Lloyd, are you sure—"

He silenced her with another kiss as he lifted her. Katie wrapped her legs around him and he knelt down, laying her back on the blanket and kissing his way down between her legs again.

Katie made no more protest. She reached over her head and gripped at a tiny new growth of a pine tree, hanging on to it as Lloyd kissed along the inside of her thigh.

"When we first met, I never knew you had such beautiful, slender legs under all those skirts," he told her, working his way back to private places no other man had ever tasted, not even her first husband.

"And I never dreamed I'd let a man do such brazen things with me." She gasped with desire as Lloyd worked his magic. They hadn't had a chance to get back to this since Lloyd had to leave her in the loft, and he was anxious to finish what they'd started there. He worked his way back over her belly, moving fingers inside of her and feeling the pulsation of her climax. He tasted her breasts again, moved to her neck. "I'm sorry I had to leave the other day."

"You didn't have any choice," she answered softly.

"I felt so sorry for you. I love you for doing that, Katie."

She cried out when he moved inside her, wrapping an arm under her left knee and bending her leg up so he could push even deeper.

"Let's make another baby," he told her, kissing her behind the ear, over her eyes, ravishing her mouth with his own.

For several minutes there was only the pure joy of mating, rhythmic thrusts matching rhythmic groans and gasps until finally his life spilled into her.

"Stay right here," he told her. "I'm going to stay inside you and do this again."

His hair fell around her face as he tasted her neck, moved to her breasts again, back to her neck while he kept a powerful arm under her leg and began the mating all over again. He loved the way she had of pulling him inside, and he deliberately held back a need to come until he felt her climax again.

"God, Katie, it feels so good." His life surged into her again, and in the next moment, he relaxed on top of her, kissing her behind the ear. "Yes, you *are* my captive, and I've just claimed my woman."

"Lloyd, the way you talk." Katie smiled, reaching up and pushing some of his hair back behind his ears. "I swear you have a wicked side to you."

"Of course I do. I'm a Harkner, aren't I?"

Katie sobered. "Yes, and that's what scares me. That terrible man who got out of jail wants to kill you, Lloyd."

He kissed her again. "Don't you be worrying about that. You know I can take care of myself."

"Lloyd—"

"We aren't going to talk about it." He got to his knees, then picked her up and rose, carrying her to the pond. Katie's screams of protest did no good. He dropped her into the water and dove in with her. "I'll race you to the other side."

"Lloyd Harkner, your arms are longer than mine!"

He took off swimming, and Katie followed. It wasn't a big pond, and it took only a couple of minutes to reach the other side. They splashed at each other, and Katie studied her husband's magnificent build as he came out of the pond naked. She joined him as he lay down in soft grass to rest. They both stared up at puffy white clouds.

"I wish it could always be like this, Lloyd. Quiet and peaceful with no danger lurking behind the trees."

"There's no danger lurking anywhere." Lloyd traced a finger down between her breasts. "Compared to the dangers Pa and I faced every day when we were lawmen back in Oklahoma, this life is great."

Katie leaned over and kissed him. "But with that man on the loose, it's like your lawman days are coming back to visit. I hate it."

Lloyd touched the side of her face. "Katie, I said we wouldn't talk about that; but if you need reassuring, just remember that he doesn't want to go back to prison or hang, which is what would happen if he tries anything. And don't forget that I'm used to watching my back. I want you to stop thinking about it. It's not likely anything will happen, but if it does, I'll be ready for it. I just want you to be happy and to concentrate on having another baby." He grinned, leaning over to taste her breasts again, lightly sucking at them. "We have to catch up with Brian and Evie," he told her as he nuzzled her cleavage.

"Don't you dare say that in front of them."

"I wouldn't do that to my sister." Lloyd sobered. "You talk to her a lot, Katie. Is she really all right? How upset is she over this Mike Holt thing?"

Katie sighed, running a hand over his arm. "She's okay most of the time. I think she'd fall apart without Brian, though. He's her rock. So is your father. She so adores him, Lloyd, and she's scared to death what he might do if he sees Mike Holt. She's scared for you, too."

"I'll talk to her. I don't want her worrying about it. Pa and I *were* the law for a while, so we know the ins and outs of it." He kissed her again. "And you, little lady, should concern yourself only with me and little Tricia and Stephen." He caressed her hair. "Other than this mess with Mike Holt, you're happy now, aren't you?"

She smiled again. "I'm very happy."

"I know things didn't start out so good for us, but I fall more in love with you every day, Katie. I'm so sorry about what happened in Guthrie. That was a hell of a way to start a marriage."

"It's over now, and everybody is safe. Evie is healing, and you and I have discovered we're more than just the good friends we started out to be. For a while I was afraid you wouldn't be able to love me like you loved…her. But I feel it now, Lloyd. I feel your love."

He pulled her into his arms with a deep sigh. "I've had

to let go of Beth and put that part of my life behind me, just like we have to put Oklahoma behind us, and you have to leave your first husband in the past." He kissed her hair. "The baby you lost will always live in your heart. I know that. But now we have Tricia, and maybe soon another baby. And I'll always have Stephen, a part of Beth. Mom says all things happen for a reason, and we have to accept it. God knows nobody needs to learn to accept things more than my mother. She's been through so much over the years. If she can hang on and still be happy and put the bad times behind her, we can, too."

Katie kissed him again. "I once couldn't understand how she could put up with all the things your father put her through, but I understand it all so much better now. When I see how much they love each other, I can understand why your mother can bear the hard parts. You're so much like him, Lloyd, in the way you love somebody. It's just that…sometimes I see that dark side of him in you, and it scares me. I'm not scared *of* you— I'm scared *for* you."

"And I'm a grown man who can take care of himself. And I'm my *own* man, Katie—not my father. I'm not saying there's anything wrong with that, because I know he's a damn good man…but there's a part of him that can go deeper into that dark place than I ever will, because we were raised so different. But you and I will be just fine, Katie-girl."

Katie traced a finger over his lips. "Will we go to Denver together again when you're ready to take in the herd?"

"We sure will. It won't be for another six weeks or so. We need to fatten up the herd first. When we do go to Denver, we'll stay at the Brown Palace like we always do, and we'll go to the theater and do some shopping and have a damn good time."

"I kind of hate leaving Tricia and Stevie, but they

love Teresa and Rodriguez to death, and there are a lot of good men here to watch out for them."

"Sure there are. It's good for us to get away." He rolled on top of her. "And I like spoiling you on those trips to Denver. This year I'm going to buy you a diamond necklace."

"Lloyd, you are not! You can't afford that."

"Sure I can. I have plenty of money from Beth's estate. I put some away for Stephen and Tricia, and I'll use some to buy more land." He kissed her lightly. "Someday the J&L will all belong to the kids. Evie's, too. I'll not leave my sister or my nieces and nephews out of any of this." He gave her another kiss. "But I have plenty left to splurge on my beautiful wife." He glanced up toward the sun. "We have another hour or so, Mrs. Harkner."

"Then let's make the best of it, Mr. Harkner."

The lovemaking started again. In the back of his mind, Lloyd *was* damn well worried about Mike Holt, and worried about his father, too. But he was determined not to place that worry on this woman who'd already learned the hard way what life sometimes handed a man with the last name of Harkner. Too many times he'd blamed his father for the troubles that name could bring, but Jake never asked for any of it.

He released his pent-up passion and frustration on Katie, hoping the pure pleasure of this would keep her from thinking about anything that upset her. "I love you, Katie-girl," he groaned near her ear as he moved in sweet rhythm to the tune of her cries of ecstasy. When he was finished, he held her close, not wanting to move off of her just yet.

"Don't let go," she said softly.

"Never," he answered, "even when we're apart." He remembered his mother telling him once that Jake often said that same thing to her...that he was always holding her. The one thing he'd always wanted growing up was a marriage that involved as deep a love as he knew his parents shared.

He'd finally found it.

Nine

JAKE RODE INTO ONE OF THE BARNS TO PUT UP HIS horse and get a fresh mount. Pain from old wounds stabbed at weary bones as he unsaddled and removed the gear from his equally weary cutting horse.

Daily routines had changed, as they always did when spring roundup and branding became the most important chore. He hated that Randy, Katie, and Evie were kept busy helping Teresa with constant cooking for the men, but they didn't seem to mind. Rodriguez usually did the cooking out at the cookhouse, but this time of year he was busy helping the rest of the men.

As he'd promised Evie, Jake kept Little Jake with him for the first time on roundup. So far, the boy had obeyed every order, but Jake could tell he wanted to get on his own horse and ride down a calf and try to rope and brand it by himself. Maybe next year. For now he spent most of the time sitting on a fence, watching, but sometimes Jake let him ride behind him on his horse when he rode away from the main homestead to rustle up more stray cattle.

Stephen and Ben came inside also to change horses. They were big enough now to ride and do some herding themselves. Watching them learn to rope and brand was something the whole family enjoyed. Jake smiled at the fact that they were wanting to be men in the worst way. He and Lloyd sometimes had trouble convincing them there were certain things they still weren't ready for, which included carrying their own six-guns, something Jake flat-out refused to allow.

"Don't waste too much time, boys," Jake told them as he threw a blanket over a gray-spotted Appaloosa. "We have to get back out there."

"Yes, sir," Stephen answered.

The boys unsaddled their horses a little too quietly, and Jake glanced over to see them whispering.

"What's going on?" he asked.

They approached him rather hesitantly. Stephen met Jake's gaze boldly, as though he needed courage. "Grampa, you let us hunt, so why can't we learn to shoot pistols? You're the best there is. You could teach us really good."

Jake was not oblivious to the boys' attempts at flattering him into letting them have their way. "Stephen, I don't intend to discuss it. And besides that, I'm not the one to ask. Ask your father."

"He always says I should ask you."

Thanks a lot, Lloyd, Jake thought. Lloyd was just as hesitant about his son using a six-gun as Jake was, but Jake had even deeper reasons than just the danger. "Stephen, I can tell you for a fact that knowing how to use a gun can bring you a lot of heartache. And you and Ben are still way too young for handling pistols. They're a lot more dangerous than a rifle."

"Is it true, Grampa?"

Jake heaved the saddle onto the horse, then turned. Both boys stood facing him, eyes wide with curiosity. "Is *what* true?"

Stephen shrugged. "You know—about the way you used to live. About your own pa and all that? Nobody will let us read the book Jeff wrote about you. Grandma and my pa say you have to tell us when we can read it."

Jake studied them, remembering when Lloyd once asked him about his past, and he'd refused to tell him. His not knowing had led to tragedy when Lloyd was older and learned the truth the hard way. "Stephen, why are you asking this now? We're in the middle of herding and culling and branding."

Stephen's eyes actually teared. "I don't know. I just thought it had something to do with why you won't let us use a handgun. I'm sorry I asked."

"We'll get our horses saddled." Ben spoke up with urgency in the words. His eyes showed an odd fear Jake hadn't seen there before.

Ben turned to go to another stall.

"Ben!" Jake spoke up. "Stay right here." Jake left his horse only partially saddled and walked out of the stall, ordering the boys to sit down on some stacked hay. They looked at each other, then obeyed. Jake walked over and knelt in front of them. "What's going on?" he asked them.

Ben swallowed. "Nothing."

"And you just looked at me like you were afraid of me. What did I tell you the day I took you from your father and adopted you?" Jake asked Ben.

"You said...I'd be your son, and nobody would ever hurt me again."

"And did I keep that promise?"

Ben nodded, tears brimming in his eyes.

"Then why did you just now act like you were afraid of me?"

Ben quickly wiped at the tears. "I'm not afraid of you. I'm afraid something bad will happen to you 'cause of you killing all those men a couple weeks ago. Sometimes we get scared when you act like that, but nobody tells us why you can get mean sometimes. You're never mean to us."

Jake had never felt so touched. The boy's remark about being afraid *for* him was the epitome of all he'd ever wanted in life—love and family. He wondered if he would ever get used to these feelings, and he knew it was time to tell his grandson and Ben things he'd rather not talk about. He reached over and pulled a nearby crate closer, then sat down on it, facing the boys. He lit a cigarette.

"All right." He took a long drag on the cigarette, hoping he could do this without visiting that dark place that usually took over when he had to talk about his father. "It's really hard for me to talk about these things, boys, but you need to know that everything you've heard about me is true." He rested his elbows on his knees, keeping the cigarette between his lips. "When I was your age, I'd been beaten too many times to count by a father who instilled in me the idea that I was worthless. I'd already witnessed him murder my mother and my little brother." He paused to keep his voice steady, taking the cigarette from his lips. "He…uh…he made me help bury them." He struggled against the sick anger.

"Grampa, that's terrible!" Stephen told him, looking ready to cry again.

Jake took the cigarette from his lips and just stared at it for several quiet seconds. "I have scars on my back from all the beatings, often with the buckle end of a belt. Someday I'll show you the scars, but not today." He looked at Ben. "Now you know why I attacked your father, Ben—why I took you away from all that. I knew what that was like."

Ben quickly wiped at silent tears. "I won't forget what you did. I'll be a good son."

"You're a wonderful son. I don't regret for one minute taking you into our home." Jake sighed. "As far as what happened after my mother and brother were murdered, I lived in hell for seven more years. When I was fifteen, I found my father…doing something bad to a young girl I cared about. He was a big, strong, brutal man who drank too much. The only way I could think to stop him was to shoot him…so I did. I didn't mean to kill him. I just wanted to stop him."

He took another drag on the cigarette. "So yes, I killed my own father. And back then, I didn't know a bullet could go through one person into another. When I shot my father, I accidentally killed that young girl, too. I'll never forget that or forgive myself for it. I just didn't know what I was doing, and I was scared, afraid people would accuse me of murder when it wasn't that at all. I rode off scared to death I'd hang for it, so I joined up with a gang of outlaws, and for the next several years, that's how I lived—robbing and killing and learning I was damn good with a gun. I felt like a worthless murderer and figured maybe that's all I'd ever be known for, so why should I care about living any other way?"

He smoked again, then reached over to flick the cigarette into a bucket of water kept in the barn for such things. He ran a hand through his hair and rubbed at his eyes. "I didn't used to be able to talk about this, but a preacher, and Randy, helped me learn to deal with it and taught me I was better off talking about it than holding it all inside. It's up to you boys to decide how you feel about what I did. And I don't want you telling Little Jake yet. I'll decide when to tell him."

"Okay, Pa," Ben told him, his eyes wide and curious.

Stephen shook his head. "It's okay, Grampa. You were a kid like us and didn't know what else to do."

Jake smiled sadly, taking Stephen's hand. "Stephen, I hid the truth from your father till he was almost grown. He found out everything when I was arrested after years of running and they took me to prison. I didn't even do some of the things they accused me of, but I ran with some really bad men, so I was accused of all the things they did. When Lloyd found out, it hurt him really bad. He'd always looked up to me. So he went on kind of a rampage against me, because my going to prison cost him the woman he loved...your mother. Her father found out she was in love with the son of an outlaw, so he took her away. Lloyd never knew she was carrying you, Stephen, until almost five years later. That was a really bad time for Lloyd. He ran off while I was in prison, and he lived like an outlaw himself."

"Will he get mad if I ask him about it?"

"I don't think so, but let me say something to him first. I just want you to know that my not telling Lloyd the truth about my past caused a big rift between him and me that broke my heart. I lost my son for a while. I never want that to happen between me and any of my grandchildren, or to you and your father, Stephen. Your grandmother preaches to me constantly about telling all of you the truth, so that's what I'm doing—and for me to be able to talk about it at all is a miracle, and it's all thanks to Randy. There are some things you just never quite get over, boys, things that live down deep inside that sometimes come back to revisit you in bad ways. That happens to me sometimes. Randy has taught me it's okay to let people love me, because I've never felt I deserved it. Evie has also taught me a lot about love and forgiveness. She has a beautiful soul, boys, and I think it all comes from Randy. God knows it couldn't have been me. Don't ever underestimate how bad a life I led for a while, because I was as bad as they come. You might as well know it."

"Some of Aunt Evie's goodness *does* come from you, Grampa," Stephen told him. "You love all of us real good. That must mean you're good inside, too."

Jake couldn't answer right away. He swallowed before speaking again. "Well, I guess that's for God to decide when I meet my Maker." He turned to Ben. "And don't ever, ever be afraid of me, Ben, no matter what you hear from other people—understand?" He looked at Stephen. "Understand? As bad as I was in the past, I never hurt a child or a woman."

Both boys nodded.

"It's a man's job to protect and defend his own," Jake

continued. "I think both of you know what happened to Evie back in Oklahoma—or you at least have a pretty good idea. Lloyd and I killed a lot of men that day, but it had to be done. I just don't want either one of you to worry I'll go back to prison, because I haven't done anything wrong, and I *won't* do anything wrong if I can help it. But I'll damn well use my guns to protect my wife and my children and grandchildren if I have to. And it's *because* these guns I wear have brought me a lot of trouble and heartache that it's hard for me to teach you to wear guns. It's hard for Lloyd, too. Can you understand it's because we love you and don't want you to get hurt or in trouble?"

The boys nodded, and Stephen suddenly threw his arms around Jake's neck. "Don't do something that makes you have to go away, Grampa."

Jake struggled against his tears. "I'll try real hard not to let that happen," he promised.

"I heard one of the men say that Mike Holt wants to kill Pa. Is it true?"

Jake reached out to grasp Ben's hand while he clung to Stephen. "Yes, it's true. But, Stephen, your father is just as good at handling men like that as I am, so don't you worry about it, okay? Is that why you and Ben want to carry your own guns?"

"Yeah," Ben answered for Stephen. "What if you and Lloyd need protecting? He's my brother now."

Jake squeezed his hand. "Boys, I assure you that Lloyd and I can handle ourselves just fine—and we've got plenty of hired hands, all good men. This is the J&L, and nobody is going to get onto this land without us knowing it. Nobody will get near any of us. And even when we leave the ranch and take the cattle to Denver, we'll be on the lookout. Lloyd and I rode together for three years as U.S. Marshals. We know what we're doing. Promise me you'll stop worrying."

Stephen sniffed and pulled away, wiping at his eyes. "Will you still teach us someday about how to use handguns?"

"Sure I will, but not till you're at least fifteen or sixteen, understand? And in your case, Stephen, only if your father agrees."

"He likes you now, doesn't he?"

"Likes me?"

"I mean, he's not mad at you anymore about when you went to prison? You said Pa was real mad at you."

Jake smiled sadly. "Your father and I have never been closer, Stephen. We still have our differences, but I'd die for Lloyd, and he damn well knows it. And I think he'd do the same for me. I hope you and Lloyd will always be as close as he and I are. I might have had a father from hell, but one thing I learned from the man was the kind of father I *wanted* to be. It took me a long time to learn how to do that, but your grandmother taught me things about love I didn't understand when I first met her. And let me tell you something—both of you—no better woman ever walked the face of the earth than Miranda Harkner. Because of me, she's had a hard life, but she stuck through it and never complains and has shown me what love really means. I pray both of you find a woman like that someday."

Ben made a face. "We don't want nothing to do with girls."

Jake grinned. "Believe me, when you are older, you will change your mind, Son."

Stephen frowned. "Eddie Holmes told me his pa said you used to run around with bad ladies. Did you?"

"Bad ladies?" Jake couldn't help laughing. "That was before I met your grandmother, and that is a whole different subject, boys. Stephen, that's for your father to tell you about. But you shouldn't really call them that. They aren't bad. Most of them are good at heart." He sobered. "Women like that half raised me, and sometimes they shielded me from my father when he was having one of his drunken rages. One even took a beating to protect me. Many women like that have a lot of good in them, and most have had their own tragic past." He tousled Ben's hair. "You boys listen to me. When you get older, you respect all women. *All* women, understand? Don't you ever think of a woman as bad, and don't ever, ever lay a hand wrongly on a woman. That's one thing I will never tolerate. If I ever learn you've abused a woman when you get older, I'll toss you right off the J&L and disinherit you. Understand?"

"Yes, sir," Ben answered.

"You don't go with other ladies now, do you, Grampa?"

Jake tried to keep the moment serious, but it was next to impossible. He chuckled. "Stephen, if I did, I would have to answer to your grandmother for it, and believe me, I'm more afraid of *her* than I am of those seven rustlers I went up against a few weeks ago."

Both boys laughed as Jake rose. "One more thing," he told them. "Living like I did the first thirty years of my life has left me with a lot of aches and pains and scars and regrets, so live a good life, boys. You'll feel a lot better physically and be a lot happier when you get to be my age."

"Oh, Grampa, you're still a strong man," Stephen argued. "Pa says he thinks you're just as strong as he is."

"He does, does he? He's never told *me* that. He's always saying he could beat me senseless if he wanted."

"And you're always daring him to try," Stephen answered. "I see how you talk to each other. Is that because you love each other?"

Jake felt the old ache deep in his heart, remembering when he thought he'd lost his son's love. "Yeah, something like that. Let's get these horses saddled. The men out there probably think we're shirking our duties."

Just then Lloyd pushed open the barn door and came

inside, leading his horse behind him. "Where in hell have you three been? We're all out there working our asses off, and you're in here taking your own sweet time getting fresh horses." His smile faded when he noticed the boys had been crying. "Anything wrong?"

Jake turned away and went into the stall again to finish cinching the saddle on his horse. "Just having a little heart-to-heart," he answered. "Everything is fine."

Lloyd looked from the boys to his father. "You okay?"

Jake fought a distinct desire to walk up and hug his son. "Never been better," he answered. "I was just explaining why we don't think the boys are ready yet to carry handguns."

Lloyd pushed his hat back and moved closer to the stall. "What did you tell them?"

Jake didn't answer right away. He urged his horse backward out of the stall and mounted up. "Everything," he told Lloyd. "And you'd be wise to do the same. It's about time Stephen knew it all." He rode the horse toward the barn entrance.

"Pa?"

Jake reined the horse in, not looking at Lloyd.

"You know I love you," Lloyd told him.

Jake rode out of the barn.

"Why didn't he say anything, Pa?" Stephen asked.

Lloyd sighed and rearranged his hat again. "He didn't need to." He looked at Ben. "And you boys had better finish saddling fresh horses and get back to work. We still have more cattle to bring in and brand. No rest for the wicked on this ranch, boys, so get busy."

The boys eagerly obeyed. Lloyd led his horse out of the barn and mounted up again, watching Jake ride down a calf and rope it. "No rest for the wicked, that's for sure," he muttered.

Ten

Late May

"It's like watching a circus," Evie commented, laughing when Billy Dooley, who was cutting calves from their mothers, fell off his horse and got up, cussing a blue streak.

"I call it organized bedlam," Randy remarked.

Katie laughed. "It sure is that!"

The three women sat in a wagon bed in the middle of all the action on one of the J&L's busiest days. Cattle and cowboys filled the air with braying and whistling and swearing and yelling. Extra men had been hired just for roundup and the busy job of branding. Steers meant for slaughter were herded into designated pens, calves were culled out and roped for branding, and certain male calves were urged into a separate corral, where they would later be castrated. Two breeding bulls were penned well away from the rest of the herd, including mean old Gus.

Lloyd stayed busy culling out calves. The sharp turning and dodging movements of his favorite cutting horse made Katie nervous. More than one man had been thrown from his horse when it would suddenly dart in a different direction. Well-trained cutting horses did most of the work on their own.

Once Lloyd urged a calf into the branding area, Vance Kelly took over from there, riding down the calf and roping it. When he'd climb off his saddle, the back end of it would jerk up from the calf pulling on the rope tied to the saddle horn. He and Jake took turns wrestling calves onto their sides for branding.

Lloyd had decided the women shouldn't have to cook today, so he'd put Rodriguez back on duty feeding the men. Smoke wafted from the cookhouse, where the Mexican was preparing supper for what would be a bunkhouse full of very hungry men in a couple of hours. Teresa had stayed at Evie's house with both little girls to keep them out of dirt and danger.

Men rode every which way, stirring up swirls of dust as whistles and shouts filled the air. Ben and Stephen sat on a fence counting cattle, and even Brian helped, using a quirt to urge the cattle into the chute one by one. Little Jake also sat on a fence, watching the branding, obeying his grandfather's orders to stay where he would be out of danger.

"I wish Little Jake would be as obedient for me and Brian as he is for Daddy," Evie commented.

"That boy worships the ground Jake walks on," Katie replied. "So does Stephen."

"I find it incredibly comical," Randy put in. "Big, bad Jake Harkner ordering kids around—and if he ever made any of them cry, he'd be completely devastated. Someday those boys will figure out *they* could likely order *Jake* around."

More laughter. "Yes, but Jake has a way of telling the boys what to do without ever raising his voice," Katie added.

"He doesn't *need* to raise his voice," Randy answered. "He just has a commanding way about him. Even people who don't know him pick up on that *don't mess with me* air about him. You can tell by the way they react to him."

Katie laughed. "Yes, except for you, Randy. Jake is a big sap when it comes to you. Stephen told me his grampa said the other day that he was more afraid of you than all seven of those cattle rustlers he faced down three weeks ago."

Randy grinned. "Is that so?"

"Yes, and at the time, they were talking about 'bad women.' Stephen wanted to know if Jake still liked 'bad women.' Where all that came from, I have no idea, but Jake told him that if he was around women like that he'd have to answer to you, and he wouldn't want to do that."

All three women laughed again.

"He *would* have to answer to me, and I would make him very sorry," Randy told them.

"Ouch!" An extra hired hand spewed several not-so-proper expletives after being kicked by a steer. "If I had my gun on, I'd shoot your ass, you sonofabitch!"

"Hey, there's women watchin'," Charlie McGee shouted. "Watch your language."

Katie giggled, and Randy just shook her head. At this time of year she was extra grateful to have her physician son-in-law around during roundup and branding, because nearly every day someone was kicked or sometimes thrown by an extra strong and ornery calf or steer, or by a cutting horse that swerved the wrong way. There was an occasional burn from the hot coals of the branding fire, and sometimes one of the men would get something in his eye. She worried about Jake, knowing this wasn't easy work for him, but he enjoyed it, and he was amazingly tough for a man who'd stood at death's door too many times to count in his lifetime.

Most of the injuries came from any man who dared to help break one of the wild mustangs that were inevitably brought in with the cattle, and last year Pepper lost a finger when he mistakenly gripped his saddle horn just when he'd roped a calf and it jerked the rope tight. It caught his left index finger between the rope and the saddle horn and cut right through it.

Every man helped, including Charlie McGee from

Tennessee and Vance Kelly, a weathered, hard-edged man whose past they knew nothing about. Another man, named Cole Decker, limped from a wound suffered fighting for the South in the big war. Pepper was always chewing tobacco and spitting its juice, but he was a good man. He had a big belly that shook when he laughed. Terrel Adams was nice-looking and rather quiet, a hard-working man who'd appeared one day wanting a job. Right now he was out looking for more strays.

Jake had hired Teresa and her husband, Rodriguez, in Denver when they first went there after moving from Oklahoma. Jake liked having Mexicans around. He spoke Spanish himself and often had long conversations with Rodriguez. Randy supposed being around Mexicans reminded Jake of his mother. Hearing the language probably comforted him. Evita Ramona Consuella de Jimenez. That was her name. Evie was named after her.

"Mother, who's that?"

Randy looked in the direction of Evie's gaze to see five men approaching, well armed and dressed in the familiar dusters and hats that signified U.S. Marshals. "Oh no!" Randy gasped. "No! No! No!" She started to climb out of the wagon. "Evie, they've come for Jake!"

Evie grabbed her wrist. "Mother, wait! Don't go over there! The day those soldiers came for Daddy to take him to prison, you got hurt. Stay here!"

"I can't!" Randy jerked her arm away and climbed out of the wagon.

"Oh no… Daddy…" Evie followed.

Jake noticed the visitors and walked out of the corral where he'd finished branding a calf. "Lloyd, get over here!" he shouted.

Lloyd turned his cutting horse, charging the horse up to Jake when he saw what was happening. He dismounted and walked to stand beside his father. For the next few minutes, things quieted as most of the hired hands ceased their work and began moving closer to Jake and Lloyd defensively. Brian hurried over to stand near Evie. In the more distant corrals, the action stopped completely as more men quit cutting and roping and branding when they saw what looked to be some kind of showdown coming. They all moved beside Jake as though to shield him.

Terrel Adams rode alongside the approaching riders. When Randy came closer, Jake grasped her arm gently.

"Jake—"

"Get back," he ordered. He looked over at Brian. "Get her out of here, Brian—the kids, too."

Brian walked up to Randy, taking her arm. "Come on, Mom. They might just be here to talk. Let Jake and Lloyd handle this." He gently forced his mother-in-law to step back, calling to Little Jake and Ben and Stephen to come over near him. "Mind your grandfather and get over here," he ordered. By then Evie had also come too close. Brian urged her to move farther away.

Ben and Stephen jumped down from the fence near the counting chute and walked right between the armed men and Jake, glowering. Ben's fists clenched. The intruders halted their horses and waited as Little Jake went running by, but the boy stopped and walked right up to the lead marshal, putting his hands on his hips in a daring stance. "Don't you hurt my grampa, mister!" he demanded. He squinted his eyes to show how serious he was. "I won't let no sonofabitch take him away!"

"Little Jake, get away from there!" Jake commanded, the words firm but not yelled. "And watch your language. Get over by your father."

Pouting, Little Jake held a fist up at the marshal, who just grinned. The man turned to Jake as Little Jake marched away in a huff.

"No doubt he belongs to you, Jake."

Jake watched the man carefully. "He does."

"Same temperament, I see." The marshal nodded. "It's been over four years, Jake."

Jake wasn't wearing his guns. Neither was Lloyd, but some of the hired help were, and Randy's heart pounded at realizing they were ready to use them.

Jake nodded to the marshal. "Hal Kraemer, if I remember right from my days of riding for the law back in Oklahoma."

"One and the same." Kraemer removed his hat to reveal curly brown hair that was matted from the heat and the hat. He had steely blue eyes and needed a shave. "I remember you and that son of yours as two of the best at this job."

Jake ran a hand through his hair and wiped at sweat with his shirtsleeve. "What are you doing in Colorado, Hal?" he asked.

"Got reassigned. And, Jake, I don't like having to come out here and bother you, but it's my job. You know how it goes."

"You go away!" Little Jake yelled, tears welling in his eyes.

"It's all right, Little Jake," Jake told him without taking his eyes off of the marshal.

Hal Kraemer grinned. "Something tells me that kid is a handful, just like his grandpa can be."

Jake grinned darkly, and Randy saw the wariness in his eyes. He looked like a panther that had just been backed into a corner and might pounce. "My adopted son and my grandsons seem to think it's become their job to look out for me."

"I see that." Kraemer looked around, eyeing the hired hands and taking in the surrounding sight of cattle and horses everywhere. A hog-tied calf still lay kicking on the ground near the branding fire. One of the hired hands knelt down and cut it loose. The calf ambled away, and Jake folded his arms, facing Kraemer.

"Boss, they came riding in from the south," Terrel told Jake. "I sure couldn't stop them by myself, and they're the law, so I had to let them through."

"That's okay, Terrel. I know this man," Jake answered, his eyes still on Hal Kraemer. "Why all the extra men, Hal?"

Kraemer leaned on his saddle horn. "Well now, if I was coming out here to arrest you, do you really think I'd come all alone after somebody like Jake Harkner? Fact is, I would have brought a lot *more* men. I figure four men probably wouldn't be enough."

"If I was armed, I'd agree with you," Jake answered.

Kraemer glanced at Lloyd, then back at Jake. "This the son who rode with you in Oklahoma? I never got to meet him."

"It's him. His name is Lloyd, and this is mostly his ranch. You haven't answered my question. What are you doing on the J&L?"

The marshal's horse shimmied sideways, and one of his men rested a hand on his six-gun until Kraemer turned his horse and ordered all of them to move back a little. "Guns aren't necessary, boys. Save them for when they're really needed."

Randy breathed a bit easier. The five men looked well trained and ready to obey any command. Jake had been just as intimidating when he rode as a marshal. Apparently having been one was to his benefit now. He knew Hal Kraemer, but Randy had never met the man.

Kraemer faced Jake again. "Jake, I hear tell there was a bit of a shoot-out on this land with some rustlers a month or so back. The sheriff back in Denver filed a report."

"Rustlers is the word. They were cattle thieves. And you're right, it was over a month ago."

Evie clung to Brian's arm. "Brian, it's just like when soldiers came to take him to prison all those years ago," she whispered.

Brian moved an arm around her. "This is different, love. You stay calm."

"I reckon you had the right to take those men down, Jake," Hal told him, "seeing as how they were on your land and rustling your cattle. But there were seven of them, and none of them lived. That sounds like the work of Jake Harkner—maybe even alone. Was that necessary?"

"They was shootin' at him and the missus," Cole Decker spoke up before Jake could answer. "Jake had his wife with him. We came on the scene just minutes after they pinned Jake down. All of us was in on it. There ain't no way to say which one of us killed which man, so don't go pinnin' all of it on Jake here. He was defendin' his wife."

Randy felt a lump rise in her throat. Cole was trying to take the blame off of Jake.

"That true?" Kraemer asked Jake.

Jake turned to look around at his men, and they just nodded to him. He looked back at Kraemer. "Something like that."

"Pa did what he had to do," Lloyd spoke up. "My *mother* was with him!"

Kraemer studied Lloyd and quietly nodded. "I can understand that." He turned his attention to Jake again. "Thing is, no matter what these men say, Jake, the whole thing sounds more like something you would do—shoot to kill."

"They were doing the same," Jake told him, taking a cigarette from his shirt pocket. "My men came along and finished what I started. And if those men hadn't died from our bullets, they would have died with a noose around their necks, and you know it, Hal." He lit his cigarette.

Hal nodded. "The thing is, Jake, if they'd died with nooses around their necks, it would have been because the *law* made it so. In case you haven't noticed, there is a difference between obeying the law and taking the law into your own hands."

Jake took a deep drag on his cigarette, and Randy watched, wondering where her next breath would come from.

"And there is a difference between taking the law into your own hands and just plain defending yourself and someone you love," Jake told Kraemer. "That's all I did, and these men here can attest to that."

"And if we went out there and dug up their bodies, I'm betting the bullets in them all came from Colt .44s," Kraemer answered, "with ivory handles and triggers so touchy that just a cough could set them off. Usually when there is a shoot-out, at least one man lives to tell about it...unless it was Jake Harkner doing the shooting." He glanced at Lloyd again. "And I hear you can be just as ruthless and just as accurate."

"If someone is threatening what's mine? Sure I can."

"Nobody is digging up any bodies," Jake said flatly, taking Kraemer's attention off of Lloyd. "There sure as hell isn't much left of them by now anyway. The fact remains they came onto J&L land. They rustled up some of our cattle and were headed to Denver with them. As soon as I spotted them, I hurried my wife behind some rocks, because they'd seen us and were headed our way. They had us pinned down. I got a couple of them, and then Lloyd and some of my men here came along. None of us worried about aiming for places that didn't kill. They all died, and that's that. My wife even said a prayer over their graves, so they were properly buried, and we took their identifications and personal belongings to Denver to report the incident just like the law says we have to do. Nobody did anything wrong, so why in hell are you here? And why did you bring so many extra men?"

Hal grinned. "Well, Jake, it's like I said. When I'm coming out to talk to a Harkner on Harkner land and surrounded by Harkner men, I figure I might need some backup." He tipped his hat. "But I didn't come here to arrest you, Jake. I only came to warn you."

"About what?" Lloyd spoke up before Jake could. "We just told you Pa didn't do anything wrong. Now get off our land!"

"Lloyd, let him speak," Jake told him. "It might be important."

"It *is* important, Jake," Hal told him. "Seems as though one of those men you killed was the nephew of a Denver prosecutor, Harley Wicks. It's true the boy was a no-good and always in trouble, but the fact remains that Wicks would like nothing better than to nail you for this. His sister, who is one of those high-society snobs in Denver, ordered him to have you arrested. But seeing as how you are who you are, and you're pretty damn famous, and, well, you really didn't do anything wrong that they can legally pin on you, Wicks couldn't bring any charges. That's what took so long coming out here. He tried every which way to find something to pin you with, but he couldn't. I'm just warning you to look out for yourself, Jake. One wrong move, and Wicks will gladly oblige his sister's wishes that you go back to prison or be hung."

Jake drew on his cigarette and looked at Lloyd. "Am I that famous?" he tried to joke.

Lloyd shrugged. "Apparently so." He turned to the others. "Is he famous, boys?"

Most of them grinned.

"I'd say his *wife* is the famous one, for that great homemade bread she makes us," Pepper joked before spitting tobacco juice into the fire. It made a hissing sound against a hot coal. Jake and the others laughed at the remark.

Kraemer shook his head. "Just a warning, Jake. I think a lot of you, so stay out of trouble. I know about Mike Holt being on the loose. And word is he was seen in Guthrie."

Evie stiffened at the words. Brian tightened his arm around her. Jake and Lloyd came alert.

"When?" Lloyd asked.

"A month or so, I guess. They practically tarred and feathered him before booting him out, the way I hear it. I came out here to warn you that he mentioned heading west before he left town, so that could mean he's wanting to keep his promise about killing Lloyd. I figured that was reason enough to come out here…but that prosecutor did tell me to let you know he'll be keeping an eye on you."

Jake drew deeply on his cigarette and took it from his lips. "Marshal, I haven't done a damn thing wrong. And if I want to take my wife to Denver to show her a beautiful time and treat her like the elegant lady she is, I'll do it. And I'll be going there to sell my cattle, so you tell that prosecutor he can keep his nose out of my business, and I'll be sure to stay on the side of the law while I'm there. I've worn a badge, and I know the rules."

Kraemer nodded. "Jake, I hold you in high regard, but I have a job to do, so I really hope I'll never have reason to come after you. That's not something I would relish doing at all." He backed his horse. "These extra men are a fraction of what I'd bring along against the likes of Jake Harkner. Actually, we're headed for Loveland. There's a wanted man holed up there somewhere, or so I'm told. I just figured I'd do what that prosecutor asked and stop by to give you a warning."

"You've done your job, so move on," Lloyd answered. "As you can see, we're in the middle of branding, and we have to get back to work."

"I understand." Kraemer rode his horse closer to Lloyd. "They say that Holt is after you because you shot his brother in the back after the man had given himself up. That true?"

Jake glanced at Lloyd with a warning look in his eyes.

"Yes," Lloyd answered without a flinch, "but he wasn't standing there giving himself up. He turned and ran. I was the law, and it was within my rights to shoot him, so I damn well did."

"Well, your friends from Guthrie who were with you that day at Dune Hollow swear the same thing, so it's the word of several good men against Mike Holt." Kraemer leaned closer. "But I have a real distinct feeling they're all just trying to protect you, young man, so you keep in mind that even as a marshal back then, you could have gone to prison for shooting a man in the back."

Katie drew in her breath, holding Randy's hand so tight it almost hurt.

"All I know is what those men did to my sister," Lloyd grumbled. "You think about that…if it was your wife or your sister or your daughter, Kraemer. Would you give a damn?"

Kraemer sighed, backing his horse again. "No, I wouldn't, Lloyd. I just want you to be careful if you come up against Mike Holt. Do you understand me?"

"I understand just fine."

Kraemer turned to Jake and reached down, putting out his hand.

Jake shook it. "Good luck finding your man," he told Kraemer. "I'm just glad I'm not the one you were after."

"So am I, Jake, so am I—because that would mean I'd probably come out on the losing end." He glanced at Randy and the others, then back to Jake. "Take care of that beautiful family of yours."

"I'm trying to do just that."

Kraemer tipped his hat to the women and rode off, his men following behind.

Jake turned to his men. "I'm damn grateful, boys."

"Hell, Jake, we couldn't let that sonofabitch try to pin you with something," Cole told him. "You might have gone off to prison, and we'd lose our jobs. With all the consolidatin' goin' on around here and ranchers sellin' out to corporations, jobs for men like us are gettin' fewer every year."

"Yeah, we didn't do it for you," Pepper spoke up. "We did it for our own selves…and maybe for the wife. If the law took you away, your wife might leave, too, and we'd lose out on that homemade bread."

They all chuckled, and Jake thought about Randy's remark about true friends. He shook Cole's hand, then Pepper's. "You boys took a chance yourselves," he told them. "God knows most of you are probably wanted *somewhere* for *something*." He stepped back then. "Now get back to work, all of you, or you *will* be out of a job!"

The men grinned and shoved each other around before returning to what they were doing before the interruption. Jake looked at Lloyd. "Damn good men," he commented.

"They are."

Their gazes held, both realizing the thin line they walked. "Hal was right about one thing, Lloyd. Try not to react too quickly if you see Mike Holt."

"I won't have any trouble reacting if he has a gun in his hand."

"Yeah, well, that's what worries me." Jake sighed, looking him over lovingly. "Lloyd, if you happen to see that man and he doesn't do anything wrong against you, you come and find me before you make any decisions. Will you do that?"

"I don't know, Pa. It all depends on the circumstances and if Katie is with me, or if Evie is around."

Jake put a hand on his shoulder. "You have a family that needs you. You remember that. And I'm one of them."

Lloyd nodded.

"Jake—"

Jake turned to see Randy standing near him, her eyes showing a lingering terror. "I thought they'd come to arrest you," she told him, suddenly bursting into tears.

Jake pulled her into his arms. "Nobody is going to arrest me," he assured her.

Lloyd put a hand on her shoulder, and Evie also hurried up to Jake to hug him.

"Hey, I've got two beautiful women hugging me, and I'm covered in dirt and sweat and God knows what else," Jake tried to joke. "This is embarrassing."

"Daddy, I thought they would take you away!" Evie wept. "Like that day the soldiers came."

Jake kissed her hair. "You women have to stop worrying."

"Jake, it ain't fair that you get to hug the two prettiest women in Colorado while the rest of us have to get back to work," Cole shouted.

Jake gave his wife and daughter a light squeeze. "The condition I'm in, they won't be hugging me for long. I need a bath!"

"Yeah, but I bet *they* smell good," Vance yelled.

"You men get moving!" Jake shouted back, keeping his arms around both women.

He heard laughter and more shouting as things returned to normal. Jake glanced at Lloyd, who stood there looking devastated. Jake knew his son had never quite overcome the fact that he'd ridden out of his mother and Evie's lives in anger after Jake was arrested years ago. "It's okay, Lloyd."

"No, it isn't. They were alone when those soldiers came for you. I should have been there for them."

Katie walked closer and moved an arm around Lloyd, who kept watching his mother and Evie.

"Okay, you women have to stop being so upset," Jake told them. He gave them one more hug. "You go on home now and rest," he told Evie. He turned to his son-in-law. "Brian, go with her. We can get along without you the rest of the day. Teresa can take Sadie and Tricia over to Lloyd's house, and I'll keep Little Jake busy a while longer so Evie can lie down."

Little Jake ran up to them. "I thought they would shoot you, Grampa."

Jake touched his shoulder. "Little Jake, you need to learn to hold your tongue when strangers come around. I should have made you apologize to the marshal for what you said. Right now you get back to the branding. Your mother is going to go home and take a nap, so when you don't want to watch the branding anymore, you go with Teresa to Lloyd's house, understand? And you help watch your sister and Tricia."

The boy rubbed at his eyes and ran off to rejoin the men. Jake noticed Ben and Stephen standing nearby, both of them also looking concerned. Jake threw up his hands.

"Okay, enough! Everybody get back to what you were doing! Ben, you and Stephen go on back to the counting pen. Everything is okay now." He took Evie's arm and led her to Brian. "Go. That's an order."

"I love you, Daddy."

"And God knows how much I love you. I don't like you getting upset, so go."

Evie left with Brian, and Jake turned to Lloyd and Katie. He kept an arm around Randy. "Take Randy back to the house, will you, Katie? We'll be done in a little while."

Lloyd gave Katie a kiss. "Go ahead. And heat some water. I'll have a lot of dust and sweat to wash off when I get home."

Katie squeezed his hand. She walked over to Randy. "Let's go, Mom."

Randy left reluctantly, glancing back at Jake once more.

"I'll be along soon," he assured her before turning to Lloyd. "Let's be glad we got out of this one and get back to work."

"Yeah." Lloyd folded his arms. "You too old and tired now to finish out the day?"

Jake knew Lloyd was trying to lighten the mood. He rubbed at a sore shoulder. "Well, that's a borderline truth, Son, but by God, all you did was cull out those calves. I'm the one who wrestled them down, so I'd be careful calling me old. How about we change places and *you* do the wrestling for a while?"

"Hell, I told you I'd do it, but you insisted on showing off how strong you still are, so if you're hurting now, it's not my fault."

Jake gave him a shove. "Get the hell back to work."

Lloyd grinned and walked off, putting big hands at the backs of Stephen and Ben's necks and shoving them along with him.

With a heavy sigh, Jake headed back to the branding pen. Deep inside he, too, had thought he was going to be arrested. *The day somebody tries to take me back to prison is the day I die!*

Eleven

RANDY BRUSHED OUT HER HAIR BECAUSE JAKE LIKED it down. She'd washed up and put on a flannel gown, anxiously waiting for her husband. She would never quite get over the memory of the day the soldiers came to arrest him, the brutal way they'd beat him. He'd given up running, deciding not to put her through any more of it. For the next four years she'd lived with the agony of knowing the terrible conditions under which he lived in prison, fearing he would die there. After his release, Jake's job as a U.S. Marshal meant being gone weeks at a time, hunting men who would gladly kill him. Randy felt worn out from constantly worrying.

She went to the kitchen and retrieved yet another kettle of hot water, carrying it to the upstairs bedroom and pouring it into the large tin tub for his bath, wishing he'd get here soon. He was late. Why was he late? What was keeping him?

She returned to the kitchen to heat more water, then set bread out on the table and checked a pot of stew. Other than Ben, they never knew how many children would want to stay overnight with Grandma and Grandpa. Sometimes all the downstairs bedrooms were filled with kids, another irony for Jake. Randy loved it, loved children, and to this day she mourned not being able to have more after giving birth to Evie. But tonight…tonight all she could think about was Jake and the fear that the law had come for him. She wanted nothing more than to feel his arms around her. She supposed it was her constant fear of losing him that kept their lovemaking fresh and warm and needy. It was their way of proving to each other that they were together and alive and nothing could separate them. They weren't just husband and wife, but friends and lovers.

Finally, she saw him walking toward the house from the bunkhouse. She couldn't get over the fact that Cole and Pepper and some of the others had tried to take part of the blame for killing the rustlers. Now maybe Jake would understand what she meant about having good friends he could trust. When Jake reached the veranda, she noticed he didn't look all dusty and sweaty. She went to the door and opened it, seeing in his eyes his regret over the incident with the marshals. He understood what that had done to her.

In the next moment she was in his arms. He held her off her feet and whirled her around, and she burst into tears. Jake kicked the door shut and kept her tight against him, kissing her hair.

"Jesus, Randy, ever since what happened out there, I've ached just to hold you. I saw the terror in your eyes. I just felt like after what the men did to back me up, I should stay and help a while longer."

"It's okay." She breathed in his familiar scent, burying her face in his neck. "Jake, you took a bath at the bunkhouse?"

"I didn't want to have to mess with all that when I got home. I knew I'd just want to hold you, and I didn't want to be filthy when I did. That's why I'm late."

Only Jake would think like that. She couldn't stop her tears. He picked her up in his arms and walked over to his big leather easy chair and sat down in it, keeping her on his lap.

"I hate it when you cry," he told her. "Everything is fine, Randy. Please stop crying."

"All I could see were those soldiers."

"And all I could think about was that black eye that Lieutenant Gentry gave you back then." He hugged her even tighter. "I've never wanted to kill a man as bad as I wanted to kill him that day!"

"Jake, I'm worried about that prosecutor."

"Don't give it another thought. I haven't done anything wrong, and he knows it, or I'd already be in jail. I don't intend to give him reason to put me there, either, so you just relax."

"Sometimes I just want to go back to that line shack and never leave…just you and me, Jake." Randy relaxed more, kissing his cheek. He met her mouth in a hungry kiss.

"I wouldn't mind it either," he told her between kisses. "Right now we'll settle for home. Lloyd brought these clothes to the bunkhouse for me so I could get out of the dirty ones, and he'll keep Ben at his place tonight. He knew what you were going through and that maybe we should be alone."

"He has such a big heart. I wish he'd stop feeling so guilty for running off after you went to prison."

"We talked awhile," Jake assured her. "I reminded him all of that was as much my fault as his. That's another reason I'm a little late."

Randy straightened and ran her fingers through his hair. "It's time to forgive and forget a *lot* of things. We're all together now, and you, my darling Jake, have a beautiful family that loves you very much."

He studied her lovingly. "I'm just an old ex-outlaw who got lucky and found the right woman."

"Oh, you are much more than that, Jake Harkner. Sometimes I see the little boy in you, jumping up and down with joy at loving and being loved."

He grinned, moving a hand over her breasts. "I'm no little boy, Mrs. Harkner." He leaned up and kissed her wet cheeks. "Tell me you're done crying."

She hugged him around the neck. "I'm not sure."

He took her in his arms again and rose, carrying her toward the winding stairs that led to their loft bedroom. "Maybe I can do something to help you get over those tears."

She rested her head on his shoulder. "Jake, you have to be tired and aching. It's been such a long day."

"Nothing hurts so much that I can't tend to my wife." He carried her to their bedroom and set her on her feet, then closed the door.

"Jake, I went to all the work of fixing a tub of water for you, and you don't even need it."

"Well, we're both clean, so let's get in it together."

"What!" She moved back from him as he unbuttoned and removed his shirt.

"Why not? I'll give you a bath and a damn good rubdown." He sat down in a chair and removed his boots and socks, then stood up to unbuckle his belt.

"Jake, I'm not getting into that tub with you. There isn't enough room!"

"That's what will make it more fun." He unbuttoned his pants and shed them. "Get that gown off, woman. I hope you're properly naked underneath."

"I'll do no such thing!"

Her eyes widened when Jake removed his long johns. "Oh, Jake, this is silly."

"After thirty years?" He came closer. "Raise your arms, woman, and I'll strip this gown off of you."

"You're just trying to joke around with me so I'll feel better."

"Sure I am. Can you think of a better way to forget our troubles?" He smiled the handsome grin that always undid her, then picked her up and carried her to the washroom just off the bedroom, where they also had a sink with a pump and a flush toilet rigged with a water tank above it, more conveniences Jake had insisted Randy should have. Randy let out a little scream when he set her in the tin tub, nightgown and all. "Move over, woman."

He climbed into the tub with her and made her wiggle out of the nightgown, throwing the wet garment onto the floor. "Come here." He settled into the back of the tub, pulling her back against him so she was sitting between his legs. Grabbing a bar of soap on a stand beside the tub, he dipped it into the water and lathered his hands, then began massaging her shoulders and back with soapy water while kissing her neck. "There, you see? This isn't so bad." He reached around and gently washed her breasts. "Your breasts are still beautiful. You keep saying they're too big and not so perky anymore, but I love them. How many times have I teased you about your cleavage?"

Randy smiled, leaning back against his chest. "That feels good."

"I *want* it to feel good. I want you to relax and be happy, Randy, and realize that I'm here, and I'm not going anywhere. You just close your eyes and take some deep breaths and let me rub away all your troubles."

She turned her head to kiss his neck. "There is something hard pressing against my back, Mr. Harkner."

"Yeah, well, we'll have to take care of that, won't we?"

He moved strong hands to her shoulders and neck, using soap to slide his hands in a deep massage of the back of her neck, down her back, then reaching over her shoulders and moving down to her breasts again.

"At least this time when you came home already clean, it wasn't because you'd stopped at a whorehouse to take a bath," Randy chided.

He laughed. "Yeah, I kind of miss those baths at Dixie's place."

"I'm sure she misses it, too." Randy kissed his neck again. "Are you sure she didn't lather you up like you're doing to me now?"

He pulled her closer, and she met his lips while he moved a hand down over her belly and between her legs. He ran a tongue around her lips in a deeper kiss before answering. "You know better."

Randy breathed deeply from his gentle touch. "Well, according to what Eddie Holmes told Stephen"—she let out a little groan when he moved his fingers into the crevice of her body—"you run with bad women." She kissed his neck again.

He began working his magic in gentle, circular touches. "It's more fun making a good woman do bad things."

Randy didn't answer. She simply drank in the luxury of a strong hand plying her breasts while another strong hand made her whimper with pleasure. She felt her desire building when he moved his other hand down to push his fingers inside her while he continued feeling secret places until she groaned with an exquisite climax. He moved his hands back up over her breasts, to her shoulders, down her back. Without saying a word, she sensed what he wanted—something they rarely did. She leaned forward, and he raised up on his knees, grasping her hair from behind. She gasped when he filled her with stunning hardness, keeping one strong hand under her belly for support and still grasping her hair.

Water splashed out of the tub as he moved in rhythmic thrusts that made her cry out with erotic pleasure as he pushed deeper. He kept up the exquisite intercourse, moaning her name and keeping a steely arm under her until he groaned with his own deep climax. She felt his life pulse into her as he leaned over her back, wrapping his arms fully around her and pushing deep inside to finish off the pulsating pleasure. He kept a tight grip on her for several seconds as he held himself inside her. Finally, he leaned down and kissed the back of her neck, still holding her hair away from her face. "You okay?"

"Yes," she whispered, wondering how many men knew all the ways to please a woman that Jake did.

"That was beautiful. I was afraid maybe it hurt."

Randy shook her head.

"Stay there." Jake pulled away and rose, stepping out of the tub and drying off. He grabbed one of her robes from a hook on the wall and brought it to her, holding it open. "Step out, and I'll wrap this around you."

Randy rinsed herself off and climbed out of the tub. Jake wrapped her in the robe and toweled the damp ends of her hair, then carried her to the bed.

"You sure you're okay? You're awfully quiet." Jake laid her on the bed and crawled in beside her. "I worry I'll break something one of these times. I swear, you get smaller every year, Randy."

She snuggled against him. "We just don't usually... I mean... I don't know why I wanted to do it that way. I just love pleasing you."

He kissed her eyes. "And if anything hurts, you tell me. I can read your every reaction, Mrs. Harkner, and you please me just by existing. Sometimes that's all I need...just to have you beside me."

She nuzzled his neck. "Well, you did say you prefer doing bad things with a good woman."

He laughed teasingly. "I saw that beautiful bottom, and I couldn't help myself."

"Well, what you did was most disrespectful, Jake Harkner. Something tells me you prefer it that way."

He moved on top of her. "The more disrespectful, the more delicious."

"You just learned more than you needed to know in your wilder years."

"The better to please you with," he answered, "but you have to enjoy it, too."

Randy didn't object to deep kisses that silenced their talking and led to a journey down her body to her breasts, and on down to intimate places that belonged only to Jake Harkner. He had a way of making her feel brazen and alive and beautiful. She grasped his hair when she felt him warmly caress her with his tongue.

"Jake, that definitely does *not* hurt." She'd never dreamed there were so many ways to enjoy a man, and he always had a way of making love to her that made her feel adored.

Moments later she was climaxing again. He kissed and licked his way back up to her mouth and entered her again, grasping her bottom and moving in a harder rhythm, proving to her that he was really here and would damn well make sure nothing would separate them again. She could taste her own sweetness on his lips. He even had a way of kissing that made her feel like they were having intercourse, even when kissing was all they were doing. She drank in his familiar scent, his breath, his hard strength, the sureness of his love. She pressed her fingers into the muscles of his arm and arched up to his gentle thrusts, every fiber of her being wanting to love him back and to claim him as just hers. This man could have a hundred women, but he wanted only one. He needed her as much as she needed him, and when he was inside her, it was as though they were one body, sharing souls in a spirit world no one else could touch.

"*Tu eres mi vida,*" he groaned, "*mi querida esposa.*"

She'd learned the meaning of the words: *You are my life, my darling wife.* She couldn't help crying out with the ecstasy of the way he moved inside her, and she loved him even more for being concerned he might have hurt her when he made love to her in a different position. It wouldn't have mattered. He had a way of making her want to please him in every way possible, and she knew he wanted to make sure she was equally satisfied. She felt lost under his big frame.

"Jake, I love you so," she said softly. "If anyone takes you from me again, I'll die."

He pushed hard, his life spilling into her once more. He kissed her over and over. "I'll not let it happen," he groaned.

They kissed hungrily, feeling as though they couldn't get enough of each other. Finally, he settled beside her, pulling the blankets over them and wrapping a leg over her, keeping her close. "It's been one long day," he said.

"And you're hurting, aren't you?" Randy asked.

"I hate to admit it, but wrestling down calves and then wrestling down my wife have done me in."

"I didn't exactly fight you like those calves do."

He grinned. "Not exactly." Jake kissed her hair. "Did I tell you what a beautiful bottom you have?"

"In so many words. Just don't expect that too often, Jake Harkner."

"We'll see. All I have to do is touch you in the right places."

"Is that so?" Randy turned and kissed him. "Well, you're right." She kissed him again. "All I really need is that handsome smile." Another kiss. "I love you."

He caressed her hair. "In another month we'll go to Denver—you and me, Katie and Lloyd, Brian and Evie. The girls can stay here with Teresa, and the boys can stay in the bunkhouse. They get a kick out of that."

"Oh, Jake, heaven only knows what they see and hear around those men!"

He snickered. "Being around *me* isn't a whole lot better. They're itching to be men themselves. Spending time with Pepper and that bunch will certainly teach them a few things, and Little Jake will give those men a run for their money."

Randy smiled. "I can't believe the way he walked up and threatened Hal Kraemer! That child has not one ounce of fear in him. He is so much like you it's comical. Little Jake couldn't be a more fitting name."

"He's going to be something to deal with when he's grown, that's for sure."

"We've produced quite a family in spite of all the things that tried to stop us."

"Hey, it's you and me against the world, woman, and that's okay. We can handle it."

Randy studied his eyes. "When you told me the other day that you talked to the boys about your past, I was so glad you were able to do that. For so many years you wouldn't talk about it at all. Big and strong and able as you are on the *out*side, you've grown so much stronger on the *in*side."

He kissed her eyes. "*You* keep me strong."

Their lips met again, their passion no different than it was nearly thirty years ago when he took her for the first time…when he was a lost soul…when she showed him everything he didn't know about love. The only thing that could change that and bring back Jake the outlaw was if his ugly past found a way to revisit him.

Twelve

Early July

GRETTA WINCED WITH PAIN WHEN HER CUSTOMER BIT at her breast. "I don't go for that, mister, so if you're going to try to hurt me, you can just get off this bed."

The man grinned. In spite of a Z-shaped scar on his chin, Gretta found him nice-looking, but his cruel smiles made him ugly.

"Hey, I'm a payin' customer, lady."

"You paid for sex, not for hurting a woman, so get off!" Gretta shoved at him, but he grabbed her wrists and pushed them over her head.

"I'll get off when I'm *done*, lady!" He rammed himself hard, deliberately squeezing her wrists until it hurt. Finally, he released himself, then bent down to bite her breast again, this time hard enough to leave teeth marks. He finally let go of her, and Gretta quickly got off the bed and slapped him hard across the side of the face.

The man stood up and shoved her against a wall, half choking her as he held her there. "You're awful damn choosy for a whore!" he growled.

"Even whores don't like it rough," she said in a near whisper, hardly able to find her voice.

"*Some* do!"

He let go of her, and Gretta bent over, gasping for breath. "None...that I know," she answered. She reached for her robe, quickly pulling it on and walking over to her dressing table.

"I ain't got my money's worth yet," the man told her.

"You have as far as I'm concerned." Gretta reached under a handkerchief on her dressing table, where she always kept a pistol hidden. When her customer came at her again, she quickly grabbed the gun and held it straight out. "Leave!" she ordered.

The man froze in place. "You wouldn't."

"*Wouldn't* I? I have an agreement with someone very important in this town, mister. I can shoot anyone who abuses me, and I'll get away with it, so if I were you, I'd get out of here!"

"I don't believe you."

The bite on her breast made Gretta wince again. She didn't doubt she'd have quite a bruise there by morning, which would hurt her business. "*Believe* it," she answered, her voice still raspy. She cocked the pistol. "And I want your name. I usually don't bother with names, because it's easier not knowing, but I intend to warn the other prostitutes around Denver about you. Once I tell them about that odd scar on your chin, you'll be recognized by all of them, and you won't be sticking that thing into *any* of them!"

He backed away more. Gretta wanted to smile at the way his penis began to wilt. "You're real lucky, lady. I spent three years in prison for *rape*!"

"And that's exactly what you've just done to me!"

"Whores can't be raped!"

"Can't they?" Gretta had a strong urge to pull the trigger. "What's your name?" she demanded again.

"Mike Holt." He raised his chin, bragging the name proudly. "Maybe you've heard it in the news. I'm one of the few men who've gone up against Jake Harkner and lived to tell about it."

Gretta kept the gun pointed straight at him. "Seems I read something about that in the newspaper not long ago."

Mike grinned. "Sure you did. I'm practically as famous as Harkner is."

"For all the wrong reasons. The way I heard it, the woman you raped was his daughter, a fine woman and the wife of a physician."

"You *heard*? Or you *know*?"

"What's that supposed to mean?"

"Harkner has a reputation for bein' favorable toward women like you. Maybe he's paid you a visit, and you got all the details straight from him."

"I've never met the man," Gretta answered. She kept the gun on Mike through the conversation, suspecting he'd try having at her all over again if she didn't. She grinned slyly, wanting to mock Holt. "I did see Harkner in town last summer, and from what I saw, *I'd* pay *him* for a roll in the hay. God knows he'd be better at it than you are with that little pecker of yours."

Mike glowered at her. "You bitch!"

Gretta laughed, enjoying his embarrassment. "Get dressed and get out of here!"

Mike walked over to the bed to grab his long johns.

"'The handsome outlaw,' I've heard he's been called," Gretta added. "What are *you* called? Little Pecker?"

Mike pulled on his underwear. "I ought to kill you."

"Try. Please. Then I can have the satisfaction of shooting you."

Mike finished dressing. "I think Harkner *has* been here, and you know more than you're lettin' on. He likes women like you."

"The man has a beautiful wife and a big family and runs a ranch four or five days from here, or so I'm told. I've seen the wife when she didn't know I was looking, and if you had a wife like that, you wouldn't be visiting whores either. Those two look at each other like the world would come to an end if they lost sight of each other."

Mike broke into more laughter. "Ole Jake pretends to be the family man, but don't you underestimate that sonofabitch. He's mean as they come and fuckin' ruthless. I seen the article in the *Denver Post* about him killin' seven or eight rustlers not long ago. He about got himself arrested, but the article said as how he had a right. I'm thinkin' the law ain't too happy about it."

Gretta lowered her pistol slightly, frowning. "What's your interest in the man?"

Mike buttoned up the front of his long johns. "Can't you figure it out?"

"You're after him?"

Mike grunted with more laughter, pulling on his boots. "I'm after his *son*. That kid shot my brother in a shoot-out back in Oklahoma…shot him in the *back*. I aim to repay him in the same way." He looked her over. "Have you ever met the son?"

"Lloyd Harkner? Sure, I've seen him and his wife, too—same time I saw Jake and his wife. They were all shopping and walking up the street together. They didn't notice me, because I was watching out a window as they walked by, but I got a good look, and the son is even better-looking than the father, if that's possible."

"Well, take a good look next time, 'cause when you see Lloyd Harkner again, it will be for the *last* time. How often do they come to Denver?"

Gretta still held the gun on him, not trusting him for one second. "I really don't know. Not often. Most ranchers tend to stay right on the ranch most of the time, except to come into the city for supplies once in a while, or to bring in cattle. This is the time of year for that, so I wouldn't be surprised if they showed up in Denver in the next week or two."

Mike pulled on his pants. "Good. I'll be ready for 'em."

Gretta smiled. "Mister, the only reason I told you they might come around is because from all I've read about

Harkner and his son, *you'll* be the one who's dead if you try going after them, and I will truly enjoy seeing you sprawled in the street, your body riddled with bullets."

Mike reached into his pants pocket and pulled out a plug of tobacco, biting some off and pushing it down between his cheek and his gum. "Depends who sees who first. Onliest thing I know is I ain't gonna try goin' after him at his ranch. Most men I've talked to say nobody gets on Harkner land without bein' noticed, and after hearin' about them rustlers, I figured I'd wait right here. Here, he'll be out of familiar territory, and there are plenty of places to hide instead of goin' after a man in the wide open spaces."

"You'll go back to prison, you fool!"

"Not if I do it without gettin' caught."

"You're the first one they will suspect, and now *I* know your plans."

He looked her over. "Don't matter. Like you said, I'm the first one they'll suspect, but I don't intend to be found. I've staked this city out pretty good, and there are plenty of places to hide till shit blows over."

He smoothed back his hair. "The only way for men like Harkner to die is lyin' in mud and horse dung in the street, all shot to hell, their women cryin' over their bodies." He rose. "The man's daughter is as much of a looker as his son is, and she was sweet between the legs, let me tell you." He walked a little closer. "Want to know what she did after Harkner found her and shot up most of the men at Dune Hollow?"

Gretta just glared at him. "You're *scum*, Mike Holt."

He grinned. "Maybe so, but scum or not, she *forgave* us. Can you believe that one?"

"Forgave you?"

"Yup. She's the reason I'm alive. After all the shootin' and things was said and done, she told her pa not to kill those of us still alive. Ole Harkner, you could tell he wanted to blow our heads off, and he would have if there weren't men from town with him to see him do it. Even at that, I think he would have done it anyway out of pure meanness. But that daughter of his said she forgave us, and she'd be real upset if he killed us outright, so he had to bring us in for trial. The bastard wouldn't let his daughter testify, so we all got nailed for rapin' her, even though some of them didn't."

"But *you* did."

Mike rubbed at his privates. "Sure I did. But I got out of prison on account of they couldn't really prove it, and she wouldn't testify, so the judge let me go."

"You should have left well enough alone and gone someplace else to start life over."

He shrugged. "What fun would that be?" He began pulling a belt through the loops on his pants. He stepped a little closer. "You want to know the best part?"

"I don't think I do." Gretta raised the pistol again.

"The best part is, Harkner's daughter was blindfolded when I went at her. I could walk right up to her, and she wouldn't know I was one of 'em."

Gretta shook her head. "You're crazy. Jake and his son know your face. You'll never get close to that young woman."

"Oh, I'll wait till they ain't around."

"I hope they kill you. I've just met you, and *I* want to kill you! When I'm through, there won't be one prostitute in Denver who will let you touch her."

He shrugged. "Then I guess I'll have to find a woman who *ain't* willin', won't I?"

Gretta raised her chin. "If I hear of anything like that happening here, I'll report your name to the prosecutor." She stepped a little closer, holding the gun out again. "I happen to know him well."

Mike's smile faded. "So that's how it is, is it? Well, I heard the prosecutor ain't real happy with Jake on account of one of them rustlers Jake killed was his nephew. So I expect the man will be glad to find a reason to throw ole Harkner in jail—his son, too—if they survive what I have planned for them."

"And that will mean you're *dead*. Have you thought about it that way, you fool?"

"'Course I have. But I'm not worried. I've got it all planned."

Gretta shook her head. "I'm guessing you never had any schooling, because you have to be the most ignorant man on the face of the earth."

Someone knocked on the door.

"You done in there, Mike?" a man asked.

Mike looked Gretta over scathingly. "I reckon so. She ain't much good at what she does, so she ain't worth her price." He walked over and opened the door. "You get a good lay?"

The stocky, younger man shrugged. "She was okay. She likes it in the mouth, so I obliged her."

Both men laughed, and Gretta grimaced at the remark. She took a hard look at the young man at the door. He was perhaps in his twenties and built like a bull. She knew he'd picked Sondra for his lay, and she hoped the brute hadn't hurt her. Gretta liked running a clean place, mostly for wealthier men or men of prominence who knew she could keep their trysts secret. One of them was Harley Wicks, a city prosecutor who was also wanting to make trouble for Jake Harkner. She hoped Harkner wouldn't show up this year, for his own sake. She decided that if she saw him or his son anywhere, she'd warn them Mike Holt was in town. She didn't know the younger man's name, but she figured he was no better than Holt and probably also dangerous.

Holt came inside for his hat and plopped it on his head while the younger man looked Gretta over as though she were a fresh piece of pie. She just glared back at him.

"Your friend isn't a very nice man," she told the younger man. "Get him out of here."

The younger man just smiled. "What'd he do?"

"None of your business."

Mike picked up his leather vest and pulled it on. "Come on, Brad. Let's go have some drinks and find a card game."

The one called Brad tipped his hat to Gretta and left with Mike. Gretta walked to the door and closed it, then slid the lock shut. She decided neither man would be allowed in the Range Club again.

Good riddance to bad rubbish. She shuddered to think what Harkner's daughter must have gone through.

Thirteen

Mid-July

"WHICH ONE IS THE SON AND WHICH ONE IS THE father?" Pepper joked. It was his turn to drive the three-seater carriage in which Randy, Evie, and Katie rode when the family went to Denver, well ahead of the cattle drive behind them. Jake did not want any of the noise and dust of the drive to affect the women, who at the moment watched Jake and Lloyd racing two young mustangs not far away.

"Pepper, if it weren't for Lloyd's long hair, it would be difficult to tell," Randy answered him. "As far as behavior, I don't think Jake ever got past twenty himself. He behaves like a younger man and then pays for it at night."

"Well, ma'am, he's a man who's known a lot of pain. I reckon he's just learned to live with it."

The words stabbed at Randy's heart. "Oh, yes, he has a very high tolerance for pain of *all* kinds, not just physical."

"Looks like Lloyd won," Pepper said with a chuckle. "They're heading this way now."

Pepper pulled up on the horse, halting the carriage while they waited for Jake and Lloyd to catch up. Several of the regular help stayed at the ranch, taking care of daily chores and helping watch the grandsons while Teresa and Rodriguez took care of the little granddaughters. The only ranch hands along who worked steady for Jake were Pepper and Cole. The others were drifting cowboys hired out of Longmont and Boulder, as well as two younger men belonging to neighboring farmers who wanted to earn some money. Randy couldn't help smiling at one of the boy's comment that he would get to go on a "real cattle drive with Jake and Lloyd Harkner," which they considered an exciting honor.

She didn't mind traveling this way. She and the other women could have taken a train to Denver, but all three preferred what some might now call the "old-fashioned" way of reaching their destination. The carriage they used was high quality, with good springs that made for a comfortable ride.

Jake and Lloyd reached them on lathered horses.

"Wait for me here while I go get a fresh horse," Jake told Randy with a wink. "I want you to ride with me somewhere. I found a spot with a view you need to see."

Lloyd dismounted. "Pepper, get on down and take this horse back to the herd. I'll drive the carriage for a while."

Pepper climbed down. "Whatever you say. You're the boss."

Lloyd got up into the seat beside Katie, leaning close to give her a kiss.

"What's going on?" she asked.

"Pa is taking my mother for a ride, and I miss you," Lloyd answered, "so I'm going to ride beside you for a bit." He kissed her again. "And I can't wait till we get a room in Denver."

"Lloyd! Your mother and sister are sitting right behind us!"

"Hell, they understand." He turned and smiled at the other two women. "Has she told you yet?"

"Told us what?" Evie asked.

Lloyd looked at Katie.

"Not yet," she told him. "We have to be real sure."

"I'm sure enough." He turned back to his mother and sister. "The race is on, Sis. Katie's carrying."

Evie reached forward and shoved at him. "It's not supposed to be a contest, big brother."

"Well, Sadie and Tricia aren't far apart in age, and they have each other to play with. What if it's boys this time? They'll each need someone to play with, too."

"Well, it could be girls again," Evie told him, "but if I have another boy, I hope he's not as wild as Little Jake. I won't be able to handle it. *You* can have him. In fact, if you have a girl and I have a boy, I'll *trade* with you."

Lloyd laughed. "Speaking of Little Jake, here comes *big* Jake."

Jake rode up close on a big roan gelding, reaching out for Randy. "Let's go."

Randy watched him slyly. "I don't trust you, Jake Harkner."

"After thirty years?"

"That's *why* I don't trust you. I've known you too long."

"Come on. Get on this horse." He glanced at Lloyd. "Help her up here, Lloyd."

Lloyd climbed down and helped his mother out of the carriage. Randy let out a little scream when he picked her up and raised her up to Jake, who grasped her around the waist and hoisted her up to sit in front of him on the horse. "You just keep going," he told his son. "We'll catch up in time for supper. Of course, none of us is crazy about Cole's cooking, but we have to make do without Rodriguez."

"I wonder how he and the boys back at the bunkhouse are doing, trying to watch Little Jake?" Lloyd joked, winking at Evie.

"They'll be more worn out than if they were out digging trenches," Jake answered.

"Daddy, Katie and I can help with the cooking this evening."

"No. This is a hard enough trip. I don't want the women doing anything extra." Jake glanced at Katie.

"You young women need to take it easy. Lloyd tells me you're going to give me and Randy grandchild number six, not long after Evie has number five."

Katie blushed. "I'm pretty sure."

"Well, you're both making a really old man out of me."

"You'll never be old, Daddy," Evie told him. "Mom either. Look how pretty she still is."

"Oh, I am well aware of that, baby girl." He grinned and rode off with Randy.

"Jake, what are you up to?" Randy asked warily, hanging on to her hat.

"Just some time alone with my wife. I want to show you how pretty it is in that pine forest to the west."

"That had better be all you want. We are out here with the whole family and a lot of men."

Jake pressed her closer, taking her a good quarter of a mile west of the parade of buggies, wagons, and cattle and into a stand of pines where the ground was carpeted with needles and the trees offered cool shade. He dismounted, then helped her down and tied his horse. He took a blanket from behind the saddle and spread it out on a thick carpet of needles, then removed his guns and sat down. He reached up, and Randy saw the sly look in his eyes as she took his hand. "Jake—"

He pulled her down to sit beside him. "I just thought we'd have some quiet time together."

Randy breathed deeply of the pungent smell of pine. They sat in the shade, watching the distant procession of family and animals make their way over what was currently government land. They had special permits to move on through private property as they made their way to Denver.

"Beautiful, isn't it? You can see our wagons and see the cattle off in the distance. It's quite a scene."

"It is." Randy watched quietly for a few seconds as

Jake moved an arm around her shoulders. She turned to meet his eyes, seeing something familiar there—something she didn't want to see. "I know you better than I know myself, Jake. You're worried about going to Denver this time, aren't you?"

"I'm not worried about a damn thing."

"Yes, you are. You're thinking about Mike Holt, and about that prosecutor who'd like to bring you down."

He sighed, removing his Stetson and lying back. "Yeah, well, you're right. I want this thing with Holt over with. I can't help wondering what he's up to, and I'm worried about Lloyd. Evie, too. If that man gets anywhere near her, I don't know how Lloyd will react... or how *I* will react. I want this to be a nice trip, Randy. We'll go to the Cattlemen's Ball and maybe the theater, and you can shop for some new clothes and whatever supplies we need." He pulled her down beside him and rolled to his side, moving a leg over her and pulling her close. "I just want to do something extra nice, because in a few days we'll celebrate our thirtieth anniversary."

Randy smiled. "You remembered!"

"Of *course* I remembered." He moved on top of her, leaning down and kissing her softly. "Thirty years of too much hell for you."

Randy touched his hair, thinking how thick it still was, with tiny streaks of gray that only seemed to make him more handsome. "Nobody loves like you do, Jake. That's all I've ever needed, and few women can say they've been adored and cared for in all the ways I have. Yes, it's been hell sometimes, but not because of you, and never because of how you've treated me. And as far as Mike Holt, there are laws now that will take care of him if he makes trouble. You remember that and *let* the law deal its justice. He'd be sent right back to prison."

He kissed her again, this time deeply, in that way he had of disarming her. Randy knew his worry about trouble had brought this on. Jake Harkner was a man who was not good at handling any kind of threat to those he loved. Whenever he sensed such things, he always turned to her in a need to prove to himself that she was right here in his arms and everything was all right. And whenever he kissed her this way...touched her this way...needed her this way...

"My boots are still on," she groaned as he moved a hand under her dress and pulled at her underpants.

"So are mine."

She closed her eyes as he sat up slightly to yank the underwear off and over the boots.

Randy ran her hands over the hard muscles of his upper arms. "Have I told you how handsome you look in this blue flannel shirt?"

"Yes." He moved a hand back up under her dress. "And you wore your yellow checkered dress today. You know what yellow does to me."

Randy gasped when his fingers moved inside of her. "Why is that, Jake?"

He worked his magic. "I don't know. Yellow just looks so beautiful on you, and you know how I like it. You wore this dress deliberately, just to drive me crazy."

"I never gave it a thought," she said softly.

"The hell you didn't." He leaned closer to nuzzle the soft cleavage that showed at the square neckline of the dress. "I still love these breasts. They are perfect. Have I ever told you that?"

"Practically every day."

Amid deep kisses, he fondled the right places.

"You're a devil," she whispered.

"Who do you belong to?"

"A man who insists on embarrassing me by"—another kiss; Randy felt the intense ecstasy of an orgasm building—"taking me off in the woods when the whole family"—another kiss—"probably suspects what we're doing." She cried out in an intense climax, one that came on more quickly than normal because of the hint that trouble could be around the corner. The silent fear of being torn apart again always made their lovemaking more fiery and commanding than it normally would be for two people together for so long.

"Jake—" She moaned his name.

"God, I can feel your climax," he told her, pressing his fingers hard against her to help increase the intensity of the moment.

"Keep touching me there," she whispered.

He kissed her deeply as he kept his fingers pressed tightly to satisfy a climax that hung on longer than normal. He let go to unbutton his pants and long johns, then moved his hand under her bottom, pushing himself inside her while the pulsations of her climax continued pulling at him. "You still make it feel so good," he groaned as he licked and kissed her neck.

He found her mouth again and moved deeper. Randy buried her face against that part of his chest revealed by a few open buttons on his shirt. She enjoyed the feel of his weight on her, the hardness of his body, the ecstasy of his fullness pushing deep inside her, a man still able to make love in every way a woman needed. His concern over her only made her love him more…want him more. No matter how intimate they were, there was always that feeling of respect and adoration that only made him more desirable and irresistible.

He kept up the rhythm in the joining that helped both of them take strength from each other. Randy leaned up to draw his mouth back to hers, clinging tighter when she remembered how it felt to think Marshal Kraemer had come to arrest him. No one was going to take him away from her again. No one!

His life pulsed into her, and they lay there quietly for a moment, sharing soft kisses, Jake still hovering over her.

"Are we crazy, coming out here like this?" Randy asked softly.

"Probably, but after all we've been through, we have a right to do this anytime we want and any*place* we want."

"I suppose so." Randy felt him stiffen as he looked past her.

"Don't talk anymore," he whispered. "And don't move a muscle...not one finger or one toe."

"Jake?"

"Shh." He put his face down beside her ear. "There's a grizzly bear watching us," he whispered. "Don't move."

Randy tightened up in terror.

"My gun is right beside us," Jake assured her.

"Can you kill a bear with a six-gun?" Randy whispered in reply.

"Not with one shot—but maybe with all six. Be still. She might go away if we don't move. She has cubs with her."

"Oh, God, there is nothing more dangerous!" Randy whispered.

His left arm tightened beneath her while he very slowly took his right arm from under her so he could grab his gun if necessary. They lay there as still as possible, saying nothing, breathing against each other's ears.

Jake finally managed to turn his head enough to see the bear cubs cavorting nearby. His horse whinnied and reared in terror when it smelled the bear. It jerked its reins loose and ran off. The startled bear cubs took off in another direction, heading deeper into the foothills, and finally the mother bear followed.

Jake wilted against Randy. "She's gone." He raised up on his elbows. He waited a few seconds, watching the trees into which the bear and her cubs had disappeared. Finally, he looked down at Randy. "Do you realize how ridiculous we must look? I'm still inside you."

Randy met his gaze, and they both started laughing.

"Oh, for heaven's sake, get off me!" she told Jake. "The horse! It will go running back to camp, and God knows how many men will come riding up here, wondering what happened!"

Jake stayed on top of her. "We'd look pretty funny lying here like this, wouldn't we?"

"Jake Harkner, get off of me so I can fix my dress!"

"But this feels so good."

"Oh, you're so mean! Maybe you got caught this way with whores a time or two, but you're not going to get caught like this with your *wife*!"

Jake just laughed and rolled off of her. He got up and buttoned his pants. "I brought a towel for you, but the horse ran off with it. You'll have to use that blanket to clean yourself up the best you can. We don't even have a canteen."

"Oh, Jake, this is ridiculous!" Randy managed to clean herself a little with the blanket, and quickly pulled on her underwear. She smoothed her dress, then realized her hair was down and a mess. "Jake, my hair! They'll know! Oh, this is terrible!"

Jake finished buttoning his shirt. "I brought my beautiful wife out here so we could be alone. So what if her hair is down now?"

Randy sat back down on the blanket and fished for the combs and pins that had fallen from her hair. She quickly twisted the back of her hair up and shoved combs in it to hold the quick up-do in place. She plunked her hat on her head and looked at her husband, who only watched with a big grin on his face. "Do I look ridiculous?" she asked.

"You look beautiful. It's impossible for you *not* to look beautiful."

"You know what I mean." Randy stood up. "Am I a mess?"

Jake frowned. "Not bad. A few strands of hair are

hanging down, and the skirt of your dress is a little more wrinkled in front from being pushed up."

Randy gasped and looked down. "Oh my gosh! It is! Oh, Jake, this is just... I just don't know what to do!"

"Come here."

Randy looked at him. He still had a handsome smile that only made her smile in return. He opened his arms, and she fell into them.

"Just be glad we weren't mauled by a grizzly," he told her. "You've seen what a grizzly can do to cattle, and we both remember when Joe Jacobs was killed by one, so let's not worry about what anybody thinks. You are my wife." He let go of her and held her face in his hands, kissing her gently. "And in spite of not having you fully naked beside me, that felt damn good." He kissed her again.

They heard a whistle. In the distance they could see Lloyd and one other man riding hard in their direction, the other man leading Jake's horse behind him.

"Oh, for the love of God," Randy said as she quickly rolled up the blanket and held it close, looking down as the two men drew closer.

"Pa!" Lloyd shouted. "You okay? Your horse came charging back to camp like it was terrified of something!"

Jake moved an arm around Randy. "We saw a grizzly. It scared the horse."

"Jesus! Why didn't you shoot it?"

"Because it was a she bear and there were cubs with her. I didn't want to leave those cubs motherless. She didn't really threaten us. Besides, I'm not so sure you can even kill a grizzly with just a .44. I might have just made her even angrier."

"For God's sake, that bear could have mauled both of you! You know there's nothing more dangerous than a female grizzly with cubs."

"We just lay there and didn't make a move. The bear finally lumbered away with her cubs."

Randy buried her face against his chest and couldn't help laughing. Jake grinned and looked at Lloyd. "Hand me the reins to my damn horse and get back to camp."

Lloyd hesitated, then started laughing. "You mean that bear came along when—" He laughed harder.

"Holy Moses," Cole muttered with a grin.

Lloyd kicked at Cole's leg. "Get the hell out of here," he told Cole. "And don't say a damn word."

"I'll try my best." Obviously struggling not to laugh out loud, Cole turned his horse and left.

"We might as well camp the night here," Lloyd told Jake. "I'll tell the boys to keep the herd tight and be on the lookout for that grizzly." He tipped his hat. "Didn't they used to call you 'the handsome outlaw'?" he teased his father. "Mom still sees you that way, doesn't she?"

"Get the hell out of here before I beat you within an inch of your life."

"And how many times have I told you to try proving you can?"

"Don't tempt me, Son."

With a big grin on his face, Lloyd rode closer and handed Jake the reins to the extra horse. "Don't worry about it, Mom. I'm just glad nobody is hurt." He laughed again as he turned and rode off.

"Jake, this is absolutely the most humiliating situation you have ever put me in!" Randy looked up at him. "You do these things on purpose just to embarrass me, don't you?"

He put both arms around her. "Breaks up the monotony of the trip and erases all your worries for a while, right?"

"I should *never* have come up here with you."

"Woman, when have you ever said no to me?"

"I can't name the number of times I *should* have said no to you!" Randy met his gaze, and after a moment of silence, they broke into laughter. "I honestly can't remember ever saying no," Randy said. "I've spoiled you rotten." She threw her arms around his neck. It felt good to laugh. They were headed for Denver and the Cattlemen's Ball and shopping and enjoying the excitement of city life.

For a while they'd both forgotten about Mike Holt, and that was what Jake meant to do.

Fourteen

"We should make it to Denver day after tomorrow," Jake told the men. He unbuckled his gun belt and dropped it next to his bedroll.

Cole grinned. "Barring any more side trips," he teased.

They all laughed. Six men, including Cole, Jake, and Pepper, sat around a campfire, smoking, while the women remained farther ahead, making ready to bed down. Besides the cook wagon and one with supplies, Jake had brought along two covered wagons just for the women and Brian. Lloyd would stay with them tonight to stand watch, and Brian would sleep in one wagon with Evie, while Katie and Randy slept in the other wagon. Four of the men remained with the cattle, quietly riding around the herd, one of them singing softly to keep them calm, while the rest would soon bed down on the ground around the cook wagon.

"Must be nice," one of the new hires named Clem muttered in a near grumble.

"What's that?" another asked.

The man shrugged. "Bein' the boss—and bein' Jake Harkner to boot. You get to bring a beautiful woman along on a trip like this and use her like your own personal whore."

Smiles faded, and every man quieted except one, who just softly muttered the word, "*Shit!*"

They all remained frozen in place while Jake took the cigarette from his lips and tossed it into the campfire.

"God Almighty," Pepper grumbled. "Clem, you stupid sonofabitch. That's Jake's wife you're talkin' about."

Jake slowly rose.

"Hell, I was just joking." Clem shrugged.

"Calling my wife a whore is no fucking joke." The words came out in a deep menace as Jake walked closer. "Get up!"

The man slowly rose. "Jesus, Jake, you were a wanted man when that woman married you, if she married you at all. I mean, she's a beautiful woman, but everybody knows you ran with whores. You trying to tell us that's not how you met that woman?"

Men scattered when Jake landed a hard fist into Clem's face just as he spoke the words "that woman." Clem landed against a wheel of the cook wagon, and Jake jerked him up by the shirt, then slammed his fist into him again.

"I'm just sayin' what the others are thinkin'!" Clem yelled.

Jake kept hold of the man's shirt front and rammed him up against the side of the wagon. "You're just goddamn lucky I'm not wearing my guns, you foul-mouthed bastard!" He landed a hard fist into Clem's gut while one of the men ran to get Lloyd.

"Lloyd, come quick!" he hollered.

Clem doubled over, and Jake brought a knee up under his jaw, catching him hard in the teeth and sending him sprawling again. Jake leaned down and yanked him to his feet. "No man who works for me treats my wife with anything but *respect*!" he growled. On the word *respect*, he punched Clem hard against the cheekbone.

Clem went sprawling yet again, blood pouring from his mouth. "Goddamn it!" he choked. "You knocked my damn teeth out!"

Again Jake jerked him to his feet. "Be glad you aren't *dead*!" he snarled.

"Pa!" Lloyd reached them by then. "Jesus, Pa, what's going on?"

"He called your mother a whore!" he growled as he shoved Clem away and turned to Pepper. "Hand me your gun!"

"No, Pa! He's not armed!" Lloyd objected.

Jake was already reaching for Pepper's gun, but Lloyd stepped between them. He shoved at Jake. "Don't do it!"

Jake raised a fist. Lloyd put up his arm to stop the blow and grabbed Jake's shirt front. "Pa, it's *me*! Get out of that dark place, damn it! You're looking to kill the man!"

Jake froze, glaring at him. He shivered then. "I *want* to kill him! He even said maybe your mother and I never legally married! She doesn't *deserve* that! I brought her along to celebrate our thirtieth anniversary, for God's sake!"

Lloyd kept hold of his father's shirt but closed his eyes. "She goddamn well *doesn't* deserve this!" He looked at Jake again. "But you can't kill him, Pa, because it would mean you not being there for Mom, and that's worse than *anything* that could ever happen to her!"

The rest of the men remained backed away. Pepper kept a hand on his gun as Clem rolled to his knees, groaning and weeping with pain. Father and son glared at each other a moment longer. "Let *me* finish this, Pa," Lloyd said calmly.

Jake saw that spark of his old self in his son's eyes. "You remember the same thing you just told me. Katie needs you. She's carrying another baby."

Lloyd gave Jake a light shove. "Well, these beautiful women just keep interfering with our mean side, don't they?"

Jake closed his eyes. "I don't *want* you to have a mean side."

"I *have* one, whether you like it or not, but I know when to check mine...*most* of the time. You don't!"

Jake spoke through gritted teeth. "He tried to make it sound like I met her at a whorehouse! After all that woman has sacrificed for me, I can't—"

"What on earth is going on here, Jake?" Randy stepped into the light of the campfire.

"Go away!" Jake ordered, still staring at Lloyd.

"Jake—"

"Get the hell away from here!" he roared. "I mean it!" He heard a little gasp from her lips, and it tore at his gut. Never in their marriage had he raised his voice to her. Randy quietly walked away, and Jake turned away from Lloyd. "God*damn* it!"

"Go get her, Pa. I'll make sure Clem is gone before you come back here."

"I can't go anywhere!" the man protested, literally sobbing. "He knocked my goddamn teeth out!"

Jake turned dark eyes to Lloyd again. "Get rid of him, or I'll *kill* him," he said flatly. He ran a hand through his hair and turned away again.

"Jake—" Pepper called his name.

Jake stopped, his back to the men.

"You know damn well that was just a drunk man who's only heard half-truths and made up the rest. There's not a man among us who doesn't realize what a fine woman your wife is. You remember that. If you hadn't done what you did, we would have."

Jake walked off into the darkness, and Lloyd jerked Clem to his feet.

"No! Don't hit me again," the man cried. "I was just jokin'! He took it wrong!"

Lloyd slammed Clem against the cook wagon, enjoying the sight of blood pouring from the man's mouth. "This is how it is, mister," he growled. "I should kill you myself for insulting my mother, but I'm in too bad a state right now to make logical decisions, so I'm leaving for a while in order to get rid of this strong desire to blow your *head* off!" He threw the man to the ground and turned to Pepper, resting a hand on one of his six-guns. "When I come back, I don't want to see that man! Make sure he gets the message! I don't want to see him riding in the distance beside us, or behind us, or after we reach Denver, because if I see him again I might not be able to keep from *killing* him! If my father sees him first, *he'll* kill him. I'm trying to stay within the law, but right now it's damn hard!"

"We'll take care of it, Lloyd," Cole told him. "You go see to your pa. I ain't never seen a man that black-hearted mad in my life."

"You've just never seen the dark side of Jake Harkner," he answered, "until now. He fights it, but it's there. It's my mom who usually keeps him from falling over the edge." He turned to Clem. "Go saddle your horse and ride out!"

"It's dark!"

"Ride out!" Lloyd roared. He backed away and looked at Cole and Pepper. "Make sure he disappears," he told them.

Cole nodded. "Sure, boss."

Lloyd walked off into the darkness. In the moonlight he could see a figure standing bent over a few feet away, and he knew it would be Jake. The man had come so far in his ability to check his anger and keep the old Jake at bay, but Lloyd knew nothing could set him off much worse than for someone to insult Randy, and he suspected there was more…something to do with bad memories of his father. He carefully approached him.

"Pa, she'll understand. This won't hurt her near as much as it hurt you."

"I screamed at her." Jake bent over more. "I can hear my father…roaring at my mother."

"Pa, you know you aren't like him."

"But I *am*! Sometimes I still am."

"You could *never* be like him—not with your wife and the mother of your children—not with *any* woman. You never have been, and you never will be."

Jake grasped his head in his hands. "Jesus Christ, she's my *wife*! How could he say that?"

"Because he's a stupid sonofabitch who would never understand what you and Mom share. Mom knows that, too. You being like this will hurt her far worse than anything somebody else says about her."

Jake remained turned away. "I almost hit you."

"Yeah, well, you didn't. And I know it wouldn't have been me you were hitting. I'm also guessing that your hand is hurting pretty bad right now. That's the hand that's never been completely right anyway after—"

Jake turned to look at him. "After I *did* hit you—when you visited me in prison."

"I was a complete asshole to you that day. You should have beat me to a pulp."

They heard Clem arguing then.

"Ride off now, or we'll finish what Jake started!" Cole yelled.

There came the sound of a horse riding at a gallop then, the hoofbeats quickly fading.

Lloyd closed his eyes and shook his head. "Pa, if I didn't butt in just now, you'd be in trouble, like when you were out to kill young Ben's father back in Oklahoma. You would have killed Clem if I hadn't stepped in, and you'd go back to prison."

"Which goes to show you I *am* like..." He turned away again. "My father."

"Your father was a drunk and a rapist who beat and killed his own wife and forced himself on the young girl you loved. But when it comes to your loved ones, you go into that protective rage, probably because you love *too* much. So no, you're *nothing* like him!"

Jake took a cigarette from his shirt pocket. "It's the rage part that reminds me of him. Part of me says I didn't really have to kill all those rustlers, but they threatened to come for Randy, and when it comes to her, something just...snaps." He lit the cigarette. "Jesus, I screamed at her."

"You were protecting her. You wanted her away from the men just then because of what was said. She knows that, Pa. Mom knows you better than *you* know you."

Jake took a drag on the cigarette. "Yeah, she keeps telling me that, too."

"And she has stayed with you through everything all these years. Getting yelled at once in all those years isn't going to bother her one little bit."

"I heard that...little gasp...like I'd hit her or something." Jake ran a hand through his hair. "God*damn* it! I screamed at my wife. I didn't just raise my voice. I *screamed* at her. The minute I did that, I saw *him* screaming at my mother."

"Pa, you have to get *over* all that. Don't fall back into that awful place where you're the kid getting beat on and you think you have to fight back all the time."

Jake smoked quietly. "Go saddle a horse for me, will you?"

"Why?"

"I just need to be alone, that's all."

"Don't you be thinking about riding off, Pa. I know you."

"I can't talk to your mother right now."

"But you *should* talk to her. She'll *want* to talk to you."

Jake took a last drag on the cigarette and stepped it out. "I can't. I'm still too angry: not so much over what happened, but angry with myself. I don't *want* her to tell me it's all right, and I don't want her forgiveness, because I don't deserve it. What that man said...it's too personal. I never should have touched that woman thirty years ago. Who the hell was I to think I could bring a woman like that into my fucked-up life? She deserves so much better."

Lloyd sighed. "Damn it, Pa, give her some credit for knowing a good man when she sees one. And if you *hadn't* come along back then, she'd have died from snakebite, remember? Did you ever think that maybe God deliberately *put* her in your life to *save* your sorry ass?"

Jake faced him, shaking his head. "I don't deserve you, or Evie either."

Even in the moonlight, Lloyd could see tears in his father's eyes. "Well, whether you like and accept it or not, we both think we couldn't have asked for a better father."

Jake wiped at his eyes with his shirtsleeve. "I'll go get my horse."

"You need to go get Mom and talk to her."

"I can't right now. I can face ten men with guns, but that woman can completely undo me with one look or one word. That little gasp she made when I yelled at her—it was like somebody planting a knife in my heart."

"Pa—"

"Lloyd, normally she'd already be looking for me and wanting to talk. In case you haven't noticed, she *didn't* this time. That tells me I hurt her way worse than I ever have before. As far as I'm concerned, yelling at her like that was the same as hitting her. That man took something beautiful and made it ugly. Randy doesn't deserve that, and it's because of who she's married to."

"And *married* is the key word here, Pa. She's your *wife*. So nothing he said matters."

Jake turned away. "It *does* matter." He walked off into the darkness.

"Pa, what about your hand? Don't tell me it's not hurting. You should let Brian look at it."

Jake just kept walking.

"Damn it, Pa," Lloyd muttered. He turned to go back to the women's wagon when he saw Randy walking toward him, her robe wrapped tightly around her. Lloyd reached out and grasped her arm.

"Leave him alone, Mom. He'll come around in the morning."

"Where is he?"

"He just needs to be alone."

"No! That's the worst thing he can do."

"Well, he wouldn't listen to a damn thing I told him. In his mind, he as much as hit you."

Randy closed her eyes and turned away.

"You *do* know why he screamed at you, don't you? It was just his way of protecting you. That man he beat on…" He closed his eyes. "Shit," he said softly. "He called you a name."

"A whore? I've heard it before, Lloyd. In spite of explaining the truth a thousand times over, some think that's how Jake and I met, because of the life he lived then." Randy shook her head. "I know him. He blames himself for every hurt or insult to someone he loves. And when he's that angry, it makes him think about his father screaming that he's worthless and no good, and then he starts thinking his father was right."

"I talked to him. He'll get over this."

Randy wiped at her eyes. "He's riding away, isn't he?"

"You know Pa. I know you want to go talk to him, but this time you really need to leave him be and let *him* come to *you* when he's ready. He needs to learn how to deal with the bad memories on his own."

"But I've always been there for him."

"Yeah, well, maybe he needs you to *not* be there for him. Maybe he needs to face his demons on his own. And you need to get some sleep." Lloyd led her toward the covered wagon.

"How can I sleep? He's out there alone. When he gets like this—"

"*Let* him be alone, Mom. He'll be back. You have

that man so hog-tied he can hardly breathe without you. Remember what he told Jeff for that book? You are the air he breathes."

Randy looked up at him. "Doesn't he realize I feel the same way about him?"

"Sure he does, but this one ran really deep. He needs time to deal with it."

Randy looked off into the darkness. "That's what worries me." She turned away. "This was so…personal. Sometimes an insult can hurt worse than a bullet. And I have a feeling what that man said hit some kind of chord—something Jake has never told me, probably about his father." She sighed and shook her head. "I hate it when he leaves without talking to me. That's when he goes to that lonely place where I can't reach him."

"Then you need to pray for him. That's all you can do."

"I've been praying for Jake Harkner for thirty years. I hate his father so much for all the damage he did, Lloyd. Not just the physical beatings, but the mental ones."

"And God brought you into his life. He'll be okay." Lloyd urged her back to the wagon, hoping he was right.

Fifteen

THE MEN SAT QUIETLY AROUND THE MORNING CAMPFIRE, drinking coffee and eating biscuits and bacon. There was very little conversation. Jake never came back the night of his confrontation with Clem, nor last night. All wondered the same thing: Was he coming back at all?

Lloyd only drank coffee. He didn't eat. He threw the remains of his coffee into the fire, making it hiss, then tossed the tin cup at a man named Moses Crenshaw, who was their designated cook. He stood up and lit a cigarette, then noticed a rider in the distance. He knew his father's silhouette well enough to realize it was Jake.

"Well, what do you know?" Pepper muttered.

"Don't anybody say a word to him," Lloyd warned. "Just let him ride in." He leaned against the cook wagon while others finished eating and lit their own cigarettes.

Jake rode closer and dismounted, obviously weary. He pulled his rifle from its strap on the saddle, then removed the saddle and set it in the grass along with his gear. He took off the horse's bridle, then smacked the animal on the rump. "Go get some rest," he called to it. He walked into the circle of men and sat down, pouring himself some coffee. "Pepper, I'll need a fresh horse."

"Yes, sir."

Jake swallowed some coffee, glancing at Lloyd with bloodshot eyes.

"You look like shit," Lloyd told him.

Jake set down his coffee cup and reached into his

pocket for a cigarette. "I don't doubt that," he answered. He lit the cigarette.

"I only want to know one thing, Pa."

Jake took a deep drag on his cigarette, blowing out smoke as he answered. "No, I didn't go find Clem and kill him, if that's what you're wondering."

"Good."

Jake looked at the others. "We should be in Denver by this afternoon. Pepper, you and Cole herd the cattle to the stockyards and—"

"I already gave those orders," Lloyd interrupted. "Don't be concerned with the cattle, Pa. Be concerned about my mother. She's a wreck. She thought maybe you wouldn't come back."

Jake slowly rose, keeping his cigarette at the corner of his mouth. "From the look on your face, maybe I *shouldn't* have come back!"

Lloyd just shook his head. "And you're a damn fool!" He turned and walked away. Jake watched him. He'd never seen his son quite like this.

"Jake, he's just upset about his mother and sister," Pepper said cautiously. "I think it hit him hard, thinkin' he might be responsible for takin' care of the whole family on his own."

Jake rubbed at his eyes. "Sorry you men had to witness any of this. I have a bit of a problem with my temper."

"No kidding?" Cole answered. "We never noticed."

Jake looked at him and saw a grin on his face. He smiled a little himself before taking another drag on the cigarette and then gulping down the rest of the coffee. "There's something down inside me that's kind of like a dragon coming up from a dungeon to roar and spit fire once in a while. All of you know how I feel about my family. The anger is at myself and my...father...not at any of them."

"We know," Pepper told him. "And by the way,

we, uh, yesterday we rode through an area filled with wildflowers—every color in the book—so we all picked some for your wife and daughter. 'Course they cried, but I think it made them feel better."

"Thanks," Jake answered quietly.

"Jake, it's like we told you the other night," Cole told him. "Your wife is one fine woman. We hold you and your whole family in high regard."

"That son of yours is a hell of a man," Moses put in. "He's got his head on straight. And your daughter is like a damn angel. I ain't never met a woman more gracious and kind. It's just a reflection of the kind of woman who mothered her, and you raised a fine son."

Jake glanced over to where Lloyd was still walking away. "He is. We've had our differences, though, as you just saw."

"You know, Jake, that's how sons are about their mothers," Pepper told him as he rose. "If they have to choose which one to defend, they'll always choose the mother first. Ain't nothin' much more sacred to a boy than his ma."

Jake thought about his own mother, murdered before his eyes by his father when he was too little to defend her. He took another drag on the cigarette. "Yeah," he said quietly.

"I'll go get you that fresh horse," Pepper told him. "Time to get moving." He stopped in front of Jake. "And your son was right. You look like shit. You okay?"

Jake smiled sadly. "I'm okay." He rose with a deep sigh, aching all over, both his heart from regrets and his body from the raging fight and no sleep. Men began cleaning up as he walked out to where Lloyd stood next to his horse. Lloyd was untying his hair, which hung nearly to his waist now. "Someday you'll get mistaken for a renegade Indian and get yourself shot," Jake told him.

Lloyd smoothed back his hair and retied the strip

of leather at the nape of his neck. "You keep telling me that. And with this dark skin from the sun and my Mexican blood, I guess I do look like I should be wearing buckskins." He turned and faced his father, his eyes still showing anger.

"Are you going to forgive me anytime soon?" Jake asked. "I'd like us to have a good time in Denver, for the women's sake."

Lloyd closed his eyes and shook his head. "Pa, when you disappear like that, it hurts mother, and that hurts Katie and Evie. And it hurts *me*. And it makes me wonder sometimes who the hell *Lloyd* Harkner is. I'm always Jake's son, and that's fine with me. You know how I feel about that, but I'm also my own man, and I have a son and a daughter and a good wife and a ranch to run. I can't always be there for my mother when you decide you're not good enough for her and think she's better off without you. She's loved you for thirty years, Pa, so *accept* that love. She's nowhere near as upset about what Clem said as she is about you leaving without talking to her after yelling at her like that."

Jake took a last drag on his cigarette and stepped it out, turning away. "Lloyd, there are things about me I try to change but can't. That's just *me*. And you are damn well a lot like me except for that real, real deep ruthlessness that I lived with the first fifteen years of my life. You have my temper, but you know how to check it when things get really bad. I don't. Randy knows that."

"But it still hurts her, Pa, especially this time, because of how you yelled at her."

"And I never will again." Jake removed his hat and ran a hand through his hair before replacing it and turning back to face his son. "You asked who Lloyd Harkner is. Apart from being my son, I see him as a damn fine man who is all the good things I never was, the man I wish I could have been at your age if not for the kind of life I fell into. Someday the J&L will be yours, and it's most likely I'll go before your mother, considering the kind of life I've led. I have enough aches and pains for ten men. You have no idea how comforting it is to know you'll be there for your mother when I'm gone." He looked away. "God gave you to me to make up for my own lost years, and I can't figure out why He thinks I deserve such things."

Lloyd took his hat from where it hung on his saddle horn and put it on. "Well, maybe you should just face the fact that the Good Lord saw the good in you, but He couldn't figure out how to make you see it yourself." He mounted up. "So he brought Mother into your life. Accept that and be happy. Not everything bad that happens is your fault." He leaned down a little. "And I love you, but you cast a long shadow. I'm moving out from under that shadow. I'll always have your back, and I'll never desert you like I once did, but when you told Stephen and Ben about your father, I knew you'd moved on from the horror of that man and were a lot stronger—on the *inside*. God knows how strong and able you are on the outside, but it's the man on the inside that is wearing Mother down. It hurts her to see you like that, because she can't stand to see that little boy in you come out all lost and alone. The woman in her loves the *man* you are. She's your *wife* and proud of it. So nothing anybody else says is going to bother her one bit. Understand?"

Jake folded his arms. "When in hell did you get so wise?"

"Since I had to figure out my father so I'd understand him instead of wanting to *hit* him." Lloyd turned his horse and rode off, shouting orders to the men. Jake wanted to hug him for the child he used to be, but he most certainly was his own man now. *Go ahead and get out from under my shadow, Son. It's time.*

By then Pepper approached with a freshly saddled black gelding for Jake. "Here you go."

"Thanks." Jake mounted up.

"You and Lloyd get things straightened out?"

Jake lit another cigarette and caught Pepper's gaze. "He's quite a man all on his own, you know."

Pepper nodded. "That he is." Pepper sobered. "He was awful worried about you, Jake. Don't let him make you believe otherwise. He'd be real lost without you."

Jake nodded. "I feel the same way about him." He took a deep drag on the cigarette. "Right now I have to straighten things out with the wife. That might be a bit more difficult than talking to my son."

Pepper laughed. "I don't envy you there." He laughed again as he rode off.

Jake rode ahead of camp to the covered wagon and the women's buggy a good half mile ahead. He could see the three women and Brian were dressed and ready to go. Brian was cleaning up a cook fire. Randy glanced at Jake, then turned away. Jake dismounted and walked up to Brian. "How bad is it?"

Brian's eyebrows raised as he half grinned. "You're in deep this time, Jake. Even Evie is mad at you for yelling at her mother and then riding off for two nights. Considering the fact that my wife is the most forgiving woman who ever walked, let alone knowing how much she worships her father, it takes a lot of hurt for her to be upset with you."

Jake sighed and rubbed at the back of his neck. "Do me a favor and take all the women to the Brown Palace when we reach Denver and get rooms for all of us. Lloyd will make sure the cattle get counted and corralled. I'm going on in and get a bath and a shave and some clean clothes."

Brian looked him over. "Good idea. You look like hell."

"Yeah, well, you're the third or fourth person who has told me that."

"How's that hand? I see some swelling."

Jake flexed his hand. "It's been better, but I'll live."

"I'm a doctor, remember? I can tell it hurts like hell. Need some laudanum?"

"Shit, no. I'll put up with the pain. I don't need to be half drunk with that stuff when I try making up with my wife."

Brian shrugged. "Suit yourself. I'm here if you need me."

Jake studied his blue-eyed, sandy-haired son-in-law, thinking how different he was from himself and even Lloyd—quiet, patient, highly educated, a man not easily shaken, and the perfect, loving man for his very gentle daughter who rarely saw the bad in anyone. "Brian, you have always been there for all of us, and I appreciate it. I'm sorry for the extra weight I throw on those shoulders at times."

Brian grinned. "Well, you certainly make life interesting, Jake."

Jake managed a weak smile. He turned then and kept his cigarette between his lips, taking his horse's reins and walking over to the women.

"Daddy, it's about time you came back," Evie scolded. "We're almost to Denver. And you look terrible!"

Jake rubbed at his eyes. "Evie, my sweet daughter, I am well aware that I am a mess. So far, every person I've talked to has told me so."

"Well, we were all worried about you. I don't like it when you get all mean and ornery."

The remark brought a smile to his lips. He threw down the cigarette and stepped it out. "Sweetheart, for some people, mean and ornery just comes naturally, which is something someone like you could never understand. You just take care of that good husband of yours and that baby you're carrying, and I'll deal with the mean and ornery." He glanced at Randy. "All of you go on ahead and get our rooms. I'll be along later tonight."

That got Randy's attention. "*Later* tonight? What does that mean?"

"It means that, as everyone tells me, I'm a mess, and I'm going into town on my own to buy some clothes and find a bathhouse to clean up before I come to our room. You *will* let me in, I hope."

Randy looked away. "I'll think about it."

"Well now, I'd hate to have to kick the door in. I'd have to pay for it."

Randy met his eyes challengingly. "You wouldn't dare!"

"*Wouldn't* I? How well do you know me, Mrs. Harkner?"

"There are times when I wish I didn't know you at *all*!"

There was the feisty, teasing woman he loved beyond life itself. That was what he'd been waiting for. He let go of the reins to his horse and reached into the buggy, wrapping an arm around Randy's waist. She let out a short little scream as he lifted her out of the carriage. He set her on her feet and took her arm, leading her a few feet away.

"Listen to me, Randy," he said quietly so the others couldn't hear. "You of all people know how sorry I am. In thirty years, I've never raised my voice to you."

Randy shook her head. "My darling Jake, the way you reacted to Clem's remark, and the way you screamed at me—it had to have something to do with your father, not just with Clem's insult. And it's not the insult that bothers me or the fact that you yelled at me. I know exactly why you did that. You weren't screaming at me, Jake. You were screaming at *him*. And it was your father you were beating on, not Clem. Am I right?"

Their gazes held as Jake slowly shook his head. "You sure have a way of climbing into my head."

"And you need to explain things to me when you get like that, Jake. That's all that keeps you from going off the deep end. The last thing you need is for me to be upset with you, and I don't *like* being upset with you.

So tell me what this is *really* about. Get it out of your system, because when you come to our room tonight, I want to see the calm and happy Jake you were before this happened."

He sighed deeply, looking toward the distant mountains. "I've told you before that I don't think my father ever legally married my mother."

Randy folded her arms. "And?"

"And he used to…brag to other men that she was his own personal whore. When Clem said that about you and hinted that you must have been a whore when I met you…" He turned to meet her eyes. "I saw *him*, heard *him*. It's been a long time since something happened to bring that all back."

Randy stepped closer. "You should have told me that same night, Jake."

He shook his head. "I was too damn mad. When you walked into that firelight, I saw a woman who was so far above those remarks…a woman I never had any right ever touching in the first place. I grew up with whores, and that's the kind of women I should have stayed with—not something as beautiful and special and educated and sophisticated as you."

"And did you ever stop to think that I could have said no? I *did* have a choice, Jake. You offered to leave more than once, and you *did* leave more than once. Wasn't I always there waiting when you came back? My God, Jake, I need you just as much as you need me."

He rubbed at his eyes, suddenly feeling very tired. "*Lo siento, favor perdóname, mi amor. Tu eres mi vida.*"

"And you are *my* life, Jake. After thirty years I shouldn't have to keep telling you that."

He smiled sadly. "Lloyd said pretty much the same thing. He's not real happy with me either."

"He just gets tired of trying to climb over that wall you keep building around yourself, and so do I. It's because we love you so much that we get upset, because we can't stand for you to hurt."

He reached out and touched her cheek with the back of his hand. "And right now I want to hold you so bad that I ache, but like Evie and everybody else keeps telling me, I'm a mess. So I'm going to ride back to the supply wagon and get a change of clothes and head on in to Denver and get a bath and a shave. Denver is only an hour or so ahead. I'll probably meet Lloyd at the stockyards and then come to the hotel."

Randy touched his arm. "You be careful when you get to Denver. The mood you're in... I'm worried about Mike Holt."

Jake sobered. "Don't you worry about that sonofabitch. We're going to enjoy the city, and you're going to buy a new dress, and I'll be taking the most beautiful woman in Colorado to the Cattlemen's Ball. All the women there will be jealous, and all the men will be envious. And with you on my arm, I'll be the proudest man there."

Randy touched his chest, looking up at him. "And I'll be the proudest *wife* there. You remember that, Jake."

"I'll remember." He grasped the back of her neck and leaned down to kiss her forehead. "I love you."

Randy squeezed his wrist. "In spite of how difficult you make it sometimes, I love you, too."

"I wish we were completely alone right now."

"So do I, but you *are* a mess, so go ahead and find that bathhouse." She looked up at him. "Just make sure it's not in some brothel."

Jake frowned mockingly. "Now why would you think that?" He leaned down to kiss her cheek, then grinned as he turned to walk back to his horse and mount up. He looked down at her. "Will you unlock that hotel room door for me?"

Randy folded her arms and raised her chin. "Maybe."

"You might regret it."

"Something tells me I *will.*"

He grinned more. "Woman, you don't want to know what I'm thinking right now." He rode back to the supply wagon to get his things, and Randy climbed back into the buggy.

"Mother, is he all right?"

Randy patted her knee. "Evie, you are the most gentle-hearted and forgiving young woman I've ever known. Like your father told you, you just worry about your husband and children and that baby you're carrying. Right now Jake is just being…Jake. The most frustrating, confusing, self-depreciating, lonely man who ever walked." She sighed. "I'll straighten him out."

"What did he say?"

"Nothing I haven't heard before, but I know he always means it. Your father can be quite the romantic when he thinks it will soften me up, and it always does. Sometimes I just want to hug him and hit him at the same time."

Evie smiled. "You can't stay mad at him, can you?"

"Evie, I can't stay mad at that man any more than I can stay mad at Stephen or Little Jake or Ben, which tells you how easily I see the sorry little boy in him sometimes. I don't always know which one I'm dealing with—the boy, or the man."

Brian climbed into the buggy seat. "Ladies, I am your official driver today."

"Then I am sitting up front with you," Evie told him, climbing down and then getting into the front seat. She grasped Brian's arm and leaned in to kiss his cheek. "You *will* dance with me tomorrow night, won't you?"

"Every single dance."

Evie looked back at her mother. "And you'll look for a yellow dress for the ball, won't you, Mother? It's Daddy's favorite color."

"Yes, dear, I will wear yellow." Jake rode past them, headed for Denver. *I'll wear yellow, all right.* Randy wanted to hold him. Sometimes she wondered if in all these years she had ever really reached the deeper man, the one who, in spite of all the love he enjoyed now and all the love he gave back, was still a loner, still…lonely… in a way no one would ever be able to comprehend.

Soon he was a small dot on the horizon, and for some reason she shivered and wanted to cry. After all these years, there were times when even she couldn't penetrate that wall he'd built around his heart when he was a lonely little boy.

And that scared her more than anything.

PART TWO

PART TWO

Sixteen

"WELL, WELL, WELL, IF IT ISN'T THE INFAMOUS handsome outlaw."

Jake turned from a mirror where he'd been adjusting the lapel of a new suit. He watched a beautiful, auburn-haired woman walk right through the curtained doorway to the clothing store's dressing room without making sure first he was even dressed.

Jake grinned, holding his arms out to his sides. "What do you think? I hate dressing up, but I need something for the Cattlemen's Ball tomorrow night. Will this do?"

The woman strutted closer and looked him over, walking in a circle around him. She stepped back then and sized him up with bedroom eyes. "I think a man like you could wear a simple farmer's cotton pants and have dirty hands and need a shave and a haircut and still make a woman…uncomfortable. Even more uncomfortable if you didn't have a shirt on. Why don't you take that one off so I can better judge?"

Jake chuckled. "Well, ma'am, underneath this shirt is an undershirt, and that stays on." He guessed the woman to be perhaps thirty—a hard thirty years at that, but still beautiful.

"Yeah, well, according to that book about you, women like me raised you, so before you got married, I expect *plenty* of women saw that great body without a shirt. And something tells me you learned about the facts of life at a very young age." She held his gaze. "And my

God, you have a smile that could melt a woman right down to the boardwalk."

Jake folded his arms, scrutinizing the blue eyes with lines about them. Her still-trim figure showed full breasts that mushroomed from the low-cut neckline of a blue taffeta dress with ruffles in all the right places. She wore tiny diamond earrings and a feathered hat that matched the dress. "Let me guess," he told her. "Gretta MacBain?"

She nodded. "And how do you know my name?"

Jake removed the suit coat, hanging it on a hook. "Oh, I know your kind very well, and from the way some of my men have described you, I just figured you had to be Gretta."

"Well, I hope they were complimentary in their descriptions."

Jake winked at her. "*Very* complimentary."

Gretta laughed again. The store owner hurried into the dressing room, glancing from Gretta to Jake and back to Gretta.

"Gretta MacBain, how many times do I have to tell you to stay out of this store?" The short, balding man reached over and nervously took the suit coat down. "Sir? Do you intend to buy this?"

Jake kept his eyes on Gretta. "I do. Just give me a minute."

"I'm sorry this woman intruded on you like this," the owner told Jake, turning to glower at Gretta over spectacles that had slid down his narrow nose.

"I don't mind at all," Jake answered. "In fact, why don't you go out there and do whatever you need to do? I'll get the rest of this suit off and be along in a minute."

The man sucked in his breath, then scowled at Gretta again as he walked to the curtained doorway and looked up at Jake. "Sir, are you sure you should be alone back here with...with this woman? I mean, if she's bothering you—"

Jake grinned broadly. "Am I supposed to be afraid of her? Should I strap on my guns?"

Gretta laughed heartily and deliberately gave the owner a hungry once-over. "Henry Porter, when are you going to come on over and see me? I can show you things I'll bet your wife never even thought of doing to you."

Henry blushed. "Gretta, you *have* to stop coming in here!"

"Hell, it's good for your business." Gretta looked him over again. "Or are you afraid people will gossip and say you spend time here in the back room with me? Maybe you really *want* to come back here with me."

Henry sniffed. "You are shameless and...and you have a dirty mind!"

"Yeah, and I'm having fun with both."

The man turned even redder before turning to dart through the doorway. "It's your reputation, Mr. Harkner!" he called back.

"Mister, don't you be worrying about my reputation. There isn't a damn thing anyone can say about me that hasn't been said before, and most of it is probably true." He looked Gretta over appreciatively as he spoke, and they shared more laughter. "It's like you just said," Jake told Gretta. "Women like you raised me. I have some very good friends who are of your...profession."

She let out another bawdy laugh. "I'll just bet you do! What did you do—ask around the first time you came to Denver to find out who the best whores were and where they could be found?"

"I didn't have to ask. Men down at the stockyards talk."

"Did they tell you I own a whole house full of ladies who know most of those men?"

"Something like that." Jake removed the tie. "And how did you know who I am?"

She walked closer and took the tie from him. "Honey, do you really need to ask that? I mean, *look* at you!

Everybody knows who Jake Harkner is. The only man in this whole state who might be a tad more handsome is that son of yours." She began unbuttoning his shirt for him. "You have a way of making everything and everyone else in a room just disappear. All eyes turn to you. I did see you once last year. You were out shopping with your family. Everybody knew who you were, and I probably would have guessed, even if someone hadn't told me." She pulled the shirt down over his shoulders, revealing sleeveless underwear that accented his muscled arms. She ran a hand over his chest and down over his stomach suggestively. "Damn, you smell good."

"Just came from the bathhouse—got a shave and a haircut, too. I was a mess from bringing in a herd of cattle, and a couple of nights of no sleep."

"Now why on earth would you go two nights with no sleep?"

Jake let her pull off the shirt. "Personal. And what the hell are you doing in a men's clothing store?" he asked as he pulled his hands out of the sleeves.

"Looking for men, of course."

"Me in particular?"

"Maybe." She licked her lips. "And unlike Henry out there, I'll bet there isn't one thing I could say that would embarrass you one little bit."

"No, ma'am. I've seen it all and done it all." Jake put his hands on his hips. "So, should I buy the suit?"

"Mister, when you walk in to the Cattlemen's Ball in that suit and that silver brocade waistcoat I see lying over the chair there, women will faint. And I've seen your wife. She's a beautiful woman. You will make quite a pair."

Jake nodded. "If I make women faint, my wife will make men's jaws drop. Their cigars will fall right out of their mouths when she walks into the room."

Gretta laughed again. "I like you, Jake Harkner.

How many men would stand half dressed in front of a prostitute and talk about how beautiful their wives are?"

Jake lit a cigarette. "I would. I had my share of prostitutes a long time ago, Gretta. Then my wife came along and showed me a man only needs one good woman—although right now she's probably still a bit peeved at me."

"Is that so? Well, I find it hard to believe that any woman, wife or not, could stay mad at *you* for long."

Jake sobered. "Yeah, well, *believe* me, I'm not always easy to live with."

"Oh, I have no doubt about that." Gretta leaned against the doorjamb. "Let's see…you were running from the law when you two first met, and I'm betting you were an ornery sonofabitch back then, and the last thing you wanted was a woman hanging around—a *good* woman, that is. You preferred the kind you could take to bed and leave the next morning, only that wife of yours wouldn't let go. And then there were all those shoot-outs and then prison and then putting up with the dangers of you being a U.S. Marshal." Her gaze grew sincere. "She must be quite some woman."

Jake leaned against the other side of the doorjamb, also sobering. "They don't come any better."

"So, why is she peeved at you?"

Jake turned and picked up the shirt he'd worn into the store. Gretta noticed the scars at the back of his shoulders where the skin was exposed from the sleeveless undershirt. *From his father's beatings*, she thought. The man had quite a storied past—had killed his own father. She could tell there were likely a lot worse unseen scars under the shirt.

"Someone insulted her, and I beat the hell out of him," Jake answered Gretta. "Then I yelled at her for the first time in our almost-thirty years together. I left afterward and stayed away a couple of nights because I don't like being around my wife and family when I'm that angry. She's not happy that I didn't stay and talk to her." He pulled on his blue cotton shirt. "Let alone yelling at her like I did." He sighed. "It's been quite a while since I was that mad, and she worries about me when I kind of turn into the old Jake, if you know what I mean." He took another drag on the cigarette, then laid it in an ashtray provided in the dressing room.

"I can guess," Gretta answered. "And it's easier for you to talk to somebody like me than to her when you're that way."

Jake nodded. "You must have read that book pretty close to know so much about me."

"You're an intriguing man, Mr. Jake Harkner. What did that man you beat on say about your wife?"

He looked at her darkly. "He called her my personal whore. No offense."

"None taken."

"There are a lot of women like you that I respect, but Randy Hayes Harkner is no whore and doesn't deserve to be called one in the way that man said it. It hurt her bad, and I should have stayed and talked to her, but that remark made me feel like I didn't deserve to touch her at all."

"And you think women like me are the only kind you have any business being with."

He picked up the cigarette and drew on it again. "Sometimes." He grinned. "But I'll be damned if I can keep my hands off of her. She's got me tied to railroad tracks with a train coming, and I just lay there and don't even try to get loose."

"And you'd *let* that train run right over you if it meant never hurting her again."

"I would."

"Lucky woman."

Jake shook his head. "*I'm* the lucky one." He studied his cigarette a moment. "She changed my life years ago, but changing the real me isn't so easy. Some things are just beat into you until…" He looked Gretta over. "Here we are—just now met—and I'm talking to you about things that are none of your business."

Gretta put a hand on his arm. "Honey, I'll just bet that wife of yours never stays mad at you for long."

Jake couldn't help a smile. "Generally not."

She stepped closer, patting his cheek. "Of course not. You reek of sex, Jake Harkner, and she just can't resist that."

"Reek?"

"Reek. Sex just oozes from every pore of your body."

Jake laughed. "I've never heard it put quite that way."

Gretta looked him over again. "You damn well know it's true. And I would give my right arm to find out what you're like in bed."

"Ma'am, you pose a mighty strong temptation," Jake answered with a grin. "I appreciate the offer, and I appreciate the talk, but I have a wife waiting for me in a room at the Brown Palace."

Gretta pouted, stepping back. "How about that son of yours? He available?"

Jake set the cigarette aside again. "Lloyd is *also* happily married."

"Woe is me," Gretta joked.

Accustomed to women like Gretta, Jake had no qualms about removing the new suit pants in order to pull on his denim ones.

Gretta gladly studied the way Jake's knee-length long johns snugly fit firm thighs. She took a deep breath at the bulge between his legs that suggested a well-endowed man. He handed out the suit pants, and she took them as he picked up his denim pants.

"Maybe you can help me some other way," Jake told her as he pulled on his pants.

"How's that?"

He tucked his shirt into his pants as he answered. "Let me see your hands," he said after buttoning the pants.

"My *hands*?"

He reached out. "Your hands."

Gretta obliged, enjoying the soft way he touched her hands and rubbed the backs of them. He felt her fingers, studying them. "Where's the best jewelry store in town?"

"Bush and Company. That's where the snobs of Capitol Hill shop."

"Come there with me. It's our thirtieth anniversary, and I want to buy my wife the wedding ring she should have had all these years. Your hands are the same size as hers, so you'll need to try on whatever I pick out."

She squeezed his hands, leaning in close. "And you know every inch of her body, I'll bet."

Jake grinned. "Every inch. Intimately."

"If you want me to help you, you owe me a kiss. Just one kiss, Mr. Jake Harkner."

He leaned down and only kissed her cheek before pulling away and grabbing his gun belt from where it hung on a hook. "The only woman I kiss the way *you* want to be kissed is my wife. Believe me, if I kiss *you* like that, she'll know, and she won't unlock that hotel room door." He strapped on his guns.

"So, those are the infamous .44s."

"They're just guns."

"Not when they belong to Jake Harkner."

Jake tied the holsters to his thighs, then pulled on a suede jacket he'd purchased at another store earlier. He put out his cigarette in the sand-filled ashtray. "Where is that jewelry store?"

"Seventeenth Street—just a block over."

"Let's go then. I'll have Henry fold and pack these clothes, and I'll pick them up on the way back, along with my horse and my other belongings."

"So you're going to be seen walking the street with

me…Gretta MacBain, who runs one of the fanciest brothels in Denver? It's called the Range Club, by the way."

"I know all about it."

She shook her head. "Of course you do."

Jake put on his wide-brimmed Stetson and took her arm. He started to lead her out of the dressing room.

"Wait," she told him, pulling back. "There is something you should know."

"Yeah? What's that?"

Gretta glanced at the curtained doorway, then pulled him farther back into the dressing room. "I had a visitor a couple of weeks ago," she told him, her voice lowered. "He's the real reason I followed you in here." She took a deep breath before continuing. "He called himself Mike Holt." She watched Jake's whole demeanor change. The charming smile was gone.

"And?"

"And he bragged about…about being freed from prison and about…" She looked down, hating her next words. "About…your daughter…and about how he was going to kill your son for shooting his brother in the back." She looked up at Jake and was startled at the complete change in his demeanor. "I'm so sorry, Jake. I thought you should know he's probably still in town somewhere. He knew you'd be coming in with cattle. You need to be really careful." She watched Jake's jaw flex as he obviously struggled with repressed anger. He took a deep breath to calm himself.

"I'd already received a wire from Guthrie some time back, telling me he'd been there boasting about coming after me and Lloyd. It helps knowing for sure he's been here." He looked her over, stepping closer and putting a hand to the side of her face. "I appreciate the warning, but that man is an animal. Did he hurt you?"

Gretta's eyes widened in surprise. "Good Lord, you *care*?"

"Of course I care. After what those men did to my daughter? Men like that have no respect for *any* woman, and in my book, prostitutes aren't any different from any other woman when it comes to a man hurting them."

Gretta felt an urge to cry. "Well now, aren't you something, Jake Harkner?" She took a deep breath and blinked back tears. She pulled the bodice of her dress down enough to show him a bruise on her left breast. "He likes to bite." She re-covered her breast. "I kicked him out and told him never to come back and that none of the other girls would do business with him. Same with his friend."

Jake's eyes grew even darker. "Friend?"

"I think Mike called him Brad."

Jake turned away. "Jesus!"

"You know who he is?"

"I killed his father and two brothers back in Oklahoma when I was a marshal there. And I beat the hell out of Brad Buckley and left him in a bad way. If he's teamed up with Mike Holt—" He shook his head. "My God, that was four years ago. I figured we were done with all that." He faced Gretta. "I'm more worried about my daughter than anyone else. It's taken her all this time to totally recover from what happened to her…and I'm not sure she really has. Her only saving grace is her deep faith and a very good and very kind and understanding husband."

Gretta took his hand. "I hate having had to tell you all this."

"You did right." To Gretta's amazement, Jake pulled her close and put his arms around her. "I'm just sorry for what he did to you," he told her. "I should have killed that bastard when I had the chance, but my daughter— who thinks I walk on water—begged me not to go back to my old ways, so I let him live. That was a mistake."

"Well, it got me into the arms of Jake Harkner. I don't mind that at all."

Jake gave her a squeeze before letting go. "Yeah, well, now I have to figure out how to go to my wife later and pretend I'm not upset. After what we've just been through, she needs a break from worry, and I want her to enjoy herself tomorrow night at that ball."

"Then let's go buy that ring. Nothing softens up a woman like diamonds." She looked him over with a grin. "Although I have a feeling you don't need diamonds to soften a woman up. All you have to do is smile at her."

Jake managed a soft grin. "Yeah, after thirty years, she knows me all too well. Just a smile won't do it." Jake led her through the curtained doorway. "Come on. I have a feeling you know a lot about diamonds."

"You bet I do." Gretta paused. "Are you sure you want to be seen walking with me?"

Jake led her out. "Gretta, I long ago stopped worrying about what people think of me, and it's too late to try to change their opinions." He glanced at Henry. "Package up that suit, Henry, and I'll be back for it." He walked over and plunked the leather satchel with his other belongings in it on the counter. "Watch this till I get back." He took Gretta's arm and headed out. "I also need to find a florist and a garden supply," he told her on the way through the door.

Henry just shook his head. He couldn't wait to tell others he'd met the infamous Jake Harkner, and that the man had walked out of his store with Denver's most notorious harlot—after spending time with her alone in the dressing room and changing his clothes right in front of her!

Seventeen

RANDY HEARD THE TAP ON THE DOOR.

"Randy, it's me."

Her heart pounded with both relief and irritation. She pulled her robe close around her and tied it, then went to the door. "I'm tempted to leave you out there in the hallway," she called.

"I don't blame you. Come on, baby, let me in."

Baby. Randy closed her eyes and sighed with frustration. He knew the use of that word undid her. She unlocked the door, stepping aside as he walked in, his arms full with his personal leather bag, something wrapped in brown paper, and one hand wrapped around the paper-covered stems of a dozen yellow roses. It was already dark out, and by the soft light of two gas lamps, he looked strikingly handsome, filling up the room with his tall frame. "Well, you certainly look better than you did this morning," she told him, "and you apparently found a bathhouse."

"And a shave and a haircut, and I bought a new suit of clothes for tomorrow night." He set aside his leather bag and the package of new clothes, then handed out the roses. "Your favorite color. And I found a place where we can buy all the rosebushes you want to take back to the ranch. For now, here are these. Happy anniversary."

Every last bit of determination Randy had of staying upset with him vanished. She reached out and took the roses, smelling them. "Jake, they're beautiful!"

"Tomorrow, I want you to buy yourself the fanciest

dress in town, as long as it's yellow, and get your hair done up. I'll be taking the most beautiful woman in Denver to the Cattlemen's Ball."

She looked him over, trying not to cry. She turned and set the roses in a pitcher on the washstand. "Well...I already bought a dress, but I'm not so sure I want to go. After taking all this time to get to our room, you just come walking in as though nothing has happened, and you hand me yellow roses and pretend everything is just fine."

"Isn't it?"

Randy faced him. "Where have you been, Mr. Harkner?"

Jake leaned against the door, folding his arms. "I just told you. I got cleaned up and went shopping. It takes time to try on clothes. Then I went over to the stock-yards to see how Lloyd did. By the time we got through with the buyers, it was getting dark. And, by the way, we made a killing. The price of cattle is up right now, so we picked the perfect time to bring them in. We even talked to that government agent about buying that land with the old fort on it, which is why I'm later than I planned. Lloyd just went to his room and wants to go out to eat. Do you want to go?"

Randy frowned. "No! I mean, *look* at me. For heaven's sake, I'm not even dressed."

He raked her over with his eyes. "I noticed. And you know how much I love your hair brushed out long like that. I guess maybe we should stay here in the room tonight at that."

Randy stepped back. "Well, they do have room service here."

Jake looked around. "Damn nice room, isn't it?"

"Yes. And they brought up a bathtub for me, and a maid even washed my hair. The service is wonderful, and it feels good to be pampered after that long trip. Even better, after going through what I went through the last couple of days!"

Jake grimaced as though she'd just hit him. "I was hoping for a better reception."

"I'm sure you were." Randy studied him closely. "Let me guess," she said, watching his dark eyes as she stepped closer. She breathed deeply through her nose. "I am getting the distinct smell of perfume, and it's not the kind I wear. You've been with a prostitute, haven't you?"

He just stared at her a moment. "Jesus, woman, how in hell do you always know?"

"Because I know *you*, especially when things go a little haywire in that head of yours. You fell back into that mood of thinking you aren't good enough for me. When you get like that, and especially when that rage against your father comes out in you, you turn to the kind of people who used to understand and make you feel better. Dixie is still in Oklahoma as far as we know, so who was it this time?"

He stepped closer, grasping her face in his hands. "Gretta MacBain, and she runs a place called the Range Club. And I did *not* go there. And I didn't even go looking for *her*. *She* found *me* at the clothing store where I was trying on that suit over there. She knew who I was, and we struck up a conversation. I told her what happened, and that's all there was to it. I always say it like it is, Randy. When have I ever lied to you?"

She let out a long sigh and grasped his wrists. "It's not that, Jake. That has never bothered me, because I understand that little boy down inside the magnificent man you are. But I'm right here, Jake, and I've *always* been right here. You don't need to turn to someone else when these things happen—not to Lloyd or to Evie or some prostitute."

He moved his hands into her hair. "I had to leave those couple of days because I was afraid I'd yell at you again. I'm so damn sorry, *mi amor*. What Clem said made me sick inside. I couldn't even *look* at you, and I hated any of the *men* looking at you."

She closed her eyes. "Jake, what do you ask me every time you make love to me?"

His breathing deepened, and her need for him rushed through her with heated force.

"Who do you belong to?" he replied.

"And what do I answer?"

"Jake Harkner."

"And you always say…'every inch of your beautiful body.' And I *do* belong to you. I'm your *wife*, Jake, so anything you do with me you have a *right* to do as the man who loves me, as long as I *want* you to do those things to me. And I *do* want those things, because you make me feel beautiful and wanted and needed. How many times have I told you that I only feel safe when I'm in your arms?"

He cut off her words with a deep, hot, groaning, almost savage kiss as he walked her backward to the bed.

"Jake, we aren't done talking," she tried to protest.

"*I* am." He pulled off her robe. "I want to make love to you, Randy. I *need* to make love to you."

"Jake—"

He grasped her nightgown at her hips and pulled up. "Get this thing off."

"This isn't what I planned."

"Didn't you?"

"No. I mean, not right away." She was forced to raise her arms as he pulled off the nightgown. She was naked under it.

"Do you still want to tell me you didn't plan this?" He enfolded her in one arm as he pulled down the bedcovers. "You're the one who said it was all right for me to do whatever I want with you because you belong to me."

She grasped his arms, studying his eyes. "Only if you're all right now."

"I wouldn't be here if I wasn't all right. That's why I waited. I'm always all right when I come to you."

"Then *do* that. Come to *me*. I only like making love to the Jake who is in the present, not the past, but I can help the old Jake when I need to, and you know that."

He drank in the sight of her. "Woman, I am definitely in the present." He picked her up and laid her on the bed, then threw aside his jacket and unstrapped his guns. He sat down on the bed and pulled off his boots. "You want to know what Gretta told me?" He stood up and unbuttoned his shirt, taking it off.

"I'm not sure I want to know," Randy answered, pulling the covers over her nakedness. She could see the strong, loving Jake moving back into his eyes, the one who loved to sometimes tease her relentlessly and use just the right words to make her give in, even when he'd done something to upset her.

Jake unbuckled his belt and pulled off his pants, taking his underwear off with them. He removed the sleeveless undershirt and crawled into bed.

"I am waiting for your answer," she told him. "What did that woman say to you?"

He moved on top of Randy and braced his elbows on either side of her, grinning. "She said I reek of sex. How's *that* one for you?"

Randy couldn't help responding to the masculinity that was Jake Harkner, nor to the way he was smiling at her now. The Jake she loved most was back, and that was all that mattered. "*Reek?*"

"Reek."

"Interesting description."

"Her word, not mine. I just wondered what you think of that."

Randy smiled slyly. "You reeked of sex that first time I found you lying wounded in my bed back in Kansas. Actually, you reeked of sex when I saw you in that store the first day we laid eyes on each other. I could feel the man in you as you moved around, picking up the things you needed. That little store was filled up with Jake Harkner."

"I felt the same thing in you."

"That I filled up the room?"

"You know what I mean. The woman in you signaled to me like a damn warning bell. I should have *heeded* that warning."

"I felt a signal, too—but it was more like the deep, long whistle of a locomotive, telling me to stay away. I should have heeded *that* warning."

He grinned even more. "You did. You *shot* me."

"Yes, well, we know how that worked out. Here we are almost thirty years later, lying naked in bed together, when I really should have slapped you when you came in for taking so long, let alone spending time with a prostitute. In fact, I should have sent you over to her place of business, but then when you came back, I'd have to shoot you again for actually going there."

"I wouldn't have gone, and you know it. Why would I leave the bed of the most beautiful woman in this city? I don't deserve her, but if she's willing to be with me, I'm sure as hell not going to say no. What man would?" He leaned down and kissed her throat in the ticklish, butterfly way he had.

"I am supposed to still be mad at you," Randy reminded him.

"What can I do to change that?" He kissed her throat again.

"You're already doing it." She felt his penis pressing in that crevice where the top of her leg met more private places. "And I hate you for it."

He moved to her mouth, groaning as he ran his tongue deep in a long, delicious, passionate kiss. By the time he finished, she felt as though he'd already invaded every part of her body. He had a way of making love to her mouth that completely undid her. He left her lips only long enough to kiss her cheek, her ear, her neck, then back to her lips yet again, searching deep. His kisses sometimes made it feel like he was already having intercourse with her. Again he left her mouth, kissing her eyes gently. "If this is hate, I can't wait till you decide you still love me."

Randy grasped his hair. "I'll always love you, even when I hate you, if that makes any sense."

He moved to her throat again. "Sure it does."

"Maybe it's because you *do* reek of sex."

"Whatever works." He kissed his way to her breasts, savoring the taut nipples as though they were sweet cherries, making her groan and arch toward him. He ran an arm under her neck and moved to her side so he could run his other hand over her belly and down to the place that had always belonged only to Jake Harkner.

And you damn well know it, Randy thought as he moved his fingers inside her suggestively, drawing out the silken juices that prepared her for what was to come. He moved his lips over her belly then. She parted her legs as he found his mark. It made her feel wanton as he kept teasing her with his fingers while his tongue worked its magic in private places that truly did belong only to this man.

Oh, how she wanted to stay mad at him…and oh, how impossible he made it. That little part of her that made her jealous of the woman who'd told him he reeked of sex made her offer herself with total abandon. She would damn well please him like none of those women ever had. Those days were over for him, because she always made sure there wasn't one thing the man needed that she couldn't give him.

"My God, Jake," she whispered as a deep, aching climax engulfed her. He had a way of tasting her in these moments that only prolonged the climax until she literally cried out from the nearly painful ecstasy. He kept his fingers pressed tightly against her throbbing clitoris as he worked his lips back up to her throat. The man knew every move there was to please a woman.

"Still mad at me?" he teased.

"Yes."

He met her lips as he moved on top of her. She could taste herself in his kiss. "Still?" he said softly.

"Yes."

He moved inside of her then, filling her full and deep. Randy gasped as she raised her hips in response.

"Still?" he asked.

"No." She leaned up and caught his lips again with her own, wrapping her arms around his neck and pulling him down while he moved his hands under her bottom to support her and rocked in and out of her with perfect rhythm.

"Who do you belong to?" he asked.

"Jake Harkner."

"Every beautiful inch of your body," he answered between kisses.

Between groans and gasps she replied, "And you belong to *me*, Jake Harkner. Every…single…inch of you."

The talking stopped as the deep kisses continued and their bodies remained locked in perfect movements, now so familiar that neither of them needed to wonder if what they were doing felt good to the other.

"Don't stop," Randy begged.

"I'm trying…not to," he answered. "It would help… if you weren't such a beautiful woman…and if I didn't… adore everything about you." He kept up the erotic invasion for several more minutes before his life spilled into her in several hard, groaning shoves. His whole body shuddered, and he kept her under him. "I want to do this all night."

Randy kissed his neck, breathing in his familiar scent. "We have to eat sometime."

He fed her several delicious kisses. "Once more. Then we'll eat. Then we'll do this again." Another kiss. "And again." Already she felt his growing hardness against her thigh, but he sobered on the next words. "When I make love to you, I feel stronger." He kissed her breasts. "Calmer."

"Jake."

He met her gaze again, and she detected tears in his eyes.

"What is it, Jake? You're leaving something out."

"I don't want to tell you."

"Jake, I can feel some of that anger and restlessness still there. What's wrong?"

He sighed, collapsing to the pillow beside her. "Gretta had a visitor. That's why she looked me up—to warn me."

"Mike Holt?"

"Mike Holt. She thinks he's still in town somewhere waiting for me and Lloyd. Last she knew, he had a friend with him...named Brad."

"Oh no!" Randy turned onto her back. "Brad Buckley?"

"It has to be."

"Does Lloyd know?"

"I pulled him out in the hallway and told him before I came here to our room. I hated telling him, because he's so happy about the good money we made today." He ran a hand into her hair and toyed with it. "Gretta said Holt even bragged about that thing with Evie. I didn't tell Lloyd that. It would have been too hard on him."

Randy felt his hand tighten on her hair. "We can't tell Evie any of this," she told Jake.

"Of course not, but we're going to have to be very watchful when we shop tomorrow, and at that ball tomorrow night. Men like Holt won't likely get in. It's invitation only, but it's a big event, so you never know. At least it will be right downstairs in the hotel lobby, so we won't have to walk through town to get there." He sighed. "I promised you a wonderful time, and now this. I should have killed Mike Holt when I had the chance to get away with it."

"It would have broken Evie's heart," Randy reminded him. "She still worries about you. Earlier today she told me she hated to see you so lonely. It's amazing how sweet she still is after what happened to her."

Jake closed his eyes. "There's an angel inside of her. She can't possibly be mine."

"Are you saying I had an affair?"

He enveloped her into his arms. "Did you?"

Randy smiled. "Why would any woman who belongs to you want any other man?"

"I can think of a *lot* of reasons."

"Well, I can't think of even one." Randy kissed him. "Maybe we should just go home to the kids, Jake."

"No. Katie and Evie are looking forward to the ball, and Brian wants to take Evie to the opera. They're young and excited and need to feel beautiful and have some social enjoyment away from the loneliness of the ranch. Lloyd feels the same way." He raised up and kissed her eyes. "And you need a chance to show off some new jewelry."

"What new jewelry?"

Jake rolled off of her and reached for his jacket, taking out a small box and handing it to her. "This."

Randy's eyes widened, and she scooted to sit up.

Jake rested on his side as he watched her open the box and gasp. "Happy anniversary, baby."

"Jake! We can't afford this!"

"Yes, we can. For years I have wished you had a fancier wedding ring than that plain gold band I gave you back at Fort Laramie when that priest married us a lifetime ago."

"I love my plain gold band."

"And you deserve something more. I want you to

wear that tomorrow night at the ball. Everyone's heads will turn when we walk in, because I'll have the most beautiful woman in Colorado on my arm. And she'll be wearing a ring that damn well proves she *did* legally marry me all those years ago. And now she's just as rich and important and elegant as the high-class snobs in Denver who think they're better than everyone else."

Randy removed a gold band from the box. It sparkled with one large diamond in the center and four smaller diamonds on either side, with a swirl of eight more tiny baguettes crossing over the band. She slipped it on her finger. "Oh, Jake, it's…it's too much!"

"Quit worrying about that."

"It's so beautiful! So exquisite."

"Like the woman wearing it."

"And it fits perfectly! How did you—" She looked at him slyly. "Someone must have helped you pick this out."

Jake just grinned. "Her fingers were the same size as yours." He pulled her farther down under the covers again. "I could tell just by touching her fingers they were exactly right."

"The woman who said you reek of sex? What else did you touch?"

Jake kissed her. "Nothing else. She knows a lot about diamonds."

"I'll just bet she does. She knows a lot about men, too." Randy fingered the wavy strands of hair that brushed his forehead. "How is it that some men age so well?"

"It's the ones who have a good woman by their side." Jake moved on top of her. "I want you to know that I picked out that ring myself. Gretta didn't have anything to do with it, other than to try it on for fit. That ring is all me, and I love you, Mrs. Harkner. No man could be prouder of his wife than I am of you."

"And I love you…for better or for *worse*."

He nuzzled her neck. "It's been mostly for worse. I know that. I'm sorry these past thirty years involved so much heartache at times."

"These past thirty years brought me two beautiful children, a dear adopted child, and four wonderful grandchildren with more on the way. They brought me a man far more loving than any other man I might have chosen. It's all been worth it." She held her hand up and studied the ring as he continued kissing her throat. "Thank you for the ring, Jake. I can't wait to show it off tomorrow. "

"And I can't wait to show *you* off."

"Maybe we *should* go out to eat. I want to show the ring to Evie and Katie."

"Too late. I'm too deep into wanting my wife right here in bed."

Randy reached up and wrapped her arms around his neck, pulling him down to her as their lips met in a deep, delicious kiss.

No foreplay was needed this time. She opened herself to him, and he guided himself inside her, pulling her to him with a strength that told her how easily he could hurt her, yet a gentleness that told her he never would. Not this man who adored women, and especially adored the one most special to him. When they were together like this, she could hardly believe that dark, ruthless side of him even existed…but it did. She couldn't get over her belief that she had to keep that side of him at bay… or lose him.

❧

Katie pulled down the netting from her hat and over her forehead. "Do you like my hat?" She turned to Lloyd, studying his brawny chest. She walked up and kissed it before he could finish buttoning a white shirt.

"It's beautiful, but no one is going to notice that hat." He put a hand to the side of her face. "All they will see is this delicate face and your beautiful green eyes and these luscious lips." He leaned down and kissed her deeply, groaning as he pulled her close. He moved his kisses to behind her ear. "Let's go back to bed."

"Lloyd Harkner, we made dinner plans with Brian and Evie, and we are already running late."

"Yeah, well, maybe my sister and her husband are having the same problem we are. We've all gone quite a few days without a nice soft bed we can share together."

Katie pushed at him. "Well, you didn't waste any time getting me back into bed, and now I'm hungry. So finish dressing. Should we see if your parents want to go?"

Lloyd grinned as he finished buttoning the shirt. "Katie, the reason Pa pulled me out in the hallway a while ago was to tell me he wanted to be alone with my mother tonight. So no, they won't be going with us. They have a lot to talk about, and if I know my father, he'll find a way right back into my mother's soft side in no time at all. He probably already has." He pulled on a waistcoat over the shirt and buttoned it, deciding not to tell his wife the real reason Jake had wanted to talk to him. Mike Holt was somewhere out there, looking for revenge, but Lloyd decided he wasn't going to let that spoil things for Katie. "Let's get dinner over with sooner than later. I'm anxious to get back here."

Katie smiled and had to reach up to get her arms around his neck. "You look so incredibly handsome in a dress shirt and waistcoat." She kissed him, then fussed with his silk tie. "Of course you don't need clothes to make you look handsome. Actually, I prefer you with no clothes at all. You have the build of a god, Lloyd Harkner."

"Yeah? Well then, that makes you a goddess."

"Thank you, but I'll have a hard time keeping you to myself tomorrow night. Do you know how many women will try flirting with you at that ball? I see how they look at you."

"And I will have eyes only for the mother of my beautiful little girl and the woman who is carrying another one of my children in her belly as we speak. You're all the woman I need, Katie Harkner, and when we get back from dinner, I'll show you just how *much* I need you."

She smiled. "You already did that."

"And I'm not through with you."

Katie blushed. "I want a massage next time. You are wonderful at that. You have such strong hands."

"Oh?" He grasped her shoulders and gently moved his hands over them. "I'll massage every inch of your body." He leaned down and kissed her again, then stepped back to look her over. "You picked the perfect dress. The color blue is beautiful on you."

She turned for him, holding out her arms. "Isn't it lovely? I got it at a store that sells dresses made in Paris!"

Lloyd watched her lovingly. "Yeah, well, it won't be long before it will be too small in the waist, thanks to that new baby."

She smiled. "Well, for now I'm not showing, and wait till you see the dress I'm wearing tomorrow night! It's mint green, your favorite color on me. And your mother bought the most beautiful yellow dress. You know how Jake likes her in yellow."

Lloyd nodded as he pulled on a black frock coat with silk lapels. "I'm surprised my mother was in the mood to shop."

"She wasn't, but Evie and I made her. We both knew Jake would find a way to make things better. He always does."

Lloyd put on a black silk bowler hat. "Yeah, well, Pa has a way with women."

Katie folded her arms. "And so do you." She sighed. "Lloyd, you look wonderful."

"What about my hair? Is it okay just pulled back at my neck like it is?"

"You look fine."

"Pa would say I look like an Indian dressed up like a white man." He turned and took one of his guns from its holster and slipped it into a special pocket in his vest.

Katie lost her smile. "Why are you taking a gun?"

He forced a casual air. "I'm a Harkner, Katie-girl." He put out his arm. "Let's go eat."

She took his arm. "Lloyd, is something wrong?"

"Not a damn thing." He led her to the door.

"Are any of the ranch hands coming with us?"

Lloyd grinned. "Sweetheart, we raked it in at the stockyards today, and I paid the men off. I have a feeling they have other plans for tonight with all that money in their pockets. Whiskey, cards, and women, most likely."

She looked up at him, sobering a little. "Do you miss that life, Lloyd?"

"Hell no." He pulled her close. "I've got a beautiful wife and family and a ranch to run. I've never been happier." He took her arm again and led her to the door. "Now, let's get Evie and Brian and go eat."

Mike Holt be damned, he swore inwardly. Katie deserved this. So did Evie and his mother. He could handle the Mike Holts of this world. Still, he'd be glad to head home…to the J&L, to peace and quiet…away from the noise and filth and smoggy air of this city. To his own home deep in the hills that looked down on the homestead. To his son and daughter and his own bed where he'd shared so much pleasure with his wife. "I love you, Katie-girl."

Katie touched his chest. "Lloyd, when you made love to me, it was with such passion, as though it was the last time or something. What's wrong?"

He shook his head. "Nothing." He started for the door.

"Lloyd, you are just like your father. When there is

trouble around, it's written all over your face. He can't fool your mother, and you can't fool me. It's that Mike Holt, isn't it?"

He sighed deeply. "Katie, Denver is a big city with law and order, and we are going only to the best restaurant and staying in the best hotel and will shop in the best district—places where lowlifes like Mike Holt don't hang out. In a city this size, it would be very hard for Holt to track us down."

"But that's why you brought a gun, isn't it?"

"Don't worry about it. I can take care of myself, as you well know."

"Well, guns aren't allowed at the Cattlemen's Ball tomorrow night. So we have to be extra careful."

"With me and Pa there, you have nothing to worry about. It's a closed-door dance, by invitation only, so we'll be fine. In a couple of days, we'll head back to the ranch."

Katie stepped back, taking his arm. "I love you, Lloyd. I don't ever want to have to live without you."

"And I'm not about to let that happen." He kissed her and headed for the door, almost hoping Mike Holt *would* show up. After what he did to Evie, he'd like to shoot the sonofabitch and have it over with.

Eighteen

RANDY ENJOYED WEARING SOMETHING ELEGANT FOR once, after months of plain cotton dresses or riding skirts for ranch life. The light yellow dress she'd purchased earlier in the day was designed in New York City. Its pleated bodice was set off by a wide yellow satin bow, and the skirt fell in lace-trimmed panels with a flounced hemline of white puffed organdy.

She and Jake whirled around the dance floor, and she was secretly delighted that women were watching her very handsome husband and gossiping behind fans, some of them finding excuses to come and introduce themselves.

"Hugh Draper and his wife are here," she told Jake as they turned to a waltz. "I think his wife is hoping you'll ask her to dance."

Jake grinned. "Why would I ask anyone else to dance when I'm with the prettiest woman here?" His gaze dropped to the off-the-shoulder neckline of her dress. Her ash-blond hair was swept up into curls topped with a tiny satin hat trimmed with white feathers. "You wear that dress like you were a governor's wife, and I can't wait to dip my hands into that bodice when we get to the room later."

"Well, I intend to have several more dances before we do that, Mr. Harkner, so it will be *much* later. I am truly enjoying myself, especially the fact that I am with the most handsome man at this ball. You look absolutely stunning in black silk tails and that silver waistcoat. You could *be* the governor! Maybe you should run for office."

Jake pulled her closer than most men danced in public. "I hardly think people would vote for an old ex-outlaw for governor."

"Every woman in this city would vote for you if they were allowed, and you are holding me embarrassingly close."

"You're my wife."

"And we aren't dancing in a brothel, Mr. Harkner."

"If we were, we'd be having a *lot* more fun."

Randy couldn't help laughing. "Isn't Katie beautiful in that mint green? Her dress is from Paris, and she's absolutely giddy over the diamond necklace Lloyd bought her. And Lloyd is absolutely beautiful in that suit. Not handsome. Beautiful."

"Yeah, well, don't tell *him* that. He'd probably leave so fast you wouldn't see him for dust, and like me, he'd rather be in denim pants and leather boots and riding on the back of a big mustang out on the J&L."

"Well, I love seeing you that way, too, but it's not often any of us Harkner women get to see our men looking so dapper, let alone dress up ourselves. Even Brian doesn't wear suits as often as he used to back in Guthrie when he was doctoring full time. Since we moved to the ranch, he's taken to denim pants and cotton shirts just like the rest of you, but doesn't he look wonderful tonight? He's such a handsome man in his own right."

"Woman, you do carry on."

"Well, you've produced such a beautiful family. I'm so proud of all of them."

Jake scowled a little. "It's all due to you, not me." He whirled her past a group of stout women who just stared. "Tomorrow we'll go to that landscaping business and buy the rosebushes you want," he told Randy.

"Mostly yellow ones. I want to plant them around the veranda."

Brian and Evie turned past them. "You two look wonderful!" Evie called to them.

Jake cast her a smile before looking down at Randy. "My baby girl seems to be having a wonderful time. I'm so glad for her and Brian."

"So am I. And doesn't she look wonderful in that coral chiffon dress? It beautifully accents her dark skin."

"She looks ravishing."

The music ended, and Jake took Randy's arm and led her to the small table where a candle burned and a bottle of free champagne sat, along with two flutes. "I'm missing the grandkids," Jake said as they sat down. "We'll head home the day after tomorrow. I'm sure Little Jake is giving the men quite a time of it."

Randy smiled and began removing her elbow-length gloves as Jake stopped a waiter.

"Bring us some water and coffee, will you?" he told the skinny young man. "Take the champagne to some other table."

"But, Mr. Harkner, it's the best there is, compliments of Prosecutor Harley Wicks, who would very much like to meet you."

Jake's affable demeanor instantly changed, and Randy stiffened.

"Is that so?" Jake asked. He straightened in his chair. "You tell Mr. Wicks that I appreciate the gesture, but I don't drink, especially not around my wife. Neither does my son, so you can give someone else his champagne, too. And if Mr. Wicks wants to meet me, all he has to do is walk over here."

"Yes, sir." The waiter took the bottle of champagne. "And I'd like to say I'm privileged to meet you, Mr. Harkner."

Jake sighed and shook his head. "I don't know why you consider it a privilege, young man, but thank you."

"Well, you're…you're pretty darn famous, sir."

"And you read too many books."

The words came from behind the waiter, and he turned to see Lloyd standing there. "Well, I'm glad to meet you, too, Mr. Harkner."

Lloyd glanced at Jake and grinned. "I'm getting anxious to get out of here, but I guess we have to put up with this."

"The women are having a good time, so let's give them a few more dances," Jake told him, looking him over. "You're looking like quite the gentleman, Son."

"Yeah? 'Gentlemen' isn't usually the term people use for me and you, is it?"

"You are every bit a gentleman," Katie told Lloyd.

"Well, I might not be such a gentleman when we get back to our room," he told her. Lloyd kept an arm around his blushing wife and moved to a table beside his father's as the waiter removed the champagne from both their tables. "And here comes one more beautiful woman to join us."

A smiling Evie approached on Brian's arm. "Daddy, Brian is taking me to the opera after this. Can you and Mother go?" She looked at Lloyd. "You, too?"

"I'd love to go!" Katie put in.

Lloyd gave his father a pained look. "*Opera?*"

Jake shrugged. "It's their night." He looked at Brian. "You agreed to go?"

"Your daughter's wish is my command, Jake. You know that."

Jake grinned. "And I appreciate that." He reached out and squeezed Evie's hand. "This lovely woman deserves to be spoiled. How are you feeling, angel?"

"I feel good, and I'm having a wonderful time." She put a hand over Jake's. "And I can't say enough how beautiful mother's ring is! Daddy, that was so romantic of you to surprise her with that ring. I'm so glad everything is all right. Mother was so worried about you, and so was I."

"Evie, you have to stop worrying about everybody else. You just take care of yourself, and if you want us to go to the opera with you, we'll go. I'm sure your mother and Katie would enjoy it."

The music started up again, and Brian kept an arm around Evie's waist. "You told me you wanted to dance every dance, my love, so I'm holding you to it, as long as you feel up to it."

Jake noticed a short, rotund man coming toward them and guessed it was Prosecutor Wicks. To his relief, Evie let go of his hand and joined Brian on the dance floor. Women turned to another waltz, swirling around the dance floor in beautiful gowns in dozens of colors and designs.

Jake rose, towering over the man coming his way, a big-boned, haughty-looking woman walking with him. She wore diamonds at her neck and a dress that fit too tight in the waist and forced her large bosom to bubble up at the bodice and jiggle as she walked with an arrogant air about her.

"Well, at last we meet, Mr. Harkner," the man said when he came closer. He put out his hand, but Jake just kept his arms folded.

"I don't shake a man's hand until I know his name," he told the rosy-cheeked man.

Lloyd slowly rose to stand beside Jake.

"How dare you snub an important man like my brother!" the woman sniffed.

Jake turned to Lloyd. "Did I snub the man?"

"Seems to me you only asked who he is," Lloyd stated.

A few people nearby quieted and watched the confrontation. Jake and Lloyd's sizes and demeanor made Wicks look like a chubby little boy.

"Let me start over," the rotund man, whose vest was too tight over his belly, told Jake. He put out his hand again. "I am Prosecutor Harley Wicks, and this lady beside me is my sister, Arlis. Of course, everyone knows who *you* are."

More people stopped talking, and some stopped dancing. Evie noticed and started to rush over to Jake, but Brian kept hold of her arm.

"I'm sorry, Mr. Wicks, but why should I shake your hand?" Jake boldly asked. "I got a visit from Marshal Kraemer a few weeks ago, and he told me you'd like to arrest me. So why are you here wanting to shake my hand?"

Randy glanced at Katie, who quietly rose and moved to go sit beside Randy. The two women clasped hands.

Wicks pulled back his hand. "Mr. Harkner, I just want you to understand that I'm not a man who holds a grudge. Marshal Kraemer cleared up the situation over the shooting out at your ranch."

"*Did* he?" Jake moved a little closer, causing the prosecutor to back up a little. "Let me tell you the situation, Mr. Wicks. Seven men tried stealing my cattle, and I'm sure there are plenty of ranchers here who would have done the same thing I did if they caught rustlers stealing from them. My wife happened to be with me at the time, and they threatened to come after her. I did what any man would do."

"You murdered my son!" the woman beside Wicks told Jake, her dark eyes glittering.

All music stopped, and this time everyone turned. Just then Jake noticed, of all people, Gretta MacBain coming through the doorway. He moved his gaze back to the woman who'd accused him of murdering her son. Her nostrils flared with indignation, and her large bosom heaved with her deep breaths of fury.

Jake met her gaze boldly. "Ma'am, I shot back at someone who was shooting at *me*. That's called self-defense. And I had no idea who any of them were."

"You could have just wounded him!"

"And what was an obviously wealthy and probably spoiled young man doing out at the J&L rustling cattle in the first place?" Lloyd asked. "He didn't need the money, and he must have been raised to know better."

"My nephew had fallen in with the wrong bunch of men, who convinced him they could show him a good time," Harley Wicks answered. "I'm sure they intended it as just a prank."

"A *prank*?" Jake seethed. "What I saw was no prank, Wicks, and even if it had been, I wouldn't have known who was who. When you play with guns around me, you've picked the wrong man!"

"Are you saying it was a lie then, when some of your men claimed they came along and did some of the shooting?"

Randy squeezed Katie's hand, praying Jake wouldn't lose his temper in front of the very man who would like to jail him.

Lloyd joined the confrontation then, always ready to step up in defense of his father. "They were out to kill both my parents, you sonofa—"

"Lloyd!" Jake interrupted his son, keeping dark eyes on Wicks. "What I'm saying, Wicks, is that seven men came onto my land and stole my cattle and then came at me and my *wife*! I'm not sure how many of them I shot myself. I only know I had to stop them from getting to *her*, so that's what I did! If some of my men came along in time and took care of some of the others, then that's what happened. I was pretty damn preoccupied at the time, and one of their bullets got me across the back and would have hit my wife if I hadn't been shielding her. I'd say that warrants shooting *back*, wouldn't you?"

Flash powder exploded nearby as a newspaper man managed to get a picture of Jake and Lloyd confronting Prosecutor Wicks. Jake kept his eyes on Wicks as he raised his voice for the others. "Any of you cattlemen here disagree with what I did?" he asked.

There came a few "hell nos" and "certainly nots," most of the replies quietly mumbled.

"There's your answer, Wicks." He looked at Arlis. "Ma'am, I'm sorry about your son, but I don't know for sure whose bullet hit him, and I don't understand why he went out there in the first place. And to this day, I don't even know which one he was. What happened is something I couldn't have controlled. Life hands us some pretty bad things sometimes. Believe me, I know that better than most. What happened to your son is no one's fault but his own."

Arlis stiffened, her eyes tearing. "Somehow, some way, I'll see you *hang*, Jake Harkner!" She turned and stormed out.

Jake turned his gaze to Harley Wicks. "What was your *real* reason for creating a scene?" he asked the man.

Wicks put his thumbs into his vest pockets. "I simply wanted to meet you, Mr. Harkner. All the other times you've been to Denver, we've never met, but then I didn't have reason to care. But after what happened to my nephew, I thought it was time we got acquainted, since someday I might have the privilege and pleasure of prosecuting you and sending you back to prison—maybe not for what happened with my nephew, but I'm sure something else will come up. After all, you're Jake Harkner, and no man can truly escape his past, can he?"

A few quiet gasps could be heard.

"What are you after, Wicks?" Jake kept his voice steady.

"I can break you, Harkner. And I can keep you from getting that extra land you want south of your ranch."

"Too late! I already bought it," Lloyd answered for Jake. "Signed the papers this morning."

Wicks looked taken aback. His face reddened with

repressed fury and with embarrassment at having been beaten to the punch. "I told—"

"You told that government representative not to sell it?" Lloyd interrupted. "Isn't that underhanded and illegal, Wicks? Is that how you use your power? To screw people out of their rights?"

Wicks's chest heaved with deep breaths as the man stood there speechless. "You Harkner men think—"

"Now, now, folks, let's not spoil the fun here," Gretta quickly spoke up, sauntering toward Jake and the prosecutor. "Mr. Harkner here and his beautiful family are a real bonus to our first Cattlemen's Ball, don't you think? We've got somebody famous here." She shimmied between Jake and Harley Wicks. "Harley, why don't you go rejoin your *wife*?" she suggested. "You're one of Denver's finest, so trying to start trouble with Jake doesn't suit you. And you're surely embarrassing the missus." Gretta raised her hand and signaled the orchestra leader, who got the band of several violins, a flute, drums, and a bass playing another waltz. She glared at Wicks. "Everybody is here to have a good time, Harley. Save your prosecutor's threats for the courtroom."

Wicks backed away as couples began dancing again. "What are you doing at a dance for decent people?" he asked Gretta.

Gretta put out her arms, showing off a lovely blue form-fitting dress that actually had a high neckline. "I'm dressed like a proper lady, and I'm a business owner in this town, and so far that business is still legal."

Wicks gave her a dark glare. "I can always change that."

Gretta sobered. "And I can destroy *you*, and you know it!"

Wicks looked as though he'd just been slapped. He turned his gaze to Jake. "You're walking a thin line, Jake Harkner."

"I always have," Jake answered.

Wicks turned and walked away, and Gretta turned to Jake, lowering her voice. "Harley and I have kind of an understanding," she told him. "He doesn't kick me out of Denver, and I don't tell his *wife* on him, if you know what I mean."

Jake grinned. "You're a clever woman, Gretta."

"Pa, you know this woman?" Lloyd asked.

"Lloyd, this is Gretta MacBain. She runs—"

"Don't tell me." Lloyd nodded to Gretta. "I've heard of you, ma'am."

"I'll just bet you have." Gretta looked Lloyd over. "My God, are there more Harkner men like you and your father back at the ranch?"

"Just ones who are too young," Lloyd answered, giving her a wink. "Thanks for stepping in when you did. I'm not going to ask how you know my father. Let's just say I'm not surprised." He turned to Jake. "Right now the ranch is sounding real good."

"That it is." Jake glanced at a confused-looking Katie. "Go dance with your wife," he told Lloyd. "She looks kind of lost and scared."

Lloyd nodded to Gretta. "Nice to meet you, ma'am. Thanks for stepping in when you did." He glanced at Jake again and just shook his head before taking Katie's arm and urging her away from the table and back to the dance floor.

"Lloyd, I thought that man was going to try to arrest your father," Katie told him.

"Well, he didn't."

"Who's that woman?"

"I'll tell you later."

"Is she—"

"Yes." Lloyd put his hand to her waist and began turning to the music.

"Kind of hard to stay out of trouble when you're Jake Harkner, isn't it?" Gretta asked Jake.

Jake nodded. "Sometimes." He turned to Randy. "Randy, this is the woman I told you about."

Randy got up from her chair and touched Gretta's arm. "Thanks for smoothing things over."

"Well, Harley Wicks can be a real sonofabitch," Gretta answered, glancing over to see Wicks talking with the local sheriff. "He likes to act important, but I have a few things on him that I can use sometimes to knock him down a notch or two, know what I mean?"

Randy grinned. "I believe I do." She grasped Jake's arm. "And you must be the one who told my husband he reeks of sex."

Gretta paused and sobered. "He *told* you?"

"Jake tells me everything."

"And you aren't upset?"

"I know Jake all too well. And thank you for helping him pick the right size ring." She held out her hand, and Gretta studied the ring. She met Randy's eyes then in a mutual understanding between two women leading very different lives.

"Ma'am, you should know that Jake picked out that ring. He just wanted me to try it on to see how it fit. You shouldn't think that someone like me chose something so special. It was all Jake." She glanced up at Jake, who just smiled.

"I told you she was quite a woman, Gretta."

Gretta met Randy's eyes again. "Mrs. Harkner, most women in this room turn their backs when I get anywhere near them. They are probably all gossiping about you right now because you're talking to me."

"Why shouldn't I? You warned Jake about Mike Holt, and I appreciate that. And Jake has always had friends among women of your…profession."

Gretta threw her head back and laughed, turning to grasp the arm of the man who'd accompanied her to the dance. "Sam, meet Mr. and Mrs. Jake Harkner."

The man nodded to both of them. "It's a privilege." He put out his hand, and Jake shook it.

"Sam here kind of manages my place. Kicks out the no-goods."

Jake studied the huge, burly man. "Well, Sam, you look like someone who could kick out a grizzly if he had to."

"I do my best to protect the lovely ladies," Sam answered with a grin that showed a missing eye tooth.

"And Gretta pays you well?" Jake asked.

"*Very* well," Sam answered enthusiastically.

Both men laughed, and Jake turned to Gretta. "I'd better take Randy and do some visiting with some of the other cattlemen here."

"You go right ahead." Gretta took Sam's arm. "Let's dance, Sam. The other women here need something to talk about behind their fancy fans and gloved hands."

The next hour was spent mixing and mingling. While Jake and Lloyd talked business with other cattlemen, their wives and daughters nearly swarmed around Randy and Katie. Randy ached for Evie, who avoided the gatherings and stayed near Brian. She knew Evie feared how some of them would look at her and wonder what it was like to suffer what she'd suffered.

"Oh, my dear, the things you have been through," Olivia Draper soothed Randy. Mrs. Draper was the woman who had a flirtatious eye for Jake. "I can't imagine what it's like to be married to a man like Jake Harkner."

"Actually, it's quite wonderful," Randy answered proudly. "Jake is a good husband and father, very loving and caring. Oh, and look at the new wedding ring he bought for me!" Randy eagerly showed the ring, enjoying the chagrined look on Olivia's face.

"Oh my, it's quite beautiful."

Several of the other women gathered around to look. "How long have you been married to the man?" one of them asked.

"Thirty years. Actually, this dance is part of our anniversary celebration."

"Well, you both look so young!" another put in. "You have a beautiful family, Mrs. Harkner. With your newfound fame, you should move to Denver. There are so many social societies you could join, and some feel your husband would make the perfect sheriff for our county. I've heard some of the other men say so."

Randy shook her head. "Jake is done with that kind of work. I've spent most of our marriage wondering if and when Jake was coming home, or if he would make it home at all. We are perfectly happy with the peace we have found on the J&L." Randy glanced over at Lloyd and Jake sharing laughter with several of the men.

"*Perfectly* happy? That's not what I heard from Henry Porter," another said snidely behind a fan. "I've heard your husband has an affinity for prostitutes."

There came a few gasps.

Randy faced her squarely. "Oh, you must mean Gretta MacBain," she shot right back, wanting them all to know she wasn't the poor, abused wife who was ignorant of the truth. "Men like Jake have unusual friends, and there is a reason, Mrs. Lane. Perhaps you wouldn't trust your own husband around such women, but I totally trust mine."

The woman's eyes widened with indignation, and she marched away.

"Don't mind her, Mrs. Harkner," another spoke up. "That's Corinne Oates, and she's the worst gossip in all of Denver."

The rest of them twittered and laughed.

"What's he *really* like?" another asked. "I can't imagine being married to someone so handsome and able but with such a reputation. How do you handle a man like that? Is he as ruthless as they say?"

Randy was getting tired of all the questions. She just smiled and shook her head. "Only when he is protecting his own or if..." She sighed. "Down inside he's just another man who wants to be loved and who is good to his family." She decided to give them what they were after. "And he *adores* women. He can be quite the gentleman, and he's *very* good at... Well, let's just say he's good at making a woman feel beautiful."

They all giggled and some blushed. Jake walked over to rejoin Randy then, and the women all gawked at him, some blushing harder. Jake smiled and nodded to them. "Ladies, I would like to dance with my wife again."

Obviously flustered, they backed away as Jake pulled Randy out onto the dance floor. "The tension was a bit thick over there," he told her. "You okay?"

"I am wonderful," Randy answered with a smile. "They are all properly curious and imagining all kinds of things about you and me. I gave them an earful."

He pulled her close again. "Well then, let's add to their curiosity by dancing too close." He whirled her around the floor again as Brian walked Evie over to the table where punch and champagne and cookies were being served.

"You sure you want to do this?" Brian asked Evie.

"All us women need to take a turn serving. I'll be fine."

He kept an arm around her and kissed her cheek. "I'd like to talk to Dr. Cook over there about some new findings on pain drugs. I'm getting rusty."

"Brian, if you want to move closer to town and restart a practice, I'll make do. I'm taking you away from what you really want to do."

He kissed her lightly. "I want you to be where you feel happiest, Evie, and that's with your family. I'll manage just fine. I just want to find out what books and articles I might be able to take back with me to study." He squeezed her hand. "Don't be concerned about my practice. I certainly get plenty of chances for doctoring on the ranch." He looked around as if to check to see if anything was out of the ordinary. "I won't be long."

He left, and Evie turned to another woman at the table. "You can go join your husband for a dance, if you would like," she told her. "I'm Evie Stewart. I thought I would take my turn serving punch."

"Oh, thank you! You're Jake Harkner's daughter, aren't you?"

"Yes."

"I've heard what a kind woman of faith you are. My husband is a preacher here in Denver. Daryl French. I'm Linda French. Whenever you come here and want to go to church, you come and visit us, Mrs. Stewart. It's the Methodist Church on the east side of town."

"Thank you! I would like that."

"Well, from all I've heard, you are a great testament to faith and forgiveness. Please don't take offense, but many of us, especially the women, respect you for how you've risen above...what happened to you."

"I don't take offense at all. Thank you for the invitation."

Linda French left, and Evie began pouring punch into glasses with a large dipper. Several people came and went, all kind and smiling, some asking what it was like to be the daughter of a rather infamous man.

"My father is wonderful," she would always answer.

"Well, he has a very beautiful daughter," one man told her. "You're even prettier when a man can see those big, dark eyes."

Evie frowned at the neatly dressed and decent-looking man. His teeth were a bit yellow, and one eye tooth was missing, but he seemed clean and gentlemanly. "Excuse me?" she asked. "I'm not sure what you mean."

He moved around the table, standing closer. "You have beautiful eyes. I couldn't see them that day back at Dune Hollow, when you were blindfolded."

Evie felt as though all the blood was running out of her through her feet.

"Something wrong?" he asked. "You look pale in

spite of that lovely dark skin," he told her. "I've always thought women with Mexican blood were more beautiful than most."

Evie stumbled backward, reaching for something for support but grabbing the punch bowl instead. It tipped over and went crashing to the floor, drawing everyone's attention.

After that, her whole world changed—as did that of her whole family.

Nineteen

SECONDS.

Everyone turned at the sound of the crashing punch bowl.

Brian saw Evie standing speechless, gaping at a man near her. He knew instantly who it was. "My God!" He charged toward her, unaware the music had stopped, or that people gasped and backed away, or that he shoved some of them out of the way as he ran to Evie.

Seconds.

Lloyd was faster. As soon as the punch bowl crashed and he turned to see why, he, too, headed for Evie. Somewhere in the unreal events unfolding, Brian heard Lloyd roar, "Get away from my sister, you sonofabitch!"

Someone else shouted, "Everybody down!" Was that Jake?

Lloyd reached Mike Holt, bolting right over the food table and sending food and punch cups flying.

More crashing sounds.

Brian and Lloyd reached Evie at nearly the same time.

Holt had already drawn a gun that just one second earlier no one knew he even had.

Seconds.

Brian grabbed Evie and literally tackled her to the floor, staying on top of her to shield her. Even as they went down, he heard the loud boom of Holt's gun... heard people scream.

"Oh my God! Lloyd! Lloyd!" Was that Katie screaming? More people screamed. People were running out of the room. Brian saw someone duck behind chairs in one corner of the room, and at the same time Lloyd's body came crashing down close to where Brian held Evie on the floor.

Seconds. How many had passed? Two? Three?

"Lloyd!" This time it was Evie, screaming at the sight of Lloyd lying there with a bloody hole in his chest. He didn't move. In wide-eyed terror, Brian saw Mike Holt move to stand over Lloyd, preparing to shoot again. "How does it feel to be shot down when you're unarmed?" he screamed.

A dark figure loomed close then.

"How does it feel to have your head blown off when you *are* armed?" a voice growled.

Jake.

The room became dead silent.

Holt froze. "I was told no one could bring guns to this dance," he told Jake.

"I'm never *without* a gun, and you are fucking *dead!*"

"My gun is cocked!" Holt told Jake, panic in his voice. "You shoot me, and it will go off—another bullet into your son or maybe your daughter or some innocent—"

He didn't get a chance to finish. In an instant, Jake grabbed the man's wrist and shoved his gun hand upward. Holt's gun went off, skimming across Jake's shoulder.

More screams.

"Jake, no!" Randy screamed from somewhere.

Seconds. Jake didn't even flinch when Holt's bullet ripped through his upper shoulder. In a black rage he shoved Holt to the floor, his knee in the man's chest and his .44 pressed against his forehead. "I wouldn't want my bullet to go through your skull and into someone else," Jake growled, "so it's best you're against the floor when I pull this trigger!"

Holt stared at him in wide-eyed terror.

"Daddy, don't!" Evie screamed. Too late...and

fruitless. She watched in horror as Jake fired the gun. The boom of the famous .44 made people jump and scream.

Evie broke into terrified sobs as she buried her face into Brian's shoulder. "Daddy! My God, Daddy!"

Mike Holt lay there with a huge, gaping hole in his forehead while blood streamed from under his head.

Jake rose, his shoulder bleeding, smoke coming from the barrel of his gun.

"Lloyd!" Katie screamed again, running across the room to kneel beside her husband. "Oh my God! Oh my God! Lloyd! He's dead! He's dead!"

In a moment, Randy was beside her. Jake looked around at those remaining in the room, all staring as they stood frozen in place, women whimpering.

"Some of you want to know what Jake Harkner the *outlaw* was like!" Jake roared.

Evie clung to Brian. "Daddy, stop!"

"You've just *met* him!" Jake finished. "Anyone comes against me right now, and this gun goes off again!" He slowly moved the gun around the room.

No one moved.

"Brian, see if my son is"—Jake's voice wavered—"dead or alive."

Brian moved off Evie and scuttled over to kneel beside Lloyd. Evie curled up and wept. Jake pointed his gun at a group of cattlemen. "You! If Lloyd is still alive, I'm asking some of you to please help get him"—his voice wavered again—"to his room."

Jake watched everyone carefully as Brian ripped open Lloyd's white ruffled shirt, now stained with blood. He checked for a pulse.

"Lloyd. Oh God, Lloyd," Evie continued sobbing, her words and tears mixed with Katie's.

"Tell me he's still alive," Jake asked Brian, his voice gruff with rage and sorrow.

"He is," Brian answered.

"Some of you men get over here and help carry Lloyd up to his room!" Jake roared. "Brian, you go with them. Evie, Katie..." Jake took a moment to glance at Randy. The devastation they both felt hung thick between them. "Randy...all of you go with them!"

"Jake, this isn't something I can handle alone," Brian told him. "There is a doctor here I was just talking to. He's one of the best. I'd like him to go with me."

"Which one of you is he talking about?" Jake demanded, again keeping his .44 pointed at the crowd.

Dr. Graham Cook stepped forward, swallowing nervously. "Me."

"Are you any good with bullet wounds?"

"Yes, sir. It's my specialty."

"Then go with my son-in-law!" Jake ordered.

"Mr. Harkner, I'll have to run over to the hospital first and get instruments and supplies, and something for pain."

"Then *do* it! And you'd better by God get back here *alone*! And *fast*! My son is likely"—the word caught in Jake's throat, and he struggled not to break down—"*dying*!"

"I'll be back fast as I can," the doctor told him, hurrying out.

Jake looked at the cattlemen he'd asked to help carry Lloyd to his room. "Move!" he roared. "Time is important! Get Lloyd up to his room so my son-in-law can do something for him!"

They quickly obeyed.

"Jake," Randy said softly, moving beside him. She dared to touch his arm. When he was like this, even she feared setting him off so he'd do something worse—not to her...never to her—but this was the ruthless Jake she'd first met, and when he was in that dark place, he was unpredictable. "He's still alive," she said in a shaking voice, wanting to scream Lloyd's name in anguish. She had to stay calm… "Please put your gun away before someone innocent gets hurt."

Jake looked at her, and again Randy nearly gasped at the rage she saw there. He was the Jake she'd shot thirty years ago because she was so afraid of him—the Jake who'd blown a man away in the supply store where he first set eyes on Miranda Hayes. "You and Katie go on up to the room with Brian and Evie like I told you," he told her firmly. "And I'm damn well not putting this gun down! Not yet!"

"Jake." She nearly groaned the word.

"Go!" It was a quiet command. Randy knew there was no arguing with him—not when he was like this. She wanted to scream and weep and collapse to the floor, but she told herself to stay strong for Katie and Evie… and for Jake.

"I'll be along," Jake told her, his eyes gleaming with the look of an outlaw, his voice cold.

There was nothing she could say. Evie and Katie were beside themselves, weeping over Lloyd, who truly looked more dead than alive. Randy felt stunned and helpless. With an aching heart she turned to help Evie and Katie up as the cattlemen came over to pick up an unconscious Lloyd. It took six men to lift him, and the women followed as they carried Lloyd out of the room amid whispers and gasps and weeping. Brian hung on to Evie, who was so devastated that she couldn't walk on her own.

Randy kept an arm around Katie. She glanced at Gretta as they walked past her. Gretta was crying. "I'm so sorry," she told Randy.

"Murderer!" Harley Wicks's sister Arlis screamed at Jake. "You didn't need to blow that man's brains out! He could have been arrested!"

Randy's heart pounded. She didn't like leaving Jake behind when he was in the mental condition he was in right now, but she had no choice. Katie needed her. Evie needed her. Either of them could lose a baby over this.

"Who let that man in?" Jake roared, walking closer to Arlis. "*You?*" He pointed his gun at her. "You *bitch!*"

"Jake—" Randy whispered. She glanced at him, but right now he wasn't seeing or hearing her. She hurried Katie out of the room, wanting to scream in fear for what might happen to her husband.

"You let him in here, didn't you?" Jake seethed at Arlis. "Let me hear you *deny* it!"

God, keep him safe! Randy prayed as she left the room.

Those left behind saw a darkness about Jake Harkner that no one dared to challenge, not even Harley Wicks. Arlis gasped, putting a hand to her chest and stepping back from Jake.

"You're goddamn lucky you're a *woman!*" Jake roared at her. "Otherwise, you'd already be *dead!* In all my years and all my crimes, I never *once* hurt a woman, but by God, I want to hurt one now! I'll see you go to *prison* for this! It's aiding and abetting! If my son dies, you're no better than a murderer yourself!"

"*You* will go to prison for taking the law into your own hands again!" Arlis screamed back daringly.

Jake turned his gun on Harley Wicks. "Try arresting me, and you'll regret it!"

There came a loud *poof!* and a flash as the reporter attending the event took a picture of Jake holding his gun on Wicks. Jake whirled, aiming at the reporter, who quickly turned and ran out. Jake kicked over the tripod that held the camera, then kicked the camera across the dance floor. He turned back to Wicks. "I am going upstairs to my son's room," he told him, "and I'm *staying* there! If you send anyone to arrest me, I'll *shoot* them, understand?"

Wicks nodded.

"I'm not leaving my son's side until I know he'll be all right," Jake added. "I'll kill anybody who tries to take me out of there!" He looked over at Sam and Gretta. "Do me a favor and stay close," he told Gretta. "It's room eighteen on the second floor. I might need you to help my family in some way."

"Sure, Jake." Gretta hurried out after the others.

"Mr. Harkner, let us help, too."

The words came from the preacher's wife Evie had relieved at the punch table.

"I'm Linda French, and my husband is a Methodist minister. I met your daughter just before all this happened. I'd like to go and be with her, and my husband might...he might be able to help in some way, even if it's just prayer."

Jake looked her way. "I appreciate the offer," he told her gruffly. "It's not likely that God of yours will listen to any of *my* prayers now, but maybe He'll listen to *yours.* And my beautiful daughter has a real deep faith, but right now she's suffering after having to face one of the men who..." His voice wavered again. *My God, Evie...my beautiful Evie! I'm so sorry! And Lloyd! My son! My son!* "Where is your husband?" he asked Linda.

"I'm Reverend Daryl French." A young man with blond hair and blue eyes stepped forward.

"Take your wife and go see what you can do," Jake ordered him.

The reverend hurried over to Linda and took her arm, leading her out of the room.

Jake continued to hold the gun steady, studying the crowd closely as though looking for someone. "Has anybody here ever heard of a Brad Buckley?" he asked. "Ever seen him around?"

Most shook their heads, a few mumbled the word no.

"If you do, you tell me, understand? Buckley and that dead man over there were both plotting to come after me and my son, so if anybody runs into him, you tell the sheriff and have him arrested! I guarantee he had something to do with this!" He waved his gun at Arlis again. "Have *you* seen him?"

"No!" she answered quickly. "I swear! I've never even heard of him."

"You belong in jail for what you've done!"

"I just... That man over there...that dead man...I did let him in, but he only said he had a score to settle with...with you and your son. I thought he'd make trouble, but I didn't want...I didn't want your son to get shot! It...it should have been *you*!"

Jake struggled against an urge to pull the trigger of his .44. For the first time in his life, even when he was at his worst in his younger years, he wanted to shoot a woman. "It *should* have been me, lady! It should have been me clear back in that shoot-out in California. It should have been me shot on the Outlaw Trail! I should have died in *prison*! It should have been me in the shoot-out in Guthrie, or when I rescued my daughter! It should have been me a hundred times over! And if my son dies, it *will* be me! You'll get your wish, because I'll put this gun to my *own* head!" He stepped closer. "And may you rot in *hell*!" he told her.

The look in Jake's eyes terrified Arlis so badly that she suddenly fainted. Harley caught her as she went down amid more gasps.

"You'll pay for this, Harkner!" Harley told him as he laid his sister out on the floor. "What you did to that man over there was nothing short of an execution!" He rose, facing Jake with a cocky look on his face.

Jake walked closer, pressing the gun against Harley's cheek as more people gasped and a couple of women screamed. "He shot my *son*! Lloyd wasn't wearing a gun. And Holt was prepared to fire again! Was I supposed to stand and watch him murder my son?"

"You illegally carried a gun to this event, and you used it to deliberately blow a man's brains out when you already had him down!" Harley answered weakly, sweat breaking out on his forehead.

"Get one thing straight, Wicks," Jake sneered. "I am never *without* a gun! And when I think it's right to use it, I'll *use* it!" He shoved the man backward, using the barrel of his gun still pressed to Harley's cheek. Wicks stumbled and fell on his rump. "Now," Jake told him, "I'm going up to Lloyd, and you'd better pray he doesn't die, because if he does, you'll see a side of me that hasn't shown itself in thirty years, except when Mike Holt and about eighteen other men kidnapped my daughter back in Oklahoma! A lot of men died the day I found her, and I'll kill again if anyone comes to that room to try to take me out of there! Got that?"

Wicks nervously rubbed at a sore cheek. "I'll leave you alone...for now. But I may well arrest you for taking the law into your own hands...again."

Jake coldly stared him down, then turned and walked out of the room to find his son.

Randy stood at the balcony outside Lloyd's room. The doors to the ballroom below were open, and she'd heard every word Jake had said. She knew he meant them. She watched him storm across the lobby and head up the stairs, his .44 still in his hand. When he reached Lloyd's room, he looked at Randy, and at that moment, she didn't know him. He stood there with blood staining the front of his shirt as it flowed down his chest from the shoulder wound, but he didn't seem to care. Randy realized he was too angry and devastated to even notice the pain.

"Come into the room with me," he said gruffly, "and lock the door behind you." He turned away and went into Lloyd's room. Randy followed, not sure whom to mourn the most: her son...or her husband.

Jeff Trubridge looked over the top of his spectacles to see his secretary standing in front of him, holding a piece of paper. Jeff recognized the yellow note as a wire.

"I think you need to see this," the young man told him.

Frowning, Jeff took the wire and read it.

> *Lloyd Harkner shot in cold blood at a cattlemen's ball in Denver. Might not live. Jake Harkner took down the shooter, Mike Holt, with a shot point blank to the forehead. In spite of warrants for his arrest, Harkner is holed up in a hotel room with his son and doctors.*

It was signed by Liam Davis, a fellow reporter for a Denver newspaper called *The Evening Post*.

"Oh my God," Jeff exclaimed softly. "Not Lloyd! Not Lloyd!" A lump rose in his throat, and he fought tears.

"A picture came through also," his secretary told him. He handed Jeff a picture of Jake holding a gun on someone. "That's a Denver prosecutor," the man explained. "They say Jake is holed up in Lloyd's room at the Brown Palace and is threatening to shoot anyone who tries to come and arrest him."

Jeff closed his eyes and leaned back in his chair. It took him a moment to find his voice. "Get me Attorney Peter Brown on the phone, will you?" he finally asked. "I think we need to go to Denver." He paused, his shoulders jerking in a sob. "Jake is going to need some legal help, and I want to be there if"—his voice caught in his throat—"if his son dies."

"Yes, sir," the young man answered.

This is going to kill Jake, Jeff thought. *He'll never survive if Lloyd dies.* He couldn't help the sudden tears.

He'd never admired a man more than he admired Jake Harkner. Lloyd, too. And Randy. Poor Randy!

Memories flooded over him like a waterfall. He'd never seen a father and son who were closer than Jake and Lloyd Harkner. He didn't need to wonder what this was doing to Jake…to the whole family.

"Attorney Brown is on the phone, sir," his secretary told him. "Over at my desk."

Jeff was surprised at how weak his legs suddenly felt when he stood up. He had to hold on to the desk for a moment before walking over to the phone. He picked up the base in his left hand and put the horn of the phone to his ear. "Peter?"

"Yes. What is it, Jeff?"

"It's…Jake."

"Jesus, what's happened?"

"Lloyd's been shot…and Jake killed the shooter. I have a feeling he could be in a lot of trouble. I think we should go to Denver."

"For God's sake, yes! Is Randy all right?"

Jeff grinned through tears. He'd expected the question, coming from Peter. "I have no idea. I'm sure she's a mess. A person can only take so much. Same for Jake."

"Make the arrangements. I'll meet you at the train station tomorrow morning."

Jeff hung up the phone. As far as he was concerned, he couldn't get to Denver fast enough.

Twenty

"THE MAN WON'T LEAVE THE ROOM." DR. COOK HAD
agreed to speak with reporters outside Lloyd's room at
the Brown Palace. "He isn't talking, and he rarely lets go
of Lloyd's hand."

"Is he still carrying that gun?" one of the reporters
asked.

"He most certainly is, and I believe him when he says
he'll use it on anyone who tries to come in there after
him. The man is devastated. His mental state isn't good."

Amid gasps and shaking heads, reporters rapidly
scribbled on pads of paper.

"Wasn't Jake wounded, too?" someone asked.

"Yes, but it's just a flesh wound at the top of his left
shoulder. I stitched it up. He refused pain medication
when I stitched his wound because he was afraid the law
would come in and take advantage if I put him to sleep.
He just gritted his teeth and let me stitch him up. He's
one tough man."

"How is Lloyd?" another asked. "Will he live?"

A very tired Dr. Cook rubbed at the back of his neck.
"I honestly don't know. I did the best I could—went in
through his side and removed a bullet lodged near his
spine. It missed vital pulmonary veins, and luckily, his
heart, but that area of the spine controls a lot of body
movement. It could affect his ability to walk or to use his
arms or maybe even his ability to speak. He's breathing
on his own, so that's a good sign. He had a collapsed
lung, and it's been extremely painful for him to bring it

back up. He seems to still be in a lot of pain, but he hasn't truly regained full consciousness yet, so it's difficult to tell just how much damage has been done. Jake has had to hold him down a few times to keep him from thrashing around from the pain. Too much movement could make the injury worse."

"Do you think Harkner would shoot one of us if we tried to go in there?"

Dr. Cook glanced at the young reporter who'd asked the foolish question. "You willing to try finding out?"

The reporter swallowed. "I guess not."

"Smart decision." Cook rubbed at his eyes. "I have to say that Jake Harkner practically worships that son of his. For all his ruthlessness, I can already see the kind of family man he is. The agony in his eyes is heartbreaking. Mrs. Harkner isn't in any better shape. For the last two nights they have both just stayed right by their son's bedside, along with Lloyd's wife and his sister. All of you should leave or at least get away from this door, so the women can come and go without you harassing them with questions. Both Lloyd's wife and his sister are carrying, and this has been dangerously traumatic for them. I finally convinced them to go lie down in another room, so that's where they are now, but they will want to come back here at times to check on Lloyd, so all of you stay out of their way. Jake's son-in-law is a doctor, and he's in his own room now tending to the two women. I'm leaving for a while to go home and clean up and change, but I'll be back. I'd suggest for your own health that all of you clear out of here. Jake Harkner is still in a dangerous mood, and he's getting tired of all of you milling around out here. He could start shooting through that door at any time, believe me, so leave. If you don't, I'll get the police to *make* you leave."

"Are they going to arrest Jake?" another asked.

"How would I know that? I haven't been out there

in the streets to find out. You're the ones who would know something like that. Why don't you go talk to the prosecutor and police chief?"

Brian came out of his and Evie's room, where Katie was sleeping in an extra bed brought in for her so Brian could tend to her and Evie both. He shoved one of the reporters aside. "Get out of here! Go on! All of you get out of here! Nothing is going to happen any time soon, so if you don't want to get shot, get the hell out of here!"

The reporters finally began to disperse, and Cook told Brian he was leaving for a while but would be back. "You need some rest, too," he said.

"I'm more concerned about my in-laws and my wife," Brian answered wearily. He knocked on the door. "Jake, it's Brian. I'm coming in."

A couple of remaining reporters tried to peek inside as Brian slipped through the door, but he quickly closed it before they could see anything. Brian walked up to Randy, who sat in her usual spot—a chair beside the bed. Her head and shoulders were reclined on the side of the bed, and she had hold of Lloyd's hand, while Jake sat on the opposite side, holding Lloyd's other hand. He glanced at Brian with dark, bloodshot eyes. "Did you get rid of those sonsofbitches outside the door?"

"Most of them."

"When you go back out, you tell them that I'm going to take a look myself soon, and if there is one stranger standing out there, he'll be shot."

Brian sighed, touching Randy's shoulder. "I'll tell them."

Randy looked up at Brian with eyes puffy from crying. "Brian! How is Evie?" She got to her feet and embraced him.

"She's better. I held her as she slept for a while. That helped."

"At least she has you," Randy told him as he let go of her.

"I'm worried about you and Jake. You both need to get out of here and get some *real* rest and get some food in your stomachs."

"I'm not going anywhere!" Jake spoke up.

Brian sighed, keeping hold of Randy's arm. "Jake, you have to believe Lloyd will get through this, and if he does, he's going to need his father for a lot of things. You won't be any good to him if you continue not to eat or sleep. You're killing yourself."

"That obviously doesn't matter."

"Doesn't it? Don't forget you have a beautiful daughter who needs and loves you. You're breaking her heart behaving this way, let alone her watching you blow a man's brains out. And you have grandchildren who will need their grandfather, especially if Lloyd doesn't make it. And you have a *wife* who needs you. You aren't the only one suffering, Jake."

Jake let go of Lloyd's hand and rubbed at the back of his neck. "I should have seen it coming. I should have spotted that sonofabitch sneaking in! This all comes back to the same thing...*me*! Jake Harkner—the man who brings trouble and heartache every place he goes!"

"It only goes as far as that bastard Mike Holt."

"Who hated me and Lloyd. We *knew* he could be around. I never should have taken it for granted that just because it was a closed-invitation event that Holt couldn't have found a way in." He rose, picking up his gun and walking to a window. "All the things I've been through in this life, I should have died a hundred times over, yet here I stand while it's my *son* who's dying, and my daughter lies in the next room, suffering ungodly memories after seeing one of those bastards who raped her. And all...because of who her *father* is!" He turned and glared at Brian. The Jake he'd become gave Brian chills. "You should have let me die of pneumonia back at that prison all those years ago."

"I saved you for *Evie!*" Brian barked. "My wife loves and needs her father. She thinks the world of you, Jake. Lloyd isn't your only child, and you know what a soft-hearted angel she is. It's killing her, the way you're behaving. She's been in here with her brother, constantly praying, not just for him, but for *you*. She hasn't said much, because you're like a stick of old, damp dynamite right now, the kind that explodes way too easily. I don't like what this is doing to my wife after what she and I have already been through, especially in her condition. I don't often speak up to you, but I feel I *have* to now, because Evie wants to come in here and talk to you, Jake. She won't sleep well until she does, so you're going to *let* her talk to you, and you are *not* going to behave like the bastard outlaw you used to be! You're going to behave like the father you are *now*—the good man she still calls Daddy."

Their gazes held, and for a moment, Brian thought he'd gone too far. This was not the Jake Harkner he knew or had ever known. He'd never been around Jake when he was a man wanted for bank robbery and gun running and God knew what else. At the moment, he couldn't imagine that his mother-in-law had seen through the man he was looking at now. He'd only known the Jake that Evie worshipped as her father, the Jake who loved with great passion—almost too much passion. That's what had brought him to where he was now, a man devastated by the possibility of losing the son who was his life's blood.

Jake sank back into the chair beside Lloyd's bed. "Go ahead and send her in."

"I don't want her to see Jake the outlaw when she comes in here, Jake."

Jake reached for a cigarette on a table beside him. "I'll do my best," he told Brian with obvious sarcasm in his voice. He lit a cigarette, and Brian moved an arm around

Randy. "Come on, Mom. Get out of here for a little while. Get cleaned up and change. Pepper is out in the hallway. He wants to talk to you." He looked at Jake. "In case you hadn't noticed, your wife also needs you. Lloyd is *her* son, too."

"Brian, don't," Randy protested. "I'll be all right."

"No, you *won't*—not without Jake's support. You're suffering, too. You need each other."

"We're *all* suffering," Randy told him wearily. "Let it go for now. I'll go talk to Pepper."

Brain cast Jake a warning look and started to leave.

"Randy." Jake spoke her name with a tone of agony. "I'm...sorry." He didn't look at her. He just sat there staring at his .44. "I know..." He didn't finish. "I just... can't right now. *Lo siento. Favor perdóname.*"

"I know, Jake. I'm here. You come for me...or you send for me. I'm here." Her voice choked, and she hurried out.

Brian glanced at Jake once more. "You be careful how you talk to Evie," he warned again. He left to get Evie.

Out in the hallway, Randy found Pepper and Cole waiting for her, both with obvious sincere concern in their eyes.

"I'm going to get Evie," Brian told Randy. "Will you be all right?"

"Yes."

"Promise me you will go into your own room and clean up and change. I'll bring you something to help you sleep."

"I shouldn't leave Lloyd—or Jake, for that matter."

"Your son needs you healthy and rested, and Jake can make his own decisions. Lloyd needs *him* healthy and rested, too. I'm hoping Evie can make him see that. He usually listens to her."

"I hope so, Brian. I want him to get out of there for a while."

Brian left her with Pepper and Cole, both of whom stood there in the hallway, looking a bit lost. Pepper nodded to Randy. "Ma'am? We, uh, we got rid of a couple of reporters who were still hanging around."

"We came by to see what you want us to do, Mrs. Harkner," Cole added.

Randy walked up and hugged them. "Thank you for coming," she told Pepper with the embrace. "Right now it makes me feel better to see someone from the J&L." She spoke the words brokenly. "I wish we could just go home and have all of this behind us."

When she embraced Cole, he gingerly hugged her, as if not quite sure if he should, considering the mood Jake Harkner was in. He looked at Pepper with wide eyes. Both men looked at her a bit sheepishly when she pulled away.

"Ma'am, I just... I mean, me and Cole was wonderin' if you want us to go back to the ranch and tell everybody there what's happened," Pepper told her. "Them kids back there will be awful upset, especially the oldest ones. They might have already got the news."

Randy glanced at the door to Lloyd's room, then pulled Pepper farther away, motioning for Cole to follow. She thought how strange it was to be relieved to see men who were likely from the outlaw world, just like Jake was. It was even stranger that she felt she could trust them implicitly. "Just the thought of the grandchildren helps my heart." She wiped at tears with a shaking hand.

"Ma'am, you look so tired," Cole told her. "We heard what happened and what Jake did and... God, we're awful sorry, Mrs. Harkner, for what you're goin' through. We waited a couple of days to let things calm down, but the gossip outside this hotel is pretty wild. A lot of people keep millin' around to find out what's going to happen next, and if Jake is gonna go on some kind of shootin' rampage or somethin'. Is it true, how bad Lloyd is?"

Randy broke down, and Cole and Pepper looked at each other. Pepper took her arm. "Come over and sit down on this bench here," he told Randy, indicating a bench in the hallway. He sat down next to her. "Ma'am, Lloyd is a big, strong kid with a lot to live for. Just think of all the things Jake has been through. Lloyd just like him, maybe even stronger, because he's got a wife and kids and a big ranch to run. Jake didn't even have them things when he was Lloyd's age."

Randy nodded, blowing her nose into a handkerchief that was already overused. "I have to hope you're right."

Cole folded his arms, leaning against the banister. "Mrs. Harkner, your family is one of the tightest and strongest I've ever seen. That boy will be fine. We just wanted to tell you we think we should go back to the ranch and make sure things are okay there—tell them there what's happened, and keep things goin' while Jake and Lloyd can't."

"Yes. You should go and take care of things. You know what to do." Randy glanced up at Cole, thinking what a good-looking man he would still be if not for his hard life and his drinking. "Cole, Jake is in a bad way. I hope Evie can get through to him." She wiped at her eyes. "He's in such a dark place right now." She struggled against more tears. "I think it would be good for him to see the grandchildren. It will help him remember what he has to live for even if…the worst happens." She grasped Pepper's gnarled hand. "I want you two to go home and bring the grandchildren back here. Stephen has a right to be with his father, and it might be good for Jake to see Ben…and especially good for him to see Little Jake. I suppose the little girls should stay at the ranch. They won't understand what's happening. Teresa and Rodriguez can stay there with them.

Explain everything to the other men and give them orders on what to do while we're gone. And...I can give you a note to take to the bank where Lloyd put the money from the cattle sale. He paid you and the other men, but the men at the ranch should get paid, too, and Teresa and Rodriguez. I want you to take enough to pay all of them when you get there, and leave some money for supplies. In fact, get some supplies to take back with you. I'll give you a list."

Pepper frowned. "You're trustin' us with that much money?"

"Of course I am. Besides—" She glanced at Cole. "Do either of you really want to test Jake's wrath if you run off with his and Lloyd's money?"

Cole grinned, and Pepper chuckled. "You've got a point there, especially considerin' the mood Jake's in now."

"I am going to clean up and change, and I'm sure Brian is bringing me something to help me sleep. Come back in the morning, and I'll give you the list and a note for the bank so you can get started. The sooner you get back here with the grandsons, the better for Jake...and for Lloyd. I'm praying that by then, Lloyd will be awake and able to talk to them. And we all have to pray he'll be able to move his legs. Right now he's still unconscious, but you can tell he's in a lot of pain. It's so hard to watch. He groans almost constantly. We're trying to keep Katie in bed for fear she'll lose the baby, and we're so afraid Lloyd might be paralyzed." She rose again. "Do the two of you have a place to stay?"

The men glanced at each other, looking uncomfortable. "Yes, ma'am."

"Are you at Gretta's place?"

Pepper visibly reddened. "Yes, ma'am."

"You tell Gretta I'm grateful for her offers of help."

"I...ma'am... You know Gretta?" Cole asked.

Randy managed to smile a little through her tears. "Cole, who am I married to?"

"Jake Harkner."

"And Jake generally knows every prostitute in every town he's ever been to. Yes, I know Gretta. Back in Guthrie it was Dixie James. It's too long a story to explain, but it's all right to talk in front of me about Gretta." She wiped at more tears. "At any rate, yes, bring the grandsons here. Little Jake will be a bit difficult, but he'll mind us if we tell him it's what Grandpa wants. I am thinking that wild little boy would be good for Jake. Maybe seeing him and Stephen and seeing his own son, Ben, will bring Jake out of this darkness and remind him how much he has to live for."

Cole tipped his hat. "We'll head on out then and come back in the mornin' for your list and that bank note," he told Randy. "You and the women take care of yourselves. And if anybody can bring Jake back to the here and now and pray Lloyd back to health, it's that daughter of yours. I swear she's right up there with the angels."

"Thank you. I hope you're right."

Both men left just as Evie came out of her room, Brian holding her arm. Evie flew into her mother's arms, and both women wept.

"Evie, you be careful how you approach Jake," Randy warned. "Are you sure you're up to this?"

"I just want Daddy to come back from that awful place he's in," Evie sniffed. "I just have to get through to him. He can't give up, and he has to be strong for Lloyd and for… Oh, Mother, I heard they want to arrest him! They want to take Daddy away like they did all those years ago!"

Randy hugged her close. "People will see that he had reason for what he did. We have to pray for that, Evie, but it won't help Jake's cause for him to stay in this mood, especially if there is a trial. He has to show people the wonderful man he really is. You can bring that out in him."

"I'm going in there with her," Brian told Randy. "I need to check on Lloyd, and I'll otherwise stay out of the way, but I'm not sending Evie in there alone—not in her condition. She's still shaken from seeing Holt in the first place."

"I understand how you feel," Randy told him, "but when it comes to Evie, Jake is a pushover, even when he's like this. She'll be fine." She looked at Evie. "Try to get him out of there for a while, Evie. Send him to our room. I need my husband back. He has to understand we are in this *together*. He's got to share this with me and not keep it all to himself."

Evie nodded. "I know." She wiped at her eyes and took Brian's hand. Randy watched as they walked to the door to Lloyd's room. Brian knocked.

"Jake, its Brian. I have Evie with me."

When there came no reply, Evie opened the door and marched inside.

Twenty-one

JAKE TURNED FROM THE WINDOW AS EVIE RUSHED OVER to kneel beside her brother's bed. She took his hand and bowed her head and began praying, while Brian moved to the other side of the bed to get out his stethoscope and listen to Lloyd's heart. He checked the bandages for bleeding and felt Lloyd's forehead for fever.

"I changed the towels," Jake told him, "and that pad underneath him. His bladder is still working okay. That's good, right?"

Brian checked under Lloyd's closed eyelids. "*Anything* that appears to be working right is a good sign."

"You tell Katie that," Jake told him, more in the tone of an order rather than a request. "For a while, taking care of him is going to be a lot of work, some of it backbreaking because of his size. The best thing she can do is stay in bed and hang on to that baby. I know she feels like she should be in here doing some of these things, but if he comes around and finds out she lost that baby, it's going to take him twice as long to recover... *if* he recovers."

"I think she understands that, Jake." Brian faced him. "But Dr. Cook and I will continue to help, and Gretta said her Sam can help, too. You can't keep doing this around the clock. It's going to catch up with you, and you're going to go right to the floor and be no help at all. You're killing yourself, just like you almost did when you rode like a maniac going after Evie, and you were nearly four years younger then."

Jake looked at his daughter...his beautiful, precious daughter. "I couldn't save my mother, and I almost didn't save Evie. In fact, I *didn't* save her from those bastards before they—" He turned back to the window. "At least she lived. Lloyd might not. Either way, I can at least be here for him."

Brian sighed. "How's that shoulder?"

"I'll live."

"Well, whether you like it or not, I'm changing that bandage tomorrow. For now, I'm going to leave Evie alone with you for a while, because that's what she wants, but at the moment, being around you is like being around the loveless, hardened, wanted man you used to be, and she's not designed for that. She only knows the Jake who raised her, the Jake who loves almost *too* much." He glanced at Evie as she rose from the other side of the bed and came around to sit on the edge of the bed closest to where Jake's chair was.

"You sure you want to stay here?" Brian asked her.

Evie watched her father, who stood with his back to her. "I'm sure." Jake was wearing a pair of Lloyd's denim pants and Lloyd's favorite blue-paisley shirt. He'd refused to go back to his room to change into his own clothes. "I'm fine." She turned to look at her husband. "It's okay. You can go."

Scowling, Brian walked to the door. "I'll be in the next room, Jake. I'm going to give Randy something to help her sleep, but her best medicine would be getting her *husband* back. She needs holding, and not by any of the rest of us." He spoke the words with the hint of an order, then started out.

"Brian," Jake called.

Brian hesitated.

"Thank you." Jake faced him. "I can't recall seeing you truly angry before, and I don't blame you. There were times when you were the one who held this family together, and right now you're doing it again. You're a hell of a doctor and a hell of a son-in-law...and a hell of a husband."

Brian managed a hint of a smile. "I have a hell of a wife. She's behind pretty much everything I do."

Brian left, and Evie covered her face with her hands. "Daddy, he's so good to me," she said, softly crying.

Jake sighed deeply and sat down in the chair beside the bed, facing her. He set his gun on a table beside the bed. "Evie, I'm sorry for what you saw the other night."

She wiped at her eyes and studied him, his dark eyes stricken with grief and anger. "I've never seen anything like what you did to that man. I know it was awful—him coming there to kill Lloyd. But when you shot him—" She shook her head. "I've seen you angry...but I've never seen the Jake you were back when you met Mother—the man you became when you put your gun to Mike Holt's head. I'm not even sure how Mother saw through that man, but I'm glad she did. All I know right now is that I don't like that other Jake. You still have so much rage down inside, Daddy, and I wish I could help you get rid of it."

Jake rested his elbows on his knees. "Evie, sometimes that man *has* to come back in order to protect those he loves."

"But you weren't like that after...after you found me at Dune Hollow."

"Baby girl, I was *exactly* like that! You just didn't see the things I did before I got there. And after all the shooting and I grabbed you up, you were in too bad of shape to see the real Jake who'd come after you. The only thing that stopped me from killing every last one of them was you begging me not to, but I wanted to, Evie. I *wanted* to! When things like this happen, the old Jake immediately turns off all feeling. That's the only way I know how to survive the hurt."

Evie reached out to take his hands, but he pulled away. She studied him sadly. "Daddy, the only way *I* survive is to forgive. You've still never learned how to do that, even though God has forgiven you for everything you did before Mother came along."

Jake shook his head, the dark bitterness still there in his eyes. "When I was a little boy, I quickly learned that loving and forgiving didn't work if you wanted to survive, Evie. Hate and self-defense and learning not to care about anything—*that's* all that helped me." He rose and walked to the window again, lighting a cigarette. "The old Jake is still down inside, Evie. He'll never really go away." He took a deep drag on the cigarette. "You have to stop seeing me as perfect, because I am *far* from that. I can't let myself care about anything or anyone. This is what happens when I do."

"But that's the whole point. You *do* care. It's okay to care, Daddy. And sometimes love does hurt, but God can—"

"Evie, don't! I can't…allow myself to think about it."

Lloyd let out a deep groan. Jake turned and looked at him, then faced Evie. "Do you hear that? My son is in so much pain—pain he shouldn't be suffering! It rips my heart out every time I have to hold him down because of that pain. I can't stand seeing him suffer! I failed him, Evie! I failed my *son*! All those years we rode together and had each other's backs…and then we go to a simple, civilized affair, and he's gunned down right in front of me! That man took my precious son in cold blood, and I *killed* him in cold blood! The old Jake came roaring back, and he put a gun to that man's head and pulled the trigger! So now you know the man who fathered you, and you see why I can't believe something as good and beautiful as you even came from my seed. I am what I am, Evie, and everything I touch gets hurt."

He walked back to the chair and reached over to snuff

out the cigarette, then faced her again. "It should be *me* lying in that bed, Evie. *Me!* It should be…*me!* That's what my father would tell me, because I'm *worthless*. That young man lying in that bed is worth *ten* of me—a *hundred* of me!" His voice began to break, and he put his head in his hands.

Evie reached out and touched his hair, but he jerked away again. "Daddy, that man who raised you might have physically fathered you, but he's not your *real* father. Your real father loves you a hundred times more than you love me and Lloyd…a *thousand* times more! And He doesn't want you to hurt, and He knows you are worth all the gold in heaven. No human being can love as much as God Himself loves us, and He must love Jake Harkner an awful lot to have brought Mother into your life—and then Lloyd and me. *He's* your real father, and you don't need to put up all those walls around your heart, because God isn't going to take away any of the good things He's given you. Satan is trying real hard to keep you from all the love that surrounds you, by constantly bringing up the past, Daddy, but God is so much stronger than Satan…and so are you."

Jake rubbed at his eyes and met her gaze. "There is just no getting through to you what I really am down inside, is there?"

"I *do* see that man, Daddy. I saw him when you put that gun to Mike Holt's head and pulled the trigger. But I refuse to recognize that man as my loving and gentle father. He's not the man who is married to the most devoted and gracious woman I know—the man who has grandchildren who need to see their grandpa come back home to the J&L, and when he does, they need him to be the only kind of man they've ever known as their grandfather."

Jake sighed, rubbing at his eyes again. "Right now I hardly know that man."

"He's there, Daddy, down inside you, and I pray for him all the time. You keep saying you should have died many times over. You *did* die. The old Jake died when he met my mother. And right now she's feeling so alone. Go in that other room, and you be with Mother. You hold her, and you show her that this time she doesn't have to suffer alone. Brian is going to bring Katie in here to spend some time with Lloyd. When he does, you go over there and talk to Mother. *Share* this with her. God gave her to you so you *could* share the hurt. This is hard for her, too, Daddy. What you're doing now is the same as when you yelled at her—or when you ride away every time something bad happens. You can't keep doing that to her. Lloyd wouldn't *want* you to, so go see her—for *his* sake. If he was able, he'd be scolding you something awful right now."

Jake's eyes teared. "I can't—"

"Yes, you can! What you *can't* do is keep burying your feelings, because they are too strong and too deep now. *Pray* with me, Daddy. Take my hands. I'll do the praying, but you have to open your heart and believe Lloyd will live. You have such *powerful* emotions, Daddy. Put them into faith and prayer, and God will hear you. I pray for you all the time. Give me your hands and pray with me, Daddy."

Jake put his head in his hands again. "No. I'm not a praying man."

"And that's a lie! You wear your mother's crucifix all the time. Don't tell me you don't pray, Daddy. I know better! Give me your hands!" He still held his head, and Evie daringly reached out and grabbed his hands away. He jerked again, but she refused to let go. She met his eyes squarely. "Keep it up, and you'll hurt my arms!" she told him. "Is that what you want? To be that outlaw who hurts people? Or can I just hold the hands of my *father*? Which is it? I'm not afraid of either one!"

For a brief moment, Evie almost gasped at the look in his eyes—a glimpse of the man her mother met thirty years ago—the man who scared Randy so badly that she shot him. He suddenly softened then, his grip gentler. He rubbed the back of her hands with his thumbs. He leaned down then to rest his head against her hands. "I should go to her."

"Yes, you should. But first we're going to pray, Daddy. I'm praying right now. I'm asking God to please, please let Lloyd live." She squeezed her father's hands. "He's still so young, and he's such a good and loving son and brother, a good husband and father. Please, Lord, let him live. And protect my father. Bring him back from that dark place and show him the light. Help him understand You've forgiven his past and that all the good things around him now are Your blessings, and he deserves those blessings, because deep inside the man, there is that little boy who just wants to be loved, that little boy who never asked for all that horror. Help him see and accept all the love we have for him."

Jake let go of her hands and rose. "Just pray for Lloyd, baby girl. I'll manage on my own."

"God has been with you every step of the way, Daddy, and you don't even know it. Do you have any idea how hard God works to wrestle down that other man inside you? He's very difficult to deal with, but he doesn't scare God one bit, and he doesn't scare me either. I just realized Mom felt that way, too. She actually *met* that other Jake, and she stood right up to him, didn't she?"

He managed a smile. "Your mother can be quite the opponent once she decides to put up a fight. She's surprisingly brave and strong willed when she's mad, especially for someone so small."

"And big, bad Jake Harkner wouldn't harm a hair on her head. If she came at you with a frying pan, the worst you would do is cover your head with your arms."

"And I have no doubt she has fantasized about using that frying pan on me more than once."

Evie took hope in the remark—a sign of the sense of humor her father possessed when his dark side retreated. She rose and faced him. "Go see her, Daddy. She needs you… the strong and sure husband you are, not that other man."

Lloyd groaned again, but this time he called out, "Pa…" Jake hurried over to the side of the bed as Evie moved around to the other side, touching Lloyd's cheek.

"Lloyd? Hey, big brother, are you awake?" she asked softly.

Lloyd put a hand to his head and bent one knee.

"He moved his leg!" Jake exclaimed, grasping Lloyd's hand.

"Oh, Daddy, I *told* you prayer helps!"

Lloyd opened his eyes and stared blankly at both of them for a moment, then locked his gaze on Jake. "Pa?"

Jake leaned closer. "I'm here."

Lloyd moaned. "Everything…hurts bad…real bad."

"I know, Son. We can get more laudanum for you."

Lloyd kept his eyes on Jake. He frowned. "You… look terrible."

Jake grinned and pulled the blankets higher over Lloyd's shoulders. "I *should* look terrible. You've kept me awake for almost three days straight. Your mother and Evie, too. And Brian and Katie aren't in much better shape."

Lloyd looked around, bending up his other knee.

"Oh, thank you, Jesus!" Evie whispered. "Daddy, he's moving both legs!"

"What…happened?" Lloyd tried to sit up but cried out from pain.

Jake gently pressed his shoulders. "Take it easy, Lloyd. You were shot. We weren't sure you'd even live. You're still in a lot of danger, so you have to lie still. We can't be positive infection won't set in." He leaned closer, kissing his forehead.

"Jesus, Pa…what the hell…was that for?"

"Because I love you."

"Well, if somebody is going to…kiss me…I'd just as soon…it was Katie. Where is she? Where's…my Katie? Is she…okay?"

"She's fine."

Evie wiped at tears and leaned down to give her brother a kiss on the cheek.

"That's more like it." He suddenly scowled. "Wait! Evie! You…that man! I…remember now." He reached for Evie and tried to sit up again.

Jake held him down. "It's okay, Lloyd. Evie is all right."

"I'll go get Katie," Evie told him.

She started to rise, but Lloyd grasped her hand. "You really…okay?"

Evie smiled for him. "I really am. And Katie will want to know you're awake. Just lie still, big brother, and I'll go get her." Evie glanced at her father. "You stay calm, Daddy. God is with us. As soon as Katie gets in here, you go see Mother." She started to leave.

"Wait." Jake walked around the bed and pulled her into his arms, his embrace saying everything.

"It's okay, Daddy."

Jake took a deep breath, keeping her close. "You have a way of taking the gun out of my hand. I'm so sorry… for the things you've been through."

Evie felt his whole body shiver as he hugged her tighter.

"Don't you be sorry for one thing, Daddy. Not one thing. Just promise me you'll get out of here and get some rest and be with Mother. She needs you so much."

"I promise." Jake kissed her hair and let go of her, wiping at tears with his shirtsleeve. "You do the same thing. Get some rest. Your husband is already mad enough at me. I don't want him blaming me for you losing that baby."

"I'll be just fine." Evie leaned up and kissed his cheek.

"I'll go get Brian and Katie." She left, and Lloyd groaned the word "Pa" again.

"I'm right here, Lloyd." Jake hurried back over to his side.

"I remember something. Evie...looked so scared." He closed his eyes. "Jesus, now I remember. Evie! Pa, I tried to stop him..."

"It's over, Son. Mike Holt is dead."

Lloyd met his eyes. "You?"

"Me."

"You in...trouble again?"

"Probably."

Lloyd closed his eyes. "Shit." He grimaced. "Pa, I can't...keep getting you...out of trouble."

"I'll handle it. Your job is to just get better."

"Everything hurts, Pa."

Jake leaned over and fluffed his pillow as best he could. "It will get better. And I'll be here to help Katie. So will Brian. And we've had the best doctor in Denver taking care of you. He took the bullet out. You have no idea how good it is to see you moving your legs and arms. We weren't sure you'd be able to move at all. The bullet ended up pretty close to your spine."

"Katie," Lloyd whispered. "Tell me she's okay, too."

"So far."

"The baby—"

"She's hanging on to it." Jake leaned closer again, grasping the brass rail at the head of the bed with one hand and taking Lloyd's hand with the other. "I love you, Son. I'm sorry as hell that sonofabitch got to you before I did. I would have shot sooner, but Evie was in the way, and then *you* were in the way. When Holt fired that gun and I saw you go down..." His voice broke, and he took a deep breath. "I went down with you."

Lloyd grasped his wrist. "I'm sorry I...got mad at you...after that thing with Clem."

"You had every right to be mad. I am well aware that I can be a real sonofabitch sometimes. You're a hell of a man, Lloyd. You'll get through this, and someday you'll be the biggest landowner in Colorado, and you'll carry the Harkner name with a lot more respect than I ever could."

Lloyd clung to his wrist. "I'll never be...*Jake* Harkner, Pa," Lloyd answered weakly. "There's a damn lot of pride in that...too. You...remember that."

The words tore at Jake's heart. "You're as bad as Evie when it comes to making me out to be more than I am."

"No. Evie...sees you through special glasses that...filter out the bad. I...see *all* of you...but I...love you anyway."

Jake grinned through tears. "I guess that's one way to put it."

Lloyd grasped at the sleeve of Jake's shirt. "Why are you...wearing...my favorite shirt?"

"Because I haven't left this room since you were shot, and I had to change out of that fancy suit I wore to the ball." Jake straightened. "It had a little blood on it."

Lloyd looked him over. "Were you...hurt?"

"I'm all right. I had a little scuffle with Holt before I took him down, and his gun went off. The bullet skimmed across my left shoulder. Not all the blood on that good shirt I was wearing was mine, though. Things get a little messy when you shoot someone point-blank."

"Pa? Oh...God!" He grasped Jake's arm tighter. "You *are* in trouble...aren't you? I...know you. You...went crazy...didn't you?"

"A little."

"A *little*?"

"That man shot my son! My *unarmed* son!"

"You weren't...supposed to have a gun..."

"I'm Jake Harkner. I *always* have a gun."

Lloyd covered his eyes. "Jesus, Pa."

Brian came into the room then with Evie and Katie.

"Lloyd!" Katie hurried to his side and sat down on the bed to lean over and kiss his lips.

"Hey, Katie-girl. I'm in...no condition for this," he joked.

Brian turned to Jake. "I told Randy to give Katie some time with Lloyd before she comes in here," Brian told him. "Go see your wife, Jake. She's been staying with Katie and Evie, but I told her to go to your room and wait there. You've been with her in here for most of these three days, but you haven't *really* been with her."

Jake ran a hand through his hair. "Yeah." He glanced at Lloyd again. Both his sister and his wife were fussing over him.

"Too many...women," Lloyd teased.

Jake grinned. "Son, I assure you, you can never be surrounded by too many women." He walked around and touched Katie's shoulder. "Katie, don't do anything but be here for him. You let me and the doctors do the hard work, understand? And don't let him move around too much. He still has a long way to go."

Katie stroked Lloyd's hair. "He's already falling asleep again. I can stay here by him, can't I, Brian?"

"Sure you can."

"Thank God he came around," she wept. "What would I do without him?"

The words reminded Jake of things Randy had said to him too many times over the years. *Randy. My God, Randy, I've left you out again.* He picked up his six-gun and headed out, looking into the hallway first to make sure no one was out there waiting for him. He hurried into his and Randy's room to find Randy standing there in a robe and looking anxious.

"Jake, is it true?" she asked, looking ready to pass out. "He woke up? He moved his legs?"

"It's true."

She searched his eyes. "And how are you? *Who* are you? Do I have my husband back?"

He turned and locked the door. "Not completely. I'm trying, Randy."

"I've been living with an outlaw the last three days, Jake."

He looked down at the gun in his hand, then met her gaze. "Last I remember, it's the *outlaw* you fell in love with."

She shook her head. "I fell in love with the man underneath all that. And right now I need him in the worst way. Don't shut me out, Jake. I can't do this by myself, and neither can you. When Jake the outlaw rode out of my life once after we first met, I just wanted to die."

He saw the love in her eyes, thought about all she'd been through, being the wife of Jake Harkner. He set the gun aside and walked up to her, pulling her into his arms.

"Well, he's here for now."

Randy rested her head against his chest and wept. "I didn't even take the medicine Brian brought over to help me sleep. I hoped you'd come here and just hold me, and I wanted to be awake for it."

Jake kissed her hair. "I'm sorry I've left you out. I just..." He squeezed her tighter. "God, Randy, I thought I'd lost him! I feel like I failed him, Randy. All those years we rode together back in Oklahoma I never once failed him. When I saw him go down..." He began to stumble. "It should have been me! It should have been me!" He rambled between Spanish and English.

"Jake, I can't hold you up."

They literally helped each other to a bed. Jake felt himself nearly collapsing. He pulled her onto the bed and crushed her close. "I shouldn't have left you alone in this." He ran a hand into her hair and kissed the top of her head. "*Que Dios te acompane, mi amor. Yo te amo.*"

"And I love you, Jake. It's going to be all right now. I know it is. Tell me that when this is all over we'll go back to that line shack, Jake, just you and me."

"We'll go back." He clung to her then…and wept.

"He'll be all right," Randy soothed. "He's in God's hands."

"¡Mi hijo! ¡Le falle!"

Randy recognized the words *my son* and *fail*. "You did not fail him, Jake. No one knew. No one knew. You did what you could."

"¡Mi hijo, favor perdóname!"

"There is nothing to forgive. Lloyd will never blame you for this." Randy held him tightly as his tears soaked her neck and the pillow beneath her. He needed this. The Jake who'd refused all feelings could not deny that they were there. All she could think of was the horror it must have been for him as a tortured little boy with no one to hold him. Her own tears mingled with his as they both wept until they fell into an exhausted sleep.

Twenty-two

RANDY FINISHED PINNING UP HER HAIR. "BUTTON ME up," she asked Jake.

Jake walked up behind her, wearing his own clothes now, a white shirt and denim pants. He'd just pulled on his boots after his daily ritual of shaving and scrubbing his teeth with baking soda—things he'd neglected while sitting at Lloyd's bedside for nearly four days.

Randy watched him in the mirror. "I see some remnants of an outlaw, Jake, and I feel it in the way you are jerking at those buttons."

He frowned. "They're going to try to arrest me, Randy. You understand that, don't you?"

She closed her eyes. "Maybe they won't."

"They will. And I'm still not leaving here—not until Lloyd is standing and walking. And there is one other thing we haven't talked about."

"I don't want to think about it."

"We *have* to. Brad Buckley is still out there somewhere, so if I get hauled away—"

"Don't say that!" She stood up and turned to wrap her arms around his middle. "Jake, I just want to go home to the J&L."

"Believe me, there is nothing I want more."

Someone tapped on the door then. "Jake? Mrs. Harkner? It's me—Pepper. Cole is with me."

Randy pulled away, wiping at her eyes. "Just a minute!" she called out. She turned around so Jake could finish buttoning her dress.

"Jake, I told them they should get the grandsons and Ben when they go home, and bring them back here."

Jake finished her buttons and walked over to pick up his gun belt. "I don't want my grandsons involved in this." He buckled the gun belt.

Randy hurriedly straightened the still-unmade bed. "Stephen has a right to see Lloyd, Jake, and having him here might help Lloyd heal faster. And Ben will be worried sick once he finds out what's happened. He gets so scared when he thinks he might lose you. He and Little Jake will both want to see you're okay. I want them here, whether you like it or not."

Jake scowled. "Well, those precious little granddaughters should be left at the ranch."

"I agree."

"Anybody out there in the hallway?" Jake called to Pepper as he approached the door.

"No. Just us."

Jake opened the door and quickly let in the two men while Randy opened a carpetbag and retrieved the papers they needed. The men glanced around the room nervously, feeling uncomfortable in Jake's private room. Pepper looked Jake over as though fearing he might pull a gun on him.

"Relax," Jake told them. "I only blow the heads off my enemies, not my friends."

"Well then, I reckon we're glad you consider us friends," Cole joked, trying to lighten the moment.

"We're damn sorry about Lloyd, Jake," Pepper told him. "It's a goddamn shame. I ain't never had a kid—none that I know of anyway—but anybody can see how close you two are. And Lloyd is a damn fine man."

Jake nodded. "Thank you." He took a cigarette from a tin on a nearby dresser and lit it.

Pepper and Cole removed their hats and nodded to Randy. "Ma'am, this must be awful hard on you and Jake both," Cole told her.

"We are all praying for him," Randy answered, "and you know God will certainly listen to Evie's prayers, if no one else's."

"Yes, ma'am," Pepper told her. "No doubt about it."

"Lloyd woke up and moved his legs last night," Jake told them, "so we're hopeful."

"Good! That's damn good," Cole told him.

"And right now you need to run a few errands," Jake added, taking a drag on the cigarette. "Randy already told you what you need to do. She has a note to give you for the bank. After you pick up supplies, I want you to go to that garden supply place over on Eighteenth Street and buy as many yellow rosebushes as they have. Take them home and have Rodriguez plant them all around the veranda of the main house. A few red ones are okay, but mostly yellow. I want them there for Randy when we get home."

"Yes, sir."

Randy felt like crying over the fact that in the midst of all that was happening, Jake remembered her roses.

Pepper watched Jake tie his holsters to his thighs. "You okay, Jake?"

"I will be when Lloyd is up and walking. He spoke last night and moved around quite a bit."

Cole nodded. "You've got everybody scared to death after what you did to Mike Holt," he told Jake. "Not even Denver's finest police want to come up here and try to arrest you."

"Good." Jake took a drag on the cigarette as Randy handed Cole the papers.

"Lloyd has a long way to go," Jake told them, "and I still might be facing an arrest, so I don't know what's going to happen or how soon we'll make it back to the J&L. Make sure the men there are taking proper care of everything, and give my baby girls hugs for me."

"You trust us no-goods to be huggin' those little angels?" Pepper asked.

"Of course I do. And I don't want them to know that anything bad has happened. Make up whatever story you want to tell them, and make sure Stephen and Ben and Little Jake understand they're not to tell those girls anything that would make them scared or make them cry."

Cole nodded. "We'll tell them."

Pepper shook his head. "I never knew a man who could blow—" He hesitated. "Who could do what you did and then worry about somebody givin' hugs to two little girls."

"Yeah, well, I guess I'm two different men, and my poor wife has to live with *both* of them. I try to be the good Jake, but the bad one just can't help some of the things he does."

"They surely won't send you to jail, Jake," Cole assured him. "For God's sake, the man shot your unarmed son. Lord knows if Lloyd had had his own gun with him, that never would have happened. He's as good with a gun as you are."

"I just wish I'd realized what was happening sooner. That sonofabitch should never have been allowed into that dance. I'll see to it that the woman who let him in goes to jail herself for aiding in an attempted murder."

Pepper nodded to Jake then. "Well, in the meantime, we'll get those roses and other supplies to the ranch and come back here with the grandsons. I'm sure by now the rest of the men will be glad to give Little Jake over to us for a while."

That got a grin out of Jake. "I don't doubt that one bit." Jake took another drag on the cigarette. "You don't need to be in a big hurry. After a couple of days of excitement at seeing a city, those boys will get bored real fast, and we know Lloyd has a good two weeks of recovery ahead of him, maybe a lot longer. Nothing is going to happen anytime soon."

Pepper nodded and put his hat back on. He started

to leave, then hesitated. "Oh, by the way, there are a couple of men downstairs askin' about you, Jake. One's a fancy-lookin' dude—like a big city lawyer or somethin', and I heard the other one say he was a reporter from Chicago. Wears round wire glasses and looks more like a kid than a man."

Randy gasped. "Jake! It must be Jeff!" She looked at Pepper. "Jeff Trubridge is the reporter from Chicago who spent time with Jake and Lloyd back in Guthrie and wrote the book about Jake. He came to visit once the first year we settled here, before you and Cole even worked for us."

"Well, him and the other man was askin' your room number, but the clerk downstairs said he wasn't allowed to give it out," Pepper told her.

"Go ahead and tell them where we are," Jake told them. "The man with Jeff—" He shared a look with Randy, strong memories of another man who'd loved her hitting home. "He's probably a lawyer friend we also knew back in Guthrie. His name is Peter Brown."

"We'll take care of it," Pepper told him on his way out.

Both men left, and Jake locked the door and leaned against the wall beside it. "I'll be damned. We haven't seen Jeff in a couple of years, and we've never seen Peter Brown since—"

Since he left for Chicago because he loved me too much to stay in Guthrie, Randy thought. She saw the same thought in Jake's eyes. "Jake, he must be here to try to help us. Hear him out. Personally, I'll be relieved to see both of them. It gives me a little more hope."

Jake looked her over with a strong hint of "you belong to me" in his eyes. "Maybe he's just here for *you.* If things go bad, you'll need someone to turn to. I'm sure Peter would gladly help out."

"Jake, don't start. Jeff told us in that letter a year ago that Peter's married now."

"That doesn't change how he'll always feel about you." He walked over to a dressing table and snuffed out his cigarette. "Don't worry. I'll be good."

"He did so much for us."

"I am well aware of what he did, and I'm also aware he did it all for you."

"And if he's here to help you, it only shows what a good friend he is to us—*both* of us. He does care about you, Jake. That was obvious when he worked so hard on that petition to get your sentence shortened."

Jake raked her over with his gaze as she walked closer. "I love you," he told her.

Randy saw the flash of past regrets in his eyes. "And I love you, way more than you can ever imagine."

Someone tapped on the door. "Jake? It's Jeff Trubridge. I have Peter Brown with me."

Jake kept the cigarette between his lips. "Anybody else?"

"Just us."

"This had better not be a trick. There are a few people out there who'd like to see me hang."

"Jake, for God's sake, how well do I know you?" Peter spoke up. "You'd still like to shoot me, and I have no doubt you are wearing guns right now. Do you think I'd add to your wrath by bringing someone up here to try to cart you away?"

"Well, I don't know, Peter." Jake winked at Randy. "If they hang me, that leaves Randy a widow. Pretty convenient for you, wouldn't you say?"

"It would be if I wasn't already married to someone else."

Randy smiled.

"Jake, stop joking around and let us in," Jeff spoke up. "I have coffee with me, and it's still nice and hot."

"Well, since Peter is married now, I guess it's okay." With his back still to the wall, Jake opened the door and peered into the hallway, seeing no one else. "Come on in."

The men walked inside, and Jake closed and locked the door. He fought old jealousies and reminded himself Evie was praying for miracles. If Peter Brown was here to try to keep him out of prison, maybe Peter was just another answer to those prayers. Keeping him out of prison this time *would* take a miracle.

Twenty-three

JAKE JUST WATCHED AS RANDY EMBRACED PETER, keeping his feelings in check. Peter Brown was responsible for his being released from his sentence to serve as U.S. Marshal in Oklahoma so he and the family could finally come to Colorado. He was responsible for a lot of help in other ways…but Jake knew it was all for Randy.

"Oh, Peter, it's so comforting to see old friends right now," Randy told him. "You did so much for us back in Guthrie. Did you bring your wife? I so want to meet her."

She pulled away from Peter but kept hold of his hands, while Jeff set a silver tray that held a decanter and four coffee cups on a dresser.

"Not this trip," Peter answered. "I figured I'd wait until things are back to normal for you and we're sure you and Jake can go home. Then maybe I can bring Treena out to the ranch for a visit. Jeff has told me how beautiful it is."

"He's right, Peter! It *is* beautiful!" Randy agreed.

Jake watched Randy finally let go of Peter's hands and turn to Jeff for a hug. He caught the way Peter watched her then. Yes, the man was most certainly still in love with her.

"I'd love to see *both* of you and your families come to the J&L," Randy was telling them, grasping both their hands then. "Once all this is—" She hesitated, her smile fading. "Over." Her eyes suddenly teared. "You did come here to help, didn't you, Peter?"

"When I heard the news, I knew I *had* to come."
Peter turned to Jake. "I'm so damn sorry about Lloyd,
Jake. Sorry about *everything*. Jeff and I came as soon as we
could. We took a train from Chicago. Thank goodness
we can travel to places a lot faster than we used to."

Jake nodded. "Yeah."

Jeff turned and looked up at Jake. At six feet four
inches, Jake towered over his five-foot-eight-inch frame.
He reached out to shake Jake's hand, and Jake jerked him
closer, slapping the young man on the back.

"Jeff, it's damn good to see you! *Damn* good!"

"You, too, Jake, but I don't like the circumstances
that brought me here."

"Well, my good friend, you are always looking for a
headliner story. You know me. I can always provide one
for you." Jake stepped around him and closer to Randy.
"It's been a mess."

Peter noted the tired, strained look in Jake's eyes.
"We knew this would be hell for you, Jake." He glanced
at Jake's guns. "I have to say you're looking a bit intimidating at the moment. Are things really so bad that you
have to wear those guns?"

"They are. You must know by now everything that's
happened, and I'm not leaving this hotel until I know my
son is completely well. These guns are keeping the law
from coming for me." Jake put out his hand. "Thanks
for coming."

Peter took his hand a bit hesitantly. He knew Jake
Harkner well, and that meant being careful when he was
in the kind of mood Peter guessed him to be in. Neither
of them needed to say it. Peter had come as much for
Randy's sake as anyone's. They shook hands firmly…
two men in love with the same woman…two men as
different as sand and water. But that woman had eyes
for only one of them, as devoted a wife as a man could
ask for.

"Jake, you're in every headline in every newspaper across the country by now," Jeff told him. "I know for a fact you made the *Chronical* in San Francisco and the *St. Louis Post-Dispatch*. It hit the papers in Chicago the very next day after the shooting, and Peter and I knew right away you might need some help out here. Thanks to the railroad, we were able to get here in just a couple of days."

"Oh, my goodness, I didn't know half the country knew about this," Randy exclaimed, putting a hand to her chest. She cast Jake a worried look.

"There are people milling around outside and in the lobby," Jeff added. "Mostly reporters, all of them wanting to get a look at the infamous Jake Harkner. Half of them expect some kind of shoot-out."

"There *will* be if they try to come for me before Lloyd is up and walking," Jake told him. "He'll need a lot of care, and he's a big man. Katie and Evie are both with child, so I need to be here to help move and lift Lloyd and help keep him bathed and all the other things that need doing for something like this."

Peter smiled softly. "So, you have two more grandchildren on the way."

"We do. I always have trouble believing our growing family is really mine. That's something I never dreamed would happen to me." Jake turned to Jeff. "I'm not leaving my son's side, Jeff. You know how it is between me and Lloyd."

"I know all too well," Jeff answered. "A man doesn't ride with the likes of Jake and Lloyd Harkner like I did and forget it anytime soon."

"Jeff, how is your wife?" Randy asked. "We were so happy to learn you got married."

"She's fine. She is also going to have a baby. I was afraid the trip might be too much for her, so I left her back in Chicago."

"You be sure to let us know when the baby is born," Randy asked. "We'll want to send a gift."

"Congratulations, Jeff," Jake told him with a grin. "That's good news. It won't be long before babies are popping out all over the place."

"Yeah, well, Peter is here to see that you're around to welcome all of them."

Randy put a hand to her forehead and turned away. Jake took her arm and led her to sit down on the edge of the bed. "Jeff, pour us some coffee. Sorry, but there are only a couple of chairs in here. If we'd known you two were coming..." He sat down with Randy on the bed. "You can take the chairs." He put out his cigarette in an ashtray on the bed stand, noticing how Peter looked at Randy with love and concern. Jake moved an arm around her. "How's married life, Peter?"

Peter smiled at the instant possessive embrace and the obvious hint in his question. "Very good. Katrina is a beautiful woman. I knew her when she was married to a friend of mine, a business acquaintance who died a few years ago. Katrina hired me for some legal work involving one of his businesses, and, well, one thing led to another, and now we're married. We have a home north of Chicago, and my practice is flourishing."

"I'll say!" Jeff put in. "His home is more like a stone castle." He handed some coffee to Jake and Randy. "I visited him there once when..." Jeff hesitated. "Well, when Mike Holt was released, I thought I'd go talk to Peter about it. We were both a little concerned, Jake. Turns out that concern was well placed."

Jake sobered. "Yeah." He drank some of the coffee.

Randy did the same, clinging to the cup and closing her eyes to enjoy the warm steam that helped her relax. "It's been a nightmare," she said softly. "That man walked right up to poor Evie and..."

Jake tightened his arm around her. "Evie nearly

passed out," Jake continued. "I don't even know yet what he said to her, but you can bet it was something that brought all that ugliness back for her. Lloyd noticed what was happening, and so did Brian. Both ran to help her. By then, I couldn't shoot because they were both in the way. It all took place in maybe three or four seconds. That sonofabitch turned on Lloyd and fired."

The room hung quiet for a moment until Peter spoke up. "And you, being a man used to dealing his own justice, decided then and there to be judge and jury and executioner of the shooter." He spoke the words more with sorrow than condemnation.

Jake stared at his coffee cup. "I thought Lloyd was dead. He's my *son*! All I could think of was that sonofabitch robbed me of the chance to even..." His voice caught in his throat. "*¡Me quito a mi hijo y ni siquiera tuve la oportunidad de despedirme de él!*"

"I know you sometimes turn to Spanish when you're upset, Jake, but I need English," Peter told him.

Jake breathed deeply and rose, walking to a window. "He took my son from me, and I didn't even get a chance to say good-bye. That's what I was thinking. I didn't get to...hold him and tell him I love him... before he died. That's what was going through my mind. *¡Debería de haber sido yo!*"

Peter looked helplessly at Randy.

"He said—" Her eyes teared. "It should have been me."

Jake wiped at his eyes while his back was to the rest of them, and Randy put her head in her hands. Jake cleared his throat before continuing. "The man deserved to die!"

"Of course he did," Peter answered. "But you're no longer a U.S. Marshal, Jake, and even if you were, that wouldn't give you the right to hold the man down and blow his head off. That's just a fact that I know is hard for a man like you to live with."

Jake turned, the "outlaw" back in his eyes. "I didn't

kill Holt the other night just because he'd shot Lloyd. I killed the man who blindfolded my beautiful, angelic, Christian daughter and *raped* her! No man who does what he did should exist!" He took another deep breath. "And then there lay my son…my *life*! Lloyd and Evie are the only good things I've ever contributed to this world. If I didn't know Randy like I do, I'd swear they came from someone else's seed, but they're *mine*—something I did *right*! So, yes, I shot the bastard who didn't hurt just one of my children. He hurt *both* of them! If Evie hadn't asked me to spare their lives, I would have killed every last man back there at Dune Hollow, and this thing wouldn't have happened, because Holt would already have been dead."

Jake's wrath permeated the air to the point where the room began to feel much too small.

"Jake, when we go before a judge you can't be in the kind of mood you just showed me," Peter told him. "You *can* tell the judge what you just told me because it's very touching and helps people understand, but you can't say it with that dark, menacing way you have about you when you're upset. And you shouldn't mention that you would have killed the rest of the men left alive back at Dune Hollow if it weren't for Evie. That just makes you look more ruthless." He shook his head. "Not that you *aren't* ruthless at times."

"A judge? Do you know something I don't?"

"Jake, we've already talked to a prosecutor and a judge about this," Jeff told him.

Jake straightened in a defensive mode. "I hope the prosecutor you talked to wasn't Harley Wicks," he said with obvious anger. "This is partly *his* fault."

Peter always felt nervous around an angry Jake Harkner wearing six-guns. He ran a hand through his hair. "Jake, you are less intimidating when you sit, so please do me that favor. I can tell you're getting worked up again, and you need to learn to control that for what I have planned. If you will sit back down I'll explain. And no, it wasn't Wicks."

With a deep sigh, Jake walked back to the bed and sat down next to Randy.

Peter met his gaze sternly. "Have you forgotten I'm actually good at what I do? And I know you all too well, Jake. Jeff got the scoop on what happened and what Wicks had to do with it, so I talked to a different prosecutor. With the help of a young attorney here in Denver named Hawk Monroe, I got this whole thing removed from Wicks's control. And Mr. Monroe helped me gain permission to practice here in Colorado so I can represent you."

Randy let out a little gasp. "Thank you, Peter!"

"I've heard of Hawk Monroe," Jake told him.

"There is a book about the Monroe family here in Colorado. It's called *Savage Destiny*. The Monroe name is well known here. The father, Zeke, was half Cheyenne and very involved with the Indian problems here years ago. He once owned quite a big ranch in southern Colorado. Hawk Monroe is his grandson. He had to go out of town, or I would have brought him with me to meet you. Be that as it may, I can represent you if that's what you want, Jake."

Their gazes held in mutual understanding. "You helped me get out of that job from hell in Oklahoma so Randy and I could find some peace in Colorado, Peter, but peace doesn't seem to last long wherever I go. And I do know you're good at what you do, so yes, your help is welcome. Like you said, you know me better than most men, so maybe you know a way to keep this from looking as bad as it really is."

"Peter, Harley Wicks's sister let Mike Holt into the dance that night," Randy explained, "hoping to cause a ruckus and get Jake kicked out or in trouble for fighting.

She said she didn't know Holt had a gun. I don't know if that's true or not."

"I heard," Peter told her. "That's how I got Wicks off the case." He turned his attention to Jake. "I told Wicks that if he backed off of this, you and Lloyd won't press charges against his sister for letting that man into the ballroom."

Jake nodded, suddenly rising and wiping at tears. "I'm sorry, Peter. The last four days have been a nightmare. Seeing Lloyd lying near death just about put me in my own grave."

"I understand completely, believe me. It would be the same for Lloyd if it had happened to you. I saw him after you were shot in Guthrie, and he was devastated. I know how close you two are. The bond is admirable, and it might help you in this."

Peter shuffled through some handwritten notes while Jake stood at a window and lit yet another cigarette.

Jeff got up and poured more coffee for everyone.

"Like I said, I spoke with a prosecutor named Randall Prescott," Peter continued, "and I consulted with a judge. Both agreed to hold a hearing, not a trial. The public can be there, but there won't be a jury. The judge will decide whether or not to actually bring charges against you. He said he can't just let you off without some kind of chance for others to have their say and without some kind of public explanation. It wouldn't look right, and judges are voted in, so he obviously wants to please the citizens of Denver. And until the hearing, you can stay right here with Lloyd, as long as you promise not to try to leave Denver."

Jake drew on the cigarette, staring absently out the window. "I'm not going anywhere, especially if Lloyd is still in that bed." He turned to Peter. "Things might get ugly at that hearing."

"I know that, but it will get uglier if you go off on one

of your rants and show the darker side of Jake Harkner. The judge has to think it was a crime of passion, one most people can easily understand. But you can't give the impression it could happen again. You're supposed to be a *reformed* outlaw, not just one biding his time until he kills again."

"It won't happen again, because when this is over, I'll be going back to the J&L where I can enjoy some peace well away from people who want me dead." He walked back to the bed and sat down wearily beside Randy again.

Peter set his papers aside and leaned forward, resting his elbows on his knees. He studied Randy lovingly, thinking how beautiful and poised she was in spite of being married to a man like Jake for thirty years. He glanced at Jake then and realized Jake had caught him looking at Randy. Peter held his gaze firmly. He'd never denied his love for Randy Harkner, although she'd never returned his affections. The woman was blind to her own beauty and how other men looked at her.

"Jake, let me explain something, and I hope you'll understand this." He sighed before continuing. "You feel you did nothing wrong, and God knows you probably did similar things when you were a marshal in Oklahoma. But you were a *lawman* then. Now you're just another citizen, and one with a unique reputation you'll never live down. Maybe you think nothing of blowing a man's brains out, but for the common person who has never seen anything worse than a dead raccoon or a deer they've shot, or maybe an aging parent dying, something like what you did is an incredible shock. It's hard for them to accept, and the fact remains you apparently had Mike Holt on the floor and could have held him there until he was arrested. Instead, you chose to put a gun to his forehead and pull the trigger. Plus, you had a gun on you, which was against the rules in the first place."

Jake kept the cigarette between his lips. "When practically anyone you meet could be out to make a name for himself, you arm yourself at all times."

Peter rubbed at the back of his neck, then stopped to drink some coffee. "Well, we have to rely mostly on that judge understanding your relationship with Lloyd and how hard that was for you. Obviously Mike Holt committed murder and would have hung anyway. You were just a bit out of order when you took care of things the way you did." He shook his head. "You are one complicated man, Jake. I still find it amazing what a good family man you are. We will point that out. It will work in your favor."

Jake grasped Randy's hand. "Do we have a date for this hearing?"

"Two weeks, unless Lloyd's condition is still questionable. The judge wants this over with as soon as possible, because it's causing a lot of contention and disagreements in town and more publicity than Denver cares to have."

"You sure they aren't going to try to arrest me?"

"I'm sure."

"How did you manage that?"

"I told the judge and the prosecutor about that petition I circulated in Guthrie and that over three hundred people signed it, agreeing you deserved to have your sentence reduced. I told him what an excellent job you did as a U.S. Marshal—you and Lloyd both—and all the dangers you faced bringing in the worst of them and having to go into No Man's Land to do it. And after what happened to Evie, you damn well deserved to get out of that life and out of Oklahoma."

"Your rather questionable fame from that book I wrote will probably help," Jeff added. "For every person who thinks you should pay for this, there are twenty who are rooting for you."

Jake rubbed at his eyes. "Jesus," he muttered. He met

Peter's gaze. "You didn't need to do this. God knows that even though you're married now, you're doing this for Randy, but I'm grateful anyway. I'll be forever indebted to you, which probably pleases you greatly."

Peter smiled sadly. "It doesn't please me at all. What pleases me is being able to help—at least I *hope* I'm helping. That's yet to be seen. In spite of our differences and the hard feelings over certain things, I like you a great deal, Jake. And I *respect* you even more than I *like* you. You're one of a kind and becoming a bit of a legend. Jeff, of course, thinks you're the greatest human being who ever walked. I just see you as a man who was dealt a really bad hand early in life, and I admire your strength in overcoming some of that."

"Yeah, well, most of that is thanks to Randy." Jake moved an arm around her again. "Like the wife here said, if this works out, that invitation to come to the J&L is always open. You won't regret the visit, and you might even want to stay in Colorado. It's beautiful, beautiful country." He squeezed Randy closer. "Living out here has been everything we hoped it would be. Since we left Guthrie, we've been blessed with two new little granddaughters who crawl all over me with hugs and kisses, and now two more grandchildren are on the way. Evie, of course, is hoping she doesn't give birth to another boy who turns out like Little Jake. He's quite a handful."

Peter chuckled. "I remember well."

"He hasn't changed," Jake answered with a grin. "I'm pretty much the only one he minds."

"Probably because you share the same soul," Jeff put in. "That kid is nothing more than a little Jake—so his name definitely fits him."

"He's wonderful," Randy spoke up. "He's fearless and brave and bold and full of energy."

"Does that remind you of anyone?" Peter asked.

She smiled. "Yes, and that's fine with me. He is also

incorrigible and wild and has a bit of a temper...which also reminds me of someone else."

Jake rubbed her shoulders before rising and walking over to put out the second cigarette. "So, what do you think, Peter? Do I have much of a chance of getting out of Denver without some kind of sentence? I wouldn't be surprised if some want to hang me."

"I don't think that will happen, but there are no guarantees. That prosecutor is required to do his best to make you look bad. That could mean asking questions he knows might get a rise out of you. You can't let that happen, Jake, understand? Even if he brings up Evie or your past outlaw ways or your...father. And he *will* bring that up. He will want to show people what a short fuse you have and try to convince the judge that you're a danger to society because of it."

Jake stood at the window and watched buggies going back and forth in the street below, as well as a couple of horseless carriages. He thought about the fact that people could talk to each other now from far away just by speaking into a telephone—something they didn't have on the ranch. If only Randy could have telephoned him the times they were apart.

"Peter, I come from an era when there wasn't even a Denver yet. People were still recovering from the war and moving west to find new lives—and I was riding with some of the worst men who ever walked, and drinking and gambling and running guns and robbing banks and trains and... Hell, I don't even remember all of it. I just figured my father was right that I was worthless, so why should I try to be anything better than all of that?" He felt a tug at his heart. "Until a lovely young widow came along and changed it all for me." He turned and faced Peter. "I have to go home, Peter, with my wife and my son and the rest of my family. If I go back to prison...or worse...it will kill Randy; so you do this for *her,* just like in Guthrie when you circulated that petition and got my sentence reduced—for *her.*"

Randy looked at him with tear-filled eyes. "Jake—"

"We all know it's true." Jake's eyes were still on Peter. "I know you're married, and I'm sure you love her and that she's a lovely woman, but I know the real reason you're doing this. If I were you, I'd be doing the same thing…for the finest woman who ever walked. I think you know why this is so important."

Jeff scribbled notes the whole time.

Peter rose. "I know why." He turned and closed his briefcase. "I'm doing everything I can, Jake. But my best defense is you not losing your temper in front of the judge, understand? No matter *what.*" He faced Jake. "And the day of the hearing, wear a suit—and no guns."

"Do you know how many people are going to be waiting for me to walk out that door without any guns?"

"No guns! Do you want to intimidate that judge or *impress* him? And guns aren't allowed in court anyway. It's most likely the point will come where the judge tells the police to come and take your guns. If they do, you hand them over without putting up a fuss. I promise they won't be coming to take you away. They have agreed to let you stay with Lloyd until he's better. And if you want to stay alive and out of jail, you've got to convince the judge that most of the time you are a law-abiding family man."

"*Most* of the time?"

Peter grinned. "In your case, Jake, no one is going to guarantee you're a law-abiding man *all* of the time. The only thing I can guarantee is that you are definitely a very devoted family man. You just get a little too protective of that family sometimes, and those of us in this room know why you so fiercely defend them. Just give me something to work with and do *not* lose your temper when the prosecutor questions you. I ran into a couple of your men downstairs, and when I asked them a few things, they mentioned what you did to one of your men on the way here."

"He insulted Randy."

Peter rubbed at the back of his neck. "Lord God, Jake, this is what I'm talking about. And I heard about you and those rustlers and why you ended up on the bad side of Harley Wicks."

Jake shrugged. "They were stealing my cattle and threatened to come for Randy. Was I supposed to let them do both?"

"Have you ever heard of shooting to *wound* rather than *kill*?"

"I don't pay much attention. I just shoot to stop them from shooting back."

Peter looked at Jeff. "Maybe I should just go home."

Jeff grinned. "The man doesn't bend easily."

Peter faced Jake. "You're going to have to bend on this one, Jake. You're the one who said Randy can't lose you, so you're going to have to do what I ask if you don't want that to happen. Now, let's go see Lloyd. Maybe he'll heal faster, knowing his father has some help in getting out of this and going home. Jeff is anxious to see him, too."

"Randy and I were heading for his room when you two showed up. I'd like to go see him first and make sure he wants visitors," Jake told him.

Peter nodded. "All right. We'll wait here."

With a sigh, Jake walked up to Randy, leaning down to kiss her. "Just give me a few minutes. Have some more coffee and try to relax."

"Jake, I'm so anxious to see him."

"I know." Jake turned to Peter and Jeff. "I appreciate what both of you are doing. I never expected you two to show up—especially you, Peter."

Peter shrugged. "I went to all that work to get your

sentence reduced. I couldn't let this one go and risk you being sent right back to prison."

"Yeah, well, some people expect the worst from me, and I guess they got it the other night." Jake lit another cigarette and turned to Jeff. "Come with me, Jeff. You can help with Lloyd. He won't mind, and he'll be thrilled to see you again." He turned to look from Peter to Randy. "I'm sure you two wouldn't mind a couple of minutes alone."

"Jake—" Randy started to protest as she rose.

"It's okay. I'll come back in a few minutes." He opened the door, taking a good look around before going next door into Lloyd's room.

Randy met Peter's gaze. "He's been doing almost everything for Lloyd. He bathes him and changes the dressing on his wound and cleans his teeth and shaves him and even takes care of more personal things. The contrast between the Jake who put a gun to Mike Holt's head and the Jake who's been nursing Lloyd is stark. People need to know what kind of a father he is, Peter."

Peter nodded. "I'll do my best to make sure they see that. Maybe if Lloyd is healed enough by then, he can testify himself and make an impression on the judge as far as his father's devotion to his family." He walked closer. "And you look like you need to sit back down."

Randy wavered a little, and he hurried up to embrace her. Randy hugged him in return. "Thank you, Peter! Coming all the way here so quickly just shows the kind of friend you are, and I'm so happy you've found someone. I can't wait to meet Katrina."

Peter pulled away, smiling sadly. "And she's anxious to meet you. She knows the whole story, Randy. She's a very gracious, understanding woman. We're very happy."

"I'm so glad!" Randy studied his handsome blue eyes, thinking how Peter Brown was such a good man in his own right.

Peter kept hold of her arms. "We all deal with the what-ifs, Randy, but in your case, I don't think you have ever once asked yourself, 'What if I'd let Jake Harkner ride out of my life? What if I'd married someone like Peter Brown?'"

Randy shook her head, smiling sadly. "God put me in Jake's path for a reason, Peter. There are things about him that make him constantly on the defensive, but those same things make him easy to love."

"Notwithstanding the fact that he is still an extremely handsome man who has a way with women and worships the ground you walk on."

Randy smiled more and leaned forward to kiss his cheek. "Something like that." She stepped back and squeezed his hand. "Peter, Jake will spend his whole life being on the defensive, because he spent his childhood the same way—trying to shield himself from his father's blows…and trying to shield his mother and little brother from that man's cruelty. John Harkner left a lasting effect on Jake that he struggles with to this day. I shudder to think what the little boy Jake suffered."

Someone knocked on the door then, and Jeff called to them. "Randy, Jake says to come to Lloyd's room. He's standing up!"

Randy sucked in her breath with surprise and joy, letting go of Peter and rushing to fling open the door. She hurried out, and Jeff glanced at Peter.

"Kind of hard to face certain old memories, isn't it?" Jeff asked him.

Peter nodded. "Jeff, this has to work—for *her* sake."

"Jake is really moved that you came, Peter. It's hard for him to admit it to you, but in spite of the fact that he knows why you are doing this, he is really grateful. He told me he can hardly believe you came all this way to help out."

"Well, I'm not sure I'll be any good at all, but it isn't

just for Randy. I've never met a man I wanted to hate so much but *liked* so much. He's the kind of man you have a lot of trouble imagining being gone from this world."

"A lot of people would miss him, Peter—even those of us who only see him once in a while."

Peter sighed and left with him, going into Lloyd's room to see Lloyd sitting on the edge of the bed with Jake's arm around him for support and Katie on his other side. Brian was getting something out of his medical bag. Lloyd wore cotton pants and no shirt, heavy bandages around his chest. In spite of his condition, his impressive muscular build was obvious.

Lloyd met Peter's gaze, and in that moment, Peter saw Jake Harkner. The resemblance was uncanny. Evie had her arms around her mother, and the whole family was teary-eyed with joy. Peter wished the judge could see them. This was not the Jake Harkner who'd held a man down and fired point-blank into his head.

He shivered at the thought. That would not be easy to defend.

Peter turned to Jeff, who was already scribbling something down on a pad of paper. It wouldn't be long before half the country knew Lloyd was going to live. Everyone would be watching the headlines then to see what would happen to his notorious father. "Jeff?" he spoke up. "I am suddenly feeling a very heavy weight on my shoulders—something about six feet four inches tall and weighing probably two hundred forty pounds or so."

Jeff just smiled.

Twenty-four

RANDY BRUSHED OUT HER HAIR, STILL DAMP FROM A long bath. She breathed deeply against the anxiety of knowing that the hearing would finally take place tomorrow. She dreaded it. In the past two weeks, Jake had come to their room only three times to sleep. He'd kept a nearly constant vigil with Lloyd, sleeping in his and Katie's room at night to make sure Katie did not overdo herself by trying to help Lloyd on her own. Jake was adamant she not do any heavy lifting.

Randy could tell without asking that Jake ached more than he was willing to admit from caring for his son day after day, but Lloyd had made great progress. He could get out of bed on his own now and had begun to fully dress each day and go for walks up and down the hallway, supported for most of those walks by his father.

Everything they did was under the watch of Denver police, who had taken Jake's guns in a very tense moment of showing Jake a judge's order that he not be armed until after the hearing. Peter came with them, urging Jake to turn over his guns without any trouble, to show the judge he was not dangerous. They had taken Lloyd's guns also so Jake could not get to any weapons, and when Peter and Jeff visited to talk about the hearing, they were always searched.

The Brown Palace, though the most beautiful hotel in Denver, had become their prison. From their windows they could see the crowds gathered in the streets every day, hoping to get a look at the famous Jake Harkner.

The two grandsons and Ben arrived three days ago, running to Jake and nearly tackling him to the floor in their enthusiasm, but breaking into tears that their father and grandfather might go back to prison...or worse. Stephen cried all the first day after seeing his father bedridden, scared he would die.

Now that Lloyd was better, waiting for a hearing date was agony, and the boys were growing restless. Little Jake, of course, was the biggest problem. Pepper and Cole were kept busy finding ways to entertain him, including playing cards and marbles. Jake insisted the boys stay in the hotel, because he didn't trust the crowds outside. It still concerned him that Brad Buckley could be out there somewhere.

All three boys clearly sensed the gravity of Jake's situation. Ben hardly left Jake's side and insisted on sleeping on the floor right beside Jake's cot in Lloyd's room at night. And Stephen wouldn't leave his father, so he slept in a stuffed chair near Lloyd's bed. Little Jake insisted on sleeping beside his grandfather too.

No one had any privacy. Jeff and Peter each took a room of their own, and to relieve too much crowding in Lloyd's room, Jeff kept Ben and Stephen in his room the last two nights. The whole situation had created a bit of family chaos, but the kind of chaos that was heartwarming and supportive. Randy thought how incredibly close they all were, their family unity only strengthened by all that had happened. She set down the brush, wondering if and when she and Jake would get back to a normal life, if ever. Her heart ached at the memory of that line shack where they had shared such a beautiful, quiet time alone...so happy. Jake was so much fun when he was like that, but that handsome, genuine smile was gone now. There was no joy in those dark eyes except when he saw his son walking on his own.

She glanced at the door when she heard it being unlocked.

"Jake?" she asked.

"Yeah." He quietly came inside and closed the door. "Ben and Stephen are with Jeff, and Little Jake is with Brian and Evie. I left Katie with Lloyd. He's sleeping pretty hard, so she should be all right."

He set the key aside and walked over to the bed and sat on it to remove his boots. He grimaced as he began wiggling his feet out of them. "I ache everywhere. Thank God Lloyd can do most things on his own now."

Randy watched his every movement, wondering if this was her last night to see and touch him. She watched as he jerked off his boots. She loved his arms, still so strong and hard. She studied his broad chest when he removed his shirt and a sleeveless undershirt, noticed how flat and hard his stomach still was when he rose to unbuckle his belt and remove his denim pants and his socks. Unlike most men his age, there was nothing soft about him. He was as hard as a rock, and sometimes he liked to pretend he was hard on the inside, like he was doing now. It terrified her that he could go to prison. He'd nearly died from beatings and pneumonia those four years he did time, and he was younger then. When he was wild and free and working the ranch, he was in his own element, but the poor food and medical care of prison life could kill a man his age.

"I appreciate what Peter is doing," he told her as he finished stripping to his long johns, "but we both know the real reason he's doing it. You'd fit right in at that palace of a home he owns back in Chicago. When I think about the kind of life you could have had—"

"All I want is a big log home in the foothills of the Rockies," Randy interrupted, "and a big, strong man taking care of it all—a man who can handle himself in any situation and protect and defend me and his family, a man who needs nothing more in life than *me* and his family."

Jake looked away, rising and laying his clothes over a

chair. He walked to the window. "I know I'm not an easy man to live with, Randy."

"Jake, don't try to sell me on what a good life I could have without you. I know what you're doing. You're trying to make what might happen tomorrow easier on me."

He stood there quietly, studying the streets below, lit up by gaslights. "I'm still not sure it's good for the boys to be at the hearing," he said then, obviously trying to avoid the inevitable.

Small talk, Randy thought. He was going for small talk. Casual, *I'm okay* talk.

"They are going to hear things tomorrow maybe they shouldn't hear," he added. "Peter wants them there, says it will impress the judge to see the family, but I hate for those boys to hear what that prosecutor will say about me and my past."

"They know about your past," Randy reminded him. "Nothing will surprise them. And I think Peter is right. We have a beautiful family, and the judge should see that. And when he sees how those boys look at their grandfather with so much love, it will give him reason to pause in deciding what to do about you."

"Maybe. Who knows? I'm just worried what it will do to the boys if I'm hauled away right in front of them."

"I have to believe you won't be, or I'll go crazy."

"Yeah, well, my biggest hope is Evie. She's praying for me. If God doesn't listen to her, then there *is* no God." He sighed deeply. "What I hate most about tomorrow is Evie will be there, too. What happened at Dune Hollow is sure to come up, and that's not good for her *or* the boys." He glanced at Randy, his gaze raking over her brushed-out hair and the silk robe she wore. "You look extra beautiful tonight."

Randy struggled not to break down in front of him, but it was becoming impossible. "Probably because…

because you think this could be our last night together for a while." Her lips quivered, and a tear slipped down her cheek. She looked away, feeling sick inside, wanting to stay strong for him. "They sent up your suit, cleaned and pressed."

"Good." The room hung strangely quiet for an awkward moment. "I'm not sure how Brian and Evie are going to keep Little Jake in line tomorrow," Jake finally commented.

Randy felt as though both of them were just searching for a way to avoid the terror. If the judge wanted to be truly famous and felt it was time to rid the "new" West of its "old" outlaws, he could sentence Jake to be hung.

"He's so full of energy," Jake continued. "I'm worried he'll fidget around and distract things and irritate the judge. Nobody can control that kid."

"Except you." Randy faced him again. "He worships the ground you walk on."

"Yeah, well, that admiration is a bit misplaced. He'll understand that when he's older."

"He will *always* love his grandpa. And all you have to do tomorrow is give him orders to sit still, and he'll do it—for you. Just tell him it will help you if he's very, very well behaved."

Jake smiled sadly. "I'll do my best."

"He's such a good and loving little man. He's just full of vinegar and sass—like someone else I know. And right now I need that someone's arms around me."

Jake smiled sadly. "Maybe that someone needs *your* arms around *him*."

Randy couldn't help the tears that came then. "Jake, I can't do this anymore! I can't pretend to be strong about this. This is different from when you left to chase after outlaws in Oklahoma," she wept. "At least then you had your guns and your skills and the ability to fight back."

Jake walked over and reached for her. She took his hand, and he led her to the bed. "This time we just have to fight back a different way," he told her. He sat down on the bed and pulled her onto his lap.

"You can't lose your temper on that stand tomorrow, Jake," Randy reminded him.

"Peter has made sure I am well aware of that." Jake kissed her hair as he held her tight. "Let's not talk about tomorrow, *mi esposa*. Let's talk about tonight. Let's pretend there is no tomorrow."

He pressed a big hand to the side of her face, and Randy met his lips. They kissed hungrily, almost savagely, as he laid her back on the bed. They didn't bother turning down the covers. There wasn't time. It seemed as though there wasn't near enough time for anything—for this, for talking, for looking at each other, for touching, for remembering, just for being.

Jake pushed open her robe, and they kissed...desperately.

They touched...desperately. In moments they were both fully undressed and on the bed making love...desperately.

Randy grasped the bed rails as her husband took her. He seemed to be everywhere on her body, having intercourse with her, then stopping to kiss his way down her body to her belly, her legs, running his tongue inside her until she gasped in a climax, then back to intercourse, taking her...desperately.

Randy thought how strange it was that they seemed to have come full circle. He started out a wanted man, and their first time was just as desperate thirty years ago in a covered wagon somewhere on the plains of Nebraska...or was it the Dakotas? Maybe Wyoming. She couldn't remember. She couldn't think at all.

Now this. It had all come around to this. In a sense, he was a wanted man again, and it was tempting to think about running again...but now there was a whole great big family to think about. Back in that wagon all those years ago, they never dreamed it would come to two children and four grandchildren with more on the way—an adopted son—a fifty-thousand-acre ranch…all from that one night in a covered wagon when they were so much younger.

Jake moaned as he climaxed inside of her with several hard, pulsating pushes, and she whimpered his name. She kept her legs wrapped around him.

"Don't stop," she whispered, grabbing him around the neck and kissing him wildly.

"My God, Randy, I love you so damn much," he groaned. "I'm hurting you. I'm so afraid this is our last time to be together like this that I'm moving too fast and not being gentle enough."

"No!" She kissed his neck, his throat, his chest. "I *want* it to hurt. I want to remember this."

He met her mouth again, searching deep until he was swollen yet again with the want of her, the desperate need of her, the aching realization that this truly could be their last chance to do this—after all the years; after all the other separations and all the worry and all the gunfights and all the running and all the places they had lived and all that homemade bread he loved coming home to; after the past four years on the J&L when, for the first time in their married lives, they thought they could be happy and at peace the rest of their lives; after that lovely time at the line shack.

Randy grasped the headrails again as he raged inside of her, and she arched up to him as though she couldn't get enough of him. Jake finally slowed down and rocked against her in the way he knew, stroked her in the right places until he felt her climax intensely yet again, the pulses pulling him deeper so he took her harder again, licking at the tears on her cheeks, keeping hold of her bottom with strong hands in an almost forceful crush she couldn't have gotten out of if she'd wanted to—and she most certainly did *not* want to.

"I don't want the night to end, Jake," she groaned. "I wish we could stop time."

He took her slowly, wanting to savor every lovely moment, wanting to fulfill her every need, wanting the night to last forever as much as she did. Sometimes he wondered how he could literally crave her with just as much intense desire as he'd felt back in that wagon all those years ago. She was his life. She'd *saved* his life. He loved being inside of this woman who never should have settled for the likes of Jake Harkner. Yet here she was, still wanting and pleasing him after all he'd put her through. He loved returning that pleasure, loved knowing that if the day came when they couldn't do this anymore, it wouldn't matter. All that mattered was being together and being able to hold and to touch and to love.

He grasped her hair and kissed her deeply as again he released inside of her with erotic thrusts that made him realize it didn't get any better than this. He stayed on top of her, and they clung to each other for several minutes until he reached down and grasped the bedclothes from the side and pulled them over them, rolling her over so they were wrapped up in them side by side. Randy smiled.

"I feel like we're in a cocoon."

Jake managed to move a hand to her breasts in spite of the tight wrapping. He ran a thumb over one nipple while kissing her forehead. "When we emerge from this cocoon, a beautiful butterfly with ash-blond hair and green-gray eyes and the body of a nymph will show herself."

"And what will you be?"

He caressed her other breast and smiled. "I'm not sure. Maybe the big, bad lizard, or whatever it is that eats butterflies." He stroked her hair. "And I could eat you right now. Tell me I didn't hurt you."

"Did I protest?"

"No, but in this case, you wouldn't, and I just felt like I couldn't get enough of you—like I had to make sure

I remember us this way for a long time in case I *have* to remember us this way."

"You won't, Jake. God can't let that happen. By tomorrow night, we'll be right back here in this room, doing this again."

"And the next day we'll all head back to the J&L and our big house and the great smells of meadow grass and your roses, and best of all, your bread baking in the oven."

She kissed his chest. "Right now I'd settle for the smell of horse manure if it meant we were home."

Jake grinned and kissed her hair, her ears, her eyes. "Well, when we get there, you will see rosebushes blooming all around the veranda, just like you wanted. Pepper told me Rodriguez planted those roses for you, and he's taking good care of them."

"Rodriguez has a talent for those things." Randy blinked back tears. "I miss those baby girls so much, Jake. I don't want to go home without you. They'll be looking for their grandpa, and they will be so disappointed if you don't come home with us." She couldn't help more tears. "How can I go into that house or sleep in our bed without you?"

"Because we're always together, even when we're apart. That's how it was when I was in prison, and how it was every time I had to ride out on the job in Guthrie, and that's how it will be this time. Only we have to believe it won't happen, because Evie is praying her head off, and that's akin to the Mother Mary Herself praying for us."

Randy had to smile through tears. "You keep saying she couldn't be from your seed, Jake, so maybe she's the product of immaculate conception."

That got a good laugh out of him. He rolled her back over, unwinding the bedcovers. "There was nothing immaculate about it, Mrs. Harkner."

Randy studied the rare smile. "*All* your seed is good, Jake. Just look at Lloyd and the boys and those precious little girls. We have a wonderful, devoted family, and it's all from you. You be proud of that tomorrow. And you remember that nothing they say in that courtroom will sway one family member from how much they love you. They won't hear anything they don't already know."

He sighed, kissing her lightly. "Who do you belong to?"

"Jake Harkner."

"Every bit of you, inside and out. *Yo te amo, mi querida.*"

"And I love you, Jake. This is where I feel safe. I want to fall asleep right here in your arms."

He sat up long enough to reach down for an extra blanket at the foot of the bed and drew it over them, pulling her into his arms, not about to let her see the tears in his own eyes. He'd given thought to trying an escape tomorrow if things went bad, but he couldn't do that to her. No more running. Tomorrow things would be over—one way or another.

Twenty-five

> *In Guthrie, when Jake Harkner would ride into town, towing killers and thieves and violators of women behind him, crowds always gathered, following him like the Pied Piper, wanting to get a look at him and be able to say they knew the man. Today is much the same.*

JEFF SCRIBBLED THE NOTE AS FAST AS POSSIBLE IN HIS own form of shorthand. He'd grown used to writing while walking, and Jake had insisted on walking the several blocks to the courthouse. The whole family was enjoying the chance to get out in fresh air and sunshine. So many people surrounded them that it was almost like a parade, and Jeff saw the event as the continuing story of Jake Harkner that could be serialized in his newspaper column. He would write about this with that in mind, giving more details than a normal news article. He just hoped that wouldn't mean writing about a hanging.

> *Police are all around. Jake is in the lead with his arm around his wife, who looks ravishing today in a beautiful yellow dress. Behind them is his son, miraculously able to walk but looking thinner and obviously in pain. He came most of the way by buggy but wanted to walk the last block with his father. He is supported on one side by his sister, Evie Stewart, and on the other by his wife, Katie.*

Following is Evie's husband, Brian, holding hands with a very fidgety Little Jake, seven now, and with Lloyd's son, Stephen. Out ahead of Jake is his adopted son, Ben, and on either side of Jake and his wife are two of J&L's cowhands, who seem to be posted there to protect Jake and his wife.

"Mrs. Harkner!" someone shouted. "What's it like living with a man like Jake Harkner?"

Jake kept a tight arm around Randy. "Terrible!" Jake answered for her with a wide grin. "I beat her every night! That's why she's stayed with me for thirty years!"

The crowd laughed, most of them seeming to highly enjoy watching the entourage.

Jake is in a surprisingly jovial mood, Jeff noted. *I am guessing it's a cover in order to lighten the gravity of this situation for his family.*

Jeff stayed behind the family with Peter.

"Hey, Jake, who has your guns?" another man yelled.

"I'm not sure, but whatever happens today, my family had better get them back! Those guns are willed to my grandson, Little Jake!"

Little Jake jumped up and down, looking up at his father and grinning as more laughter moved through the crowd.

"You behave, Little Jake," Brian warned. "Once we get in that courthouse, it's very important that you sit still and be very, very good, understand?"

"I will, Daddy," the boy answered, upon which he jerked away from Brian and ran up to walk proudly in front of Jake alongside Ben.

Jake spotted Gretta in the crowd, wearing a dark green ruffled dress and carrying a parasol with ruffles around the edge. Her red hair was piled into neat curls, and the bodice of her dress was cut just low enough to give a man a good idea of what she had to offer. "Gretta!" Jake shouted. "Come on over here and walk with us!"

There was a mixture of gasps from women and laughter from the men. Gretta marched right up to Jake, and he put his free arm around her.

"If I end up in prison or worse," Jake told the crowd, "I might as well go down with two beautiful women in my arms!"

More roaring laughter.

"The man knows how to win over a crowd, doesn't he?" Jeff told Peter.

"Jake Harkner does and says exactly what he wants to," Peter answered. "There is never any doubt about where he stands on anything. I just hope that doesn't hurt him today, because the prosecutor is going to bring up all kinds of things to get a reaction out of him. And I'm wondering if the prosecutor plans to use Gretta in some way."

"Hey, don't it bother Jake's wife that he has his arm around a notorious prostitute?" one man asked as he rushed up alongside Peter.

Peter looked over at Jeff. "You want to answer that one?"

Jeff laughed. "No, it doesn't bother her. Jake is just being Jake. You have to know him well to understand, and nobody knows him better than his wife."

The man shook his head. "Complicated man, but he sure attracts people like a magnet."

"Now there's a good description," Jeff answered. "Magnetic. I never seem to run out of adjectives to describe the man."

"Jake! We're all rooting for you!" another man shouted.

The walk to the courthouse had turned into a circus atmosphere. Some of Gretta's girls followed along, as did a few well-known cattlemen and businessmen. A group of women standing on a little stage near the courthouse began singing "Amazing Grace."

Jake stopped walking, and the whole crowd followed

suit. He'd paused to light a cigarette, and Jeff thought how grand he looked today—a clean shave, his hair lying in neat waves to the collar of a clean white shirt under a neatly cut suit with a string tie. He spotted gold cuff links when Jake raised his wrists to light the cigarette. Jeff looked down at highly polished black leather boots. Randy's yellow cotton dress fit her still-lovely figure perfectly. Back in Oklahoma, when Jeff got to know Jake so well, it was not unusual for Jake to mention his wife's beautiful cleavage, and today it showed fetchingly at the square-cut, lace-trimmed bodice of her dress. Her blond hair was drawn back at the sides and tied at the crown, where tiny flowers were stuck into it. Few men failed to notice how incredibly lovely she was, and Jeff grinned at the suspicion Jake wanted her looking extra beautiful in front of the judge.

Lloyd wore black pants and shined boots with a white shirt but no suit jacket. Deep worry showed in his dark eyes, but he had that aura of "Jake's son" about him that hinted he was no man to mess with. He looked thin and tired today, obviously still not a well man.

Evie's dark beauty was accented by a soft-pink dress and pink flowers in her dark hair, while Katie wore a dark-blue dress and a little, round straw hat. Both women showed only a tiny hint of growing waistlines from the babies they carried. Brian was his usual neat, well-dressed self in a gray suit with a black silk vest under the jacket.

Ben and Stephen wore suits, although when Jeff first saw them coming out of the hotel, he could tell the boys hated having to dress that way. Little Jake wore black cotton pants and a white button shirt, but he had a way of always looking ready to go play in a mud hole.

Jake and his wife are the epitome of a handsome couple, Jeff noted. *They don't come much more handsome than Jake, or more beautiful than Miranda, but I see the fear and dread in her eyes and in the way she clings to her husband with one arm*

*around his back. She knows these could be her last moment.
with him. Jake knows it, too. He's covering. I know him too
well now. He's ready to explode on the inside. This should be
an interesting day.*

"Jake!" Katie called out in alarm.

Jake turned to see Lloyd beginning to sway a little
He let go of the women and threw down his cigarette
hurrying over to Lloyd and putting an arm around him
His entire jovial countenance was now gone.

"Lloyd, you don't have to be here."

"Yeah, Pa, I do. I'll be okay…once we get inside
where it's cooler. Once I sit down…I'll be all right."

"I'll help you up the steps."

"Pa." Lloyd held back. "You know I love you. Katie
and I prayed for you half the night, and you know damn
well how hard Evie's been praying."

Evie began wiping at tears, and Randy went to her
side. Gretta graciously and quietly left the scene.

"I'll be fine, Lloyd, no matter what," Jake told his son.
"I can't think of a better man to take care of Randy and
all that's mine than you, so if it ends up that way, I'll rest
easy. You stay strong, and you remember whose son you
are but that you're also your own man now, and a hell of
a lot better man than your father ever was."

Lloyd shook his head. "They don't come any better
than you."

Jake tightened his arm around Lloyd. "You're going
to be a bigger name than I ever was. Maybe you'll even
be the damn governor someday. You'll be well known
for far different and far *better* reasons than your old man.
And I'll be watching, whether here on earth or someplace
else." He helped Lloyd up the steps. "And right now I
can't get emotional, understand? Peter says I need to stay
steady on that stand, which means ignoring my emotions,
so this isn't a good time to talk about who's the better
man. And if we ever duked it out, I still say I'd win."

"Bullshit," Lloyd answered. "The only chance you'd have…is if you tried it right now…while I'm still injured and weak."

The Christian women nearby continued their hymn singing.

"Let's get inside," Jake told Lloyd. "The atmosphere out here rings a little too close to a setup for a hanging." He turned to the rest of the family. "Let's get this over with," he announced. He kept a supportive arm around Lloyd while bringing Randy close again with his other arm. "Randy, have I told you how utterly beautiful you look today?"

"Several times."

They climbed the steps to the courthouse.

"If nobody cared about that man, this wouldn't be so important to me, Jeff," Peter told the young reporter. "If it was anyone else but Jake Harkner being questioned today, I could be pretty sure how things would go, but Jake is the most unpredictable client I've ever worked with. He goes entirely off his emotions and his ideas of what's right and wrong. I just hope he can keep that temper of his in check."

The crowd followed, some grumbling when courthouse guards wouldn't let all of them inside the courtroom.

Jeff followed. *I thought I was done writing about Jake Harkner*, he scribbled, *but with a man like Jake, the story never ends. If I'd known all this was going to happen, I would have saved it for my book.*

He turned to see how many were left behind, and then he saw a familiar face. "Good God," he muttered, feeling light-headed.

It was Brad Buckley.

Twenty-six

EVERYONE FILED INTO THE COURTROOM. JEFF GRASPED
Peter's arm and pulled him aside, glad that the flow of the
crowd caused Jake and the family to continue on inside.

"What is it?" Peter asked with obvious irritation.

"Peter, I saw Brad Buckley in the crowd outside!"

"*What!*"

"It could spell disaster for Jake if he spots him inside
that courtroom! Should we tell him?"

Peter removed his hat. "Holy Mother of God, I don't
know which would be worse—telling him now or letting him see the man by surprise! For all I know, the
prosecutor plans to call him up for some reason."

"I think we should tell Jake now so he's prepared."

Peter turned to a court guard. "Send Jake out here,
will you?"

The man left to get Jake, and Peter ran a hand through
his hair as Jake came back out looking concerned.
"What's going on?" Jake asked.

"Jake, I—" Jeff started to speak up.

"Listen to me, Jake," Peter interrupted. "It's vital that
you stay calm in there no matter what. You understand
that, don't you?"

"Of course I do."

"No matter *what*. They might bring up Dune Hollow
or the shoot-out in Guthrie or even go back to other
shoot-outs or bring up your daughter or—"

"What the hell is wrong, Peter? We've already talked
about this a hundred times."

Peter looked around the crowd that remained close by. "You stay calm when I tell you this, all right? Don't react!"

Jake looked at Jeff. "You started to tell me something?" he demanded.

Jeff sighed and stepped closer, keeping his voice low. "Jake, just before we came inside, I saw Brad Buckley in the crowd."

He waited, along with Peter, as Jake stood there, glaring back at him. Jake turned, scanning the stragglers who couldn't make it into the courtroom. They all stared back, some grinning and nodding at Jake.

"Good luck, Jake," one of them called out. "We're all on your side in this."

Jeff could swear he heard thunder somewhere, but it was a sunny day. Jake looked from him to Peter. "He's offered to testify against me. I guarantee it."

"But what could he possibly say that would matter in this case?" Peter asked.

"I killed his father and two brothers. He'll find a way to make it look as bad as he can make it look."

"But you were a marshal then," Jeff spoke up.

"They'll say I overstepped my duties."

"*Did* you?" Peter asked.

The dark outlaw look moved into Jake's eyes. "His father raped a fifteen-year-old farm girl, and then he tried to shoot it out with me. I did exactly what I had to do. And Brad's brother Bo was part of that shoot-out in Guthrie that left me in the street likely bleeding to death, so no, I didn't overstep my duties at all."

"Well, you just let me do the questioning if it comes up. If that man shows himself, you sit still, got it? You'd better tell Lloyd and make sure he does the same. He can be as bad as you when it comes to men like the Buckleys and Mike Holt."

Jeff could see Jake already struggling with his temper. Jake took a deep breath, and they walked into the courtroom. Before sitting down, Jake leaned over and spoke into Lloyd's ear. Lloyd immediately started to rise, but Jake pressed his shoulder. "Stay calm," he told him quietly. "If you don't, I won't be able to either, and I *have* to, Lloyd." He squeezed his shoulder. "It will be all right."

Randy was still standing, and she faced Jake in near panic. "What's wrong?"

Jake leaned close, talking softly into her ear. "Brad Buckley is somewhere in the crowd."

Randy put a hand to her chest. "Oh, Jake!"

"It's okay. At least I know it. Come sit down beside me, and don't you give one thought to that bastard." He scanned the row of seats…Little Jake on the end. The boy gave Jake a smile, and Jake winked back at him. Next came a very anxious-looking Brian, who Jake knew was very worried about Little Jake's behavior. Beside Brian sat Evie, then Lloyd, Stephen, and Katie. Ben sat on the end, looking ready to cry. Jake walked along the railing that separated their front-row seats from the table where Jake would sit. He reached over and tousled Ben's always-tangled-looking blond hair. "It will be okay, Ben." He couldn't help the grip at his heart at seeing his big, beautiful family…all the things he once never dreamed could be possible for him. He missed his precious little granddaughters and wondered if he'd ever see them again, feel their arms around his neck and their sweet kisses on his cheeks.

He moved back down to the aisle seat where Little Jake sat and knelt down. "You be very, very good, understand?" he said quietly. "Don't wiggle, and don't whisper."

Little Jake pressed his lips tight, and a tear trickled down his cheek. "Are they gonna take you away today?"

"We'll try real hard to make sure that doesn't happen," Jake told him. He leaned in and kissed the boy's cheek.

People whispered.

Jake took Randy's arm and moved to take his place beside Peter at the defendant's table. Randy sat on Jake's other side, and Jeff sat next to her. Peter stepped to a table across the aisle and shook hands with the prosecutor, then moved back beside Jake.

"That's Randall Prescott," he told Jake quietly.

Jake glanced at the man, stiffening when he saw Harley Wicks sitting next to Prescott at the prosecutor's table.

"What is Wicks doing here?" he grumbled to Peter.

"He has a right to be here, but he can't ask you any questions."

"I'd like to knock the man across the room. Having him over there feeding questions to Prescott doesn't help my ability to stay calm."

"And they know that. That's why he's here. You remember that. One blow-up from you, and they've won, Jake."

Jake seethed inside—not just knowing Wicks was here but also realizing Brad Buckley was around somewhere and might even testify in some way. In spite of a crowd stuffed into every corner of the courtroom and hanging over banisters above, everyone quieted when the court bailiff entered the room and with a booming voice ordered that everyone rise and be silent for the entrance of Judge Thomas P. Carter. The judge stepped up to his chair and pounded a gavel, telling everyone to be seated and warning them that he did not intend for this procedure to turn into some kind of circus.

"Anyone who causes a commotion will be immediately removed!" he announced.

Jake studied the tall, austere, and graying man, catching honesty in his blue eyes. One thing he'd learned over the years was how to read a man. The judge glanced at Jake, and both men studied each other a moment.

"Jake Harkner," the judge spoke up then. "Please rise."

Jake stood up. Peter also rose, as did Prosecutor Prescott.

"Do you understand why you're here, Mr. Harkner?"

"I do, Your Honor."

"And you and your attorney have agreed to allow a hearing before me, rather than a trial by jury, in the matter of a shooting that took place three and a half weeks ago at the Brown Palace in which a man named Mike Holt was shot dead?"

Peter nodded and answered for Jake. "We agree."

"And you also agree that I reserve the right to either demand a trial by jury or to sentence Jake Harkner myself without a trial if I so choose?"

"We agree," Peter answered. Jake nodded.

The judge turned to the prosecutor. "Mr. Prescott, do you agree to this?"

"I do, Your Honor, as long as the prosecution is allowed to call a few witnesses and to question Jake Harkner."

"And, Mr. Harkner, do you understand that I could sentence you to anything from first-degree murder—"

Jake heard Evie gasp. "Daddy!" she whispered.

"—to simple self-defense?" the judge finished.

"As long as Mr. Harkner has a right to appeal your decision to a higher authority, Your Honor," Peter replied. "However, I believe when we are through that Mr. Harkner will be exonerated of any and all charges."

"So be it. Everyone may sit down." The judge pounded his gavel again.

Jake reached behind him and took Evie's hand, squeezing it reassuringly as the judge turned to the prosecutor.

"Mr. Prescott, you may call your first witness. And please keep in mind, Mr. Prescott and Mr. Brown, that I have requested neither of you bring a parade of witnesses to repeat the same story over and over. This hearing is simply to state the facts and to allow Mr. Harkner a chance to refute any and all accusations in a cross-examination. And I might remind both of you that I reserve the right to question Mr. Harkner myself."

The prosecutor and Peter nodded.

"I would first like to call two witnesses to the stand to testify to exactly what they saw the night of the shooting," Prescott told the judge. "They are not character witnesses but are here strictly to explain what happened."

"Fine. I wasn't there, so I'd like to hear an eyewitness account," the judge told him. He looked at Peter. "Do you have any objections, Mr. Brown?"

"Not as long as they simply state facts."

"Call your witnesses, Mr. Prescott."

Two different men testified to what they saw—both telling the same story about how fast it all happened. They testified that after Jake blew a hole in Mike Holt's head, he then rose and told everyone in the room that if they wanted to know what the outlaw Jake Harkner was like, they'd just met him. That he waved his gun at everyone in the room and demanded help for his son and warned that if anyone tried to take him away for what he'd done, he'd kill them.

"It all happened in seconds," the second witness, Seth Kramer, told the spellbound audience. "I've never seen anything like it. Mr. Harkner was like a roaring grizzly bear. It's hard to explain the way he looked and acted."

"Did he look like a madman? A murderer?" Prescott asked.

The witness glanced at Jake. "I wouldn't say that. He looked more like...like... Well, I said he was like a grizzly, so I guess you'd compare it to how a mother grizzly rips into anyone she thinks is threatening her cubs—something like that."

Peter glanced at Jake and smiled softly. He quickly wrote a note.

That will help you.

Peter rose then. "Mr. Kramer, are you saying the whole incident looked more like a crime of passion?"

"Well, I guess so. I mean, the man just saw his son murdered—or at least he surely thought the boy was dead, and what Mike Holt did *was* deliberate murder. I have a son, and I'm not so sure I wouldn't have done the same thing Mr. Harkner did if the situation presented itself."

"Thank you, Mr. Kramer."

Prescott stepped closer to the witness. "And if you *did* find yourself in the same situation, Mr. Kramer, and you were able to wrestle the culprit to the floor like Mr. Harkner did, would you have blown his head off? Or would you have held him there and waited for the authorities?"

The room hung quiet. The witness, a small, balding man who seemed honest, glanced at Jake again. "I don't know for sure. I like to think I'd wait for the authorities, but I'm not Jake Harkner."

"You mean you're not a *murderer*!" Prescott urged.

"Your Honor, I object to that statement," Peter interrupted. "Mr. Prescott is leading the witness."

"I agree," the judge answered. He looked at Kramer. "Explain what you meant by saying you're not Jake Harkner."

"Well—" Kramer swallowed. "I didn't mean that he was a murderer. I just meant that he's lived a hard life and then was a U.S. Marshal in a really dangerous place where he faced some of the worst outlaws and such. It... it would probably be easier for a man like him to kill someone than for a man like me. And it was his son lying there. I think maybe he just reacted more like a lawman than an outlaw. He did have the look of an outlaw about him, but he was in kind of a rage over his son. He even—" Kramer hesitated.

"Even what, Mr. Kramer?" Peter asked.

"Well, I don't want to embarrass a man like Mr. Harkner, seeing the reputation he has, but...well...his voice broke up really bad when he was giving those orders to help his son. It was like he…like he was trying not to cry. I don't see that as something a murdering outlaw would do."

"Oh, for heaven's sake," Prescott muttered.

Peter grinned. "Thank you, Mr. Kramer. You've been very helpful."

The judge told Kramer to step down, and Peter turned to Jake, still smiling. He gave him a nod.

"I believe you have some character witnesses, Mr. Prescott," the judge told him. "Just be sure what they have to say has true bearing on what happened."

"It does, Your Honor." He turned to face the audience. "The prosecution calls Mr. Henry Porter."

Whispers moved through the crowd, and Jake just closed his eyes and shook his head as the owner of the clothing store where he'd bought his suit took the stand. Prescott established that Henry Porter was the owner of Porter Men's Wear on Sixteenth Street in Denver and that the night before the Cattlemen's Ball at the Brown Palace, he sold a suit to Jake Harkner. "And please tell us, Mr. Porter, what happened while Mr. Harkner was in your store."

Porter held his chin high as though greatly pleased to gossip about Jake. "Well, he was in the dressing room, not even fully clothed, when Miss Gretta MacBain walked into my store—which that harlot is prone to do, flaunting herself in front of my male customers in an effort to advertise her house of ill repute."

"And what did Miss MacBain do?"

"She walked right into the dressing room, and Mr. Harkner made not one objection! In fact, I heard laughter!"

A few gasps spread through the room, mostly women, while a couple of men chuckled. Jake reached under the table to take hold of Randy's hand, squeezing it tightly.

"Your Honor, what on earth can Miss MacBain paying Jake Harkner a visit in a clothing store have to do with the shooting in question?" Peter interrupted.

The judge looked at Prescott. "You want to answer that?"

"I am establishing Mr. Harkner's well-known penchant for running with lawless, sinful people of ill repute, Your Honor."

The judge frowned, and Jake rubbed at his mouth in an effort not to laugh.

"I still fail to see a connection," the judge told Prescott.

"Judge, men who run with the worst of them might think nothing of murdering someone. It's all part of their lifestyle."

The judge shook his head. "Step down, Mr. Porter."

"But...that man spent time alone in my back room with Denver's most famous harlot!" Porter argued.

"Step *down*!" the judge said louder.

A shaking Henry Porter left the stand, and Judge Carter frowned at Prescott. "I want an explanation."

Prescott sighed, his face flushed. He was a thin, balding man with not an ounce of fat on him, which made his face muscles visibly flex in his frustration. "Your Honor, Jake Harkner has run with the worst of them. Practically the first thing he did after coming to Denver was meet up with none other than Gretta MacBain, and the next thing you know he blows a man's brains out in front of a crowd of innocent people. I am just showing his basic makeup, an ex-outlaw who once rode with the worst of humankind and had a bounty on his head."

Peter rose. "Your Honor, this is enough! Mr. Harkner's past is his past, something he paid for years ago. He's broken no laws since then."

"I agree," the judge told Peter. "Do you want to cross-examine Mr. Porter?"

Jake wrote something on notepaper and shoved it in front of Peter. Peter turned to him with a frown. "You sure?"

Jake motioned for him to lean closer. "How well

do I know women like Gretta?" he spoke quietly in Peter's ear.

Peter sighed. "I won't argue that one."

"Call her as a character witness. Ask her why she was in that dressing room."

Peter hesitated, and Jake just grinned. "Ask her."

Peter straightened and faced the judge. "No, Your Honor, I have no questions for Mr. Porter. I think we've established that he's a useless witness."

A few people snickered, and the prosecutor glared at Peter.

"I would, however, like to call Gretta MacBain to the stand," Peter added.

That brought a mumbling throughout the crowd, and the judge pounded his gavel to quiet them. A few women gasped with indignation when they realized Gretta was indeed in the room, sitting in the balcony. Some of the women got up and left, as though Gretta would somehow taint them. Gretta marched down the steps to the main room and up to the witness stand, swearing to tell the truth. She looked at Jake and smiled. Peter remained seated as he questioned her.

"Miss MacBain, I think most people in this room know who you are and what you do, so I'm not going to ask you to repeat either one."

Gretta scanned the crowd. "A lot of men in this room are *very* familiar with who I am and what I do," she answered, grinning at a round of nervous laughter. A few women glanced at their husbands questioningly. Even Peter grinned. Again, the judge had to pound his gavel.

"Miss MacBain, tell us in your own words about meeting Jake Harkner in that clothing store."

"Sure." Gretta crossed her legs. "*I* looked *him* up. Jake didn't seek me out. He was very gracious, and he didn't chase me out of that dressing room because he is well acquainted with women like me, but not for the reasons the dirty-minded men in this room are thinking. Anyone who's read the book about Jake knows he grew up with women like me. They often took him in as a boy and protected him from a brute of a father who beat him regularly, so he sees women like me as friends and even as good people."

"And why did you go looking for Jake?" Peter asked.

"Because I knew he was in town to sell cattle, and not long before that, I'd had a customer named Mike Holt, who—" Gretta hesitated and lost her smile, glancing at Evie. "He bragged about the fact that he was going to go after Jake's son, Lloyd—claimed Lloyd had shot his brother in the back. He also bragged about...things he'd done to Jake's daughter in Oklahoma. Vile things no woman should have to suffer, not even women like me. I thought Jake should know Holt was out there somewhere looking for his son, so I followed him into that clothing store to warn him. That's all there was to it."

"And how long were you alone in that back room with Jake?"

Gretta grinned. "Not long enough. I mean, *look* at the man! If I could talk a handsome, well-built specimen of man like Jake Harkner into my bed, I sure as hell would take a lot longer than five minutes with him in a back room."

The room erupted into laughter, and a few more women walked out. Jake glanced sidelong at Randy and noticed she was smiling. She squeezed his hand. The judge pounded his gavel again. "This is not a circus!" he again reminded the crowd.

Peter quickly tried to smooth things over. "Your Honor, I only wanted to establish the fact that Miss MacBain wasn't in that room long enough for anything of an illicit nature to take place."

"Well, I have a feeling Mr. Jake Harkner is a man who takes his time with a woman," Gretta repeated, "but I can name a few men in this crowd who *would* only need a couple of minutes."

Even more laughter filled the room. Evie covered her face, and Lloyd just shook his head and grinned.

"Lord help us," Brian muttered.

Katie couldn't help smiling.

Again came the pounding gavel. Jake leaned over and said something more to Peter.

"I think we get the picture, Miss MacBain," Peter spoke up when things quieted. "You only sought out Mr. Harkner to warn him about Mike Holt, a man who had bragged about violating a decent, Christian, young wife and mother, and bragged about intending to murder Lloyd Harkner, which establishes the fact that Mike Holt was a reprehensible rapist and murderer and a man the world is better off without! And I believe you mentioned another name to Jake that day."

"That's right. Mike Holt had a friend with him named Brad Buckley. When I told Jake, he said as how this Buckley fellow was as bad as Mike Holt and that he, too, might be out to get him and Lloyd."

"Just a minute!" Prescott rose. "This is completely out of order! Mr. Brad Buckley happens to be one of my character witnesses! Jake Harkner must have gotten wind of it and thinks he can malign my own witness before I get a chance to call him!"

"Cattlemen call it cutting a man off at the pass," Jake said wryly.

A few people laughed, and the judge again had to pound his gavel to quiet the crowd. He sighed, telling Gretta to step down. Gretta rose, then hesitated. She looked straight at the judge. "Judge Carter, I want to add that when I told Jake about Mike Holt, the first words out of his mouth were to ask me if that man had hurt me—me, the kind of woman most people don't care about! He was worried about how Holt had treated me.

That's the kind of man Jake is. He actually cared I might have been hurt. And I'm telling you right now that nobody knows men better than I do, and that man over there is a good and honest and caring man. He might be a bit brash and waste no words when it comes to his opinions, but he's a good father and a good husband, and apparently a good grandfather. Just look at that beautiful family sitting behind him. Does that look like a family that belongs to a cold-blooded killer?"

"He *is* a cold-blooded killer!" Prescott protested. "He proved it at that ball when he held Mike Holt to the floor and put a gun against his forehead and pulled the trigger! Then he stood up and told the crowd that if they wanted to know Jake Harkner the outlaw, they'd just *met* him! The man killed his own *father*, for God's sake!"

The crowd broke into bedlam, and Jake squeezed Randy's hand so hard it hurt. She could feel him wanting to charge right into the prosecutor. Peter reached over and pressed on Jake's forearm. "He's doing this on purpose," he reminded Jake. "You'll get your turn, I promise."

Randy fought tears, and Jeff scribbled wildly in his notebook.

Harley Wicks just sat quietly grinning.

"Did your father beat you near to death almost every day of your life as a young boy?" Gretta yelled at Prescott.

The judge pounded his gavel fiercely for a good thirty seconds until the crowd finally quieted again. "One more outburst like this one, and I will clear this room!" he announced. He turned to Gretta. "Miss MacBain, you will please step down." He turned his attention to Prescott. "And you, Mr. Prescott, will refrain from referring to things that happened thirty to fifty years ago and refrain from spouting your own opinions about Jake Harkner! You are the *prosecutor*, not a witness! Am I understood?"

His face much redder now, Prescott nodded. "Yes, sir."

"I don't give one whit about Jake Harkner's past. I only care about the here and now. What happened at that shooting and *why* it happened! Now—do you have any other witnesses? If you do, they had better have more to offer than gossip and personal opinions and jokes."

Prescott raised his chin and ran a finger under his collar. "Your Honor, I would like to call Mr. Brad Buckley to the stand."

Jake started to rise. "Damn it, stay put!" Peter told him.

"That man shouldn't be in the same room as my family," Jake growled.

"Jake, please stay calm," Randy whispered. "They want you to get angry." She clung tightly to his hand.

Lloyd leaned forward and touched Peter's shoulder. "That sonofabitch has nothing to do with any of this! Get him out of here!"

"Lloyd, please!" Katie grasped his arm. "You still aren't completely well."

"Do we have a problem, Mr. Brown?" the judge asked Peter.

Peter pushed down on Jake's shoulder as he himself rose. "Your Honor, Brad Buckley comes from a family of outlaws Jake had to deal with in Oklahoma. His word can't be trusted."

"Mr. Buckley can testify as to Jake Harkner's brutality," Prescott insisted.

"I'd like to show him some of that brutality right now," Jake muttered under his breath.

"I will allow Mr. Buckley's testimony," the judge told Prescott, "but if one person in this courtroom bursts out with disruptive argument, he or she will be evicted." He looked directly at Jake. "I will remind you, Mr. Harkner, that you will have your turn to rebut any comments made against you."

Jake shifted restlessly.

"Grampa, you said to sit still," Little Jake blurted out.

The whole courtroom roared with laughter. Even the judge laughed. The whole Harkner family covered their faces and laughed, and Jake looked back at Little Jake and winked. "You're right. Thanks for reminding me."

Peter grinned and shook his head, scribbling the words "Score One!" on his notepaper and shoving it over to Jake. Jeff laughed as he frantically wrote down what just happened.

Randall Prescott scowled. Brad Buckley took the stand as the judge managed to quiet the crowd again. Brad glared at Jake and Lloyd, a victorious look on his face as he grinned at them.

"Hello, Jake. Good to see you and Lloyd again."

Jake could hear Lloyd breathing heavily behind him, and he knew it wasn't just from pain. He wanted to land into Brad Buckley, and it was all Jake could do himself to hold back.

"The witness will refrain from addressing the defendant directly," the judge ordered Brad.

Brad just kept grinning. "Yes, sir."

Prescott asked Brad how he knew Jake.

"He killed my pa *and* my two brothers," Brad sneered. "He used a marshal's badge to give him permission, but he killed them nonetheless—carted my pa into Guthrie wrapped up like a sack of potatoes and dumped him in the street. The man is a killing machine. He killed more of my relatives and half the Bryant family when he went after them for a robbery, and more of them when they shot it out with him in Guthrie. Jake Harkner doesn't shoot to wound. He shoots to *kill*, and he doesn't feel a thing afterward. Any man who kills his own father isn't gonna have any feelings for any other man he kills, reason or not. And he nearly beat me to death once back in Guthrie—broke my breastbone with the butt end of his rifle and then fired that rifle right next to my left ear so's now I can't hear out of it. He killed a *lot* of men when he was a marshal back in Oklahoma. He don't give a man a chance, and he used that badge to be nothin' more than an executioner. Don't let his family fool you, Judge. Jake Harkner ain't got no heart. I didn't see that shooting at the Cattlemen's Ball, but I'm guessin' he could have let Mike Holt live. Yet he went ahead and blew his brains out anyway 'cause that's how it works with Jake." He leaned forward, sneering. "Ain't that right, Jake?"

A look moved into Jake's eyes that made Brad sit farther back in the chair again.

"You see that, Judge?" Brad said. "See that look? That's Jake Harkner, the outlaw, and if you let him go, he'll kill again."

And it will be you, Jake wanted to reply. He forced himself to look away and wrote something on Peter's notepad.

Brad stood up. "If they let you go, Jake Harkner," he shouted, "and something happens to me, everybody will know who did it, and you'll *hang!*"

Again the crowd mumbled, and women drew in their breath. The judge pounded his gavel.

"That will be enough of your antics," Judge Carter ordered Brad. "Sit down!" He turned his attention to Prescott again. "Mr. Prescott, I expect your witnesses to just state facts, not stand and point fingers and shout their personal grudges."

Brad was still standing, and again the judge ordered him to sit down.

Brad grudgingly obeyed, glowering at Jake, who deliberately refused to look at him, because he couldn't hide the darkness he was feeling. The judge asked Peter if he had any questions.

Again Peter remained seated, glancing at Jake's note. "Mr. Buckley, can you tell us what you did that caused

Mr. Harkner to crack your breastbone with his rifle butt? Did he do it just to be mean, or did you instigate the matter?"

Brad glanced at the prosecutor. "Answer the question," Prescott told him.

"Well, hell, the man came riding into Guthrie with my pa's dead body draped over a horse. Naturally I was upset—*real* upset! Right then I hated Jake Harkner, so I called him out. I dared him to draw on me."

"You actually were stupid enough to challenge Jake Harkner to a *gunfight*?" Peter asked. "Surely you knew you couldn't possibly beat him."

"He's gettin' old. I figured I could. But before I could draw on him, he swung his rifle around and slammed it against my face and then into my chest and sent me sprawlin' against some barrels. And then he swung the rifle again and held the end of it right against my ear and pulled the trigger. I was layin' there in terrible pain from the gunshot so close to my ear, and I couldn't breathe on account of he knocked the breath out of me. On top of that, he picked me up and threw me off the boardwalk and into the street."

"And did he say anything about why he didn't just shoot you?"

Brad hesitated.

"Mr. Buckley?"

Brad scowled. "He said as how I was young enough to be his son, and he didn't like killin' somebody so young, so he knocked the shit out of me instead."

A few snickers could be heard in the crowd.

"So Jake Harkner had enough good conscience to not want to shoot someone so young, even though he could easily have done so, and had every right to do so, because you were going to draw on him, right?"

Brad pouted. "I reckon."

"No more questions," Peter said. Brad made ready

to rise, but Peter spoke up again. "Oh, by the way, Mr. Buckley—how much do you weigh?"

Brad shrugged. "I'm not sure. Two hundred twenty-five, something like that."

"And you're quite a stocky, strong-looking young man. Yet this man was able to move fast enough to knock the air out of you and keep you from drawing on him, and then was strong enough to throw you into the street like a rag doll. That doesn't sound like an old man to me."

People chuckled.

"I've seen how Jake Harkner is built," Gretta shouted from the balcony, "and he is definitely no old man!"

More laughter. The judge pounded his gavel and ordered Brad to leave the stand. "I think it's best that you also leave the room," the judge added. "You have obviously been planted here to get a rise out of Jake Harkner. And I would like to warn you that you are walking a thin line. One might be led to believe you were in on the shooting that took place—that you planned the whole thing along with Mike Holt."

"I didn't!" Brad objected, suddenly looking very worried. "I mean, Mike told me he wanted to kill Lloyd Harkner, but he never said when or how. I swear it!"

The judge studied him closely. "It sounds to me like you would be wise to stay completely away from Mr. Harkner while you're here in Denver," he told the young man.

"Your Honor," Peter spoke up. "It might be best if Mr. Buckley was escorted completely out of Denver. Mr. Harkner has had his guns taken away from him, and his first thought is always for his family. I know he's worried about what Brad Buckley might try, and it might be better if Mr. Harkner and his family didn't have to worry about the man skulking around in the shadows."

"You can't order me around like that!" Brad protested.

"Yes, we can," the judge told him. "I'm ordering that the bailiff go out and find a couple of policemen who will help you gather your things wherever you are staying, Mr. Buckley, and make sure you get on the next train out of Denver, either east or west, as long as you leave town."

Brad looked ready to explode. He glanced at Jake. "Our time is comin'," he sneered. "I know where to find you!"

"Mr. Buckley, you will leave this courtroom without another word or be arrested for contempt!" the judge shouted. "Bailiff, take that man out of here."

Giving Jake one more scowl, Brad left. The judge looked at Prescott. "Do you have any more witnesses before you question Mr. Harkner?" he asked.

"Yes," Prescott answered. "This is not a hostile witness, obviously, but I have a couple of questions for him. I'd like to call Lloyd Harkner to the stand."

More gasps and whispers moved through the crowd, and Jake grabbed Peter's arm. "What the hell does he want with Lloyd?"

"I don't know." Peter scowled. "Stay calm, Jake."

"I can't!"

Randy felt panic rising. "God, keep him calm," she prayed.

Twenty-seven

"LEAVE MY SON OUT OF THIS!" JAKE SPOKE UP. "HE'S just recovered from the brink of death and is still in pain."

"He made it to this courtroom," Prescott reminded Jake.

Peter rose. "Your Honor, I fail to see why I should allow the prosecution to question someone who is obviously here for the defense," he argued, "let alone the fact that it's a miracle Lloyd Harkner is here at all. He is still far from recovered from a grave wound that should have killed him."

"Your Honor, I don't intend to badger the young man," Prescott retorted. "I just have one or two questions to clear something up about Mike Holt."

"Leave him alone!" Jake repeated. "He's in a lot of pain!"

"It's okay, Pa," Lloyd spoke up. He grimaced as he stood up. Brian rose with him and let Lloyd lean on him as he walked to the stand. Lloyd sat down as people whispered and waited with baited breath to see what Prescott intended to do.

"Lloyd—let's establish that you *are* Lloyd Harkner and that Jake Harkner is your father, right?" Prescott asked.

"Well, Mr. Prescott, look at Jake, and look at me. I don't think there is much doubt about who my father is." A few more people chuckled.

"And when you lived in Oklahoma, you rode with Jake Harkner as a Deputy U.S. Marshal, is that so?"

"I did."

"So you learned a lot on the job, so to speak, from your father?"

Lloyd shrugged. "I already knew a lot about guns and outlaws from when I—" Lloyd hesitated. "I went down the wrong pathway myself for a while after my father went to prison. I never knew about his past, and I was angry and young and stupid. But yes, I learned a lot riding with my father. For over three years we had each other's backs in some pretty dangerous situations." He looked at Jake. "If you're going to be caught going up against a gang of thieves and killers, you can't do any better than to have Jake Harkner backing you up."

"And did your father teach you that it was all right to shoot a man in the back?"

People gasped, and Jake went very still. Lloyd didn't seem at all ruffled. He glared at Prescott, and the room was completely and uncomfortably silent for a few seconds.

"Hell no," Lloyd finally answered. "I'm not even sure my father has *ever* shot a man in the back, so if you're trying to accuse him of that, you're barking up the wrong tree. There isn't a man living who can outdraw my father straight-up! Jake Harkner doesn't *need* to shoot a man in the back!"

"But *you* did, didn't you? Back at Dune Hollow, you shot Mike Holt's brother in the back, and that's why Holt was determined to seek you out and kill you. Fact is, his brother wasn't even armed when you shot him, was he?"

More silence. Jake straightened in his chair, his fists clenched.

Like father, like son, Jeff quickly wrote, observing a sudden darkness in Lloyd's eyes. *When Jake Harkner dies, he won't be gone from this world at all. He'll live on in his son.*

"Answer the question," the judge told Lloyd.

"Yes," he said flatly, "I shot the man in the back, and he was unarmed. He'd given up his weapon, but then he decided to run, and under the law, when you run from a lawman, you risk being shot, so I damn well *shot* him."

"Without hesitation?"

"You bet! He and about fifteen other men had violated my sister in the worst ways, for days, and they tortured my little nephew by burning him with cigarettes—so yeah, I shot the sonofabitch without hesitation! And that was *my* decision, and I was within my rights as a lawman! So don't go trying to make this out to be a father teaching his son to kill, because it's *never* been that way. My father would have preferred I never even *held* a gun, because he knows the heartache that can come with violence. And when it comes to being a father, there isn't a man in here who can hold a candle to Jake Harkner. They don't come any better, and I was proud as hell to ride with him. You got any more questions? Because as far as I know, *I'm* not the one who is the subject of this hearing!"

Evie was softly crying.

"I'm sorry, Evie," Lloyd told her. "I didn't want to bring all that up." He glanced at Brian, who still waited to help Lloyd off the stand. "Go sit with her. I'll make it off this stand just fine on my own." He glared at Prescott as Brian hurried over to sit down next to Evie. He moved an arm around her, and she cried against his shoulder.

"I'd like to take my wife out of here," Brian told the judge.

"No!" Evie straightened. "I want to stay with Daddy until this is over."

People whispered.

"*Daddy?*" someone muttered. "She calls Jake Harkner *Daddy?*"

Evie assured Brian that she was fine, while Randall Prescott slumped a little at the realization that his attempt at making Jake out to be a back-shooting murderer had failed.

The biggest mistake the prosecutor made was to call up a family member, Jeff wrote in his notebook. *I could have told him that. The man's entire family adores him. All Prescott just did was show the kind of father Jake is.*

The judge told Lloyd to step down, but Peter stopped him. "Lloyd, tell the audience what the supposedly ruthless and notorious Jake Harkner has been doing these past three weeks."

Lloyd met Jake's eyes. "He's been taking care of me, night and day, sometimes with no sleep those first few days, or so I'm told. I was passed out most of that time, but I damn well felt my father with me, and I knew he was holding my hand and bathing me and changing my bandages and helping with personal things, because my wife is carrying, and he didn't want her straining herself." He looked at the judge. "But mostly he was doing it out of love for his son. My pa grew up in hell with a father who was Satan himself. When he became a father, I think he just decided to be the kind of father he always wished he'd had. He goes almost overboard loving us sometimes, and he wouldn't allow my mother to ever spank us or even slap our hand, and my sister and I have never hit our own children. Pa would never stand for that."

The room grew quiet again, and Jake squeezed Randy's hand. She knew he was struggling with a myriad of emotions.

"So," Peter spoke up, "I think we have established that the big, bad, ruthless ex-outlaw Jake Harkner is a loving, devoted father and grandfather who has never laid a hand wrongly on his wife or his children or grandchildren. We've also established that he is a faithful husband." He leaned forward and looked over at Jeff. "That man there is Jeff Trubridge, the award-winning reporter from Chicago who wrote the book about Jake that a lot of people in this courtroom have probably read. Jeff rode with Jake for a while when Jake was a lawman. If we're judging character, I'd like to ask Jeff what he thinks of Jake. He's seen both sides of the man—the family man and the, yes, sometimes ruthless lawman."

Jeff rose and faced the judge. "Your Honor, a man

couldn't ask for a better friend than Jake Harkner. It takes the man a while to warm up to you and decide whether or not he trusts you, but once he does, he'll do anything for you, and he has friends out at the J&L who would do anything for *him*. Jake is the most honest, straightforward man I've ever known. I've seen the ruthless side of him, but he'd never hurt an innocent person, and he's a wonderful family man. I'm proud to call him a friend."

The judge sighed and looked at Lloyd. "Go ahead and sit back down with your family," he told him. "Bailiff, come help this man back to his seat."

Lloyd grimaced with pain as he stepped down and walked back to his seat. He sat down next to Katie and moved an arm around her.

"Your Honor," Prescott spoke up, "before all this got out of hand, my questioning of Lloyd Harkner was merely to establish the reason Mike Holt sought him out and shot him. Lloyd Harkner had shot Holt's brother in the back. What Holt did was a crime of passion caused by the kind of ruthless things both Harkner men apparently are capable of. And the fact remains that Jake Harkner had the better of Mike Holt the night of the shooting and could have held him there until the police came, but instead he took the law into his own hands and shot Mike Holt point-blank in front of a crowd of stunned onlookers who'd never seen anything like that before and normally never would in their lifetimes. He is no longer a lawman who can use his badge for his own form of justice, and he needs to learn that being an executioner isn't how it's done in today's times. He should realize some kind of punishment for what he did, and as far as the prosecution is concerned, he should hang or at least go to prison, because when it comes to men like Jake Harkner, this could happen again!"

"Not to an innocent person," Peter answered, rising.

"*All* people are innocent until proven guilty," Prescott shot back.

"Mike Holt served time for being at Dune Hollow," Peter reminded the judge.

"And he was let go early because there was no proof he actually participated in violating Evie Stewart!"

"The man bragged about it to Gretta MacBain! *Bragged* about it! He went so far as to admit he blindfolded the woman first!"

Jake stood up so fast that his chair fell over. "Get my daughter out of here—*now*!" he roared.

"No!" Evie rose. "Let me say something, Judge Carter."

The prosecutor threw up his hands, and the judge sighed, running a hand through his hair. "State your name, please, for the record."

"Evie, don't," Jake said softly.

Evie met his gaze. "I have to." She left her seat and approached the judge's bench. "I am Evita Louise Harkner Stewart, named after my beloved grandmother, Evita Ramona Consuella de Jimenez, who was murdered in front of my father when he was only eight years old— by *his* father."

Jake pushed his way past Peter and walked up to his daughter. "Evie, stop this," Jake told her, putting a hand on her shoulder.

"I'm okay. The judge should understand what you've gone through to become the good man you are now." She faced the judge the whole time she spoke. "My father is a better man than most anyone else in this room. I can tell you *myself* that Mike Holt *was* one of the men who violated me, because I remembered his voice. When you go through what I went through, you *remember* things like that!"

Brian got up and rushed to her side. "Come on, Evie."

"No, wait!" She stood rigidly facing the judge. "The only reason they couldn't prove Mike Holt was one of them is because my father wouldn't let me testify. He knew back then that I couldn't handle it, and he loves me too much to put me through that. But I'm stronger now, and I'm telling you that if I could have testified, I would have told them Mike Holt *was* one of them, which means he would still be in prison. The night of the Cattlemen's Ball, Mike Holt came up to me and threw it all in my face, telling me how much prettier I was without a blindfold over my face!" She wavered a little, and Brian grasped one arm while Jake took hold of the other.

"Evie, *please*," Brian begged.

She ignored him. "Lloyd saw what was happening, and he ran over to get Mike Holt out of there, and Holt pulled a gun on my brother, who was *unarmed*! Holt shot Lloyd in cold blood, and if my father hadn't gotten to him in time, he would have murdered Lloyd for certain, because he had his gun pointed straight at Lloyd's head for a *second* shot! Your first two witnesses failed to mention that. And you want to blame my *father* for shooting that man? What would *any* father do in a situation like this?"

She broke into tears and stumbled. Brian took full hold of her. "Come on. You've had your say, and you need to lie down."

"But I have to know what they decide," she wept.

"You will know one way or another. I'll not take no for an answer, Evie." Brian turned with her to leave, but she stopped to hug her father. Jake embraced her.

"Go on. Do what Brian tells you, Evie. I'll be all right."

"What if this is the last time I get to hug you?" she sobbed.

"It won't be. Please go, Evie. It will be easier for me if you aren't here."

Randy quietly wept, and a few women in the crowd could be heard sniffling.

"Yes, you should leave Mrs....Stewart, is it?" the judge asked.

"Yes," Brian answered. He glanced at Jake. "We'll be at the hotel."

Jake nodded, fighting an urge to strangle Prescott.

"I want everyone else to sit down where they belong," the judge ordered. "What just happened is far beyond protocol for this hearing, and I'll have no more of it."

On his way out with Evie, Brian took Little Jake's hand to take him with them, but the boy jerked away. "No! I wanna be with Grampa!" he insisted, breaking into tears and running over to Prescott, holding up a small fist. "You leave my grampa alone!" he ordered through gritted teeth.

Soft laughter filled the room. Little Jake started to run to Jake, but Prescott grabbed his arm. "You'd better go back and sit where you belong, son," he ordered Little Jake.

Little Jake tugged, and Prescott squeezed tighter.

"Oh my God!" Randy whispered.

"Get your hand off my grandson!" Jake spoke the words calmly but in a low growl.

Brian and Evie turned and froze in place.

The room became completely silent again.

Prescott looked up at Jake and paled at the look in his eyes.

"You have about ten seconds to let go of that boy," Jake warned, "or I'll forget every rule set in this courtroom! My grandson went through enough back at Dune Hollow! Nobody lays a hand on any child related to me! Let go of him!"

Randy reached over and grasped Jeff's arm, squeezing it almost painfully. "Don't do it, Jake," Jeff heard her whisper.

"Prescott, I have a feeling you'd better let go of that boy," the judge advised.

Right now you could hear a piece of dust drop in this room, Jeff scribbled with his left hand while Randy continued to grip his right arm.

Prescott let go of Little Jake and straightened. The boy ran to his grandfather and threw his arms around Jake's hips because he wasn't tall enough to reach his waist. His eyes still on Prescott, Jake picked up his grandson. The boy burst into tears and hugged him around the neck.

Brian and Evie breathed a sigh of relief. "Come on," Brian told his wife softly. "Let's hail a cab and get you back to the hotel."

"I should stay," Evie protested again.

"No. Little Jake is fine with his grandpa. I want you out of here." He gently but forcefully led Evie out of the courtroom.

Jake finally carried Little Jake back to his chair beside Randy. "Little Jake, you can't do this," Jake said quietly. "What did I tell you?"

"I don't care!" the boy cried. "I'm not gonna let them take you away." He clung so tightly to Jake that Jake didn't have the heart to make him let go. He sat down, and Randy reached over to stroke Little Jake's dark hair.

The judge pounded his gavel again. "Mr. Harkner, I believe I'd like you to take the stand. I have a few questions, and then we'll get this over with, but you need to pry that little boy from around your neck first. I promise no one else in this room will touch him."

Jake patted Little Jake's back. "Little Jake, you have to let go, understand?"

"No!"

"Do you love Grandpa?"

"Yes." His slender body jerked in a sob.

"Then let go, Little Jake. Sit on Grandma's lap and be good. If you want to help me, you have to let go."

The boy pulled away, wiping at tears on his cheeks. "Are they gonna shoot you?" he sobbed.

Jake smiled through tears. "No, they won't shoot me. I promise."

"They should give you your guns. *Nobody* can hurt you when you wear your guns, Grampa."

The room rippled with a mixture of soft laughter and women sniffling.

"Well, sometimes they can, but we'll talk about that later. Come on now. Mind what I tell you." Jake moved the boy over to Randy, who took him onto her lap and wrapped her arms around him, kissing his hair.

"It's okay, Little Jake," she told him, looking at Jake with tear-filled eyes. People whispered when Jake leaned over and kissed her, then kissed Little Jake's cheek. He turned to glance down at a note Peter had written. "Our best witness," it read.

Jake grinned and nodded.

"I'm sorry I blurted that out about Evie," Peter told him aside.

"Couldn't be helped." Jake walked around Peter and up to the stand, where the bailiff swore him in. "I *always* speak nothing but the truth," Jake answered. "Anyone who knows me knows I don't waste words or try to hide anything."

A ripple of whispers moved through the crowd, and the judge pounded his gavel again. "Let it be known that I want no further questions from either the prosecutor or from Attorney Brown," he told everyone. "I actually just have a couple of questions, and we'll be finished here. I'm sure Jake's wife is getting tired, and his son is obviously not completely healed yet and needs to rest, so I do not intend to drag this out."

He pounded the gavel again. "Jake, take a seat."

Jake sat down and breathed deeply for self-control, noting the warning look in Peter's eyes. Little Jake's shivers from the aftermath of crying tore at his heart.

"Mr. Harkner, you do admit that the night of the Cattlemen's Ball, you held Mike Holt down on the floor, put your own gun to his head, and pulled the trigger. Is that right?"

Jake kept his eyes on Randy. "That's right."

"Can you tell us in your own words why you did that?"

Jake scanned the crowded room then. "Because the man deliberately upset my precious daughter, who he'd viciously violated four years ago. Then he turned on my son, who was unarmed, and shot him point-blank in the chest. He even said to Lloyd, 'How does it feel to be shot when you're unarmed?' He'd hurt both my daughter and my son in the worst ways. A man can take only so much, and I'm a man who protects his own. It's my nature to go after anyone who dares to harm those I love. My family is my lifeline, my sanity, and my strength. And when I thought Lloyd was dead, all I could think about was that Mike Holt had even taken away my chance to tell my son I love him before he…died. And I truly did think he was dead."

Jake zeroed in on Prescott then. "Holt pointed that gun at Lloyd again, aiming to shoot him in the head and make sure he was dead, but I got there before he could pull the trigger. For a moment I considered holding him there like everyone thinks I should have done, but he pulled back the hammer of his gun to shoot Lloyd again. I grabbed his wrist and pushed up so he couldn't shoot him. His gun went off and went through my left shoulder. I've been in a lot of gunfights, and you have to think lightning fast. I knew that if I fired while Holt was standing, my bullet could go through him and into a bystander, so I shoved him to the floor first. And yes, again I considered not pulling that trigger, but all I could think about was the hideous things he'd done to my daughter—and that he'd just shot my son and deserved to die…so I shot him because he'd taken my son from me."

Randy watched Jake pause to take a deep breath. He swallowed and shifted restlessly, a sure sign he was trying to get through his testimony without going into a rage. She tried to tell him with her eyes to stay calm.

"In that moment it didn't matter if I hung for shooting Holt. I pulled the trigger because I thought I didn't have anything left to live for. Once I realized what I'd done, I knew I might be wanted at least for questioning, but my son-in-law had told me Lloyd was still alive. I couldn't risk being carted off to jail because I knew Lloyd would need me in the worst way, which is why I threatened to shoot anyone who tried to take me away from him. All those years we rode together back in Oklahoma, I always had his back. This time I'd failed him, and I can hardly live with that." He quickly wiped at his eyes and leaned back in the chair. "He went through so much pain we had to hold him down several times, and all I could think of was…it should have been *me* lying there. *Me!* I'm the old one. I'm the father. Sons aren't supposed to…die… before the father. *I'm* the one who deserves to die like that…not my son."

He cleared his throat and shifted in the chair yet again. He glanced at the judge.

"You know the rest. My family is my only reason for existing. I've protected them with my life for years. It's who I am, and there is no changing it. And now all any of us wants is to get the hell out of Denver and back to the J&L and back to normal living…" He stared absently at his hands. "If anything can be called normal when you live with Jake Harkner." He glanced at Lloyd. "It's not an easy name to carry, but my son has brought a lot of pride and respect to the name."

"You've done that yourself, Pa," Lloyd told him.

The judge pounded his gavel again.

"Judge Carter, can I point out just two things before you make your decision?" Peter spoke up.

Carter took a deep breath and leaned back in his chair. For a moment there was nothing but silence in the room. "Make it quick," he finally told Peter.

Peter rose. "Judge, in Guthrie, I managed to get over

three hundred signatures on a petition asking a judge in St. Louis to shorten Jake's original sentence to serve as a marshal in the most god-awful and dangerous country you can imagine. All three hundred of those people agreed Jake had done an excellent job of keeping the peace in the Guthrie area, and believe me, in a lawless place like Oklahoma was then, that wasn't easy. He risked his life over and over, and it cost him and Lloyd a lot of time away from their families. They ended up making enemies that continue to hunt them and try to make trouble for them, which is just what Mike Holt was doing. The point is, three hundred people admired and respected Jake enough to help me petition the judge in St. Louis to shorten his sentence and let the man live in peace. That's all Jake and his wife want—to live in peace now." Peter stood there hesitantly, then finally sat down. "Thank you, Your Honor."

The judge leaned forward then, pausing to weigh his words before finally speaking up. "Ladies and gentlemen, this has been the most unusual hearing I have ever held, unprecedented in some of the things that happened and were said here today, completely disorderly, at times humorous, and at times far from humorous. Through it all I've sat here and watched the love this man's family has for him, and in return, I've sensed the devoted, passionate side of a man whose reputation defies all of that. I believe he is just a man who loves his family beyond measure, but he is also a man who needs to remember we live in a new era of law and order, and that we deal with justice in a different way from the kind Jake Harkner and his son dealt as marshals in Oklahoma. I am giving him the benefit of the doubt only because he grew up in different times…totally lawless times. He was raised knowing only brutality and the outlaw way. For a man to overcome a past like that says a lot about what really lies inside. He has shown himself to be a good family man, a devoted husband, a loving father and grandfather, and a friend to those who earn his respect and those who respect him in return."

He turned to Jake.

"But you have to understand, Jake, that in this day and age, a man can no longer live just by the gun. There are laws and men who are appointed to carry out those laws, and regular citizens have to *abide* by those laws. Is that understood?"

Jake glanced at Randy and Little Jake. "The safety of my family is a different matter."

"I understand that, and I don't believe that you are any kind of danger to the general public. You even considered that when you held Mike Holt down so your bullet wouldn't injure a bystander. That sounds strangely contradictory, I know, but it's a fact. And overall you are well liked by most people and can be quite affable and productive most of the time. The fact remains that you *should* be punished."

The judge hesitated, while everyone waited with baited breath to hear his decision.

Twenty-eight

RANDY THOUGHT SHE MIGHT FAINT FROM TERROR OVER what the judge would say next. She held Little Jake tightly, her gaze locked on Jake, who in turn watched her lovingly, telling her with his eyes how much he loved her, how much he would miss her if he was going to jail…or worse.

Judge Carter shuffled a few papers before finally continuing. "Jake, were you aware that you were not supposed to be carrying a gun at that Cattlemen's Ball?"

Jake sighed and ran a hand through his hair. "Sir, if you were me, would you go anywhere without protection?"

The judge just shook his head. "Probably not, but that's not what I asked you. Did you carry a hidden weapon at that ball when you knew no one was supposed to be armed?"

Jake looked at Peter, who nodded that he should reply truthfully.

"Yes," Jake answered.

"And for that I fine you ten dollars."

Jake looked at him in surprise as mumbles and whispers moved through the crowd. Randy sat up straighter, still clinging to a quivering Little Jake. No one could figure out if the very affordable fine was a good sign or not. Jake glanced at Peter, who just smiled.

The judge reached down and took something out from under his desk, setting a gun belt and ivory-handled guns on top of the desk. The holsters were decorated with white stitching with the letters *JH*. He reached underneath the desk again and took out yet another gun belt and guns. Jake recognized the mahogany handles of Lloyd's guns, and the fancy scrolled *L* on the holsters.

"Now, Mr. Harkner, these, as you can see, are your guns and Lloyd's. Right now they are *not* loaded."

"Well, sir, I hope whoever unloaded them was very careful. Those guns have hair triggers. You could practically fire them with a baby's breath."

More whispers and a few chuckles.

The judge closed his eyes and sighed. "Yes, believe me, they were very careful." He shoved both holsters toward the end of the desk where Jake was sitting. "I said you needed to be sentenced, Jake, so my sentence is another one hundred dollars for threats against the public and against our fine police department the night of the shooting. And for what I consider manslaughter, a year in jail."

"No!" Randy whispered, hugging Little Jake closer when he started crying harder. Peter reached over and grasped her shoulder, pressing reassuringly. Lloyd started to rise, but Katie pulled at his arm. "No, Lloyd!"

The judge pounded his gavel again. "Quiet, everyone!" He sighed deeply. He turned back to Jake. "Mr. Harkner, since you've spent the last few days a virtual prisoner at the Brown Palace, I will consider that time served. As for the rest, since you are obviously needed by your son to help run your ranch while he heals, I order that the rest of your sentence be spent on the J&L."

The crowd broke into whoops and applause, and Jake looked at Lloyd, who had a big grin on his face and tears in his eyes.

The judge again pounded his gavel, and everyone quieted. "Your sentence to stay on the J&L means I don't want to find out that either you or your son have been seen in Denver until the sentence is completed," he continued. "I don't want you back here until it's time to sign you off and release you, which will be July 31, 1897. I will allow you to go to nearby cities like Boulder and Longmont for supplies, but no loitering in saloons or"— he rolled his eyes in frustration—"brothels. The law in those cities will be notified to keep an eye on you if you go there. They will also be notified of the end date of your sentence." He rubbed at his eyes. "And one more thing."

Jake watched Randy, wanting to run over and grab her into his arms. He turned to the judge. "Yes, sir?"

"Mr. Harkner, I want your promise that if you do see one Brad Buckley, even if he comes up to taunt you in any way, you won't shoot the man. Can you refrain from doing that?"

Jake glanced at Lloyd, sharing an equal hatred for Buckley. Lloyd just closed his eyes and shook his head.

"Mr. Harkner?"

Jake glanced at Peter, who gave him a warning nod. "Yes, Your Honor," Jake finally answered. "I agree not to shoot Brad Buckley."

The room hung quiet for a moment as the judge studied Jake. "Why do I get the feeling you are leaving something out?" he asked Jake.

Jake took a moment to answer, scanning the crowd and then his family first. Finally, he turned to the judge. "Well, sir, if Brad Buckley threatens one member of my family, I can't promise I won't beat the hell out of him."

The crowd broke into a round of laughter, and even the judge couldn't help smiling, although he tried forcing it back as he again pounded the gavel. The room quieted again. "Mr. Harkner, you will refrain from bringing harm to Brad Buckley if at all possible. I've ordered him out of Denver, but if he makes trouble, I want you to do your best to hold him so the *law* can take care of him, not you. If he turns up badly beaten or dead, you *will* spend time in prison or possibly even face a noose. Is that understood?"

Jake nodded. He faced the judge. "Am I allowed to discipline men on the J&L who might turn out to be troublemakers? And what about rustlers?"

"Normal discipline is fine. And you will do your best to hold rustlers for the law. You have every right to use your guns in self-defense, but not for taking the law into your own hands. Is that understood?"

"Yes, sir."

"Now"—the judge shoved Jake's and Lloyd's guns even closer to Jake—"take your guns and go home, Mr. Harkner."

The crowd broke into cheers and whistles. Randy couldn't help breaking down with relief. She hugged Little Jake closer.

"Just a moment!" the judge yelled, pounding his gavel again for attention. He turned to Jake. "Mr. Harkner, your best defense today was that beautiful family sitting over there. No man who is responsible for a family like that can be all bad, and today they might just have saved your life."

Jake fought a desire to run off the stand and go grab up every last one of them. "I am well aware of that, Judge."

"And I have one last question."

Jake faced him. "Yes?"

"I want to know how a man like you—who was wanted for any number of crimes, a man who had his face on wanted posters all over the South, who'd robbed and killed and ran with loose women and God knows what all you did—how did you end up with a beautiful, sophisticated, obviously well-educated and fashionable woman like that tiny, lovely lady over there holding your grandson?"

Randy smiled through her tears, looking at Jake lovingly. Their gazes held for several quiet seconds.

"Well, Your Honor, I met her thirty years ago in a dry goods store back in Kansas City, where I had a shoot-out with a bounty hunter that scared her so bad she pulled a gun out of her purse…and shot me. Damned if I didn't fall in love with her then and there."

It took a moment for the crowd to realize he was telling the truth.

"You shot Grampa?" Little Jake blurted out to Randy.

The crowd burst into an uproar of laughter. The judge looked at Jake. "Give me one hundred and ten dollars, and take these guns and go home, Jake."

Jake rose and shook the judge's hand while the rest of the family hugged each other. Jake took the money out of his pants pocket and paid the judge, glancing over to see Little Jake had climbed off Randy's lap, and Randy was embracing Peter. That little stab of sorrow that she could have married better hit him again, along with the lingering jealousy that Peter Brown did all this for her because he was still in love with her.

Flash powder exploded as Jake strapped on his guns. Little Jake ran up to him, jumping up and down. As soon as Jake buckled his gun belt, he picked up his grandson, who practically choked Jake when he hugged him tightly around the neck.

Lloyd stood up and managed to walk on his own to greet his father as Jake came off the stand still holding Little Jake. With the boy in his arms, Jake reached out and embraced Lloyd, both men hugging for a long minute.

More flash powder exploded, and a reporter scrambled to reload powder for more pictures, which he managed to do several more times throughout the courthouse bedlam.

"Let's go home, Pa, soon as we can," Lloyd told Jake, keeping an arm around his father.

"I've got no argument there," Jake told him. Katie came up, and Lloyd embraced her. By then Randy was close enough that Jake set Little Jake down and pulled her into his arms. She buried her face against his chest.

"Oh, Jake, I can't believe it!"

"*You* did it, *mi amor*. You and the big, beautiful family you've given me." He kissed her hair, her cheek, her eyes, her lips. "I love you, Randy Harkner. Do you know how much?"

"Not as much as I love you." In seconds, they were joined by Stephen and Ben, both boys also crying. Jake reluctantly let go of Randy and took a moment to hug both boys and tell them everything would be all right now. Little Jake reached up, insisting that Jake pick him up again. He locked his arms around Jake's neck as Jake shook hands with Pepper and Cole.

"We're ready to head for the J&L as soon as you are, Jake," Pepper told him. "It's gonna feel real good to be back home, ain't it?"

"It sure is!" Jake answered.

Once the group hugs were over, Peter and Jeff joined in the moment. Randy turned to embrace Peter again. "Thank you so much, Peter. It was so good of you to come all the way here from Chicago." Jake kept hold of Little Jake, watching with mixed emotions.

Peter let go of Randy and kissed her cheek, looking at her lovingly. Jake caught the look before Peter managed to wipe it off his face. "I'm just happy for both of you and greatly relieved," Peter told Randy. He looked up at Jake. "I hope you know I mean that. I wanted this for you, too, Jake. I wasn't sure how this would turn out, but I had a feeling all along that Judge Carter was on your side. You and that beautiful family of yours won him over."

Jake set Little Jake on his feet and shook Peter's hand vigorously. "I don't know how to thank you, Peter. I'll pay you whatever you say I owe you, and you have to come visit us at the J&L—you and Jeff both, along with your wives. Our men will give them a royal escort to the ranch in complete safety. We'll have the biggest barbecue you've ever attended, and you'll taste the best beef in Colorado and see the prettiest piece of land in this whole state."

"I'll remember the invitation," Peter told him.

"You can come back with us now if you want," Jake told him.

Peter glanced at Randy, who was hugging Lloyd. He turned back to Jake. "For reasons you probably understand, I'd better get back to Chicago for now. I have a wife there waiting for me."

"Then I want your promise you'll come back with Treena," Jake told him.

"I'll do that. Right now I have some paperwork to file. Come back here to the courthouse in the morning before you head for the J&L, and I'll have a few things for you to sign."

Jake nodded, shaking his hand again. "You're a good man, Peter. One of the best, and you know why I hate saying that."

"Well, Jake, I hate having to say the same about you, but you have a way of growing on people. I respect your ability to survive and rise above some bad situations. I've come to know the man down under all the bravado." He squeezed Jake's hand harder. "I know I don't need to tell you to take good care of Randy, but I'm telling you anyway."

Little Jake was running in circles, shouting about going home. Jake kept his eyes on Peter. "I'd die for her, and you know it."

Sadness wafted across Peter's gaze. "I damn well do know it." He turned away, and Jake turned to Jeff, who'd just finished scribbling more notes and waited anxiously to shake Jake's hand and congratulate him.

"I'll come to the J&L again sometime after my wife has our baby," he told Jake.

Jake wouldn't settle for just a handshake. He gave Jeff a full hug and slapped him on the back again. "Jeff, my loyal Jewish friend, what can I say? I appreciate what you told that judge. And as far as the verdict, it's just what Evie prayed for all night. Has she converted you to Christianity yet?"

Jeff laughed. "I stay away from her as much as I can because I'm worried she'll manage to do just that, which would greatly shock my family."

Jake laughed and moved an arm around Randy, pulling her close.

"That daughter of yours has some powerful faith," Jeff added, sobering a little.

Jake felt a keen stab of pain to his heart. "That she does. It *takes* a lot of faith to pray for the likes of me." He ached at what Evie went through earlier, loving her even more for the proud way she told the judge her name and the way she honored the grandmother she never knew. He pulled Randy even closer. "Speaking of Evie, we'd better get to the hotel and tell her what's happened."

Bedlam followed as Lloyd grabbed his guns from the judge's bench and joined the rest of the family as they headed out of the courthouse. Jake spotted Gretta and called her over. With one arm still around Randy, he bent down and planted a long kiss on Gretta's lips. Men hooted, and women just shook their heads.

"Jake Harkner, you told me you only kiss your wife that way," Gretta teased, patting him on the cheek.

Jake never let up on his grip around Randy. "This is a special occasion," he told Gretta, "and you spoke up for me. I won't forget that."

"Hell, if I'd known it would lead to a kiss like that, I'd have said a lot more and made it worth *two* kisses!" Men around them roared in laughter.

"Come see me the next time you're in Denver, handsome," Gretta told Jake, jokingly swaying her hips as she walked away and invited men to come with her to the Range Club to celebrate Jake Harkner's release.

Jake grinned and shook his head, heading out with Randy. He noticed Evie hurrying toward him.

"Daddy, is it true? You can come home with us?"

Jake kept Randy in one arm and embraced Evie with the other. "What the hell are you doing here? You're supposed to be back at the hotel."

"I couldn't leave, Daddy! I just couldn't. I made Brian let me wait outside on the steps."

Jake hugged her close, kissing her hair. "You shouldn't have done what you did, angel. It wasn't necessary. I didn't want you to go through that."

"But it *was* necessary," she argued. Tall like her brother, she didn't have to stand on tiptoes to hug Jake. "I think God wanted me to speak up, Daddy. He's the one who gave me the courage and put the words in my mouth. I'm okay. Really."

Jake glanced at Brian. "I'm damn sorry, Brian. I didn't want her to do this."

Brian touched her shoulder. "I tried to get her to the hotel, but far be it for me to be able to stop her when she makes up her mind. We both know where she gets that from."

"My daughter is a brave, strong, determined young woman!"

"Yeah, well, I've never been able to say no to her since the day I met her." Brian gently pried her away from Jake. "Come on, honey, come back to the hotel with me."

They were outside on the steps by then, and Jake whistled for a cab. "I want Evie and Katie and Lloyd to go back in a buggy. All three of them should get some rest and *stay* in bed the rest of the night." He grasped Randy's arm. "Do you want to go back with them?"

"No, I want to stay right here with you. And the kids can all walk with us."

Brian climbed into the enclosed cab with the two

women and Lloyd. The buggy pulled away, and people continued to mingle around Jake and Randy.

"Grampa has his guns now!" Little Jake bragged. "Nobody can take him away now!"

People laughed, and Jake picked the boy up again. Randy walked ahead of him with her arms around Ben and Stephen. Pepper and Cole walked on either side, keeping a lookout for anyone who might decide to make a name for themselves, namely one Brad Buckley.

Jeff walked briskly behind all of them. *No jail time for Jake Harkner!* he wrote. He considered what just the right headline should be. He would wire the news to every newspaper he could right away. "Jake, I'll meet up with you and the family tomorrow morning," he told Jake. "All of you need some time alone."

"You be sure to come out to the J&L as soon as your wife can travel," Jake answered. "And if you and the wife need help in any way sometime, you let me know, and I'll damn well come to Chicago."

"It's the same for me, Jake. You know that, but I'm not so sure you should come to a big city again," Jeff joked.

"Yeah, well, you don't fit the J&L any more than I fit into a city!" Jake shot back.

Jeff laughed. "After riding with you for all those weeks in Oklahoma? Hell, I'm a real cowboy now. I'll come out to the ranch, and you can teach me how to wrangle down a calf for branding."

Jake laughed harder. "Please do! That is something the boys would definitely want to watch!"

"Then by God, I'll come out and do just that!" He shook Jake's hand again, sobering. "You're the best friend a man could have, Jake. I've never met anybody quite like you. I meant what I told the judge."

Jake squeezed his hand. "You're a damn good friend yourself."

Jeff nodded and let go. "I'd better get this news on the wire. You're good for my career, Jake."

Jake grinned. "Nice to know I'm good for *something*." He turned to join the rest of the family in their walk back to the hotel. He answered questions and joked with others the whole way, finally setting Little Jake down. The boy ran to catch up with his grandmother while Jake lit a cigarette and took a deep drag on the smoke, secretly thanking God for his freedom. *I don't know why You keep getting me out of trouble*, he prayed. *I'm sure you did it for Evie.*

He watched Randy walking ahead of him, loved the yellow dress she wore and the gentle sway to her hips. He'd never loved her more than at this moment, for all she'd gone through to give him this beautiful family he didn't deserve.

There was a time when he didn't have a clue what love was about. Little Jake ran back to him, and it hit Jake that the boy seemed the epitome of the love he'd never known at that age. He drew on the cigarette again, shaking off ugly memories as he picked Little Jake up while keeping the cigarette between his lips.

"Can I smoke, Grampa?"

"Hell no!"

"*You* smoke."

Jake scowled at him. "Little Jake, you and I need to have a good talk. I absolutely do not want you trying to be like your grampa in all the wrong ways."

"Mommy says I should be proud you're my grampa."

"Yeah, well, your mommy sees a lot of things through rose-colored glasses."

Little Jake frowned. "Mommy doesn't wear glasses."

"I'm talking about Mommy thinking everybody is good."

"Aren't *you* good?"

Jake shifted him to one arm and took another drag on the cigarette before taking it from his lips. "I'm good to grandsons who mind me. That means you can't smoke, and you can't say bad words in front of your mother. She is a very special woman with a big heart and a special faith, and she doesn't like hearing bad words."

"Sometimes you say sonofabitch in front of her."

"Yeah, well, I try real hard to watch what I say around your mother, but I grew up hearing bad words, and nobody taught me not to say them, so now they come out of my mouth sometimes when I don't want them to. You are young enough to start teaching yourself right now to watch what you say in front of nice people."

Little Jake scowled. "Did you really kill your daddy like that man said in the courthouse?"

Jake set him on his feet and crouched in front of him, tossing his cigarette aside. "Little Jake, that's a long story, and it's not something we can talk about right now, okay? I promise to explain another time."

Little Jake touched his face. "Was he real mean like Ben's daddy was?"

Jake struggled with memories that once would have taken him into hell's darkness. "He was a thousand times worse, Little Jake. Some people don't know anything about love." He kissed the boy's cheek. "Not like I love you and your daddy and mommy and Lloyd and this whole family. We all know about love, don't we?"

Little Jake nodded, throwing his arms around his grandfather's neck again. "I'm sorry he was mean to you, Grampa."

Jake rose and tucked the boy under one arm as they walked, causing Little Jake to squeal with glee at hanging off his grandpa's side like a sack of potatoes. Jake couldn't help wondering what it might have been like to have a father who'd loved him.

He took a deep breath and forced back the black memories, noticing Randy was surrounded by women asking questions. He set Little Jake down and told him to go walk with Stephen and Ben and not let go of their hands. He hurried closer to Randy, putting an arm around her. "Ladies, my wife is done answering questions. Thank you for your concern."

"Thank you," Randy told him, putting an arm around his back. "Jake, I can't believe we walked out of that courthouse together."

He leaned down and kissed her lightly. "I'm sure it's due mostly to the power of our daughter's prayers." He decided not to mention Little Jake's question about Jake's father. He was determined not to think about that now. This was a time for happiness. He swept Randy up into his arms. "Let's get to our room, woman. We have a private celebration ahead of us!"

❧

At the railroad station, Brad Buckley, holding a hastily packed carpetbag, watched a young man run through the crowd.

"Did you hear?" the boy shouted. "That judge let Jake Harkner off and told him to go home!"

Several people in the crowd whistled and cheered. Brad watched from the steps to the passenger car he was boarding.

"Goddamn lucky sonofabitch!" he grumbled through gritted teeth. He climbed the steps and went inside, taking a seat. *I'll still find a way to make you pay for killing my father, Jake Harkner! I'll do it right under your nose, and you won't be able to do a damn thing about it, because if they find me dead, you'll hang!*

Twenty-nine

KATIE HELPED LLOYD UNDRESS, PULLING OFF HIS SHIRT. She ached at the bandages still wrapped around his chest. She hated the thought that there would be a scar, yet he was still so magnificent in every other way and getting stronger every day. "I hope this is our last night in this hotel room," she told him.

Lloyd sat down. "You aren't the only one."

Katie removed his boots and socks. "Stand back up, and I'll help you get these pants off," Katie told him.

Lloyd rose and unbuckled his belt. "I hate needing help."

"Of course you do. Men like you are used to doing for yourselves." Katie pulled off his denim pants, and he stepped out of them.

Suddenly, Katie couldn't get back up. It hit her then that she'd almost lost him. She could easily be a widow now instead of having her husband standing here in front of her, walking and talking and breathing. The trying day caught up with her, and she covered her face and wept.

"Baby, don't," Lloyd told her. He reached down and helped her to her feet, then pulled her into his arms and pressed her close.

"I'm afraid I'll hurt you!" she wept.

"You won't hurt me." He led her to the bed. "Lie down beside me, Katie. I want to start sleeping with you again. I miss you beside me at night."

"We can't—"

"Yes we can." He scooted onto the bed and kept an arm around her middle, wrapping her into his arms.

"Sometimes I wake up in the middle of the night and see you sleeping on that damn cot all alone, and it drives me crazy," he told her.

Katie couldn't stop the tears. "Oh, Lloyd, when I saw you go down that night…" She curled against him. "I thought my life was over! I've tried to be strong through all of this, but it's so hard."

"You've been wonderful. God, Katie, we've hardly talked, and you've been through so much. I was so afraid you'd lose the baby."

"For those first few days, I thought the baby would be all I had left of you."

"Well, I'm here now, and it won't be long before I can show you I'm back in every way." He met her mouth in a long, deep kiss, then moved his lips to her eyes again, licking at her tears. "Don't cry, Katie. Everything will be all right now. We'll go home to the J&L and our baby girl and our own bed, and we'll pick up where we left off the last time we made love in that bed." He moved his lips down to kiss at the lovely mounds where her breasts peeked above the bodice of her dress.

Someone tapped at the door. "You two need anything tonight?"

It was Jake.

"Hell no!" Lloyd answered. Katie laughed again, and he pulled her closer, moving one leg over her. "Go away!" Lloyd added. "I've been looking at your ugly mug every day for over three weeks, Pa. I'm looking at someone prettier right now, and if you come in here, I'll fire you from the J&L!"

He heard his father laugh as Katie pushed at him and chided him for the remark.

"You couldn't run that place without me," Jake answered.

Lloyd rocked Katie in his arms. "Watch me try!" He and Katie both broke into more laughter, and Lloyd quickly yanked part of the covers over them. "All you have to do is come through that door, and you'll have to find a new place to live!"

Jake laughed again. "You two had better be able to get up in the morning because we're leaving for the J&L. I'm not staying in this damn dirty city one more day. I'm ready for some fresh air."

"Hell, I'll leave tonight if you want to," Lloyd answered. "Fine with me."

"Get some rest," Jake ordered. "*Both* of you! Don't overdo anything."

"Just go pay some attention to my poor mother!" Lloyd teased. "And if I were you, I'd kiss her the way you kissed Gretta MacBain earlier, or *she* might kick you out. Mom needs your attention way more than I do."

Outside the door, Jake smiled and breathed a deep sigh of relief. "You're damn right there," he muttered. He turned, a lump in his throat at the fact that his son was alive and back to his jabbing remarks, which meant he was definitely getting better. He went to his own room, going inside to see Randy removing her hat.

"Our son is healing fast." He closed the door.

Randy walked over and helped him take off his suit jacket.

"Jake, ever since we got back here and all through dinner, you didn't tell me what it did to you to have that prosecutor practically scream out that you killed your own father. Are you all right?"

"I'm fine." He finished unbuttoning the shirt himself. "I'm glad Ben and Stephen already knew, so they weren't shocked. When we were walking back, Little Jake asked me if it was true. I told him I'd talk to him about it another time but that some people just don't know how to love. I think he's okay with it for now, but I definitely need to explain more to him. Right now, he just thinks my father was a really mean man like Ben's father was." He pulled off his shirt. "Ben's father was a saint compared to mine," he added with obvious venom. He looked Randy over. "My God, you're beautiful. Have I told you that yet today?" He walked up to her and moved one finger down into her cleavage. "I love this spot." He leaned down and kissed her there.

"Jake, you are deliberately changing the subject."

He walked her backward toward the bed. "The way this dress fits every beautiful curve of your body drove me crazy all day today. I kept wondering if I'd ever get to take it off you."

"Jake Harkner, if you need to talk about things that were said today, then talk about it. I know what it must have done to you when Little Jake asked about your father."

"I *don't* need to talk about it." He pulled her full onto the bed. "I just want to celebrate the way that hearing went and enjoy the fact that I am free to be with my wife tonight in our own bed in our own hotel room—and that we're free to go home."

Randy stroked his hair away from his face. "Are you sure you're all right?"

"I'm sure." He leaned down and covered her mouth with his in a searching kiss, grasping her hair at the back in a strong, commanding grip. He moved his lips to behind her ear. "I've wanted to kiss you like this all day."

"Oh?" She playfully pushed him away. "That was a pretty good kiss you planted on Gretta MacBain's lips earlier."

Jake grinned, grasping her shoulders and turning her over to unbutton her dress. "For your information, she wanted me to kiss her in the back room of that clothing store, but I refused. Then I figured after the way she stood up for me today, she deserved that kiss. Call it compensation for her services."

"Compensation? Are your kisses worth money now?"

Jake laughed. "I don't know. You tell me." He continued releasing button after button.

"Well, I can think of a lot of women who would gladly pay for the chance to kiss the notorious Jake Harkner. They are all curious to know what it's like."

He got off the bed. "Stay right where you are."

She lay facedown as he yanked the dress down over her shoulders. "And what do *you* say those kisses are worth?" He jerked the dress down over her hips and threw it over a chair, then pulled off her slips.

"Well, I always get those kisses for free, so I wouldn't know how to put a price on them," Randy quipped.

Jake pulled off her shoes, then pulled down her stockings. "Free?" He yanked off her underwear, down over her feet, then kissed the back of her legs. Randy shivered when his kisses trailed up to her backside. "My God, you still have the prettiest bottom," he said softly. More kisses. "It's perfectly round and small, and it drives me crazy." He rolled her over and began unlacing her camisole. "Baby, you don't get my kisses for free. You pay for them every time with this beautiful body."

"Well, whatever they cost, I'll gladly pay for it—for *your* services."

He kissed her hard and deep, stroking her legs, her bottom, between her legs, over her belly, up to her breasts as her camisole spilled open. He pulled her to a sitting position and tossed the camisole to the floor.

"Are you saying you're paying for *stud* services?"

Randy reached up and began pulling pins from her hair as he got off the bed to finish undressing. "Something like that. Right now, just touching you and knowing you're here and free is thrilling enough in itself. I'm so happy, Jake! I just want to be sure you don't go into that dark place over things that were said today."

"I am very much in the light, Mrs. Harkner. And right

now all I want is to be inside you. Just give me a minute to get the rest of these clothes off."

Randy shook out her hair. "Oh, I am enjoying the show, Mr. Harkner." She scooted farther back on the bed and wrapped her arms over her breasts. "Are you sure you don't mind that these breasts aren't so perky anymore?"

"Baby, your breasts are beautiful and full, and the best part is they belong just to me." He shed the rest of his clothes and climbed back onto the bed, pulling her down underneath him and reaching under her hips. "So does this sweet bottom."

Randy breathed deeply. It seemed everything about her husband was still big and hard, yet he could be so gentle it seemed to defy his size and the ruthlessness he could sometimes show others. He was all over her then, hands and lips touching and caressing and tasting, rolling her over to again kiss her bottom. He massaged her back to work out the tenseness of the day, then turned her back over, sending desire through her blood as he kissed at her neck, her breasts, her belly, down to secret places. She became totally lost in the need to please this man she had no right falling in love with all those years ago. This man she couldn't even begin to imagine living without.

She cried out his name in an almost painful climax and grasped his hair as he worked his lips back over her belly to her breasts and finally her mouth.

"Do you know how much I love you?" he asked between kisses.

"It had better be a lot for me to let you do such disrespectful things to me."

Jake grinned. "I love your wicked side." He searched her mouth, trailed his lips to her throat, then began kissing her everywhere again—her eyes, her ears, her neck, between her breasts, her nipples, her belly, back down to press his tongue against her swollen, aching privates to refresh her climax, teasing her in a way that made her mad with the want of him.

"You didn't get enough of this last night?" she teased in a groaning whisper as he kissed his way back to her throat.

"That was desperate, terrified lovemaking, and I wasn't gentle with you," he answered. "I'm sorry, *mi esposa.*"

"Right now I don't *want* you to be gentle." She leaned up and kissed his chest. "And if you don't get inside of me right this minute, I'm going to die of frustration. You are deliberately making me crazy."

Jake kissed her again as he entered her, grasping her bottom and shoving deep. He groaned from the most intense love and satisfaction he'd felt in a long time.

"Jake, you're really here!" Randy couldn't help the tears as she wrapped her arms around his neck and cried out with the agony and the ecstasy of having him inside of her, filling her deep and hard. Always there was the terror inside her that she might lose him. He grasped her hair and moved in a gentle rhythm until finally he groaned with his own climax, wondering how a man could make love to the same woman for so many years and still find it so satisfying.

He knew the answer, and it wasn't just because she was so beautiful on the outside. It was because she was so beautiful on the inside…because she'd loved the unlovable…because she'd forgiven the unforgivable… because she'd waded through hell with him and never once complained…because she'd taught him about this glorious thing called love.

He held her close. "I've decided not to wait another day," he told her. "Let's head home tomorrow. Lloyd is well enough to at least ride in the buggy or in the covered wagon, and Brian can take care of changing his bandages and keeping an eye on that wound. Besides, the best medicine for him is what's probably going on in that room next door right now. Going back to the J&L will heal him even faster."

"Oh, yes, let's go home: to our beautiful little grand-daughters who must wonder if we're ever coming back, to the valleys and the mountains and the horses and the cattle and that big log home and our own bed." Randy ran her hands over his firm biceps and into his hair, drawing him down to meet her mouth in another delicious kiss. She smiled when the kiss ended. "I guess I *would* pay for these kisses if I had to."

"Oh, you'll pay, all right." Jake moved inside her again. "Get set for a wild ride, baby," he told her, "and I don't mean tomorrow on a horse."

Thirty

BEN AND STEPHEN RODE IN CIRCLES, CHASING EACH other off and on as the whole family headed home after disembarking a train at Boulder. The horses that originally brought them to Denver, along with the wagons and buggy, had also been loaded onto the train so the family could bring everything back home. Now they were on Harkner land, wagons, buggy, horses, and all, heading for home and family and peace. Jake, Lloyd, Cole, and Pepper had their own mounts, and Lloyd bought two more horses in Boulder so the boys could ride. All three women and Lloyd rode in the buggy with Brian driving, and Cole drove the covered wagon.

Today was warm and sunny. Lloyd asked the women to put down the folding top of the carriage for a better view. They were getting close to home base, and he wanted to drink in the sight.

Little Jake rode with his grandfather, and he seldom left Jake's side when off the horse. When they passed Fire Valley, the boy insisted on getting down to collect a few rocks. Jake had to dismount and yank him back from peering a bit too far over one area that had a steep, rocky drop-off.

"Little Jake, do I have to tie you to a tree to keep you from doing these crazy things?" He plunked the boy back onto his horse.

"That's my valley, Grampa—all that great big hole with all that yellow grass."

Jake remounted. "Who told you that?"

"Mommy told me. She said someday her and Daddy would rename it Little Jake's Valley." He yelled to Evie. "Didn't you, Mommy? You and Daddy said this was my valley."

Evie smiled. "We haven't discussed that with your uncle Lloyd yet."

"Your mother can call this valley anything she wants," Lloyd called to the boy.

"I think there is gold in it," Little Jake shouted in reply. "Maybe me and Grampa will find it together."

"And maybe we'll just stick to ranching," Jake told him, pressing him close. "Grandpa has climbed around enough rugged places like that and slept on the ground off and on for too many years, Little Jake. I prefer the comforts of home."

"Aw, you're tough, Grampa," the boy answered, holding up a fist. "Did you use places like that to hide out when you were an outlaw?"

Jake just shook his head. "We definitely need to talk."

"Go fast, Grampa! Catch up with Ben and Stevie!"

Jake kicked the horse into a faster lope, and Evie shook her head. "Mother, that boy might as well live with you and Daddy full-time so Daddy can have complete control of him. He wants to be just like Daddy, including being an outlaw."

"Jake will straighten him out," Randy answered. "He's just a little boy who sees his grandfather as a hero and doesn't understand how bad it really was for Jake." She took her daughter's hand. "Don't worry, Evie. Little Jake has your goodness in him, and three good men in Brian and Lloyd and Jake to teach him how to be an equally good man."

"First we have to cure him of cussing and wanting to smoke," Lloyd spoke up.

"Oh, and you and Daddy are great examples," Evie teased.

"Sure we are," Lloyd answered, "although right now I could use a cigarette."

They laughed, and Randy couldn't remember feeling happier. She reached into the back seat and grasped Lloyd's arm. "We're going home, Lloyd. It feels so good to be on J&L land!"

"It sure does." Lloyd yelled out to Pepper, who rode nearby, "Saddle me a horse, Pepper!"

"Lloyd, no!" Katie objected. "You aren't strong enough yet."

"I damn well am! Stop the carriage, Brian."

"Lloyd, you really shouldn't—"

"I can't think of a better cure!"

Reluctantly, Brian halted the carriage, and Lloyd climbed out. "Give me *your* horse, Pepper! Go saddle one of the extras for yourself. There are two new saddles in the supply wagon anyway, and they need breaking in."

"You sure about this?" Pepper climbed down.

"Damn sure!" Lloyd stepped into the stirrup. Grimacing with pain, he mounted Pepper's big roan mare.

"Lloyd, please be careful," Katie called out.

Lloyd took the leather tie from where his hair was wrapped into a tail at his neck. He shook out his hair. "Thanks, Pepper!" he yelled as he rode off to catch up with Jake, letting out an Indian-like war whoop.

"Oh, Brian, do you think he should be doing that?" Evie asked her husband.

"He's a Harkner." Brian turned to meet her gaze. "Have I ever been able to stop *you*, or even Little Jake from having your way?"

Evie smiled. She leaned over and kissed his cheek. "And you are the most patient man on the face of the earth. Do you know how much I love you?"

Brian wouldn't let her get away with just a peck on the cheek. "I think I do." He grasped the back of her neck and kissed her warmly on the lips.

"Would you two like to go ride inside the covered wagon?" Katie teased.

Evie smiled, grasping Brian's arm as he snapped the reins to get the buggy moving again. "We can wait till we reach home. I can't think of anything more wonderful than being in our own house tonight, can you, Mother?"

"No, I can't, Evie." She watched Lloyd catch up to Jake, getting more anxious to reach her own home and to bake bread again and hold her beautiful granddaughters and have the whole family together. She watched Jake turn his horse to greet Lloyd. They exchanged words, and she knew Jake was likely telling Lloyd he shouldn't be on a horse yet. Ben and Stephen caught up with the men, and they all rode side by side, Little Jake still riding proudly with his grandfather.

"Those boys are turning into men," Randy told Katie. "I think Stephen will be tall like his father, and I'll bet Little Jake won't be so little in a few years."

"What a sight," Katie answered. "I hope Lloyd will be okay."

"I think getting on a horse and heading home is better medicine than anything else could possibly be," Randy told her.

For the next two hours, they rode over rolling foot-hills, cattle grazing here and there in scenes that seemed more like paintings. Anxious to reach home before dark, they didn't stop to eat or take breaks. Even though it was late July, the surrounding mountains still showed white caps, some of the snow streaking down into deep, still-cold purple crevasses. The tree line of dark pine and white aspen decorated the mountainsides in colorful glory. Before them lay a sea of green and yellow grass, and here and there huge boulders lay piled up as though God had taken them from the nearby mountains and placed them there by hand. Wildflowers in red and purple were

scattered everywhere, and the sun came out to light up
the colors in a welcoming scene that had never looked so
good. They crested a rise…and there it was.

Home!

"Oh, Mother, what a sight!" Evie exclaimed.

Below lay the three homes, the biggest one nestled
into pines at the edge of the valley. There were the white
clapboard outbuildings, the bunkhouse, fenced corrals
with beautiful horses running around in some of them,
old Gus grazing in another corral, a few milk cows with
calves scattered here and there.

"Yee-haw!" Pepper shouted, charging past them to
catch up with Jake and Lloyd, who along with the boys
were already riding hard down the hill toward the valley,
all of them yipping like Indians. Some of the men below
mounted horses and rode out to greet them.

Randy put a hand over her mouth and cried.
Shopping and fancy balls and going to the opera meant
nothing compared to this. She was sure Peter's mansion
of a home in Chicago couldn't compare either…not to
this. Her log home was just as much a castle as any in
Europe, and the J&L was their own personal kingdom.

"Mother, this is God's creation. It's not like anything
man can build, is it?"

Randy could barely talk. They were home. Jake was
free. Lloyd was actually well enough to ride a horse. And
now, even from the distance as Brian drove the buggy
downhill, she could see two little girls running from the
main house to greet their grandfather.

Brian drove the buggy through the main gate, over
which hung the sign *J&L RANCH*, and underneath *Jake
and Lloyd Harkner, Owners*.

"Let me out, Brian," Randy told her son-in-law.

Brian slowed the buggy to a halt.

"Mother, you're crying!" Evie exclaimed.

Katie moved an arm around Randy. "She's just

happy. You want to walk in the rest of the way, don't you, Mom?"

Randy nodded, not quite able to find her voice.

"I'll walk with you."

Katie and Randy climbed out, and Brian drove the buggy slowly beside them. Moments later, Jake and Lloyd turned their horses and started riding back toward them, each of them with a little girl in his arms. Little Jake had stayed below to go to the barn and get his own horse.

"Mommy! Mommy!" Both girls were squealing the word. Jake stopped and left Sadie off with Evie, who pulled the dark-haired little girl into the seat between her and Brian. Lloyd rode up to meet Katie, Tricia's bright red hair such a stark contrast to her father's dark skin and long black hair it was almost comical. No one who didn't know better would ever believe the girl belonged to Lloyd. Katie reached up and took Tricia into her arms, and the little girl wrapped her arms around Katie's neck.

"Come on up, and I'll ride both of you down," Lloyd told Katie with a grin.

"Lloyd, you'd better get off that horse and lie down as soon as you get to the house," Randy told him. She thought how happy he looked, but he needed to gain some weight, and right now, she could see pain in his eyes.

"Well, this time I'm not going to argue with you, Mom," he told her. "I'm feeling pretty shaky at the moment. Pepper is coming over to help with Katie. I just want to ride in together."

Pepper reached them and dismounted to lift Katie up behind Lloyd. He handed up Tricia, and Lloyd turned the horse to head back down the hill at a slow walk.

Randy saw Jake coming closer. He rode up to her and reached down. "How about a ride the rest of the way in with your husband?"

Randy smiled through tears. "Gladly." She reached up, and Jake lifted her as though she weighed nothing.

She settled in behind him, wrapping her arms around him and resting her head against his back. "Jake, I can hardly believe we're back home. I don't want to go into a city as big as Denver again for a long time."

"Well, for the next year we don't have much choice. I'll settle for Longmont and Boulder. Pepper and some of the others can take the cattle in next summer." Jake turned the horse and headed down. "Damn pretty sight, isn't it?"

"I've never appreciated home more. The J&L is everything we dreamed about for so many years."

Jake wished he knew for sure what had happened to Brad Buckley. Jeff had promised to wire Guthrie and tell friends to get a message to Jake if Brad showed up there. Right now, at this very special moment, he wasn't about to bring up Brad Buckley in front of anyone in the family, but he knew Lloyd was just as concerned.

He ran a hand over the arms Randy wrapped around him. "I've never loved you more. That big bed in the loft is going to be well used tonight."

Randy smiled and hugged him tighter. "We'll see."

"We'll see? What does that mean, woman?"

"It means I'm very tired." She rested her head against his back.

"Then we'll just *sleep* in that bed."

Randy smiled more. "We'll see."

PART THREE

PART THREE

Thirty-one

> *"Rock of ages, cleft for me, let me hide myself in Thee.*
> *Let the water and the blood from Thy wounded side*
>   *which flowed,*
> *Be of sin, the double cure, save from wrath and make*
>   *me pure."*

EVIE FINISHED THE HYMN BEFORE PRAYING. THE
gathering for at least one hymn and prayer had become
a Sunday ritual for the family ever since living close in
Guthrie—a big dinner, usually chicken, mashed potatoes,
a vegetable, and apple pie, followed by prayers that
Evie offered up as easily as if Jesus Himself were sitting
among them. She sang another hymn with no bashful
reservation, her voice lovely and her faith something she
loved to share.

The entire family occupied every chair and settee in
the great room, Jake sitting in the big, red leather chair.

"Daddy, I wish you would let that traveling preacher
baptize you the next time he comes around," Evie told
her father after she finished the second hymn.

Jake glanced at her with a deep sigh. "Since you keep
asking that, baby girl, I guess you should know I've
been baptized."

The entire family looked at him in astonishment, even
Randy. He'd never mentioned any such thing. Evie put
a hand to her mouth in a tiny gasp. Lloyd frowned in

surprise, and Ben and Stephen glanced from Jake to each other, confused. Jake lit yet another cigarette and shifted in his chair before looking at his entire family, who all sat practically gawking at him. He inhaled deeply, then set the cigarette in an ashtray. "For crying out loud, don't anybody pass out over it," he joked.

"*When?*" Evie asked.

Jake looked away, taking up the cigarette again.

"Your father doesn't have to talk about it if he doesn't want to," Randy told Evie.

Jake glanced her way, and in that moment, she saw what sometimes showed through the man. She saw the boy.

"I was eight," he answered, keeping his eyes on Randy as though it was only there he could find the strength to talk about it. "My father wouldn't let my mother go to church, but in the rare times he'd pass out from drinking—and I say rare because the man could drink a whole fifth of whiskey or a bottle of tequila straight and still function…" He shifted in the chair again.

"Pa, you don't have to tell us any of it," Lloyd spoke up.

Jake took another drag on the cigarette and set it back in the ashtray. He leaned forward with his elbows on his knees and stared at the braided rug in front of his chair. "It's all right." He paused, and Randy ached for what she knew was something hard for him to talk about.

"Anyway, when my father was passed out, my mother would sneak out and go to a nearby Catholic mission so she could take Communion. She always took me and my brother with her because she refused to leave us alone with…*him.*"

"Grampa! You had a *brother?*" Little Jake asked.

Jake studied his namesake. "I did, but he died."

"How?"

Jake glanced at Randy as though to ask for help.

"Little Jake, me and Ben already know," Stephen told the boy authoritatively. "Grandpa said he'd tell you when he's ready, so you shouldn't ask him."

"It's just hard for Grandpa to talk about," Brian gently told his son, seeing the concern and disappointment in Little Jake's eyes. "Let him tell you another time, all right?"

Little Jake puckered his lips. "I'm sorry, Grampa."

Jake met the boy's curious gaze and smiled sadly. "You don't have to be sorry. It's a natural question, and I *will* tell you, but you have to let me decide when. All right?"

The boy pressed his lips together and nodded.

"Maybe we'll go for a ride tomorrow out to Fire Valley and talk about it. How's that? Just you and Ben and Stephen and me. I'll let all three of you shoot my rifle, but only under my say-so. Maybe we will find a few wild mustangs while we're at it and bring some in. And we can officially rename the place Little Jake's Valley."

Little Jake brightened. "Okay!"

Jake looked at Evie. "To answer your question, it was one of those times she snuck out for Mass that my mother asked the priest to baptize me. He baptized my little brother also. I remember it because the next day my father—" He suddenly stopped talking and reached for the cigarette. "Let's just say that my mother and little brother were no longer with us the next day. You know why. The end result of that baptism is why I've never talked about it. It's not something I care to revisit too often. I remember how much Mass meant to my mother. That's why I wear her rosary beads under my shirt. After she…died…my life went to hell, so I figure already being baptized wouldn't help much. If I get the chance to meet the Lord when I die, before dark angels take me elsewhere, I'll just have to hope already being baptized will save me from the flames."

The room hung silent except for the sound of steam softly drifting from a kettle on the stove and quiet giggles from Tricia and Sadie, who played with dolls in a far corner.

"Daddy, I know without one doubt that God will welcome you with open arms when the time comes."

"Well, I guess that's something only I will know, isn't it...and probably sooner than later."

Little Jake kept his big, dark eyes focused on his grandfather. "You didn't like your daddy very much, did you? He wasn't very nice. And that mean man in that courtroom yelled that you killed him," the boy said.

More silence. Jake never took his eyes off Little Jake. "Do you think that makes me a bad man?"

Randy closed her eyes and looked away. She knew what the conversation was doing to Jake.

The boy slowly shook his head. "No. *He* was the bad man. Did your daddy kill your mommy? I bet that's why you said her and your brother were gone the next day."

"Little Jake!" Brian scolded. "Your grandfather told you to wait with your questions!"

Jake still held his grandson's gaze, amazed at the boy's insight and seeing himself in those dark eyes.

Thick tension over how Jake might react to the conversation permeated the room. Jake said nothing for several long seconds.

"Yes," he finally answered honestly. "My father was the meanest man I've ever known, Little Jake, and I've run with some of the meanest. I was pretty damn mean myself for a long time after I killed him. I want you to understand that, Little Jake. You're anxious to get your hands on my guns, and some day they'll be yours, but by God, you are going to learn to respect them for what they are and never think of them as something to play with or that they're famous just because I was good with them. I've done a lot of bad things with guns, things

I'm *not* proud of. I don't want you or Ben or Stephen bragging what a great man your grandfather was, because he wasn't. I wasn't anything more than a lost young man who robbed and looted and gambled and drank—and when I drank, I sometimes got as mean as my father did. That's why you've never seen me drink around any of you, and you never will. And you need to realize that when you kill a man it stays with you, sometimes forever. I hope to hell none of you ever has to know that feeling. People think it doesn't bother me, but it damn well does, more than anybody knows, except possibly your grandmother. I just never talk about it."

Jake pointed to Randy. "That beautiful woman over there saved my life, Little Jake. I didn't know a damn thing about love until she came along. She is the only thing that keeps me from falling right back into that old life. When I start falling, she pulls me right back. They don't come any better than your grandmother. I want all three of you boys to remember that, and you respect her and love her like nobody's business. Understand?"

All three boys nodded, wide-eyed.

"The same goes for your own mothers. I can tell you for a fact that a good and loving mother is something to be treasured and respected and loved and cared for. If my mother were alive today, she'd be living right here in this house with me, and she'd not be allowed to do a lick of work. And if she wanted Mass every single day, I'd find a way to make that happen. And when I'm no longer here on this earth—and it's a damn miracle I *am* still here—all you boys need to take over watching out for your grandmother and your mothers."

He looked at Ben and Stephen again. "And I want all of you to remember what can happen to people you love if you fall in with the wrong kind of men. Once you do that and you take the wrong path in life, it never really leaves you, and innocent people suffer. When it's the people closest to you, it hurts... It hurts forever." He pointed to where his gun belt hung high on a hook near the door—too high for any child to reach. "And it all started with a gun—me shooting my father. So when you start learning how to use guns yourself, you respect them for what they're meant for—hunting and protection and nothing more. Not for bragging, not for thrills, and not for committing crimes. Do all of you understand what I'm telling you?"

Little Jake sniffed and angrily wiped at tears. "Don't talk about when you aren't here to take care of Grandma," he told Jake. "I don't wanna think about you not bein' here with us. And you're *not* bad, Grampa. You're *not*! I want to grow up to be just like you 'cause there ain't nobody better."

"*Isn't*, Little Jake, not *ain't*," Evie corrected him softly. "And you're right. There's nobody better. If you want to be just like Grandpa, that's just fine." She looked at Lloyd. "What do you think, Lloyd?"

Lloyd glanced at Jake and slowly nodded. He suddenly grinned, looking over at Evie. "Well now, actually..." He scanned the room. "I could tell all of you some very interesting stories from back in Oklahoma—"

"Lloyd Harkner, be serious!" Evie chided. "I used to sock you when I was little, and I'll do it again."

"Well, there *was* Dixie's place, and—"

"Lloyd!"

"—then there was that fight in the tavern in Guthrie when Pa busted that whiskey bottle and shoved it—"

"Oh, I really *will* sock you!" Evie held up a fist.

The boys giggled.

"*Do* it, Mommy!" Little Jake told her.

"I'm just trying to be honest," Lloyd teased.

Randy knew exactly what Lloyd was doing. He always knew when his father was falling into a bad place. Katie was sitting on Lloyd's lap, and he suddenly rose, picking her up with him. "Boys, I think your grandpa needs to think about something else. Things are getting way too heavy in here."

Katie pouted. "Are you talking about *me*?"

"Well, whatever is in this belly of yours isn't any lightweight," he teased.

"She's got a baby in there, just like Mommy does," Little Jake spouted with a giggle.

Everyone broke into laughter, and Randy loved her son for quickly changing the subject.

"What's yours gonna be, Mommy?" Little Jake asked her. "A boy or a girl?"

"I just hope whatever I have, he or she minds me better than *you* do sometimes, Little Jake—and better than your Uncle Lloyd, who I *can* beat up."

"Hey, I never socked you back because Pa would have taken away every privilege I ever had and probably would have made me write down 'I will not hit my sister' about a thousand times."

"Well, speaking of babies, I am having a boy," Katie declared, wrapping her arms around Lloyd's neck and resting her head on his shoulder. "I just know it."

Jake turned to tamp out what was left of his cigarette. "I think it's time for pie and coffee," he announced.

"Sounds good to me," Lloyd answered. He kissed Katie and set her back down in the chair they'd shared. "I'm still hungry." He leaned down and whispered something in Katie's ear, and Katie shoved at him, her face turning a soft pink.

"Can't you two keep your hands off each other?" Brian joked.

"You're one to talk," Lloyd shot back. "You didn't get my sister pregnant just by holding her *hand*."

Evie let out a little screech and covered her face while everybody else broke into uncontrolled laughter.

"I'd like to remind you, Lloyd, that Evie was pregnant

first last time, and she was first again this time," Brian answered, "so I might ask you—who is the better man?"

That brought little screams of embarrassment and laughter from the three women. For Brian to make that kind of remark was highly unusual. Lloyd covered his eyes and groaned. "Brian Stewart, I sure didn't see that coming. Not from you!"

"You two be careful, or Katie and I will start comparing notes," Evie told both men.

"Stop! Stop! Stop!" Lloyd put up his hands. "Enough!"

Everyone quieted a moment until Lloyd threw in a last jab. "You should notice, Brian, that as soon as we found out about Evie, it didn't take us any time at all to catch up. When I set my mind to something, I get it done."

Katie turned beet red and bent over to hide her face, and Little Jake looked puzzled, not sure what they were laughing about.

Randy loved all of them for what they were doing. She watched Little Jake run up to his grandfather and hug him around the middle while Lloyd escorted Katie to the dining table, and Randy told everyone to sit down for pie and coffee. Evie started helping her mother cut the pie.

"I love you, Grampa," Little Jake told him. "I'll always take care of Mommy and Grandma." He leaned his head back to look up at Jake. "But I'll be a big, grown man then, 'cause you're gonna live a real long time."

Jake knelt down, wincing from the pain in his hip that often flared up from an old bullet wound suffered in the shoot-out in California. "I hope you're right, Little Jake. Right now, let's go have some of Grandma's apple pie. Nobody makes it better, do they?"

"Nope! I always have three pieces!"

"*Three!* That's a lot of pie." Jake picked the boy up and carried him to the table, plunking him into a chair.

He walked around the table to Randy, reaching around her from behind. He wrapped a hand around hers and bent close as she cut into another pie. "Have I told you lately how much I love you?"

Randy turned her head and kissed his cheek. "Yes. Just a few minutes ago, in so many words."

"I'd rather show you than tell you."

"Are you just needing to prove something in case I do share notes?" she joked.

"Woman, I don't have many years left to keep up with these younger men."

Randy laughed lightly. "The day a man who reeks of sex can't—" She stopped and broke into laughter. "I can't even begin to picture it. You can prove yourself later. I have pie to serve, so go sit down."

He kissed her lightly. "I'm going outside for a few minutes."

Randy set the knife aside and looked up at him. "Are you all right?"

"I just need to go out and clear my head. You cut me a piece of that pie, and I'll be back in a few minutes." He kissed her again and spoke softly into her ear. "And you rest up this afternoon, because you won't get much sleep tonight."

"Save it for after we're gone, Pa," Lloyd jabbed.

Jake just shook his head and walked past them and out the front door.

The jovial atmosphere around the table faded a little.

"Is he okay, Mom?" Lloyd asked. "Should I go out there?"

"No. He's fine," Randy told him. She walked to the icebox to get some milk for the boys.

"Did I make him feel bad?" Little Jake asked.

"No, Little Jake. I think you made him feel very good, and sometimes it's hard for your grandfather to accept the good things in his life." She glanced at the doorway, hoping she was right.

Outside, Jake lit yet another cigarette, his mind and heart reeling with memories he preferred not to stir. But he couldn't avoid explaining everything to Little Jake and the boys. A lot of it was in Jeff's book, but not some of the ugliest details. He leaned against a support post on the veranda and drew deeply on the cigarette, hearing a wolf howl in the distant hills even though it was midafternoon. More laughter came from inside the house, and as always, he wondered how long he could hold on to those he loved most. Hearing a wolf howl in daylight was unusual, and he couldn't help feeling as though it was some kind of bad omen.

He straightened and threw his cigarette down when he saw Cole charging toward the house on an unsaddled horse and pulling another horse with him.

"Jake!"

Jake stepped off the veranda. "What is it?"

"Trouble down at the bunkhouse. I'm scared Pepper will get himself killed." Cole slid off the horse. "I figured I'd get here quicker if I didn't take the time to saddle up. And with this bum leg, I'm not much of a fast runner."

"What the hell is going on?"

Cole stepped closer, glancing at the house. "Well... it's about your daughter. One of the newer men said as how little Sadie wasn't really Brian's kid, claimed she was the... Hell, I'm sorry, Jake—he said she was fathered by one of them men back in Oklahoma. Pepper lit into him and—"

Before he finished, Jake was back up the steps and through the front door. He grabbed his guns from the hook and began strapping them on. "Lloyd, come with me!"

Lloyd immediately scooted back his chair while Jake grabbed Lloyd's gun belt from where it hung nearby and tossed it to him.

"Jake, what is it?" Randy asked.

"I'm not sure. But you women stay here, understand?" He quickly tied his holster straps around his thighs. "Brian, you make damn sure all three women and the girls don't leave this house."

"Can we come, Grampa?"

"You'll have to run fast, because we're going to the far bunkhouse, and Lloyd and I are taking horses."

Jake charged out, Lloyd right behind him, still buckling his gun belt. The boys excitedly flew out the door after them. "Stay out of the way!" Lloyd shouted as he and Jake took off, riding bareback toward the bunkhouse.

The boys raced each other across the lawn and jumped over a fence in an effort to keep up.

Randy hurried to the front door and saw Cole walking away. "Cole!" she shouted. "What's going on?"

"Just a little tussle, ma'am. Nothin' Jake and Lloyd can't handle. You know how men can be."

Randy watched him limp away as Jake and Lloyd and the boys disappeared around a barn. "Oh, I know men, all right," she said softly.

Thirty-two

JAKE AND LLOYD CHARGED UP TO A SHOUTING MATCH outside the bunkhouse, two men holding back an enraged Pepper, and three holding on to one of the newer men, Clyde Pace. Two other new hires who'd shown up with Clyde—Ronald Beck and the other named Tucker—stood nearby, rooting Clyde on. No one knew if Tucker was the third man's first or last name.

Jake dismounted and strode up to the melee, followed closely by Lloyd. "What the hell is going on here?"

"Jake's here now, you sonofabitch!" Pepper growled at Clyde. "If you'd seen what he did to a man who insulted his wife, wait till you see what he does for insultin' his *daughter*! She's an angel if there ever was one who walked among us!"

"No woman who's been had by that many men and is still getting herself pregnant is any angel!" Clyde retorted.

Lloyd charged past Jake. "You bastard!"

Jake rushed up to grab him. "You're not healed enough to be getting into a fight!" he yelled, struggling to hang on to his arm. "One wrong blow, and you'll be in trouble!"

"I'm healed enough to beat the shit out of anybody who'd say something like that about my *sister*!"

"Hold on, damn it! He *wants* this! Can't you see it in his eyes?"

Clyde stopped his struggling, grinning. "You *bet* I want it! I'm wearin' a *gun*, ain't I?" Ronald Beck and Tucker stepped forward, all three men wearing guns. By then the three younger boys made it to the scene, stirring up dust as they stopped short, panting and sweating. Ben's blond hair was plastered to his head with perspiration.

"You boys stay out of the way!" Jake ordered.

They scrambled over to the side, watching with great anticipation. Jake let go of Lloyd, who took a stance beside his father.

"What the hell do you three want?" Jake growled.

"*You*, Harkner."

"You've been here nearly a month with no trouble," Lloyd steamed. "Why now?"

"Been waitin' for the right time," Tucker answered. "Took a while to get up the courage, but we figure out of the three of us, one of us is bound to make a name for himself."

Pepper jerked away from the men holding him. "Somebody's gonna get hurt here today, and it ain't gonna be Jake or Lloyd, you stupid sons of bitches!"

"I've been so involved with making sure Lloyd gets well and getting things back to normal, I didn't pay enough attention to you three," Jake thundered. "Who hired you?"

"*Pepper* did!" Clyde answered.

"That true, Pepper?" Jake asked.

A disgruntled Pepper stood there with fists clenched. "I'm sorry, Jake. I thought they were okay."

"Where did you find them?" Lloyd asked.

Pepper looked away. "Shit," he mumbled. He swallowed before answering. "Gretta's place."

Jake grinned, surprising Lloyd. "Pepper, you should know better. I know firsthand that when you're drinking and cavorting with whores, you don't exactly make the best decisions." He backed up a little, keeping his eyes on all three opponents as he reached out and grasped Lloyd's arm. "Step over a little, Son. You keep your eyes on Tucker. The other two are mine."

The three men straightened. "You're gettin' old, Harkner, and your son still ain't completely well."

"I'm well enough, you worthless snake!"

"They insulted Evie on purpose, Lloyd," Jake told him. "It was just a way to get us out here."

"Sure it was," Ronald Beck sneered. "But it's goddamn true. Who's ever gonna know your granddaughter ain't the child of a rapist?"

"*I* know, because she was carrying when they took her," Jake answered, his smile gone. "And every man here goddamn well knows it, too! They also know that if a man insults a Harkner woman, he'd better already have his tombstone engraved."

"You just narrowly missed getting hanged back in Denver, Harkner! You'd best think twice about killin' any of us," Tucker told him, moving his hand toward a gun. "You'll end up in a noose. That gives us an advantage."

"You're the ones who decided on this," Lloyd told them. "And you aren't facing just my father. I might still be a little weak, but my gun hand is just fine!"

The three men braced their feet and put on looks of bravery, but Jake saw right through them. "They're scared shitless, Lloyd."

"They *should* be scared shitless!" Lloyd scanned them. "If I were you, I'd be pissing my pants right about now. Do you realize who you've called out? What in God's name made you think you could take Jake Harkner?"

Clyde kept moving his hands into fists and opening them again, sweat stains beginning to show under his arms. "We've talked a lot about it," he answered. "The name it would get us is worth the risk."

This time it was Lloyd who grinned. "You idiots! Take my advice and apologize for insulting my sister before you get the hell off the J&L!"

Clyde shook his head. "No way. We came this far, and we've been plannin' this for a month! We're finishing it!"

"Then I'd advise anybody standing behind me and Lloyd to get the hell out of the way," Jake announced, "because I figure these three couldn't hit the side of a barn."

Men scattered, Pepper going over to the boys and herding them farther away.

"Pa, after what happened in Denver, I don't think you should shoot to kill," Lloyd told him, enjoying the growing fear in the eyes of the opposing men. "You might get in more trouble, and these three will never clear their holsters anyway. They just want to prove they're faster."

"I figured that," Jake answered.

"Grampa said once that when you draw against a man, you watch his eyes, not his hands," Stephen whispered to the other two boys. "Him and my pa are doin' just that. Can you see it?"

"I see it," Little Jake answered, his dark eyes glowing with anger. "And I don't like what they said about my little sister."

"They're just trying to make Pa draw on them," Ben said softly. "Lloyd, too."

"You'd *better* shoot to kill," Tucker growled, "or you're both dead men!"

More men backed away.

Ronald's eyes widened. "Maybe we should just go," he told Clyde.

"Maybe you *should*," Lloyd told him. "Real quick. Wounded or not, I really, really want to beat you till you can't even see—and *then* I'll shoot you!"

"I ain't goin' *anywhere* till I kill Jake Harkner," Clyde growled. He went for his gun.

The three boys watched in astonishment. Before any of the men could even clear their holsters, Jake and Lloyd's guns boomed. The three shots came so fast it was almost like one thunderous roar that made the boys jump. Jake shot Clyde's gun out of his hand, the bullet putting a hole through his hand from the side so it blew half his fingers off. His second bullet skimmed Ronald's holster in such a way that it fell off him and left a deep gash across the side of his hip. Lloyd's bullet went into Tucker's holster and hit the bullet chambers, causing some of the bullets to explode against the man's hip and thigh.

Clyde just stood there a moment, gawking in astonishment at his bottom knuckles where three fingers used to be. The fingers lay several feet behind him, and blood poured from the stubs. Realizing the fingers were actually gone, he began shaking and screaming curses at Jake while Ronald was already down, writhing in pain from a bleeding hip.

"I think my hip bone is broke!" he screamed. "It's broke! It's broke!" He held a hand to his hip, trying to stop the bleeding.

Tucker was also on the ground, curled up and groaning and hanging on to his thigh.

"Pepper, get their guns," Jake told him.

"Gladly," Pepper answered, marching up to take the guns and picking up what was left of Tucker's shredded gun belt.

"We need a doctor!" Tucker yelled, beginning to cry.

"The men can help you best as they can, and then they'll escort you off the J&L," Lloyd sneered.

"Your brother-in-law is a doctor!" Clyde screamed. "Get him out here! He's got laudanum!"

"After what you said about his *wife*?" Lloyd seethed. "I'm not sending him to take care of the likes of you, you worthless snake in the grass! You can lay there and *bleed* to death for all I care! I hope you *die*, and real *slow* from infection!" He looked at the other men. "Do what you can for them and make sure they're off my ranch by dark!"

"Where will we go?" Clyde screamed.

Lloyd looked at Jake. "Where do you think they should go, Pa?"

They turned away, and Jake barked at the three boys to follow them back to the house.

"What do we tell the women?" Lloyd asked. "I don't want Evie to know what they said. Brian either. Jesus, Pa, in the last five or six months, I can tell they've both really been able to get back to normal married life. You can see the difference in them."

"I know. That joke Brian made really surprised me. And for Evie to be able to go along with it really told me something. They're enjoying each other the way they *should* be able to enjoy each other." He called the boys over. The three came scurrying.

"Grampa, you really showed 'em!" Little Jake said excitedly.

"I've never really seen you draw a gun on a man," Stephen told Lloyd. "That's the fastest thing I've ever seen, Pa!"

"Yeah! Boom! Boom! Boom!" Ben put in, his blue eyes sparkling. "I'm glad you're okay, Pa," he told Jake.

Jake took them aside. "You boys listen to me. What just happened couldn't be avoided, but there was a time when I would have shot those men dead. I have to be careful now how I handle myself. I knew they'd never outdraw me anyway, so I just made sure they were hurt enough that they couldn't shoot back again, even if they tried. You just have to remember there are a lot of new laws that can get you in trouble, like how I got in trouble in Denver. Understand?"

The boys nodded. "They said somethin' bad about Mommy and my sister," Little Jake pouted. "I wanna go hit 'em! That Clyde is a sonofabitch!"

Jake looked at Lloyd. "Get over there and make sure the men know not to talk about this in front of Brian or Evie," he told them. "I'll tell the women it was just a fight over cards that got out of hand, and these men were drunk and thought they could take us. We knew they were drunk, so we just wounded them and kicked them off the J&L for causing trouble."

Lloyd nodded. "I wish this was the old days. I'd have killed Clyde and made up an excuse for doing it!"

"If he makes any more trouble, *I'll* kill him!" Jake seethed. "They'd better understand it would be best to never step foot on the J&L again."

"Oh, the men and I will make that very clear. Get the boys out of here, Pa. And explain to them not to talk about this in front of Evie."

Jake put his hands on Ben and Little Jake's shoulders and walked all the boys over behind a barn, where he stopped and knelt in front of them. "You three heard what those men said, and you know it's not true," he told them.

They nodded.

Jake turned to Little Jake. "Do you understand what they meant about Sadie, trying to say she's not really your daddy's baby?"

"I know what they meant," the boy pouted. "I ain't a kid about them things, Grampa. I seen what those men did to Mommy back in Oklahoma. I was there."

His frankness reminded Jake of himself. He closed his eyes at the memory of cigarette burns on his grandson's belly after he found him and Evie at Dune Hollow. He addressed all the boys. "All right, all three of you need to understand how bad it would hurt Evie, and Brian, too—if they knew what those men said. And I know for a fact it's *not* true. So none of you is going to say anything about what really happened, understand?"

They nodded again.

"It was just a drunken fight," Ben spoke up. "That's what we'll say."

Jake studied the young man he'd rescued from an

abusive father in Oklahoma and adopted as his own. He couldn't be more pleased at how Ben was turning out. "That's a good explanation, Ben." He looked at the others. "Stick to the same story, understand?"

"Will my dad be okay back there with those men?" Stephen asked.

Jake saw the worry in the boy's eyes. He still had nightmares about thinking Lloyd might die in Denver. "He'll be fine. He's got all the other men behind him, and by now, those three know better than to mess with your father." He rose and headed back to the house with the boys. "You boys remember that men get drunk and tend to want to strut their stuff and brag a little. Sometimes it ends up in a fistfight. You just have to keep an eye out and keep the help in line now and then. And you have to get rid of the real troublemakers. You can't run a ranch well if you have to worry about somebody always causing trouble."

"*Señor*, what is happening?" Rodriguez came running over to them from his cabin. Teresa was standing on the porch, watching.

"Just a little trouble over at the bunkhouse. We took care of it."

"I heard shooting. Is anyone hurt?"

"Oh, someone's hurt, all right. Lloyd is taking care of it. And it's your day off, Rodriguez. Go on back and enjoy it."

"*Sí, señor*. Next Friday I am planning a big Mexican cookout!" he added. "I know how much you like Mexican food, *sí*?"

"*¡Sí! ¡Bueno!*"

"Grampa, did you learn Mexican from your mother?" Little Jake asked. "Is it okay to talk about her?"

Jake felt the stabbing pain of watching his mother die. "Yes, it's okay to talk about her," he answered, "and yes, I learned Spanish from her, but mostly I remember it from growing up in Texas around others who used it pretty regularly."

"Will you teach us some Spanish?" Stephen asked.

Jake shook off the memories. "Sure, I'll teach you some Spanish. Why not?"

They reached the house, where the women were standing anxiously on the veranda.

"Daddy! We heard shooting!" Evie exclaimed. "Are you okay? Where's Lloyd?"

"Lloyd is fine. It was just some trouble between a couple of men back at the bunkhouse. They're all drinking. Whiskey and bragging and cards don't always go together too well. A couple of them decided they didn't like me and Lloyd giving them orders, so they figured they'd make names for themselves with their guns. They found out it was a pretty stupid idea."

"Jake! Tell me no one is dead!" Randy said, hurrying up to him. "You can't afford to have something like that happen so soon after Denver."

Jake moved an arm around her. "No one is dead. They're just *wishing* they were dead."

Little Jake ran up to Evie and gave her a hug. "I love you, Mommy!"

"Well, thank you! I don't get that many hugs from you, Little Jake. And maybe I should stop calling you 'Little' Jake. You are really growing all of a sudden. I swear you've grown an inch in the last week!"

Little Jake pulled both his parents aside. "You should have seen it!" he said excitedly. "Grampa can pull a gun faster than a man can blink!"

Randy grasped Jake's arm. "What was this whole thing *really* about, Jake? The men have had little tussles before, but mostly nothing serious."

Jake frowned, leaning down and kissing her cheek. "I'll tell you later."

Now the boys were babbling about how fast Jake and Lloyd pulled their guns.

"Grandma, you should have seen it!" Stephen told her.

Randy looked up at Jake. "I *have* seen it," she answered ruefully. She sighed and moved her arms around Jake. "I *have* seen it."

Jake wrapped her in his arms.

Thirty-three

Late September

JAKE FINISHED HIS COFFEE AFTER A HEARTY LUNCH AND rose just as someone outside whistled.

"Jake, you in there? Got a rider comin'."

Jake rose, grabbing his gun belt from where he always hung it over the door. He looked through the screen to see Vance Kelly standing at the bottom of the veranda steps. "Who is it?" he called out.

"It's that marshal fella who came callin' last spring."

With a worried look, Randy turned from the kitchen pump where she'd been helping Teresa with dishes.

"He alone?" he yelled to Vance.

"Yes, sir."

"Good. If he was here to arrest me for something, he'd have five or six men with him." He strapped on his gun belt. "Stay here," he told Randy.

Ben came running from his bedroom where he'd gone after lunch to read his lesson for the day. Stephen and Little Jake were with him, all there for schooling with their grandmother. "What's he here for, Pa?" Ben asked.

"We'll just have to find out, won't we?" Jake strapped his holsters to his legs and grabbed his hat. He put it on as he went out the door.

"Grandma, is it something bad?" Stephen asked.

Randy wiped her hands on her apron. "Let's hope not. You boys stay inside like he told you to do."

"I wish that man would quit coming here," Little Jake grumbled.

Randy thought how big the boys were getting—even Little Jake had taken a sudden summer growth spurt. It was obvious by the longer legs he'd sprouted that he and Stephen, who was already a head taller than Ben, even though they were the same age, were going to be Harkner men through and through—in height and coloring and with that defensive edge Jake always carried. Jake and Lloyd were grooming the three of them to run the J&L someday, and she could already see the hint of "man" trying to burst forth from the "boy" in them. She'd also noticed how much more mature they'd seemed to become after Jake and Lloyd took them out for the talk they'd promised them. It had somehow changed them—made them more serious about things.

She joined them at the window as Marshal Hal Kraemer rode in, wearing the familiar duster that reminded Randy of when Jake dressed and armed himself with the same array of weapons Kraemer now displayed as he dismounted.

Terrel Adams and Charlie McGee accompanied Kraemer.

Randy whispered to the boys to be very quiet so she could hear what was being said.

"He's a marshal," Charlie was telling Jake in his drawling southern accent. "Couldn't very well tell him he ain't welcome."

Jake leaned against a support post and lit a cigarette. "Who said he's not welcome? As long as he's not here to try to drag me off to jail, company is always welcome."

Randy watched Lloyd ride up to the veranda. Brian and Evie were approaching from their house. Lloyd dismounted and didn't stop to tie his big bay before hurrying up the steps.

Kraemer nodded to Jake. "Does your whole family always surround you when they think they smell trouble?"

Jake took a drag on his cigarette. "Like ants on sugar."

"Well then, considering your penchant for trouble, they must come running pretty often."

Jake smiled. "Just a family tradition."

Lloyd came up the steps and stood next to Jake.

"You already know my son, Lloyd," Jake told Kraemer.

Kraemer tipped his hat. "Lloyd, your reputation runs a close second to your father's, so I'll be sure not to reach for my weapons."

"Might be a good idea," Lloyd answered with a hint of a grin. "What's going on, Kraemer? We just finished lunch and have a lot of chores today."

Kraemer nodded. "May I at least get down off this horse?"

Jake grinned. "Come sit on the veranda and out of the hot sun." He glanced at Lloyd. "Didn't take you long to get here."

"I was out at the milking barn, talking to Rodriguez. Saw the marshal riding past the barn toward the house."

Inside, Randy left the boys at the window. "I'm going out there to see what this is about," she told them. "You three stay here." She patted the sides of her hair and straightened her dress, then quietly walked out onto the veranda. Jake glanced at her as he and Lloyd sat down in wicker chairs. Jake kept his cigarette between his lips and nodded toward a wooden chair nearby as Kraemer mounted the steps. "Have a seat," he told Kraemer.

Kraemer tipped his hat to Randy as she moved to stand behind Jake. "Mrs. Harkner, you're looking lovely today, as always."

Randy wished he wasn't here but decided to be cordial. "Thank you, Marshal Kraemer."

Kraemer heard whispers at the window as he took a seat. He glanced at the three young faces behind the screen. "I apparently have quite an audience."

Lloyd grinned. "The place is overrun with Harkners. And two more are on the way."

Kraemer shook his head, glancing at a very pregnant Evie as she and Brian came up the steps. He rose yet again and tipped his hat. "Ma'am, I remember how concerned you were last time I was here. I assure you I'm not here to bring harm to anyone or take your father away."

Evie glanced at Jake. "Is it okay?"

"Go on inside where it's cooler. It's okay. Sadie is waiting for you to come take her home anyway." He turned to look up at Randy. "Do you have some of that lemonade you usually keep in the icebox? I'm sure the marshal could use some refreshment."

Randy didn't want to serve the man anything, but she knew Jake was trying to keep the situation calm. "Certainly."

Evie went inside with her, but Brian took another chair on the veranda, nodding to Kraemer. "Marshal."

Kraemer nodded to him. "You're Jake's physician son-in-law?"

"I am."

"Well, if anybody needs a doctor around close, it's Jake." Kraemer glanced at Lloyd. "Son, I heard what happened in Denver, and I'm damn sorry. You look like you've recovered all right."

"I have, but it's been a hard road. I still get tired easily and have pain. Brian says it's just something that will take a long time to go away, and some of it won't."

"I know. I've been there myself, and so has your father. Comes with the territory, I guess." He looked at Jake. "I have to say I'm glad you got out of that mess, Jake. Part of me figures the man you shot damn well deserved it, considering he was part of that disaster at Dune Hollow."

"Yeah, well, I don't like to talk about that. And thanks for your concern over Lloyd." He drew on the cigarette again. "Why don't you just get around to why you're really here? Like Lloyd said, we're pretty busy."

Kraemer reached inside his duster, watching Jake move his hand closer to his gun when he did so. "Just getting out some mail," he told him. He pulled out three envelopes. "I figured since I was coming here, I'd stop off in Boulder and see if you had any mail." He handed it out.

Jake took it and laid it on a table next to his chair. "And?"

Randy came outside, carrying a tray that held glasses of lemonade. Kraemer rose yet again as she walked around to set everything on the table beside Jake. She picked up a glass and handed it to Kraemer.

"Thank you, ma'am. I'm right thirsty."

Kraemer drank down the lemonade, and Randy glanced at Jake. He gave her a thin smile. "Sit down, Randy. You've had a long day."

Randy couldn't help feeling nervous at the marshal's visit. She handed out the rest of the lemonade and walked over to sit in a wooden chair beside Brian.

"You were saying?" Jake told Kraemer.

"I'm to tell you they are having a shooting contest at the summer fair in Boulder. They'd love for you to come there and show them how fast you can draw."

Jake shook his head. "Not interested. I'm not a circus act, Kraemer. And I don't want my grandsons thinking guns are for showing off. Besides, the last time I got in a shooting contest, it drew too much attention, and I ended up in a shoot-out with about seven men who injured my wife and tried to kidnap my son."

Kraemer smiled. "Your son looks pretty big to be kidnapped."

"He was only about a year and a half old at the time." Jake drew on the cigarette and took it from his lips. "And a shooting contest and picking up mail aren't good enough reasons for a U.S. Marshal to come all the way out here. What's your *real* mission?"

Kraemer leaned back in his chair, putting a booted

foot up on his other knee and hanging his hat on his foot.
He drank more of the lemonade before he answered.
"The Cattlemen's Association has an offer for you, Jake.
They sent me to tell you about it."

"What kind of offer?"

"Range detective."

Lloyd straightened in his chair. "What the hell is a
range detective?"

Kraemer guzzled down the rest of his lemonade.
"Pretty much what it sounds like. There has been too
much rustling going on, as you well know, Jake. You've
had a run-in with rustlers yourself. And nesters are also
becoming a problem. The cattlemen have decided they
need men to ride the range looking for trouble. If anyone
can sniff out troublemakers and then handle them himself
when he finds them, it's Jake Harkner."

"No!" Randy suddenly gasped.

Jake looked her way and saw the terror in her eyes.

"Jake, no! It's too dangerous!"

Jake looked back at Kraemer. "Sounds to me like
that's work for a regular marshal like yourself."

"Not necessarily. Only another cattleman can recognize men who don't belong on his land and recognize
which brands belong to which ranchers. We keep the
law in other ways, but this is a need unique to cattlemen.
You know the wide range marshals cover. We can't be
everywhere at once, Jake. Range detectives can zero in
on particular ranches and handle rustlers and such. You
find them, arrest them, and then bring them to us. I
know that part would be hard for you, given the fact that
you tend to shoot first and ask questions later, but you'd
have to abide by the law of the land."

Jake tamped out his cigarette, glancing at Lloyd.

"I need you here, Pa."

"You run this ranch just fine without me, and it's
mostly yours."

"It pays good, Jake. You'd make a lot of money," Kraemer told him. "The cattlemen know how good you are, and they're willing to pay you five hundred dollars a month. That's a whole lot more than you ever made as a marshal, and if this ranch ever hit bad times—like a hard winter that killed off most of the cattle, or a drought that burned up your grass—you'd be able to support it by taking this job."

"I have money!" Lloyd put in. "I inherited it from my first wife, and I'm not worried about this ranch going under. We'll be just fine. I rode with my father as a marshal in Oklahoma, and every damn day I was scared some sonofabitch would shoot him in the back! All it got him was even more enemies—men who turned around and hurt my whole family. My father doesn't need to be making even *more* enemies! Just a few days ago three of his own men—"

"Lloyd!" Jake interrupted.

Kraemer raised his eyebrows. "Did you have some new trouble out here, Jake?"

"Nothing Lloyd and I couldn't handle. And if you're asking if I killed anyone, I didn't. I just hope I don't live to regret that. I've learned over the years it's better to put someone down for good than to create new enemies. But all the new laws they're coming up with now make it hard for a man to protect his own family." He leaned back in his chair. "Look at my wife, Kraemer."

The marshal moved his gaze to Randy as she wiped at her eyes with a shaking hand.

"That woman has been to hell and back—*with* me and *for* me," Jake told the marshal. "We moved out here for the peace we've been wanting the whole thirty years we've been together. We're pretty damn close, but I'm worried about the three men I kicked off the J&L a few days ago. They weren't exactly in good health when they left. And there is still the little matter of one Brad Buckley, a leftover from Oklahoma who is still wanting revenge because I killed his father and two brothers. I'm needed right here in case that man decides to pull something. Lloyd and I and the men who work for us will take care of rustlers and any other trouble on the J&L. The other ranchers can take care of it however they want, but I'm not interested. My wife went through enough in Oklahoma." He took another cigarette from a shirt pocket. "Besides, I'm getting too many aches and pains from old wounds to be sitting in a saddle all day long every damn day and sleeping on the hard ground at night. I prefer my own bed, where I don't have to fight insects and worry about a snake crawling into my boots or my knapsack while I'm sleeping. A good woman in your bed at night is a lot more welcome."

"Jake!" Randy chided. The three boys inside snickered.

Kraemer smiled. "You've got me on that one, Jake. You're one lucky man."

"I think so." Jake lit the cigarette. "You tell the cattle-men thanks for the offer, but I'm not interested."

Kraemer nodded. "You can go to Greeley and wire a message to my office in Denver if you change your mind."

"I won't."

Kraemer took his hat from his foot and put it back on, then set his empty glass on the table. He rose, nodding to Randy. "Thank you, ma'am, for the refreshment. And I didn't mean to upset you." He turned to Lloyd and put out his hand. "Glad you're going to be okay, Lloyd."

Lloyd shook his hand, and Kraemer turned to Jake.

"Jake, you're somebody worth knowing. I expect riding with you in Oklahoma was quite an adventure. I wish we could have gotten to know each other better."

Jake gave him a firm handshake. "Come and visit any time. If you and your men need a place to hole up once in a while, you're welcome to use one of the barns. We have a cook who would make sure you got some of the best steaks in Colorado."

"I don't doubt that." Kraemer nodded to Brian and walked down the steps to mount his horse. "Remember the offer, Jake. I'm sure it will still be there next spring if you change your mind." He tipped his hat once more to Randy, then turned his horse and rode off.

Jake turned to Randy. "You didn't really think I'd take a job like that, did you?"

"I wasn't sure." She breathed a sigh of relief. "I couldn't stand it, Jake. After Oklahoma—"

"I know. I don't want to be away from you any more than you want me to go."

"I'm glad you decided against it, Pa," Lloyd told him.

"God knows you'd be good at it, but taking that job would have been hard on Evie, too," Brian told Jake.

Evie came out of the house. "Daddy, it's time you were always here with us. Four years away in that awful prison, and then always being gone when you were a marshal—it wouldn't be fair to Mother for you to take that job."

"I didn't consider it for one second," Jake told her, keeping hold of Randy's hand.

"Hey, look here," Lloyd told them, scanning the mail. "We got a letter from Peter Brown." He handed it to Randy.

"It must be a thank-you letter from when he and his wife visited," Randy commented. "I'm glad they were able to come here. I think they were quite impressed, and that beautiful palomino you gave Peter's wife—she was so taken by that, Jake."

"She was taken with *Daddy*, you mean," Evie teased.

"Well, if that's so, then it's proper revenge on Peter," Jake answered. "If he can ogle my wife, I can ogle his. She was quite beautiful."

"In a rich-lady, purebred kind of way," Lloyd joked. "I thought she'd faint dead away when I talked about castration." They all laughed. "And I was beginning to wonder if she ever takes those gloves off."

They laughed more, and Lloyd noticed Katie making her way over to them. "I was going crazy over at the house, wondering what was going on with that marshal," she said as she approached.

Lloyd hurried down the steps and took her arm.

"Lloyd, I'm just pregnant. I'm not an invalid."

"I don't like you walking around in this heat. Get up here on the veranda where it's cooler. We got a letter from Peter."

"Might as well take the time to listen to Randy read the letter," Jake told them. "We've already lost half an hour talking to Kraemer." He glanced at Lloyd, their gazes holding in mutual understanding.

"You made the right choice, Pa," Lloyd told Jake. "If you'd decided to take that job, I would have had to beat some sense into you."

"Oh, sit down," Randy told him as she opened the letter. "Boys, come out here! We've heard from Peter Brown." She sat down in her favorite porch rocker and wiped at more tears as she scanned the letter. Stephen, Ben, and Little Jake came out to stand behind Jake.

Jake smoked quietly as Randy began reading platitudes of how much Peter and his wife enjoyed their visit and how impressed they were with the J&L.

"*Although your home wasn't the fancy hotel Katrina is accustomed to, she thought our room was wonderfully warm and comfortable and inviting. Jake and Randy, your whole family was the same way—warm and inviting. We are both happy you are all together and life is so much better for you now than it was in Oklahoma. Katrina is immensely grateful for the beautiful palomino. The horse more than pays for my services, which I would never have charged you for in the first place.*"

"Mmm-hmm." Jake sighed. "And we all know why he did it."

"Daddy, I think he really cares about you," Evie told him.

"I suppose. I just couldn't get over wondering if he was going to leave his wife behind and try riding off with your mother when they left here." He winked at Randy.

"Well, maybe you would have been perfectly happy if he'd left his own beautiful wife behind," Randy quipped.

Jake grinned. "She wouldn't last two days on the J&L as a true rancher's wife."

"They don't make them like Mom," Lloyd put in, reaching over to take Katie's hand, "except for my sister and Katie."

"Yes, well—" Randy stopped for a moment as she scanned more of the letter. She put a hand to her mouth and started laughing. "Oh my goodness! Oh my goodness!" She laughed again.

"What is it?" Evie asked.

Randy handed her the letter and wiped at what was left of her tears as Evie looked at it and then also broke into laughter.

"Oh, this is wonderful!" she told them. "We've got Daddy and Lloyd both on this one!"

Jake rose and moved to lean against a porch post. "All right, what are you talking about?"

"Oh, Daddy, you are always trying to embarrass us, especially poor Katie. Now we have one on you!" She laughed again. "I have a feeling Peter was wishing he could see the look on your face when we read this to you. He knows it would embarrass you."

Jake shook his head, taking the cigarette from his lips. "Get on with it, Evie."

Evie chuckled with teasing glee as she continued the letter. "*The J&L is like heaven, according to Katrina, and since Jake is always looking at me like I might try running off with Randy at any moment, I thought he should know what my wife said about him. She told me she thought Jake was*"— Evie again stopped to laugh. She could hardly stop long enough to get the words out—"*quite magnificent.*"

"*Magnificent?*" Lloyd asked.

"*Magnificent!*" Evie repeated.

They all broke into hearty laughter, including the three boys.

"Grampa's magnificent!" Little Jake screeched.

Jake just shook his head and grinned, then pulled his hat farther down over his eyes.

"I'll be sure to tell the boys out at the bunkhouse that from now on they should call you 'The Magnificent Jake Harkner,'" Lloyd teased.

"You do that, and I'll put a pitchfork in you," Jake answered.

"I'll bet women like Dixie and Gretta would agree with Katrina's description of you, Daddy," Evie put in.

"Oh, he's magnificent, all right." Randy laughed. "He has a magnificent bravado when it's necessary, and sometimes just a magnificent ego around women!"

"Oh, wait!" Evie told them. "There's more! Wait till you hear what Peter's wife says about you, Lloyd!"

Lloyd frowned. He stood up and walked closer to Jake. "I don't think I'm going to like this."

"Well, according to Katrina—" Evie broke into laughter again. "Oh, this is so hard for me to say about my own brother." She wiped at tears of laughter and read, "*Not only does she think Jake is a magnificent specimen of man, but she said that Lloyd is like a—*" She laughed again. "*Lloyd! My brother!* Oh, this is too much."

"I think we need to leave," Lloyd told Jake.

Jake moved closer to the porch steps. "I'm thinking the same thing."

"Oh, it's so much fun embarrassing you," Evie told them. "It says here that Katrina compared Lloyd to a Greek god."

The women broke into screeching laughter.

"Let's get out of here," Jake told Lloyd.

The men headed down the steps.

"You sure you can work alongside a Greek god?" Lloyd asked Jake, the ring of the women's laughter filling the air.

"As long as you can admit your father is magnificent."

"He's a magnificent sonofabitch who can't stay out of trouble. *That's* what he is."

They kept walking while the rest of the family continued their laughter.

"Do Greek gods wear their hair down to their waist and wear chaps and spurs?" Jake asked his son.

"Hell, I don't know. I never studied them much. Maybe I should start."

"Well, you have a goddess of a wife. That's a start."

"She's something, all right. Any woman who puts up with a Harkner man *deserves* to be called a goddess."

"That's for damn sure." Jake stopped walking. "Do you realize we'll never live this down if the men hear about it?"

"Jesus, I never thought about that. We're dead meat."

"Not if I threaten to shoot any man who dares to bring it up."

"Good idea." Lloyd put an arm around his father's shoulders. "Magnificent, huh?" He burst into laughter.

Jake gave him a shove. "Don't make me beat up on a Greek god."

They walked off together.

Randy watched them from the veranda. "Magnificent, indeed," she said softly. She shivered, secretly thanking God that Jake turned down the cattlemen's offer of range detective. She couldn't take one more day of watching him ride off into danger and wondering if he'd make it back.

Thirty-four

February 1897

RANDY FINISHED HER LETTER TO JEFF TRUBRIDGE by the dim light of an oil lamp. She'd always felt obligated to keep him updated on what was happening with the family. They'd received another royalty check for the book about Jake's life, and she thought how that life was still unfinished, an unfolding story that brought Jake farther and farther out of the pits of hell in his mind and saw him rise above all of it into a much stronger human being on the inside. She wrote:

> On January tenth, Lloyd and Katie had a little boy they named Donavan Patrick after Katie's father. Just a month earlier, Evie gave birth to a beautiful little girl with light hair like mine. They named her Esther Miranda after my mother and me. Goodness, if someone had told Jake back when we first met and he was still a wanted man that someday he'd have six grandchildren, he would have shot them for lying.

A grandfather clock in a corner of the great room ticked softly. It was night and very quiet. Ben was sleeping, and even Little Jake and Stephen, who were staying the night, were sleeping soundly. Jake was finishing a bath upstairs.

I suppose I sound more like I am reminiscing in a diary than writing a letter, but I know you understand like few others would. I guess age is getting to me. My Jake is sixty now, and I'm fifty. No one who doesn't know better would believe Jake's age, and he remains an energetic man who is hard to keep up with. He has his aches and pains, but he's as hard-edged as ever, still strong and sure. The streaks of gray in his hair just make him even more handsome. He still has that beautiful smile that few men his age can boast about. His secret is scrubbing his teeth every day with baking soda. I have no idea how he learned about that, but I think he is secretly egotistical about that smile of his. Some people are just blessed with certain attributes, and good health and good looks seem to be Jake's. I cringe to think I might show my age before he does, but he teases that I have ten years on him, so that will never happen. And, being Jake, he has his way of always making me feel beautiful.

Our grandsons are getting tall, and so is Ben, who has turned out to be such a blessing. I think the day Jake rescued him from his father's beating was the day Jake started growing stronger on the inside. Ben was a healing for him, his chance to live his own boyhood over as someone loved and wanted. Stephen is a young man, and Little Jake goes around holding his chin up and strutting as though he's trying to look much older. He so wants to be like his grandfather, and he will be, because that boy has Jake's spirit in him. When my Jake is gone from this earth, he will live on in Little Jake. And I surely will live on in my granddaughters, and I guess that's what family is all about.

I am happy to know you have a son now, which makes me smile when I remember the nervous young reporter who came to Guthrie with a dream of writing a book about Jake Harkner. I'll bet you never thought you'd be a part of all the things that happened after that. Once a person gets to know Jake, he or she never forgets him. It's impossible. When he rode into my life back in Kansas, I knew even then that I was lost forever...and there would be no turning back.

She stopped to reload her fountain pen, thinking about Evie and how happy she'd been to have another girl.

The ranch is doing well, but it's been a bitterly cold winter with a lot of snow, so we're worried about how many cattle we might lose.

She secretly lamented that she and Jake never went back to the line shack like they'd planned. After Denver, things got busy, because they'd been gone so long, and before they knew it, snow was falling and the holidays came and babies were born. Jake had promised that this summer, after roundup, they would finally spend time at the line shack while the men took the cattle in to Denver. Randy couldn't think of anything better than spending time alone with her husband instead of going into the city again. She wasn't sure she ever wanted to go back to Denver.

"Put that pen down and come to bed, woman." Jake came downstairs shirtless and wearing only his long johns. "It's late, and the boys are sleeping like babies."

"I only have a little left to write," Randy told him, preparing to fill her fountain pen.

"Never mind that." Jake walked over and literally lifted her right out of the chair. Randy stifled a scream and laughter as he grasped her under the hips and slung her over his shoulder. "You're coming to bed."

"Jake, the boys might wake up!"

"They're fine."

"Jake Harkner, put me down!" Randy told him in a gruff whisper. "You'll mess your back up."

He shifted her to hold in his arms. "What the hell does that mean? Are you saying I'm too old for this?"

"Well…no, but—"

"You weigh less than Ben, and by now probably even less than Stephen, and I've carried them to bed more than once. And I'm damn well not too old for what I'm about to do to you, and you aren't too old to want it."

"Is that so?"

"You know it is." He set her on her feet and closed the bedroom door, walking up to Randy and untying her robe. "You're as beautiful as ever, although sometimes I worry how small you're getting. One of these days I'll look for you under the covers and won't be able to find you." He pulled off her robe.

"Oh, you'll find me all right. You'd search for me through the jungles of Africa for sex."

He grinned. "That's what you still do to me." He untied a drawstring at the neck of her nightgown. "I was sitting in that warm water and remembering what we did that time we bathed together, and that got me to thinking about your beautiful breasts and your perfect bottom."

"I thought your hip was bothering you again."

He finished untying her nightgown and pulled it down over her shoulders. "The hot bath helped."

"Well, maybe *I'm* hurting from working so hard scrubbing the kitchen floor this morning."

"That was your mistake. You let me see you on your hands and knees with that beautiful bottom begging me to touch it. Now step out of that nightgown."

Randy obeyed, laughing softly. She reached up, and he folded her into his arms, kissing her hungrily and lifting her so her feet were off the floor. He carried her to the bed, and they fell onto it together. Jake rolled on top of her, kissing her deeply again. He had a way of waking up her deepest needs without her even knowing they were there. Just a moment ago she'd been writing to Jeff, and this was the last thing on her mind. "Mmm, you smell good from that bath," she told him when he left her mouth to caress her neck with butterfly kisses.

"Well, after shoveling horse manure part of the day, I figured I'd better scrub up good." He kissed his way down to her belly, then got to his knees and pulled off her drawers. "Don't you move," he told her then.

Randy drank in the sight of him when he got up from the bed and pulled off his long johns. No. There was still nothing old or soft about Jake Harkner.

"Have I told you lately how beautiful you are?" Jake asked, leaning down to move between her legs.

"You're a wonderful lover who tells me every day how beautiful I am, even the times when I know you don't really mean it."

"I really mean it *every* time. When have you ever thought I didn't?"

"When I'm a mess from cooking and cleaning, and all you want is to relieve your needs."

"And even when you're a mess, you're still beautiful, which is *why* I have needs. You create them." He kissed her again, softly groaning with the want of her, then moved to kiss her eyes. "Randy, if you're really too tired for this, let me know."

"Oh, *now* you ask."

He sobered. "*Are* you?"

"Too tired to have Jake Harkner in my bed? Or to have Jake Harkner inside of me? Surely you jest."

He nuzzled her neck with a growling laugh. "You

bathed while I was outside working earlier, didn't you? You smell like roses again."

"I know my husband well, and we haven't done this for a few days, so I had a feeling you might be needing this."

He studied her lovingly, smoothing back her hair. "How do you do that?"

"Do what?"

"Smell like roses. Sometimes even the bed smells like roses."

"Why do you think I insist on having a lot of rose-bushes?"

"I just figured you liked raising them and looking at them."

"Well, when I trim them, I keep the petals, sometimes the whole flower, and I crush them up and use the oil to rub over myself and sometimes over our sheets. I save enough to use all winter."

"How could I have lived with you so long and not known that?"

"A woman has to have *some* secrets."

"Oh? What else are you keeping from me?"

"I'll never tell. And I could ask you the same thing, but it would probably take the rest of the night to tell me all of it. And I would probably be horrified."

Jake moved his lips and tongue down over her breasts, her belly. "You probably would."

Randy grasped his hair. "I think I'm better off not knowing."

He moved back up to her breasts, tasting them fervently. "You're always saying these beautiful breasts aren't perky anymore."

"You have a way of perking them up." Randy breathed deeply as he kissed his way back down to secret places and moved fingers inside of her, stroking her erotically in the way he had of destroying all reservations and making her forget that earlier she thought she was too tired for this.

She felt adored sexually. Jake never asked for anything he knew she wouldn't want to do, yet had a way of making her want to give him more than she had to give. In spite of all their years together and getting older, her climaxes were as intense as always, usually because she couldn't get over the memories of all the times she'd watched this man ride away with no guarantee he would ever make it back. She couldn't imagine life without her Jake, or ever imagine any other man doing this to her.

He moved back over her body, pressing his hardness against her belly, then reaching down to move inside of her. She winced at how he filled her, with tremendous pleasure but now sometimes pain. She refused to tell him. He was too sensitive and might think she didn't want this, but she did...she did so want it and always would...always...as long as they could do this, and as long as they needed each other this way. Sometimes this was what brought both of them the strength they needed to face the past, the dangers, the lingering worry that this could end. She'd lived with that fear for thirty years. This is what kept her fears at bay.

They moved in sweet rhythm for several minutes. He grasped her bottom gently, whispering to her in Spanish. She felt lost beneath his big frame and leaned up to kiss his chest as she ran her hands over the hard muscle of his arms and shoulders until she felt his life pulse into her. He pushed harder with his release, groaning her name, then settled on top of her.

"Jake, I can't breathe," she told him.

"Shit." He rolled to her side. "I'm sorry. Did I hurt you?"

"No, but there *is* a bit of a difference in our weight."

He pulled her close, kissing her hair. "Randy, just because you love me and want to please me doesn't mean you can't say no once in a while."

"Why on earth would you say that?" she asked lazily.

"I can never say no to you, Jake. I'm happiest and feel safest right here in your arms."

He sighed. "Well, sometimes I sense things—more than I let on. You tell me if I'm hurting you."

She smiled, loving him more. "How many men would say that...or care? Only my Jake. I don't like the *reasons* you know women so well, but you're so sweet to ask."

He put a big hand to the side of her face and leaned down to kiss her eyes. "Baby, I can read your every physical reaction, whether because it feels good or because it hurts. Things change. I know that."

"Are you saying *I'm* getting old?"

"Hell no!" He moved only partly on top of her. "I'm saying I love you beyond this. I'll always want you this way, but not just because I draw strength from being inside of you or because you're so damn beautiful. I want you this way because I want to please your every need." He kissed her gently.

"Then please me again. It only hurts at first sometimes when it's been a while." She leaned up and captured his mouth, kissing him suggestively before moving to kiss his throat. "Don't be worried about hurting me. It's a nice kind of hurt." She kissed him again. "I love you, Jake. And if the day ever comes when we can't do this anymore, all I'll ever need is these arms around me. I'm safe here. So safe."

He grinned, moving between her legs again. "Yeah? Well, maybe you aren't always so safe when I'm going nuts with the want of you, whether you want it or not."

"You'd stop in a second if I asked you. I knew that clear back in that wagon when we first did this. You didn't scare me one bit."

He laughed lightly and kissed her ear. "Baby, I absolutely can't guarantee I wouldn't have kept going, even if you said no. I never wanted a woman so bad in my life as I wanted you that night. If I'd have had to wait one more day to be inside of you, I would have considered shooting myself."

He entered her gently again, moving softly, slowly. "Tell me if it hurts."

"Not a bit," she whispered.

He rocked her rhythmically, moving in that way he had of bringing on another climax without her even needing any other stimulation. This time it lasted even longer before he came again in his own groaning release.

He moved to her side and pulled her into his arms again. "Thank you...for all of it, Randy—all the sacrifices, all the waiting alone, all the forgiving and forgetting."

"You're easy to love, Jake Harkner."

"Yeah, well, not many people would agree with that remark."

"They don't know the Jake I know."

They lay there quietly together, nearly asleep when they heard it—the signal bell at the bunkhouse. It began clanging wildly.

"Fire! Fire!" someone was screaming.

Jake jerked awake. "What the hell?" He jumped out of bed, and Randy followed close behind, grabbing her robe and holding it against herself as she rushed with Jake to a window. "The horse barn!" he exclaimed.

Jake ran over to the bed to find his long johns and yanked them on while Randy stared in horror. Already she could see Lloyd running from his house toward the fire as someone kept clanging the bell and more men surrounded the barn. She turned to see Jake jerking on his denim pants. He buttoned them, sat down to yank boots over his bare feet, and grabbed a sheepskin jacket from a hook on the wall. "Make sure the boys stay in this house!" he yelled to her. "I don't want to have to worry where they are!"

"Jake, be careful!" she called after him.

Randy ran to the bathroom and quickly cleaned herself with a washrag, then pulled her heavy flannel robe over her nakedness and tied it tightly. She heard the boys talking excitedly downstairs. She hurried down. "You boys stay right here!" she ordered. "I mean it! Don't go out that door!"

"Grandma, the horse barn is on fire!" Stephen yelled.

All three boys stood at the front window. Randy rushed over to join them. "I know. Those poor horses! Midnight is in there! And some of the best mustangs they brought in the other day!"

Someone ran past the house. It was so quick Randy couldn't tell who it was. She frowned, wondering why one of the men would be so close to the house when he should be running to the fire.

Thirty-five

"GET MIDNIGHT OUT OF THERE!" JAKE CHARGED toward the flames, and Lloyd caught up with him just in time to keep him back.

"Pa! Nobody can go in there!"

"Pepper's in there!" one of the men shouted.

Three horses came galloping out, the whites of their eyes filled with terror. One of them was Midnight. The black gelding reared and whinnied wildly as Jake tried to grab hold of him. One hoof came up and caught Jake under the jaw, sending him sprawling as the horse tore away and ran off.

"Pa!" Lloyd ran over to where Jake lay rolling on the ground. He could tell his father was momentarily stunned and dizzy. Lloyd leaned over to help him up. "Pa, take it easy."

"Got to help—"

"I don't think it's going to make any difference."

Brian reached them, wearing woolen pants and a corduroy jacket and leather dress shoes he'd thrown on at the last minute. They weren't high enough for the snow that collected inside them as he ran, but he paid no heed.

"Jake!" He looked at Lloyd. "What happened to him?"

"Got kicked under the jaw by Midnight."

"Jake, stay down a minute. There's nothing you can do about that barn!"

"No." Jake moved to his hands and knees. "Pepper's in there...the horses!" He managed to get to his feet while hanging on to a fence post. For several minutes he stood there, trying to clear his head.

"What can I do to help?" Brian asked Lloyd.

Lloyd just watched the out-of-control fire consume his best barn and best horses. "Sonofabitch!" he roared.

"We have to...get the horses out," Jake repeated, still clinging to the fence post.

"It's too damn late, Pa!" Lloyd kicked at a fence board and cracked it, then paced. "Midnight got out with a couple of the mustangs," he told Jake, sounding ready to cry. "I think that's all that will make it out."

For nearly an hour, men continued their fruitless effort to put out the fire. Jake struggled against blacking out from the blow to his jaw. Dizziness kept overtaking him, so he could barely walk in his efforts to help the other men. When his head cleared more, he stumbled toward the barn again.

"What about Pepper?" He grasped another fence post to keep from falling again. "Pepper! Pepper!" he screamed at the top of his lungs.

Brian hurried up to him, grabbing his arm. "No one can help him now, Jake!"

"It's too damn late!" Cole could be heard shouting to the others. "Let it go! Let it go before somebody else gets hurt!"

"Pepper! Where's Pepper?" Jake roared.

"Jake, give it up," Brian told him. "You're too injured to do anything about this."

Lloyd left him there and ran all the way around the barn, searching for more horses that might have escaped and hoping to see Pepper. By the time he made it back to Jake and Brian, the barn was beginning to creak, and the flames had reached the highest loft.

"Pepper never came out!" Vance Kelly shouted. "And most of the horses are still inside."

The continued, near-screaming whinnying of the

trapped horses stabbed at Lloyd and Jake like a dagger in the heart. For a few more agonizing minutes, the gut-wrenching sounds continued, until finally there was nothing but the roar and crackle of the fire as the barn became completely engulfed in an orange glow. All any of the men could do was watch while the building they'd helped construct creaked and groaned, until it finally collapsed with a huge rumble that hurt the ears. Glowing sparks spiraled high into the sky, accompanied by black smoke that enshrouded the sparks as the rubble continued to burn.

"Jesus God Almighty," Jake groaned.

Lloyd held his stomach and turned away. The rest of the men filled the air with curses and shouts.

"That beautiful bay I cut out of those wild mustangs the other day was in there!" Terrel Adams groaned.

"Thank God there's plenty of snow on the ground, or that fire might have spread through the grass to other buildings," Cole commented.

They all stood around in stunned disbelief, most of them wearing nothing but long johns, boots with no socks, and an array of fur or buckskin winter jackets.

"What the hell happened here?" Lloyd seethed. "Who saw the fire first?"

"Pepper! Goddamn it! Pepper!" someone yelled. "He never came out!"

Cole noticed Jake's jaw was turning so purple it could be seen even at night by the light of the fire.

Again Jake bolted for the barn, his injury leaving him still confused. "We have to get Pepper out of there!"

"Pa, get back!" Lloyd grabbed him and pulled him back. "It's too goddamn late! There's nothing we can do!"

Jake ran a hand through his hair and turned in a circle. "Sonofabitch!" he roared so loud everyone jumped. "Who the hell was in the barn last?"

"*Nobody* was in there," Cole answered. "We was all

sleepin' when Pepper suddenly yelled that the barn was on fire."

"Jesus, we've lost over half of our feed hay," Lloyd lamented.

"And most of the best horses you were going to sell," Brian added.

"Jake, that fire went too fast to be natural," Cole told him. He turned to Lloyd. "Seems like it was all around the whole barn right away, not in just one spot. No fire breaks out everywhere at once like that unless it was set."

"Who in hell would do that?" Terrel asked.

Suddenly, Jake grabbed Cole's arms, his dark eyes on fire with rage. "You really think it was deliberately set?"

Cole cringed. "Jesus, Jake, let go of me!"

Brian and Lloyd pulled him off Cole.

"Are you sure?" Jake repeated, yanking his arm away from Brian and Lloyd.

Cole put his hands on his hips, stepping back a little. "It's the way it went," he told Jake. He turned to Lloyd. "It just didn't seem like no ordinary fire."

"I found an oil can layin' outside," Terrel told them, "and it ain't the brand we use to fill lamps and burn brush."

Jake looked at Lloyd, still seeming confused at first, then stumbling backward. He looked toward the house, then back to Lloyd. "Sonofabitch!" He began running toward the house. "Brian, go check on Evie and Esther and Sadie!" he screamed.

"Pa, I left Katie and Tricia at the house with the baby!" Lloyd yelled, hurrying to catch up with him.

"Go make sure they're all right!"

Most of the men ran right behind them.

"We have to make sure all the women and kids are accounted for!" Jake roared. "All three boys are at my house!" He ran toward the main house.

Lloyd grabbed Jake's arm. "Pa, what are you thinking?"

"Brad *Buckley*!" Jake roared. "*That's* what I'm thinking!

That fucking sonofabitch did this! You can bet on it!" He turned and kept running.

Lloyd made a beeline for his house. "Katie!" he screamed.

When he reached his front porch, Katie came out of the front door. "Oh, Lloyd, the horses! The barn!"

"Never mind that! Are you and the baby and Tricia okay?"

"Yes. Why?"

Lloyd turned and screamed for one of the men to get over to his house. One called Til Reed came running.

"Stay here! There's a rifle inside over the front door!" Lloyd told him. "Keep Katie and my daughter and baby in the main room with you, and don't let anybody in!"

"Yes, sir. What's goin' on?"

Lloyd struggled with rage. "If you'd been at Dune Hollow, you'd *know* what's going on! I can't explain right now."

He heard gunshots. More shouting. "Randy!" his father was screaming.

"Please, God, no!" Lloyd groaned. "Stay here and together!" he told Katie. He ran off the porch, shouting at Vance Kelly to get over to Brian's house and stay with Evie and the girls. "Send Brian to the main house! Somebody might be hurt!" *Stephen!* Were the boys okay? He hurried toward Jake's house, where Jake was stumbling around outside like a crazy man, shooting his rifle into the air and screaming Randy's name.

"Cole, help me stop him!" Lloyd shouted, running up to Jake and grabbing him around the middle. "Pa, calm down!"

"They took her! They took Randy!" Jake shoved him away, but Lloyd charged into him again.

"Goddamn it, Pa, you're going to shoot somebody by accident! Let go of the gun!"

Jake staggered and dropped the rifle, grasping Lloyd's arm for support. "They took her! They took your mother!"

"Pa, let's think this out! Get your head together!"

"They took her!" Jake repeated yet again, total devastation in his eyes.

"Come on inside, Pa. Maybe you're just all mixed up. Maybe she's in there. And what about the boys? Are Stephen and Little Jake still in there with Ben?"

Jake went to his knees. "Yes," he groaned. "I left Randy...in our bedroom in the loft when I ran out..."

"Well, maybe she's still up there." Lloyd struggled not to think the worst as he handed Jake's rifle to Cole.

Jake shook his head. "Just a little while ago...I was holding her. I'm supposed to keep her safe. She says she always feels...safe...with me...but I ran out...and they took her. They took my Randy."

"Pa, you're all mixed up from Midnight's kick." Lloyd helped him to his feet. "Come on inside."

"The boys...they hit Stephen...Little Jake..."

"Cole, come inside with us!" Lloyd ordered, feeling as though his head would explode. He tried to keep hold of Jake's arm, but Jake jerked away as he stumbled up the veranda steps. He turned to Cole.

"Give me my goddamn rifle!"

"Jake, we ain't the enemy. You gotta calm down."

Jake just stared at him a moment, then turned away and stumbled to the door. Lloyd followed him inside, where he reeled with horror at the sight of tumbled furniture and broken lamps. The three boys sat near the fireplace of the great room, sobbing and looking terrified. He glanced at a small table near the front window where his mother always sat to write letters. He could tell she'd started another one. A fountain pen lay near a still-open bottle of ink.

Jake screamed Randy's name, stumbling up the stairs to their loft bedroom. Even Lloyd was temporarily stunned, trying to get his thoughts straight, wondering if this was real.

"Pa?" Stephen sniffled, his nose bleeding. "They told us if we ran out...to get you...they'd kill Grandma."

"Stephen!" Lloyd felt like he was coming out of a trance. He rushed over to where Stephen sat on a ledge in front of the huge stone fireplace and knelt in front of him. "My God, Stephen, what happened?" He smoothed back the boy's hair as he leaned in and kissed his forehead.

Little Jake shivered and cried, a dark bruise forming on his right cheek, blood running from a cut on his head. Ben held his left arm.

"I think my arm's broke," he told Lloyd.

"They took her!" Little Jake seethed. "I'll *kill* 'em. We were gonna go after 'em, but they said if we went out of the house they'd know...and they'd kill Grandma."

"We weren't sure," Stephen added, "and Little Jake, he was knocked out for a while."

"Heck, I'm okay now," Little Jake insisted, his lips pouted with determination.

"Pa's gonna hate us," Ben wept. "We shoulda been able to help her. Pa's gonna give me away now. He won't want me anymore."

"Jake won't blame any of you for this," Lloyd soothed. "He'll likely blame himself, but he'll never blame you boys."

"The light from the barn fire must have helped them see to get away," Cole surmised. "They knew once that fire was over it would be too dark for us to follow."

The three boys jumped, and Lloyd looked up when Jake roared Randy's name from the upstairs bedroom. Minutes later he came stumbling out, and Lloyd saw him—the fire in his dark eyes, the thunder in his presence, the dark aura that seemed to hover around the man. His heart fell when he saw that Jake Harkner the outlaw had returned full force.

Thirty-six

JAKE CAME DOWN THE STAIRS, FULLY CLOTHED, HIS guns strapped on. He headed for a locked cabinet where he kept his shotgun and repeater, other rifles, and another six-gun. He didn't even stop to unlock it. He kicked in the glass and ripped open one of the doors, nearly making the entire cabinet fall over.

Ben started crying harder.

Jake reached inside and pulled out the extra handgun, shoving it into his belt at the back, then took out an extra cartridge belt, which he hung over his shoulder. He grabbed both the shotgun and carbine, taking them over to the kitchen table and literally throwing them onto it, along with the cartridge belt. He came back to grab boxes of shotgun shells.

The room was full of his presence. It seemed as though the whole house almost shook. Lloyd watched Jake closely.

"What the hell do you think you're doing?" Lloyd asked, slowly rising from where he'd knelt in front of the boys.

"What do you *think* I'm doing?" Jake answered darkly. "I'm going after my *wife*! *My* wife!"

Brian came in with Evie and hurried over to the boys with his doctor bag.

"Daddy!" Evie exclaimed at the sight of him.

"Don't call me Daddy!" Jake seethed. He turned and glared at her. "I'm *nobody*'s daddy right now, Evie! I'm nobody's father and nobody's grandfather, and I likely won't be anybody's *husband* after this! I'm a man none of you has ever seen, and who I am has likely destroyed the only person who made me *human*! I felt this coming! I felt it in my *bones*! This is what happens when you let people who wrong you *live*!"

"Pa, you can't go after them in the dark. You'll only mess up good tracks trying to figure out which way they went," Lloyd argued. "There's enough snow on the ground that they'll be easy to follow by morning. We can—"

"By morning my wife will be dead or wishing she *was* dead!" Jake roared. "My Randy! My reason for living!"

"Pa, use your head!" Lloyd yelled, walking closer. "We need to think this out—get some of the men together. You do this your way, and you'll end up riding into a trap—or if you succeed, you could end up back in that courtroom!"

"If I lose your mother, I don't care if they *hang* me, so do you really think I give a damn right now about going back to jail?"

"No, Jake Harkner, I don't think you *do* give a damn!" Lloyd roared back. "I think of you right now as Jake—not my father—just *Jake*! And if you want to be the man I hated when he went to prison, you go ahead and *be* that man! You show your grandsons how you are when your own father takes over and creates a mean sonofabitch who goes out and kills first and asks questions later and then goes to prison for it!"

Jake charged into Lloyd, and Evie screamed and ducked out of the way when he slammed Lloyd against a wall. Lloyd shoved back, grabbing his father's shirt and jerking him around to pin him in return. "You listen to me, Jake Harkner, or I'll put another bruise on that jaw! I'll fucking shoot you before I let you go out there and destroy everything you've taken thirty years to build—thirty years to overcome—thirty years my *mother* put up with and hung on to and loved you through!"

Jake grabbed his wrists and shoved, but Lloyd hung on, pushing back. "Go ahead! Be your father, Jake!" Lloyd seethed. "Show the boys what he was like! Now your grandsons can *meet* him! And then you can go out there and kill all those men without thinking first—and you can kill *him* all over again, just like you did with all the others!"

"Daddy," Evie softly whimpered.

Brian tried to comfort the three boys, all of them bleeding and shaking.

Jake and Lloyd just stared at each other.

"*She* said that," Jake said quietly, obviously speaking only to Lloyd. "That night in the wagon all those years ago when we..." He closed his eyes. "Let go of me."

"You going to calm down? Your grandsons are watching, Jake!"

"Just let go of me."

Lloyd watched him closely as he stepped back, letting go of Jake's shirt. He grabbed his hair and pulled it behind his back as they continued watching each other.

"Your mother said that—that first night in the wagon when I thought I could make her hate me by behaving like my father." He turned away, running a hand over his eyes. "I *wanted* her to hate me. I knew what her life would be like if she stayed with me, but the damn woman...wouldn't go away. Even those two years I left and lived with...whores and outlaws again...she waited for me, and she took me back and never asked any questions." He grasped his stomach. "Now this. This is what she gets for staying with me. I was crazy to think it wouldn't someday come back to slap her right in the face!" He let out an odd gasp and wiped at his eyes. "Lloyd, they've got my *wife*! My *wife*! The woman who is my reason for...*breathing*!"

"And she's my *mother*! Do you think I don't want to go out there and blow all of them to pieces? You can't do this alone, and you can't do it without a *plan*, which includes taking some of the men with us. At least we'll have witnesses. After what happened in Denver, we can't just go after Mom alone and kill men. Everything has changed, Pa. You're not a marshal, and there are new laws. We've already talked about that. We don't even know for sure who these men are."

"We damn well *do* know!" Jake looked at the boys. "Was one of them missing some fingers?"

Stephen sniffed and nodded.

"The one who took Grandma said to tell you"—Ben jerked in another sob—"that Brad has your...wife...and he'll make you real sorry...you killed his pa and brothers." He wiped at his nose with his shirtsleeve. "You can give me back, if you want. You don't have to keep me. I promised I'd help you look after Mom, and I didn't do it." He started crying harder.

"Grampa, are you mad at us?" Little Jake asked, still shivering in sobs. "We tried to stop them. But they were too strong!" He broke into harder crying. "I wanna *kill* 'em! Take us with you, Grampa. Let us go after 'em, too!"

Jake looked at Lloyd, then turned away again. "I damn well know better than most how it feels to try defending someone you love and not be strong enough to do it." He looked back at the boys. "I'm not angry with any of you. Understand? It's damn obvious how hard you tried to stop them. I know what that's like, and I'm proud of how you boys tried to help." He looked at Lloyd again. "It's those three we chased off the J&L last summer. That's how they were able to avoid being noticed and how they knew exactly which house to hit. They set that fire as a distraction, only they probably didn't plan on all three boys being here."

"There were five of them," Stephen spoke up.

Jake came even more alert. "*Five?*" He looked from

Lloyd to Cole. "We only kicked three off this ranch. We know who the fourth one is." He looked at the boys. "Did you catch names?"

Little Jake nodded. "Yes, there was the one called Brad. I remember those three men we got rid of last summer. They were part of 'em. But there was another one. I think he maybe used to work for us, but I can't remember for sure."

"I think one of them called him Clem," Stephen sniffled.

Jake ran a hand through his hair, his whole countenance seeming to actually rumble like thunder. "Clem Sutton!" He looked at Lloyd. "It has to be Clem Sutton, the one who called your mother a—"

Lloyd's jaw twitched in repressed anger. "We should have killed him *and* the other three when we had the chance, but we couldn't, Pa. It just doesn't work that way anymore."

"A man draws on you—you're *supposed* to kill him! And they have all drawn on me again, in another way. And I'm fucking shooting back!" Jake turned to Cole, who'd watched everything from near the doorway. "You gather some men," Jake told him. "The best ones! Have them pack some gear and plenty of ammunition and be ready to ride out the minute it's even remotely light out!"

Cole nodded. "Yes, sir. I'm damn sorry, Jake. Every man on this ranch loves that woman."

Cole walked out, and Jake turned to Evie. "Who's watching the girls?"

"Rodriguez and Teresa."

"Til Reed is with Katie," Lloyd told him.

"You go back home and pack your things and get your rifle and handguns," Jake told Lloyd.

"I'm not leaving this house until I'm sure you won't try to sneak out on your own yet tonight. I know you,

Pa, but if you go out there now, you might mess up a good trail."

"This is *Randy*! She belongs to *me*! To *me*! I'm supposed to protect her." He turned away and bent over. "*¡Lo siento, querida! ¡Favor perdóname! ¡Favor perdóname!*"

"Evie, get some washrags and hot water," Brian said quietly. "I need to clean the blood off these boys' faces."

"Grampa, we're goin' with you," Little Jake spoke up. "You gotta take us!"

Jake breathed deeply and straightened, looking over at the boys. "It might be a hard ride, and I might do things boys your age shouldn't see."

"We don't care!" Stephen spoke up. "She's our grandma, and they hit her. That one called Brad hit her so's she'd quit fighting them. She fought real good, and she screamed for you, but you couldn't hear because of the fire and all the shouting outside."

Jake planted an arm against the wall and rested his head on it. "Oh my God," he groaned. "What was she wearing?"

"Just…her housecoat," Little Jake answered, breaking into tears again. "It fell open, and they looked at her, but we looked away 'cause she's our grandma."

"Jesus God Almighty," Jake whispered.

"Daddy, just get her back here. I can talk to her," Evie spoke up.

Jake shook his head. "The two most important women in my life—first my daughter, now my wife—and because of me—"

"No, Daddy! Not because of you," Evie told him. She carried a small pan of water and a washrag over to Brian. "It's because of Satan and the hatred and vengeance he creates in people's hearts."

"Then Satan is in *my* heart, because no man has ever been more full of hatred and vengeance right now than I am!" Jake looked at Lloyd. "I can't do this. I can't *not* kill them!"

"Pa, we'll figure something out. You just need witnesses. That's all I'm saying. Don't go after them alone. That's what they want. Those three we kicked off the ranch wanted a reputation for killing you, and they're at it again. And Clem just wants revenge for that beating you gave him. I don't know how they hooked up with Brad Buckley, but they did, and we have to be smart going after them. If you go alone, they'll shoot you to pieces!"

"We're goin' with you, Grampa," Little Jake repeated. "Don't you leave us behind!"

Jake glanced his way, and in that moment he saw himself—the hurt and angry and heartbroken little boy who couldn't stop his father from beating his mother to death—the little boy who had to help bury her and throw dirt on her face. He saw his own soul in Little Jake's dark eyes. He looked at Ben, and he saw a terrified boy who feared losing the only real family he'd ever known.

"Ben, you aren't going anywhere. None of this is your fault, understand? Not any one of you is to blame for this. It's obvious all of you tried real hard, and I know how that feels. You're all going with us because you *need* to go. But it will be hard riding. Do you think you're up to it?"

They all nodded, brightening a little.

"My arm feels better." Ben sniffled. "I thought it was broke."

Brian began gently feeling the boy's arm while Evie washed Little Jake's face.

"And you need to do exactly as I say, understand?" Jake ordered.

"Yes, sir," they answered almost in unison.

"The last thing either Lloyd or I need is to lose one of you over this. You let Brian finish cleaning you up and let him do something about that cut on your head, Little Jake."

"We jumped on 'em, Pa," Ben told him. "All three of us. We tried real hard. Little Jake got a poker stick, but they knocked it out of his hands, and they swung it at Little Jake. That's how he got a cut on his head."

Jake could not control the darkness that engulfed him, remembering his father using a fireplace poker to beat his own little brother to death. Flashes from the horror of his childhood kept stabbing at him, combined with envisioning Brad Buckley and the no-goods he'd chased off manhandling Randy—his sweet, tiny, devoted, beautiful wife—his reason for living. *Randy!* Clem Sutton had called her a whore. Did he intend to try to prove it? Just a little while ago they'd made love, and it was beautiful, and he'd worried about hurting her. Now…

"Pa, I'm staying here with you," Lloyd told him. "Me and Evie and Brian. One of the men can go to the house and get my gear. Katie knows where everything is, and the men know where my saddle is. Thank God my own horse was in the other barn and plenty more outside. The men can have everything ready by the crack of dawn. I'll tell Cole to try to find Midnight. You have to stay calm and think this out. The way you went after Evie in Oklahoma just about killed you. You didn't eat, and you didn't sleep for days. Dixie thought you were dying, and so did I. If you repeat what happened then, it *will* kill you this time, and if ever my mom needed you, it's going to be after this. You can't die finding her, and you can't risk going to jail or getting yourself hung. Get that through your head!"

Jake remained turned away. "My God, Evie, this has to be hard on you. Brian, too."

"We'll get through it, Daddy. I'm a lot stronger now. And maybe…" She wiped at sudden tears. "Maybe it won't be…as bad. I'll be here for Mother when you get her back."

Jake just shook his head. "She's twenty-four years

older than you, Evie. When you're older..." *Sometimes things...hurt more.* "And what happened to you...there is no comparing any of it. It *never* should have happened in the first place! You could have died, and so could your mother. She's so...fragile. And in the end, this all comes back to *me!*"

He turned and walked past them into the kitchen to start loading his repeater and his shotgun. "Lloyd, you tell the men that as far as the outside world is concerned, we went after more rustlers. I don't want your mother's name mentioned in any of this. We couldn't keep Evie's name out of the news because the whole town of Guthrie knew what happened, but this is right here on the ranch, and it's going to *stay* right here on the ranch! I don't think your mother could take that kind of publicity...not that kind. You make sure the men understand that." He glanced over at the boys. "Do you boys understand what I'm saying? We're going after *rustlers*."

The boys nodded.

"Your grandmother is a beautiful, proud woman who can be just as...sophisticated and refined...as the best of them. She's smart...and she's..." Jake began angrily ramming cartridges into his repeater. "Hell, she...taught me like a kid who'd never been to school. She used to teach me words I called fancy. She actually made me *enjoy* learning new words. She took a worthless, no-good outlaw and showed him..."

He glanced at a fresh loaf of Randy's homemade bread sitting near the stove.

"Evie, she's so...small. But she...stood right up to me." He kept shoving bullets into the repeater. "When she took that bullet out of me all those years ago, she hid my guns. Can you believe that? She hid my guns, and no matter...how much I threatened her...she wouldn't tell me where they were."

He angrily retracted the repeater so a bullet would

be in the chamber, then set it down and opened the shotgun. "I found my guns…in a potato bin, and when she came in and saw me holding them…" He smiled through tears as he shoved slugs into the shotgun. "Her beautiful eyes…got so big…and then she just…*looked* at me…and I knew I was falling in love…but I also knew nothing *worse* could happen to her than for a man like me to love her."

He slammed the shotgun closed. "And I was fucking right!" He took one of his .44s from its holster and checked to be sure it was fully loaded. "And right now, I don't much care if I go to prison or the gallows. I'm getting my wife back, and no man who touches her wrongly is going to live to talk about it!" He got up, shoving the gun back into the holster. "And Brad Buckley isn't going to die easy! If he thinks me slamming that rifle butt into his chest and breaking his breastbone was bad, he'll find out that was like a slap on the hand compared to what I'll do to him if he's…" He couldn't finish. "I'll have him wishing he was never born!"

Thirty-seven

"I AIN'T NEVER SEEN NOBODY WHO LOOKED MORE dangerous than Jake right now," Vance Kelly said quietly to Cole.

It was barely light enough to see. Cole, Terrel, Rodriguez, and Vance rode out with Jake and Lloyd. Both grandsons and Ben were also with them, and Jake had asked Brian to come along in case Randy or one of the men should need medical help.

"He was pretty wild-looking that day he beat Clem for insultin' his wife," Cole answered. "This is gonna be a hell of a lot worse."

"The son ain't any less scary-lookin' right now than the father," Terrel added. "I reckon that's what made them a team to deal with when they were marshals in Oklahoma. I didn't know a man could tote that many weapons neither."

The three men hung back as they talked, steam coming from their mouths because of the cold air.

"I still say the look in his eyes is more intimidating than the way he's armed," Vance added.

"The whole thing is a shame," Cole grumbled. "Ain't a finer woman than that man's wife. I don't blame him for wantin' to kill those men. I want to kill them, too."

Jake rode in the lead on Midnight. One of the men had managed to find the horse before they left. Part of his tail was burned off, but the horse was fine otherwise.

Those men left behind would bury what was left of Pepper once the barn ashes were cool enough to sift through them. It was a job none of them relished. Teresa would clean up the mess left at the house. Jake had ordered two of the men to take at least two weeks' worth of heating wood and supplies up to the line shack in the northwest quarter of the J&L. "Randy wanted me to take her back there for months, and I kept putting it off," he'd told them darkly. "I'll damn well take her there when we get her back, and we'll stay there as long as it takes to—" He never finished.

After the few words Cole and Vance exchanged, no one else spoke. Even Stephen and Little Jake and Ben were somber, Little Jake's countenance almost as dark and menacing as his grandfather's. Cole admired their determination. All three boys had bruises and stitches—Stephen with a swollen lip and nose, Little Jake with a bruised cheek and a bandage around his forehead from the bad cut there, which had also puffed out into a mean bump. Ben had a black eye and could hardly pull himself up on his horse because of a badly bruised arm and shoulder.

The ride was eerily quiet because of how the snow muffled the sound of their horses' hooves. There was only the squeak of saddles and the occasional snort of one of the horses, whose nostrils flared and steamed against the cold air. Rodriguez led two spare horses packed with supplies, including clothes for Randy and a rabbit-fur coat she favored. Jake insisted on bringing it, afraid she wasn't being kept warm enough.

Jake kept up a steady pace for the next two hours, not saying a thing, keeping his eyes either straight ahead or looking down at tracks. Lloyd rode right beside him, thinking how the men they were after had left a trail that was too easy.

Jake finally slowed up, looking around.

"They didn't try hiding their trail even a little," Lloyd spoke up. "It's a setup. Mom is just the bait for the bigger prize."

"*Me*," Jake answered in a deep growl. He dismounted and studied the tracks closer. "Hard to tell which horse is carrying your mother. She's so small her weight doesn't make much difference when with a man on a big horse." He stayed knelt beside the tracks for a moment, then cleared his throat and wiped at his eyes. "Jesus," he said in a near whisper. "You could break that woman in half so easy, Lloyd. She could have broken bones."

"Pa, stop torturing yourself. Mom is way stronger than you give her credit for."

"You know the Buckleys, Lloyd. You were there when I killed Brad's father for abusing a fifteen-year-old girl. And your mother isn't fifteen. She's fifty, Lloyd. *Fifty!* No one would ever guess it to look at her, but it's a fact. How many women are that beautiful at fifty?" He rose, wiping at his eyes again. "The fact remains she might not…make it through something like this. I know every tiny inch of her body and how easily she bruises. For God's sake, even her *bones* are tiny." He remounted. "God knows if they're keeping her warm enough," he added.

"Pa, don't forget that when we went after Evie, they had a good three- or four-day start on us. This is all fresh. We'll find her a lot quicker than we found Evie. And it looks like they've kept a pretty steady pace themselves, which means they haven't had time to stop and—" He didn't finish.

Jake paused to light a cigarette. "It's like Gretta said in that courtroom, Lloyd. Some men don't *need* much time." *And your mother isn't made for that. You have to treat a woman like her with gentleness.* How many times had he worried he'd hurt her? He'd left little bruises on her bottom once from grasping her too tightly when making love to her. She said she never noticed, but that had always bothered him. He knew an older woman needed special handling. Things hurt that never used to hurt. He knew every inch of her body and every sound she made, and he damn well knew things were a little different. He hadn't missed one beat with her, and the thought of men manhandling her made him crazy.

"Keep an eye out!" he shouted back to the others. "They just might leave her off somewhere because she'll hold them up. A person can freeze to death in no time out here! We'll rest the horses five minutes and get going again!"

"They're headed south," Lloyd commented. "Looks like maybe for Little Jake's Valley. That's wide-open country. If we go riding into that valley, they'll be waiting for us and pick us off like shooting tin cans off a fence."

"None of it makes any sense," Jake commented. "They know how well we know this country—know we'll catch up to them. How can they possibly think they can get away with this?"

"Because Brad Buckley doesn't have a brain in his head," Lloyd answered. "You know he doesn't think beyond the end of his pecker. The fucker just wants revenge, and he thinks because of what happened in Denver, you can't do anything about it."

"He'll damn well find out different!"

"You still need to be careful, Pa. Mom will need you in the worst way, so you'll need to be here for her, which means not doing something that will get you arrested."

Jake glanced sidelong at him, the cigarette between his lips. "I think you tried convincing me of that back at the house last night."

Lloyd pulled a cigarette from inside his sheepskin jacket. "I couldn't let you just go riding off in a rage without thinking this out. And it was too damn dark to follow any tracks."

Jake quietly drew on the cigarette. "Are we okay?"

Lloyd frowned as he struck a match and lit his cigarette. "What do you mean?"

"You were pretty serious back there. I think you really wanted to land a fist into me."

Lloyd took a deep drag on the cigarette. "Well, Pa, sometimes I love you so much I really *do* want to land a fist into you just to straighten your ass out. If you will recall, you clobbered me pretty good when I visited you in prison."

Jake turned away.

"Why did you do that, Pa? Think about it."

Jake took another drag on his cigarette and watched the smoke combine with the steam his breath made in the cold air when he exhaled. "Because I loved you, and I wanted to stop you from going off and doing something stupid."

"And there you go. Sometimes you love somebody so much you want to hit them because you're scared for them."

Jake shook his head and put the cigarette back between his lips. "Well, if hitting means loving, then my father must have loved the *hell* out of me," he said, obvious angry sarcasm in the words.

"Yeah, well, that was a bit different."

"Oh, it was a bit different, all right."

Lloyd smoked quietly for a few seconds, aching for his father. "Do you think he loved you at all—I mean, even a little?"

"Hell no. Not even a little."

"Why do you think he let you live? He killed the rest of his family, but not you."

An almost evil darkness moved into Jake's eyes. "He kept me around for something to beat on. I was his entertainment."

Lloyd closed his eyes, finding it hard to imagine such hell, especially for a child. He couldn't even come close to imagining being that cruel to Stephen.

Jake looked over at Ben and his grandsons. "You three staying warm enough?"

"We're okay," Stephen answered.

"I want you to be prepared for just about anything. I don't know what we'll find or how I'll react, but you boys wanted to come along, and you deserve a piece of this. Just don't be surprised by anything I do, and remember that no matter what I do, you boys have to handle things like this the right way when you take over this ranch someday."

"We understand, Grampa," Little Jake told him.

Ben nodded.

"And I don't blame any of you for what happened, okay? Don't ever think I blame you or that I don't understand how you're feeling, because I damn well do."

"Thanks for letting us come, Grandpa," Stephen spoke up.

Lloyd took a good look at them as Jake remounted. "You boys sure you can do this? You're pretty beat up. Little Jake, how's that cut on your head? Do you have a headache or anything like that?"

Little Jake shook his head. He'd been in a constant pout ever since everything happened. "You're talkin' like Grandma would if she was here, Uncle Lloyd, askin' us if we're okay. She's the best grandma in the whole world."

Lloyd nodded, as scared for his mother as Jake was. "Yes, she is, Little Jake. And she's a real strong woman, stronger than your grandfather gives her credit for."

Jake shifted in his saddle, reminding Lloyd of a tightly wound spring about to release an explosion of emotional rage. He decided to try to lighten the mood, at least for the moment, partly for the boys, who still looked so brokenhearted. He wanted to cheer them up, at least a little. "Your grandma jokes with your grandpa about other women," he told them, raising his voice a little more to deliberately goad Jake.

Jake turned and scowled at him.

"You've heard stories about Grandpa and bad women," Lloyd teased.

The three boys tentatively smiled.

"Grampa says there's no such thing as bad women," Little Jake reminded Lloyd.

"Yes, well, that's your grandfather's weakness. He *does* have his weaknesses, and women is one of them. But if your grandmother ever caught him really misbehaving with some other woman, she'd give him a black eye."

"Nuh-uh," Little Jake protested.

"Oh, you bet she would. I told you she's stronger than she looks. Little as she is, she can handle your grampa like a puppy dog. She's got him right here." He held up his hand and made a fist. "Right in the palm of her hand. Big and mean as he is, she can rope him down like a calf."

The three boys giggled.

"*Can* she, Grampa?" Little Jake asked.

Jake gave the boys a half smile, as if realizing, like Lloyd did, that they needed some uplifting. "Sure she can," he answered.

"How can she do that?" Stephen asked.

Jake turned his gaze to Lloyd. "I'll let Lloyd answer that one."

Lloyd put on a very serious look. "Oh, a woman has her ways, Son. You'll find out when you're a little older."

"It's a very hard question to answer," Brian told Stephen. He smiled a little himself. "Let's just say a happy woman is much easier to live with than one who is mad at you."

Some of the men chuckled, and Lloyd thought about Katie and how just last night everything was beautiful and peaceful. Before the fire broke out, he'd been watching Katie breast-feed their new son. It had been such a sweet moment. He'd meant to make love to her when she was through. They hadn't made love since the baby was born, and right now he'd never wanted her more. He already missed her and the baby, missed the smell of the baby's little neck, missed how Katie smelled, how utterly beautiful she was when she was nursing.

Jake threw down his cigarette. "Let's get going," he told them, kicking Midnight's sides and riding off again.

"Time to get serious again, boys," Lloyd told the younger ones. "Don't any of you make one move on your own once we find Grandma. You let me and Grandpa take care of things."

"But we wanna help, Uncle Lloyd. Those men hurt Grandma."

"You just wait till Jake or I tell you what to do. I mean it, Little Jake—you most of all. You mind what we tell you. And your father has a say in this, too. Your mother is probably worried sick right now."

Brian nodded. "You mind your business, Little Jake."

Disgruntled, Little Jake got his roan mare underway to follow Jake as they took off again.

Within a half hour, Jake, who rode well ahead of the others, gave out a shrill whistle. Lloyd saw him riding hard, toward what looked like a horse—and a man on the ground beside it.

"Stay behind me!" Lloyd ordered the boys. "Rodriguez, stay with them!" He galloped ahead, and Cole, Terrel, and Vance charged their horses ahead to catch up. Rodriguez hung back with Brian and the boys, looking around cautiously. They were on open range now, with nothing for cover. "Come slowly," he told the boys. "Looks like Jake found one of them. That means we are getting closer."

Lloyd rode hard. "Holy shit," he muttered. Jake had already charged Midnight right into whoever was on the ground, deliberately trampling him.

Thirty-eight

LLOYD JUMPED OFF HIS HORSE BEFORE THE ANIMAL even came to a full stop. He ran toward Jake, who held a man by the front of his woolen jacket. "I didn't touch her!" the man screamed.

"You didn't *help* her either!" Jake kicked him hard in the privates. The man yelped and bent over, and Jake kicked him under the jaw, sending him sprawling. "You fucking bastard!"

Lloyd recognized Ronald Beck.

"Somebody stop him!" Beck begged. "I didn't touch her! I was comin' to tell you where they took her!"

"The *hell* you were!" Jake growled.

"My horse threw me!" Beck yelled through bloody teeth as he got to his hands and knees to get up. "I think my leg's broke, and I think I've got cracked ribs from you ridin' your horse over me, you sonofabitch."

He rubbed at his left thigh, which was exactly where Jake kicked him again. The man screamed in horrific pain and rolled on the ground, holding his leg with one hand and his privates with the other. "Stop! Please… stop!" he slurred through pain, spitting more blood. "I didn't plan on…him takin' your wife, Jake! I can…help you find her!"

Jake reached for him, but Lloyd grabbed his arm. "Pa, wait! Maybe he knows where they plan to hole up. That could give us an advantage!"

The rest of the men surrounded Beck, and the three boys rode up with Rodriguez. Before anyone could stop him, Little Jake got off his horse and picked up a rock. He threw it directly at Beck, cracking it against his forehead. The man cried out and cringed, wrapping his arms around his head. Brian jumped off his horse and grabbed hold of Little Jake, hanging on tight as the boy struggled to get away so he could "beat up" Ronald Beck some more.

"Let Jake and Lloyd handle this!" Brian ordered his son. "We need information, Little Jake. You calm down!"

"You're a sonofabitch!" Little Jake snarled at Beck while Brian still held him. "Grampa's gonna *kill* you for hurting my grandma!"

Stephen ran up and kicked dirt on the man, and Ben came up behind him and kicked him in the rear.

"You boys get back now," Jake told them. He walked up and shoved Beck onto his back with a booted foot, holding his foot against his throat. "You want to live?"

Blood poured from both sides of Beck's mouth, and he kept one knee bent in an effort to protect his privates, while his left leg was sprawled out oddly sideways. "My leg! My leg!" he screamed.

"I'll *stomp* on it if you don't help us find my wife!" Jake threatened. "And I don't want any lies!"

"I'm tellin' the truth!" Beck nearly sobbed. "We was just supposed to burn the barn...make sure you lost a few horses and feed for...shootin' half my hip away and blowin' Clyde Pace's fingers off!" He winced and groaned. "My leg!"

Lloyd walked around the other side of Beck. "We could legally hang you just for that!" Lloyd told him. "Pepper died in that fire, you bastard!"

Beck's eyes widened. "Oh, man, we didn't mean for nobody to die in it!"

"Too late!" Cole spoke up. "My best friend died a horrible death on account of you! If Jake don't kill you, *I'll* kill you! It won't be the first time I've killed a man. Jake knows I ain't no angel, and he won't stop me!"

"Wait!" Beck begged, looking up at Jake in wide-eyed terror. "I can help! Jake, I didn't mean for somebody like Pepper to die or for that Buckley kid to take your wife! That wasn't part of the deal!"

Jake took his foot away and pulled out his .44 and cocked it before pointing it at Beck's head. "This thing has a hair trigger, so if I think for one minute you're bullshitting me, I'll get all upset and might accidentally kill you!" he growled. He knelt down and shoved the gun against Beck's cheek. "How in hell did you get mixed up with Brad Buckley?"

Beck grimaced in pain. "Gretta's place...just before you...came to Denver and...got in that trouble." He gritted his teeth when Jake shoved harder. "Buckley was there...with Mike Holt. Me and Clyde and...Tucker... we...got to know 'em...found out about Holt wantin' Lloyd dead, and Buckley...he hated you. He told us about all the shit that happened...back in Oklahoma." He tried to scooch away, his eyes wild. "Please don't... pull that trigger! I know what you did to Mike Holt!"

Lloyd shoved a foot against Beck's back so he couldn't wiggle any farther away. "We know Clem Sutton was part of this!" he growled. "How in hell did you meet up with Clem? You never worked for us the same time he did."

Jake shoved the gun harder against Beck's cheek, and Beck cringed, making a childish squealing sound. He spit more blood.

"Goddamn it, I think some of my teeth are loose, and I think I've got some broken ribs," he repeated. "And my leg—" He broke into tears. "Please don't—" he whined.

Jake shoved the gun harder. "*Fuck* your leg! I'll break your *other* leg if you don't talk!"

"You're lucky your balls are still attached to the rest of you!" Lloyd stormed. "Did my *mother* cry like you're crying now? Did she beg Buckley to let her go?"

"I told Buckley…he shouldn't take her—"

"The hell you did!" Lloyd knelt down and grasped the man's hair, pulling hard. "Tell us how you all ended up in on this together!"

Beck spit more blood. "That night…after meetin' up with Buckley and Holt at Gretta's place…me and Clyde and Tucker went out and got…drunk with them. Buckley thought it would be a good idea for me and Clyde and Tucker to try gettin' a job…at the J&L… get to know the lay of the land so's Buckley could make plans…'cause he knew he couldn't…come on to the J&L…so he needed somebody to…help him." He looked at Jake, his eyes showing his terror. "Then you shot Mike Holt…and Buckley got run out of Denver… so me and the boys decided to get a job with you… anyway…'cause you were so famous and all…figured we could take you and make a name…for ourselves. When you…shot us up and kicked us off, we went back to Denver, lookin' for work. Clem…he showed up at that same tavern one night…braggin' as how he'd like to kill…Jake Harkner on account of you'd…beat him up bad. So we got to talkin' about…how we could all…get even with you. We'd all…worked on the J&L…so we knew winter was the best time to sneak in…when not so many men was out watchin' the borders."

Lloyd jerked his head back. "What about Brad Buckley? He was forced to leave Denver! How did you end up with him?"

"We all got jobs…at the railroad depot. Needed time to…plan and…lo and behold…Brad Buckley came back to Denver on a train one day…and we all…got back together. Buckley, he came up with the idea of… burnin' down one of your barns. He was…glad to know men who'd worked on the J&L. But I swear, Jake…the thing…with your wife… That was all Buckley's idea."

"You and the others abused my wife and beat on

my grandsons!" Jake growled. "*Boys!* Just *boys!* Nobody hurts anyone in my family and gets away with it!" Jake slammed the barrel of his gun across Beck's face, and the man cried out, staying on the ground and begging Jake not to shoot him. He curled up, bawling like a baby.

"What have they done with my wife?" Jake roared.

"N-nothin'," Beck answered. "Not…yet. Clyde and…Tucker… They don't want nothin' to do with hurtin' her." Beck's words were muffled against the snow as he kept an arm up against his head. "It's…Buckley who kept sayin'…what he was gonna do to her. I got… throwed by my horse. That's how you…found me. My leg hurt somethin' awful…and I couldn't get up. The others…just left me behind."

Jake jerked him onto his back again. A deep gash on his right cheek was bleeding profusely. "So your first story about leaving them to come and tell us where to find my wife was a *lie* to save your ass! You saw us coming and figured to make up something that sounded good." He pressed the barrel of his gun painfully against Beck's eye. "You've told us two stories, Beck! How about the *truth* this time? Where did they take my wife?" he demanded, unmoved by the man's weeping. "Is she warm? Did any of you hit her?"

"No! Not me!" Beck sobbed. "Buckley…he hit her. The more she fought, the more he hit her. He threatened…to do things…with her…but we didn't want…no part of that. They're takin' her…to that old cabin on the west side…of Fire Valley. Me and the boys…told him that was a good spot…'cause they can see you comin' from the cabin. They're gonna…hole up there and… take you down."

"And through it all you didn't do a thing to help my *wife*, did you?" An enraged Jake brought his pistol hard across the side of Beck's head, this time near the temple. He got off the man and holstered his gun, walking a few feet away and bending over in grief at the thought of Buckley hitting Randy, maybe doing something worse.

Beck rolled over again, managing to get to one knee. Blood dripped onto the ground from his mouth and from the cuts from Jake's pistol-whipping and split skin at his forehead where Little Jake had hit him with the rock. He wept from the sharp pain in his scrotum and his broken leg. "I couldn't...help her. Buckley...would have shot me!"

"Well, now *I* want to shoot you!" Lloyd seethed. "You should have taken your chances with *them*!"

"Buckley was...in a hurry! He didn't want...to wait for me." Beck reached up to put his hand against the cut on his head. Jake turned to Lloyd, and the look on his face made Lloyd fear his father was about to have a heart attack and die. "Pa, let us go on without you. We can do this. You look really bad."

"I'm *fine*!" His voice was gravelly with rage and devastation. He walked closer to Beck. "We have a right to hang this man for burning down the barn. A man *died* in that fire! That's murder. And taking your mother is kidnapping."

"No! Don't hang me! Please!" Beck collapsed. "My head! My...head!" He groaned, rolled sideways into the snow, then onto his back. He looked at Jake pleadingly before his eyes rolled back so only the whites showed. He suddenly stiffened.

Lloyd frowned. "Pa, I think he just died."

Jake pushed at his body with his booted foot and got no movement.

"Is he dead, Grampa?" Little Jake asked.

"I hope he *is* dead," Stephen spoke up.

"Brian, get over here," Jake told his son-in-law.

Brian finally let go of Little Jake, whom he'd held onto through the entire ordeal. He walked over and knelt beside Ronald Beck. He felt for a pulse, then sighed. "I think Stephen got his wish. He's not breathing." He rose. "Could be a broken rib punctured a lung, or maybe it was that last blow to the head. You came awfully close to his temple, Jake. I suspect he was bleeding inside the skull."

Jake glanced at the boys. "I told you there would be violence. I hope you boys understand a man can't always behave like this. All of you know right from wrong, and you'll likely be better at handling these things when you grow up than I am. Rodriguez can take all of you back home if this is too much for you."

"No, sir, we aren't going anywhere!" Stephen told him. "We came to help, and I think me and Little Jake can help more than you think." He looked at his cousin. "Can't we, Little Jake? Remember that big crack in the rocks we found by that cabin at Fire Valley?"

Little Jake's eyes lit up. "You mean Little Jake's Valley," he said proudly. "And yeah, I remember that big crack."

"Me, too," Ben added, his face brightening.

"Stephen, what are you talking about?" Lloyd asked.

"That time late last summer when you and Grampa took us with you to Little Jake's Valley to shoot rifles and look for wild mustangs, you let us play up at that cabin. There's a cliff right behind the cabin with a big crack in it."

"I know that. The cliff must be a good twenty feet higher than the cabin. It butts right up against it."

"Me and Little Jake and Ben looked into that crack and wanted to see how far it went. So we wiggled into it sideways," Stephen told Lloyd.

"You could have got wedged in there and been trapped!" Brian scolded.

"It gets bigger when you get in there," Little Jake told his father. "We just kept goin', and it got wider at one spot, then smaller again."

"It kept going up, and we just kept following it because we wanted to see how far it went," Stephen explained. "It ends out at the big rise that leads up to the cabin from the side. We went back the other way and ended up right back at the cabin."

"We never told you because we thought you'd be mad at us for going in there," Ben told Jake.

Jake frowned. "You saying you boys could get close to that cabin without being seen?"

Stephen nodded. "Ben can't now 'cause he got a lot bigger over the winter. But I'm still tall and skinny, and Little Jake is, too. Those men will be watching for us all to ride in across the valley—figure we'll make good targets, I'll bet. But you guys could ride around the outer rim to the north side behind trees and boulders above the cabin, while me and Little Jake sneak through that crack and come out to the side of the cabin where they don't see us. We could chase off their horses so's the men in there can't run out and get away."

"You gotta ride straight up from the valley to get to the cabin otherwise," Ben added. "This way you'd be closer without them seein' you, and you could use all those big boulders for cover. Without their horses, they'd be trapped in there."

"Yeah!" Stephen added. "You'd have to be on foot if you go around behind it up high, but at least you'd be close enough to shoot at 'em without them seeing you coming."

Jake looked at Lloyd.

"It's too dangerous," Lloyd commented. "That damn crack could have changed or moved, and they could get trapped in there, let alone the kind of men who are in that cabin. The boys could be shot. We can't risk it."

"But, Pa—" Stephen begged.

"I'm not putting any of you in that kind of danger," Lloyd interrupted. "If your grandmother lives through this, it would break her heart to realize one of you was hurt or killed over it."

The three boys pouted. "We can do it, Pa!" Stephen declared boldly. "We can ride, and we know all about takin' care of cattle and horses, and you've been teachin' us how to handle rifles and how to handle the men." He sat straighter in his saddle in an effort to seem bigger than he really was. "You gotta see we're getting to be men now, too. Grandma says we are."

"And you took us hunting last fall," Ben put in. "If I can shoot a deer, I can handle a rifle good enough to help give cover for you and Jake once Stephen and Little Jake chase off those men's horses."

"You gotta let us do this, Uncle Lloyd," Little Jake added with a dark, determined look in his eyes. He glanced at his own father, sure Brian was just as against this as Jake and Lloyd were. "We know how to herd cattle and rope calves, and we know you have to make sure they don't overgraze certain sections, and we know how to store feed and hay and how much to give the horses," he said proudly, turning to his grandfather. "You and Uncle Lloyd don't realize how much we already know, Grampa. And we'll be safe in that crack in the rock. They'll never know we're there."

"Yeah!" Stephen put in. "We promise to come right back out if we can't make it through. We won't do anything stupid. Please, please let us do it. You said we could help save Grandma."

"You *gotta* let us help," Ben spoke up. "We saw what they did to her, and I don't think I can ever forget not bein' strong enough to help her. If you ride up to that cabin to help and they shoot you dead before you can even get there, then *nobody* can help her. And if you go around behind and start shootin' from there, they can run out and ride out through the valley before you get all of them. By the time you got your own horses to go after them, they'd have a big head start."

"With Grandma inside the cabin, you wouldn't have time to go after them," Stephen added.

Jake looked at Lloyd. "They have a point. We can't waste one extra minute getting your mother out of there. Going up through the valley will take longer, and we risk being target practice for them."

Lloyd turned to Brian. "You're Little Jake's father. You have just as much say in this as anyone."

Brian sighed, turning to Little Jake and seeing the excitement in his eyes. "I haven't been able to stop my son from doing much of anything he really wants to do." He looked at Jake. He remembered the time in Guthrie when Little Jake was much smaller. He'd run out of the house and down the street when Jake was in the middle of a shoot-out. Little Jake had thought he could help his grandfather. "You know how stubborn he is. If I don't let him do this, he'll grumble and stomp and pout for weeks. And be that as it may, I think these boys need and deserve to help any way they can. They need to feel they're an important part of this. I can't believe my own words, but that's how I feel."

Little Jake grinned. "Thanks, Pa! Grampa will make sure nothin' happens to us."

Brian kept his gaze on Jake. "You know how it feels, Jake, to not be big and strong enough to stop your father from what he did to your mother. You've lived with that your whole life. Maybe we should take the chance on the boys not having to live with the same memories." He shifted his gaze to Lloyd. "I hate to say they're right, and I hope to hell I don't live to regret it, but I think you should let them try this."

Lloyd studied the boys, then turned away for a moment, torn with indecision. He looked at Jake. "What do you think?"

Jake looked down at Ronald Beck's body. He shivered from the bitter cold, again feeling sick at how cold

Randy might be right now…if she was still alive. "I think we don't have a whole lot of choice." He met Lloyd's gaze, his eyes bloodshot from no sleep. "And I think we have to hope this is due to your sister praying over this. Maybe the boys finding that crack was a godsend." He shared with Lloyd the weight of what this could mean—both of them feeling the horror of what it would mean if they lost one of the boys over this.

Lloyd took a deep breath and looked across the open land toward Little Jake's Valley. "I'm going to trust in Evie's prayers." He walked over to his horse, pulling out his repeating rifle. He handed it out to Stephen. "Take this with you—just for protection in case it's needed."

The boys squirmed excitedly in their saddles.

"Thanks, Pa!" Stephen answered, taking the rifle and shoving it into a boot on his saddle.

"These are dangerous men, Stephen," Lloyd warned. "You and Little Jake stay right inside the crack in that cliff where they can't see you if you think for one minute you can't get those horses out of there without being seen, understand? If you see your grandmother, don't go try to help her. *We'll* take care of that. You just get those horses out of there. You're men in a lot of ways, but you aren't man enough yet for the kind of men at that cabin."

"We'll be careful," Little Jake promised.

Lloyd glanced at Jake. "I don't know any other way to get to that cabin unseen than on foot, like they said."

"If we get going right now, we can get there by dawn." Jake headed for Midnight and mounted up.

"What about Beck's body?" Brian asked.

"Leave it for the wolves," Jake answered coldly. "They're plenty damn hungry this time of year. By spring there won't be enough of him left to recognize." He turned his horse and scanned the rest of the men. "And remember one thing. As far as we know, none of the men involved in this even has family. I know for a fact Brad Buckley has none left. They could all disappear from the face of the earth and no one would know or care, so it doesn't make much difference what we do with them."

Cole nodded. "We get your meanin'."

"It would be like none of this happened," Jake added. "I never want one word of this to go outside of this ranch—or for the public to know my wife was involved in any of this. I'll not have her talked about. You men keep that in mind." He turned Midnight and rode off.

The men looked at each other, thinking the same thing. None of them cared to cross Jake Harkner.

Little Jake glanced at Ronald Beck's dead body. "Is Grampa gonna kill the rest of 'em?" he asked his father.

Brian rubbed at his eyes. "I expect so."

"Good," Ben added.

"He'd probably try to handle this differently if this didn't involve your grandmother," Brian added. "And after what happened to your mother, Little Jake, I don't blame him. But you boys need to keep it straight in your heads that you can't always handle things this way."

"We know, Uncle Brian," Stephen told him.

"Let's get going," Cole told them. He deliberately rode his horse over Beck's body before heading out after Jake and Lloyd. Everyone else charged ahead to catch up with Jake, leaving a bloody, broken Ronald Beck behind for the wolves.

Thirty-nine

"ARE YOU SCARED, STEPHEN?" LITTLE JAKE SHIMMIED ahead of his cousin as they made their way through a literal crack in the earth.

"Kind of," Stephen answered, looking up a good seventy feet or more at the sunlight above. He clung to his father's rifle, trying to be careful not to scrape it against the rocks as he skimmed sideways through the crevice, which in places seemed almost impassable. "I'd be more scared if we were doing this alone, but Grampa and my dad will be out there in the rocks, covering us when we make off with those men's horses."

"I wish Ben could have come with us, but he's gettin' real big. I don't think he would have fit."

"Heck no." Both boys spoke just above a whisper.

"Will you shoot one of 'em with your rifle?" Little Jake asked.

"Pa told me to use his rifle just for self-defense if I have to."

"What if they see us and come after us? I'm gonna shoot 'em."

"How are you going to do that?"

Little Jake stopped and reached under his shirt, pulling out a Colt .45 from the waist of his pants.

"Little Jake!" Stephen stared wide-eyed at the handgun. "Where'd you get that?"

"Cole's saddlebag. I seen him put it in there for a spare when we packed to leave the ranch."

"You could accidentally shoot yourself—or *me*! You

shouldn't have that gun! Grandpa will be *really* mad! So will your dad!"

"I don't care. Them men did bad things to Grandma, and I'm gonna *kill* 'em!"

"You'll get in trouble, that's what! Or get shot!"

Little Jake shook his head. "I'm not scared at all." He put the gun back and started shimmying along the crack again. "What do you think they'll do to Grandma?"

Stephen sucked in his belly to get through an especially narrow space. "I think Grandpa is scared they'll do something men do to women only in a nice way when they love 'em. Grandpa sure wouldn't want them doin' that to Grandma, 'cause she's his and she's old and she'd feel bad. He loves her an awful lot. My pa loves Katie, too. I hear them at night sometimes. Pa says it's okay when you love a woman, but you gotta love her a lot. You're not supposed to do stuff to her if she doesn't want you to."

"What about the bad women?" Little Jake knocked away a spider. "I think they're the kind that don't care. Do you think Grampa used to be with a lot of women like that?"

They both giggled. "I think Grampa did a lot of stuff like that when he was younger. But I'll bet Grandma really would punch him if he did that now."

They giggled again, the conversation helping relieve their nervous fear of what might happen.

"It's warmer in here out of the wind," Stephen remarked. "Grampa says another snowstorm might be coming. We have to get Grandma home so's she doesn't get sick."

"How much farther do you think before we reach the cabin, Stephen?" Little Jake asked.

"I don't know. Just keep going. We have to reach Grandma before they hurt her too much. If they kill her, Grampa and my pa are gonna feel really, really bad.

I don't think they would maybe ever smile again. I'm scared Grampa might even ride away and never come back. I think he'd go crazy without Grandma."

"My mom said that once," Little Jake answered. "She prays for him all the time on account of he gets kind of crazy sometimes, like when he shot that man in Denver."

"He just loves all of us too much," Stephen told him. "That's what makes him crazy."

"I wouldn't never be happy if Grampa left us...or if he died," Little Jake commented. "Would you?"

"I don't think so. I can't even picture life without Grampa around. He's so...I don't know...*big*! It's like he fills everything up, even outside. Do you know what I mean?"

"Yeah. Uncle Lloyd does, too." Little Jake giggled again. "My mom is always complaining how he looks like an Indian 'cause of his hair. I'm glad he didn't die when that man in Denver shot him."

"My pa is tough. I knew he wouldn't die. He's a big, strong man." Stephen stopped for a minute. "Little Jake."

"What?" Little Jake looked back at him.

"Let's make a pact."

"What do you mean?"

"You and me. We'll be like Grampa and my father when we grow up. I mean, we'll get along like they do, and we'll be tough like they are."

Little Jake frowned. "Sure we will! But Grampa and your pa sometimes get in fights." He started shimmying through the rugged crack again.

Stephen followed. "That's just them carin' about each other. We might fight sometimes, too, but it won't mean we don't care about each other. We should always get along and watch out for each other like Pa and Grampa do. And we gotta remember that Grampa would want to always treat Ben like his real son. Ben had a bad father like Grampa did."

"I know." Little Jake giggled again. "Heck, I just thought about it. Grampa adopted Ben, so he's my uncle!"

Both boys laughed over that. "He's more like a brother or a cousin. I never thought of him as an uncle!" Stephen said.

They moved along silently, blinking against stone dust that kept getting in their eyes. Because of the size of the crack, they couldn't wear their hats, and their hair was starting to cake with dust. Little Jake buried his face in the crook of his arm to sneeze. The boys froze.

"Do you think they heard that?" Little Jake whispered.

"No. We're too deep in these rocks, and you muffled it. Hurry up now! We're almost there!"

Little Jake walked faster when they reached a wider area, then sucked in his belly when the crack narrowed again. "We're real close," he whispered. "I remember that big part was just a little ways from where we climbed into the crack where it comes out by the cabin."

Hearts pounding, the boys finally reached the opening. "I see it!" Little Jake whispered excitedly. "I see the cabin!"

"Do you see Grandma?"

"No. She must be inside." Little Jake peeked farther out. "I don't see nobody. I see the horses, though. They're over to the right. You ready?"

"Ready as I'll ever be," Stephen whispered in reply. "I'm scared, but we gotta do this for Grandma."

"Yeah." Stephen hung on tight to the rifle. "But Pa and Grandpa are out there waiting. Let's go!"

Little Jake didn't hesitate. He ran out, Stephen right behind him. The boys made a beeline for the horses, quickly untying them from the tether line. One of them whinnied.

"Shit!" Little Jake yelped. He couldn't climb up on the unsaddled horse he was trying to grab. Stephen laid down the rifle and gave him a boost. He handed up the reins to two horses.

"Go! Go!"

Little Jake took off, hanging on to the two extra horses.

"Hey!"

Stephen turned to see Clyde Pace standing at the corner of the cabin. "What the hell—" He stood there with no gun. "Brad! They're takin' our horses!" Clyde started after Stephen.

Stephen bent down and grasped his rifle.

"It's the goddamn Harkner kids!"

Stephen raised the rifle and fired. Clyde whirled and went down.

"What the fuck—" Someone inside yelled the words.

Stephen couldn't believe what he'd just done. Clyde started moving and got back to his feet. To his surprise, Little Jake rode back up toward the cabin and took out the Colt .45 he'd stolen from Cole. He held it with two hands and shot at Clyde but missed.

"Ride, Stephen!" Little Jake yelled.

"Get out of the way!" Jake roared the words from the rocks above. "Get the hell out of there!"

The boys heard rifle fire, and Clyde flew forward into a watering trough.

Stephen dropped his rifle and jumped onto another of the horses. He grabbed the reins to one other, leaving the last horse behind as he and Little Jake kicked their horses into a hard ride, flying down the hill as more shots were fired.

Stephen wasn't quite sure whether to be glad or sorry he'd shot a man. He remembered Jake telling them once that it wasn't a good feeling…killing a man, but at least Clyde got back up. More likely it was the second shot that killed him, and it probably came from his father or grandfather.

He could hear Little Jake behind him, whooping like an Indian. He caught up to Stephen as they neared the bottom of the hill. The boys yelled in victory and laughed.

"We did it!" Little Jake rejoiced. "We chased off their horses, and we got one of 'em!"

"Let's go find Grandpa!" Stephen yelled, turning his horse to the left and heading up into the high rocks at the side of the cabin. More gunfire rang out, bullets from the cabin, pinging against the rocks as the boys headed into them. Return gunfire was blasting the cabin to pieces. By the time the boys reached their father and grandfather, the shooting had stopped.

"Hold up!" Jake ordered. "Randy could get hit from a stray bullet! We need to flush them out of there."

"You're dead meat, Harkner!" Brad Buckley yelled from the cabin. "Leave now, or your wife is *dead*!"

Stephen saw puffs of smoke where someone fired at them from the cabin windows. Clyde Pace was still alive and trying to drag himself out of the watering trough.

"Stay back!" Lloyd screamed to the boys when he saw them climbing up toward them. "Get behind some shelter!"

The boys clambered into the trees and ducked behind a large boulder.

"You don't have a chance, Buckley! There's no place to run!" Jake yelled. "I've got Lloyd and three other men with me, and you've got no horses!"

"How'd you get up here, you bastard!" Brad yelled. "We've been watchin' clear across the valley for you!"

"Those men with you don't know this land as well as they thought!" Jake answered. "My grandsons know it even better than *I* do! *They* got us up here, you sonofabitch! You messed with the wrong Harkners this time!"

Both boys grinned excitedly, feeling like men now.

"I've got your wife, Jake! You're the one who'd better give up, or she's dead!" More shots came from the cabin. "I've hated you ever since you killed my pa and brothers, you murderin' sonofabitch!" Brad screamed. "I've got you back for it. Takin' your wife is better than killing you!"

"You'll live to regret it!"

"And you'll never get out from behind those rocks alive!"

Jake noticed Clyde still struggling to get out of the trough. He aimed his rifle and fired, and Clyde cried out and tumbled back into the water.

"Just three of you left, Brad!" Jake yelled. "Three of you and six of us! Ronald Beck is dead, too! You shouldn't have left him behind to tell us where you were."

"You always were a stupid sonofabitch!" Lloyd shouted, moving as far behind the cabin as he could get. It was impossible to get directly behind it because of the steep cliff that rose up in back of it.

"Bring my wife out of there, and we might let you live!" Jake ordered.

"Like hell! You don't never let *nobody* live, Jake Harkner!"

"You should have thought of that before you took my wife!"

"I'll *kill* her, Harkner! I'll kill her because you're gonna kill me anyway! And you're gonna live the rest of your life knowin' the last man who had her was *me*, Brad Buckley! She ain't bad for her age, Harkner!"

"And I'll fucking take three days to kill you, you bastard! You bring her out of there, or I'll skin your hide off when I get hold of you and plant you on an anthill! And I'll damn well cut your balls off and shove them in your mouth! Bring her out now, and all I'll do is put a bullet in your head!"

"That ain't much of a choice, Harkner!"

"You think about it! I never lie, Buckley! If you kill my wife, what I did to you back in Guthrie will seem like a picnic!"

Things got quiet. Lloyd moved around to confirm that there were no windows at the back of the cabin. He'd brought a rope along in case he might need it, and indeed, he realized he might be able to use it to get behind the cabin. He scurried up through the rocks, finding an area where he could slide down the cliff on sheer, flat rock and land in the small area between the face of the cliff and the cabin. He waved to Jake, then set down his rifle and tied one end of the rope to a small pine tree at the top of the cliff. It wasn't very strong, but it was his only choice. He clung to the rope and shimmied down the cliff for about fifteen feet. The sapling broke, and Lloyd fell the rest of the way, a good ten feet. He landed hard just behind the cabin but got to his feet, silently waving that he was all right.

"What's it going to be, Buckley?" Jake shouted. "Do you want to die easy? Or do you want to take two or three days to die? You've trapped yourself by your own stupidity! Dying one way or the other is your only choice!"

"You bastard! I had her, Jake. I've got that much to go out of this life with! And it wasn't the way you think! I figured I wouldn't enjoy it much on account of her age, so I shoved it in her *mouth*!" He laughed, and Jake felt like someone was ripping his heart out. "She practically choked on it, Harkner! She had to swallow Brad Buckley's shit! *Twice*! Clem's too! He figured since she was a whore, she'd probably like it. You ever do that, Harkner? Hell, a big man like you could break her jaw!"

More laughter.

Stephen and Little Jake looked at each other. "What's he mean?" Little Jake asked.

"Something real bad," Stephen answered, his hands moving into fists. "It's a dirty, low-down thing. I wish we'd been big enough to stop them, Little Jake. I can't wait till I get big like Pa and Grandpa."

Lloyd was tall enough to grab hold of the edge of the wooden shingle roof of the cabin. He stepped on a barrel behind it to give himself a boost onto the roof, then quickly removed his jacket and laid it over the chimney. Jake and the other men moved from the rocks after a few minutes and headed for the cabin. Brad Buckley, Tucker, and Clem couldn't help but run out, coughing and hacking from smoke. All but Brad dropped their weapons and raised their hands as Jake, Cole, Rodriguez, and Vance surrounded them. Lloyd quickly removed his jacket from the chimney, worried about his mother, who was surely choking on the smoke inside the cabin.

"Don't kill us!" Clem whined. "We didn't hurt her! It was Brad!"

Brad's eyes stung from the smoke, but he had to know the big figure coming toward him was Jake Harkner. He raised his gun, but before he could fire, Jake shot him in the privates—twice. He went to his knees, screaming. Lloyd jumped down from the roof. He pulled his six-gun and walked up to Clem, shoving the gun into Clem's mouth. "You fucking piece of shit! Nobody messes with my *mother*!" He pulled the trigger without hesitation. Clem's head exploded into pieces.

"Oh my God!" Tucker cried out.

"Pa!" Stephen whispered.

"I think that's what Grampa did to that man back in Denver," Little Jake said.

Cole raised his six-gun to Tucker's chest. "That fire killed my best friend, you bastard, and men like me don't have many friends!" He shot Tucker in the heart.

Still standing over Brad, Jake seemed unmoved by what Lloyd and Cole had just done. "Go inside and use something to bring a hot coal out here!" he ordered Vance. He looked at Lloyd. "Go see if she's still alive." He almost groaned the words. "I'm sorry to make you do it, Lloyd, but I need to know before I…go in there." His face was etched dark with devastation.

Brian came closer, the three boys with him. "Jake, I'll go," Brian offered.

"No!" Lloyd objected. "It's okay. You went through enough with Evie." He turned and headed into the cabin, Vance right behind him. They left the door open to clear out some of the smoke.

Lloyd hesitantly approached an old rope-spring bed where something lay curled up under blankets. He couldn't imagine life without his mother, and he said a quick prayer that she was alive. He bent closer. "Mom?"

She curled deeper into the blankets. "Jake?"

Tears of relief filled his eyes. "It's Lloyd."

"I want Jake."

Lloyd struggled not to break down. "He's outside. He's coming." He touched her shoulder, but she jerked away.

"I'm so cold," she whimpered.

Lloyd could see her shivering under the blankets. He removed his smoked-up deerskin coat and laid it over her. "Just hang on. Jake's coming." He leaned closer, noticing one of her wrists was tied to a rung of the iron headboard. "Jesus," he muttered. He quickly untied it. "I'll send Brian in."

"No! I want...Jake. Just Jake."

"He'll be right here. He's okay. Everybody's okay." Lloyd walked to the doorway. "Pa, she's alive. She wants just you."

Jake stood with a booted foot planted against Brad Buckley's bleeding privates, his gun pointed at the young man's head. "That means you get to die fast, Buckley! But not without pain!" He shouted to Vance, who was still inside the cabin. "Get those hot coals out here! This man likes shoving his shit into helpless peoples' mouths, so I'll shove something unwanted into *his* mouth!"

"Noooooo!" Brad screamed. "Just shoot me!"

"Too easy for someone who would do to my wife what you did! I always knew this time would come, Brad Buckley! I should have killed you in Guthrie when I had the chance!"

Inside the cabin, Vance tried to ignore the shivering little mound of woman under the covers as he searched for something with which to grab a hot coal, per Jake's orders. He found some fireplace tongs and used them to take a glowing piece of wood from a fire that still burned in the stone fireplace. He turned, then froze in place when he saw Randy actually sitting up on the edge of the bed and holding a blanket over herself. Her face was bruised almost beyond recognition, her hair hanging in filthy strings.

"Is Brad Buckley still alive?" she asked in a raspy voice.

Vance swallowed. "Yes, ma'am, but I expect he's bleedin' to death."

"Good." Randy managed to stand up. "Give me your gun."

"Ma'am?"

"Give me your gun!"

"Ma'am, I don't think—"

Randy walked up and jerked his gun from its holster. Vance didn't know what he should do. She looked like a crazy woman at the moment, and she was Jake Harkner's wife. If he tried to stop her from whatever she intended to do, he might hurt her. He stood there still holding tongs with the burning wood in them as Randy marched to the front door. "My God!" he muttered, turning away when the blanket fell away and exposed her backside.

Outside, Brad was sobbing. "They'll…hang you, Jake Harkner! You'd…better think about that!" He struggled to get away, but to no avail. Jake stepped harder on his privates.

"No matter," Jake answered, leaning closer. "Hearing you scream and watching you die slowly will be *worth* it!"

Cole and Rodriguez held Brad's arms down, and Terrel and Lloyd surrounded him and Jake.

"Hurry it up with those hot coals!" Jake yelled at Vance again.

"Oh my God!" Cole suddenly yelled, staring toward the cabin.

They all turned, shocked to see Randy walking toward them, holding a blanket over herself with one hand and a gun in the other. She marched up and shot Brad Buckley in the heart, then pointed the gun at his face and fired again, the bullet shattering his teeth and jaw. She just stood there for a moment, then dropped the gun and looked at Jake.

"Now no one can say *you* killed Brad Buckley, so they can't take you away from me."

She started to slump, and Lloyd caught her. Jake quickly holstered his .44 and grabbed her up into his arms. He carried her into the cabin and kicked the door shut.

The rest of the men turned to stare at Brad Buckley, his privates a bloody mess, a hole in his chest, and most of his jaw missing.

"Holy shit," Cole exclaimed.

Lloyd closed his eyes and turned away.

Stephen looked at Little Jake. "Grandma shot Brad Buckley!"

Little Jake made a fist. "I'm glad!"

Forty

Jake struggled not to fall apart. The woman who'd shot Brad Buckley didn't even resemble his wife. She'd looked like a madwoman who'd come back from the dead for revenge. The minute he picked her up in his arms, she'd fallen to pieces emotionally, breaking into pitiful sobs that ripped his heart out.

Don't think about your mother and watching her die. Don't think about Evie and how you found her. Don't think about your father! Don't think about going crazy if you lose this woman! He had to stay sane. His wife needed him in a way she'd never needed him before.

He sat down in a chair, holding Randy on his lap. He couldn't bring himself to lay her back in the soiled bed nearby, the mattress bare and stained.

"Jake?" she whispered. "Is it...really you?"

"It's me."

"Jake?"

"I'm right here."

"I couldn't...let that marshal...take you away from me," she whispered gruffly. "I can't live...without you."

"My God, Randy," he groaned.

"I knew...you'd come. Like at that...trading post. When was that, Jake?" She sobbed the words.

Jake realized her mind was wandering. He struggled against an urge to grab her tight against him but was afraid he'd hurt something. "A long, long time ago... when I first knew I loved you, *mi querida*."

"Jake, they did...a terrible thing..."

"Don't talk about it. Just let me hold you. Let me make sure you don't have any broken bones or—"

"Do you...still love me?"

"My God, Randy, why would you ask that?"

She broke into tears. "You know...why." She clung to his shirt. "Jake...you never did that to me...you never did anything that wasn't...beautiful—" She kept the blanket over her face.

"*¡Lo siento, mi vida. ¡Lo siento!*" Jake rocked her as he groaned the words.

"Don't let go of me!"

"I'm right here."

"I'm so cold!"

She was shaking, and Jake realized he couldn't do three things at once. "Lloyd, get in here and build up the fire," he called through the doorway.

"No! Don't let anyone see me."

Jake closed his eyes and breathed deeply. He wanted to walk around and scream, but he needed to be strong—for Randy. For Randy. *Hang on!* This was the kind of thing that would normally send him into that world where he had to ride out of this woman's life... this woman who'd given up so much for him. He didn't deserve her. "Randy, I need to warm things up in here. I can't hang on to you and do that, too. Someone has to come in here and help."

Lloyd came inside, carrying a leather bag with a change of clothes for his mother, and her rabbit fur coat. He saw the pain in his father's eyes. "Does she need Brian?"

"I'm not sure yet."

"No! Don't let anyone see me," Randy repeated, cringing closer to Jake.

Lloyd set her belongings on the bed and moved to the fireplace, angrily throwing wood into it. He grabbed a poker and jammed it into the coals so they flared up.

Tears welled in his eyes. "Mom, it's okay. Let me and Brian help. Pa can't do all this by himself."

Randy pressed her face against Jake's neck. "I know your scent," she whispered. "It's really...you."

"It's really me. Lloyd's going to build a fire and heat some water and fix something to eat. You're going to let Brian make sure you don't have any broken bones, and I'm going to wash you up, and you're going to eat something, and I'm taking you out of here in the morning, all right? I don't want you in this place with all its filth and all its bad memories any longer than that. When we leave here, we'll burn this cabin down!" Bracing himself against the sick horror in his heart, he pulled the blanket away from her face and struggled not to gasp at how bruised her jaw and cheekbones were. It was difficult to tell it was really his beautiful wife.

"Don't," she wept, covering her face with her hand. "They hit me...and...hit me. Jake, I want to wash my mouth. Get it out of me! Get it out of me!" She suddenly straightened and vomited all over the blanket.

"Jesus," Jake groaned. "Get Brian in here, Lloyd! And get some biscuits. See if Rodriguez has anything we can make some broth with. We've got to get something into her stomach."

"No! Just you! Just you!" Randy sobbed.

"Brian needs to tend to you," Jake told her, smoothing back her hair. "No arguments!"

Lloyd hesitated. "Pa, are you okay?"

Jake didn't answer.

"Pa?"

Jake pressed Randy closer and kept rocking her. "I don't know."

Lloyd walked up behind him and grasped his shoulder. "You hang on. And you remember how proud she is of how much stronger you are emotionally. It's her turn to pull on your strength instead of the other way around."

"I'll be better when I get her cleaned up and get some food in her. Get something from Rodriguez, and then you take care of those boys out there. I know what bad memories are like. You need to talk to them."

"Right now you and Mom need me more. I'll talk to them in the morning, and I'm sure Brian will give them an earful. I don't know where in hell Little Jake got that gun, but he'll learn real quick to never do something like that again. I'll take care of those boys. You take care of Mom." Lloyd squeezed Jake's shoulder before hurrying out.

A moment later, Brian came in with his doctor bag and canteen. He knelt beside Randy. "She's probably dehydrated," he told Jake. "Randy, you need to drink some water."

"No! No! No! Go away! I'm…filthy."

Brian looked at Jake with pain-filled eyes.

"I'm sorry, Brian. I know how hard this is for you," Jake told him.

"Try to get her to drink some water." Brian uncorked the canteen and handed it to Jake.

"*Por favor, mi querida*. Drink some water." He tipped it to her lips.

"No! Stop!" she screamed, pushing it away.

"Randy it's *me*! *Jake*! I just want you to drink some water!"

She covered her face. "Jake…they did an ugly thing…" she repeated.

"Then wash it away! Drink some water and wash it away!"

She stared at the canteen, then took it with shaking hands. She managed to tip it up, and Jake wanted to scream at the bruises on her jaw and neck. The blanket fell away, and Jake could see her arms and back were also bruised. He quickly held the blanket over her breasts while she poured water into her mouth, then suddenly spit it out. She did it over and over, drinking and spitting, her sobs deepening. "Get it out of me!" she kept crying. She drank and spit again.

"Randy, you have to swallow some of that water," Brian told her.

Finally, she obeyed, then threw down the canteen. "Jake!"

"I'm right here." He held her while Brian ran his hands over her back and arms.

"Randy, tell me what hurts. Is anything broken?"

"No. It's just…bruises and—" She began panting in a panic as she moved her hands to her face again. "My… jaw. They…" She curled up against Jake again. "Hold me! Don't let go, Jake!"

"I'm right here."

Brian reached into his medicine bag and took out a bottle of laudanum. "See if you can get her to drink some of this. It will calm her down and help her sleep." He set it on the table near Jake, then picked up Lloyd's coat and laid it on the bed. He brought over an extra blanket and laid it over Randy. "I'll leave for a bit and let you talk to her more. Try to calm her down, Jake. You won't be able to clean her up until she's half out of it with that laudanum, but I don't want her taking any of it until she has something in her stomach, so try to get her to eat. I'll come back in and help you wash her up and get some clean clothes on her once she's calmer."

Jake nodded, pulling her close and kissing her hair. "She hates being dirty. She usually always…smells like roses." His voice broke on the words.

"Jake, you hang on for her sake. You have to stay strong and stay sane, understand? Right now she needs you more than you've ever needed her. Most of your married life it's been the other way around. You get her to eat and get her to sleep. In the morning, you can take her to that line shack."

Lloyd came back inside with a gunnysack of food.

"I'll heat some water," he told Jake. "And I'll find a pan. Rodriguez gave me some bacon. He said the bacon fat will be good for her."

Jake nodded. "Stir that fire some more. It needs to be good and hot."

"Jake," Randy groaned. "Don't let go."

"I'm right here."

"Peppermint. You always…have peppermint."

Never without a couple of sticks of their favorite candy, Jake shifted enough to take a stick of peppermint from inside his shirt pocket.

"I'll cook the bacon," Lloyd told him.

Jake brushed the short stick of peppermint across Randy's bruised lips. She opened her mouth a little, and he ran it inside her lips so she could smell and taste it— something fresh and clean, something they'd shared more times than he could remember.

She licked the peppermint, grasping his hand as she did so. "Tell me…you still love me, Jake."

Her body jerked in a sob. Jake drew her close, taking the other end of the peppermint stick in his mouth. Because it was so short, his lips touched her bruised and swollen ones. He kissed them as gently as possible, then moved his lips softly over her bruised jaw. "*Yo te amo, mi querida*," he told her in a near whisper. "This is something that was always just between you and me, *mi vida*. Just you and me. The peppermint. That's just ours. Nothing has changed."

Randy moved an arm around his neck and nestled her face against him. "I want to breathe in…the smell of you," she said softly. "Don't let go, Jake."

"I'm right here," he reassured her yet again.

"I killed him, Jake. I did it…for you…so they can't… take you away."

"I would have figured out a way to keep that from happening," he told her.

"They did…a terrible thing," she repeated. "You never…made me do that."

"You're too beautiful and perfect and honorable." He kissed her eyes. "I respect you too much as the woman I love." He smoothed her hair back and kissed her forehead.

"Jake, I'm not yours anymore."

He held her tighter. "Don't ever say that again. Who do you belong to?"

She jerked in a sob. "I don't know."

"Yes, you do," he said softly. "Say it."

She hugged him tighter around the neck. "You."

"Say my name, Randy. Who do you belong to?"

She curled so tightly against him it was as though she was trying to crawl inside him. "Jake Harkner," she whispered.

"You bet. Nothing has changed that, and nothing ever will."

"Tell me you're not in trouble, Jake."

"I'm not in trouble."

"You won't go away?"

"Never."

"No one's coming to get you?"

"No one's coming to get me."

"I was always scared…you'd never come back…back in Oklahoma. Don't take that job, Jake…that…ranger job. I don't want you to go away."

"I'm not going anywhere."

"Don't let go. I love…being in your arms."

"And that's where you are right now."

"I knew you'd come."

"I'd walk through the fires of hell for you."

"Everything…hurts."

"We'll fix that." He kissed her eyes again, traced a finger over her lips, struggling against a rage deep inside over realizing the hideous thing they'd done to her. The corners of her mouth were cracked and bleeding.

Lloyd kept quiet as he cooked some bacon, thinking about how ruthless Jake Harkner could be. He'd been prepared to shove hot coals into Brad Buckley's mouth, and he would have done so if Randy hadn't shot the sonofabitch instead. Now Jake sat there holding his wife as though she were a fine piece of china. Such were the complexities of Jake Harkner. "I'm heating some extra water," he told Jake. "We have to get her to eat something and get that laudanum in her so we can clean her up."

"Brian will help me."

"She's my *mother*. *I'll* help! It's okay, Pa. Besides, this is really hard on Brian after what happened to Evie. He's been through a lot, too, over the years. I'll help, and once she's cleaned up and asleep, I'll rip that goddamn bed up and take it outside and burn it! She's not going to lay back down on that filthy piece of shit! We'll make up something for you and Mom on the floor. In the morning, the men can head back with Brian and the boys, and you and I will head for the line shack."

"Don't worry about the bed. I'm having the men burn down the whole cabin when we leave." Jake kissed Randy's hair again. "As far as the line shack, I should have taken her last summer. She wanted to go back there, but we were always too busy." Jake closed his eyes and rested his head against the back of the chair. "She's had such a hard life, Lloyd. How can I ever make it up to her?"

"You don't need to, Pa. All she wants is for you to love her, and God knows you've done that. I'm the one who needs to make things up to her. I'm the one who left when you went to prison, and she and Evie had to make do on their own. I'll never forgive myself for that. And she came with you and risked her life right alongside of you when you rescued me from that mess on the Outlaw Trail and then had to go through hell getting me off of alcohol. I'll always take care of both of you if need be, and Mom if she's left alone. That's a promise. Let me help you clean her up, and I'll help you get her to that line shack safely. I owe her."

"Lloyd, you've more than made up for all of that."

"I'll *never* make up for it."

"Jake, don't let go," Randy whispered again.

"I'm right here," he answered, wondering how many times he would have to keep reassuring her he wasn't going anywhere. He managed to reach inside his pocket to take out another peppermint stick. He traced it over her lips.

"Is it...morning?" she asked. "We usually only have...peppermint...in the morning."

Her mind was wandering to better things. Jake smiled through tears. "Not this time, *mi vida*. But we'll share some more of this soon...just you and me...in the morning." He leaned close and took the other end in his mouth, working his way to her lips again. "And I'll take it all back." He felt a tiny response in the way her lips touched his.

"Don't let go," she said yet again.

"I'm right here."

"I still have...your ring. See?" Randy held out her left hand to show him the wedding ring he'd bought her in Denver.

Her hand was bruised. Jake tried not to let it drive him crazy. "It's beautiful, baby."

Randy opened her eyes a moment, touching his lips. "You're...all bruised. Jake, you're all purple here." She gently touched his jaw. "What happened?"

"Midnight reared up and caught me under the jaw."

"The fire..." She curled against him again. "The fire! Jake...I screamed for you..."

"I couldn't hear you. I'm so goddamn sorry."

"The boys! They hurt the boys. They fought...so hard to...stop them!"

"I know. They're becoming men, Randy. They came with us, and they helped us. They were so scared for you."

"They're…here?"

"They are. They wanted to help because they felt bad they couldn't stop those men."

"They shouldn't, Jake. They tried so hard. Tell me they're all right."

"They're bruised up, but they'll be fine. They're brave young men."

"They have…your blood. Little Jake…I see you… in his eyes." She curled against him yet again. "Don't let go!"

"I'm right here. I'm not letting go."

Lloyd brought over some bacon. "I left the fat soft. She'll get more fat in her than if I fry it off till it's crispy." He knelt beside them. "Mom, eat this."

"I…can't. Lloyd, don't look at me."

"I'll damn well look at you! All I see is my beautiful mother, and she needs to eat something and drink some more water and take some laudanum. You're going to do all three."

"I don't want…Jake…to let go of me."

"He won't. Now eat this bacon."

She took a piece with a shaking hand. Lloyd noticed her hand and wrist were purple. He silently groaned at her bruised and swollen lips.

"You look like…a young Jake," she told him, "like he looked when he…found me at that trading post. Is that…where we are?"

Lloyd looked at Jake, both of them realizing her mind kept wandering from present to past. "Yeah, that's where we are," Lloyd told her. His hair had come loose, and he tossed it behind his shoulders.

"Jake, you should…cut that hair. You look…like an Indian."

Lloyd turned away, his heart breaking. "Eat all five pieces of that bacon." He set the tin plate of bacon on the table and walked over to pick up the canteen Randy had thrown to the floor. Jake kept handing her the bacon until she ate it all. Lloyd brought the canteen to Jake, and Jake urged Randy to drink more water.

"Mom? Do you know who I am?" Lloyd touched her hair.

Randy studied him a moment. "Lloyd?"

"A minute ago you thought I was Jake."

She rested her head on Jake's shoulder again. "*This* is Jake. He's holding me. He won't let go."

"No, he won't let go."

"I'm safe here."

"You bet you are." Lloyd grinned through tears. He and Jake finally got some laudanum down her, and Jake held her as she began to drift off.

"Don't let go," she said once again, the words slurred.

"I'm right here," Jake told her. He pulled her close and quietly wept.

Lloyd fixed hot, soapy water. He was worried about Jake, afraid he'd slip into that much darker place from which it seemed at times there was no return. Jake removed the soiled blanket and tossed it aside. Lloyd looked away as Jake sponged her off the best he could, repeating how small she was, how in thirty years he'd never once laid a hand on her wrongly, how you had to be careful with an older woman because she bruised more easily, how beautiful her hair still was, with not even any gray in it yet.

Lloyd handed him a clean blanket he'd brought in from their supplies, and Jake wrapped it around Randy. "They say blonds don't show the gray as soon as brunettes," Lloyd told him, fighting to keep a conversation going that would keep Jake in the present. "Katie's been finding a few gray hairs lately, and she acts like it's the end of the world."

"Katie is beautiful," Jake answered, pouring a cup full of soapy water through Randy's hair. He still held her on his lap, her head in the crook of his arm. The water ran through her hair and back into the pan of soapy water.

"Yeah, well, you know how women are always looking for their flaws," Lloyd tried to joke. "Katie thinks she'll end up stout like her mother."

"Nothing wrong with that." Jake poured soapy water through Randy's hair again, and Lloyd helped towel it off. "Clare Donavan is a wonderful woman with a beautiful spirit," Jake added.

"I agree." Lloyd figured it was best to keep a conversation going. "I want about six more kids, so Katie probably *will* end up 'robust,' as she puts it. That doesn't matter to me. It's like you told me once—the bigger the woman, the more to love."

Jake grinned. "Katie just doesn't want to lose her Greek god."

Lloyd took heart in his smile, but he knew things were boiling inside his father. He returned the smile. "I think I'll punch the next man who calls me a Greek god."

Jake sobered. The smile was quickly gone, and his eyes teared. He pulled Randy closer, and she whimpered his name. "Little as this woman right here is, she owns me, Lloyd. She's got me roped, thrown, tethered, and branded. And now I've maybe lost her."

"That will never happen, Pa. Love can survive anything, and I never knew two people who loved each other more than you two."

"Jake," Randy whispered, curling closer again.

"*Que Dios te acompane, mi amor.*"

"Don't let go."

"I'm right here."

Randy drifted off again.

"Get her clothes from that bag you brought in and

help me dress her," Jake told Lloyd. "She'll feel better if she's dressed when she wakes up."

Lloyd pulled out a simple blue cotton dress and underclothes.

"Just the dress. I'm worried she could have a couple of cracked ribs. I'm not going to cinch a damn camisole around her. Just the dress and one slip."

Lloyd took a clean towel from the satchel and toweled Randy's hair to dry it more. "Hang on to her, and I'll get the dress on her."

"Shit."

"It's okay."

Jake held her limp body straighter, and Lloyd quickly pulled the dress over her head. They worked her arms into the sleeves.

"She's like a damn rag doll," Jake groaned.

Together they worked the dress down and over the rest of her, and Jake hung on to her while Lloyd buttoned the dress. "Don't tell her I helped," he told Jake. "She'd die of embarrassment. If Katie or Evie were here, they could do this, but I'm glad they *aren't* here. This would be way too hard on Evie, and I wouldn't want Katie to have to see this either." He finished the last button. "My God, Pa, how much does she weigh? A hundred pounds?"

"Something like that. Maybe one-ten." Jake pulled her closer again.

Lloyd rose and set the pan of water on the table. "I'll fix up something by the fireplace where you can sleep and build up the fire."

"Lloyd."

Lloyd met his father's gaze.

"You're one hell of a son."

Lloyd sighed. "Yeah, well, you're one hell of a father." He touched his mother's hair. "And she's one hell of a mother...and considering the ornery sonofabitch she's put up with the last thirty years, she's one hell of a wife." His heart ached at what he knew his father was going through. Staying sane through this had to be the hardest thing he'd ever done. "She'll be okay, Pa, as long as she has you. You remember that."

Randy suddenly grasped Jake's shirt. "Jake?"

"I'm right here."

"Don't go away."

"I'm not going anywhere. I'll take good care of you, just like at that trading post."

"You came for me. I'll always remember how it felt to hear your voice."

"I came for you because I couldn't forget you. God knows I tried."

"Don't let go."

Jake pulled her close. "Never."

Forty-one

"I'LL RIDE ON MY OWN. LET STEPHEN RIDE WITH Little Jake, and I'll take Stephen's horse." Randy spoke the words matter-of-factly as Jake wrapped a blanket closer around her because she couldn't stop shivering.

"You're too weak. Just last night you could barely talk or move, and you're covered with bruises and still have laudanum in your system. It's a long ride, and it's cold out there." Jake was confused by her sudden about-face—behaving like the feisty, strong Miranda Harkner he knew she could be. After she'd clung to him all night and how sick and terrified she was, her behavior didn't make any sense.

"Don't fuss over me," she demanded. "I'm fine now. Get the boys in here. They need to see that I'm...all right. I want to talk to them."

"It's *me* you should be talking to."

"No—not yet! Not yet!"

Jake grasped her arm and turned her. "Look at me."

"No! I have to be strong now...for you...for those poor boys who tried so hard—" The words caught in her throat.

"You don't need to be strong for *any*one. I'm all right, Randy. We've had some good talks with the boys, and we'll talk some more, but they're okay. It's over. Oklahoma is behind us. The last sonofabitch left over from my years as a marshal there is dead, and we can finally have some peace! But first, you and I have to get back where we belong."

She kept trying to pull away. "We can't! They...did something...they spoiled what we...had... They...made it ugly. That's why I...shot Brad..." She sucked in her breath, obviously forcing bravery and determination. "Buckley," she finished. "My God... I...killed him!"

Jake pulled her even closer. "You listen to me. This is you and me now. You and me! We've been to hell and back, and for thirty years, it's always been you and me. It's *done* now. My past and all it did to us is over now, and I can talk about it—because of *you*. I'm alive because of *you*! I'm sane because of *you*, and it's likely I won't be going to jail...because of you. But as far as I'm concerned, no one in the outside world will ever know about this. And I'm not going to lose that special thing we have because of a couple of bastards who thought they could destroy the beautiful love we share."

"Jake!" She gasped his name. "You never... You never...asked me... You never... You've been with other women. Maybe you wanted..."

"Stop it! *¡Tu eres mi vida, mi querida esposa! ¡Yo te amo!* Nothing has changed! We're going to the line shack, just you and me, and we'll stay there as long as it takes to get it all back."

"Jake...all I could think about was...that trading post... hearing your voice...feeling you pick me up and knowing...how safe I was...but when they—" She began wiping at her mouth again. "I belong to you! I belong to *you!*"

He grasped both her hands in his grip. "You *do* belong to me, and nothing has changed! I'll take back every single inch of you, Randy Harkner, and we'll go home, and you'll bake that bread and make those pies and love on your grandbabies and be my partner in everything I do. This is Jake Harkner you're talking to, and there isn't one thing in life I haven't seen or experienced or been through. So none of this can hurt me, Randy. And this time I'm not strong just on the outside. I'm strong on the *in*side, again because of you. Now you have to *let* me be the strong one! You've been carrying the load for too many years, and it's going to end, understand?"

She shivered. "You're my Jake."

"I'm your *magnificent* Jake."

She jerked in a little burst of laughter through her tears and turned, burying her head against his chest. "How do you do that?"

"Do what?"

"Know when to…make me laugh."

He grasped her hair and kissed it. "I just know women, I guess."

She wrapped her arms tightly around him and sobbed and laughed at the same time. "That remark…should make me hate you…" She cried harder then. "Do you know…how many times I wanted…to hate you?"

"Probably at least once every day. And you'd have to get in line with quite a few other people."

Her sobs mixed with laughter again. Jake just held her, realizing that right now her words and actions came partly from hysteria and partly from a groggy, confused state from the laudanum.

"Jake, I'm sorry! I'm sorry!"

"Sorry for what?"

"I tried to fight them. It's always been…just you… just you…"

He kissed her hair again. "Don't be apologizing for something you couldn't help. It's *still* just me. And you're all mixed up right now. We'll talk more when we get to the line shack. Lloyd is going to ride there with us, and before we even came after you, I had some of the men go there and take enough heating wood and supplies that we can stay there as long as we need to."

"You remembered."

"I should have taken you there a long time ago. I'll not let anything get in the way of that again."

"That's our special place. I want us…to be buried there, Jake—you and me…high on that hill overlooking the J&L."

"Let's not be talking about where we'll be buried just yet. God knows I've come too close to that a hundred times over. I think He saved me just so you'd have someone to hold you, so He kept me around."

"Tell me you still love me."

"I shouldn't have to tell you that, *mi querida.*" He touched the side of her face. "Look at me, Randy. You haven't actually looked at me since we found you."

"I can't."

"Look at me."

Tears still streamed down her cheeks as she finally raised her head and looked up at him.

"Who do you belong to?"

"I want to still belong to you," she wept.

"Then say it. Who do you belong to?"

"Jake Harkner."

He leaned down and very gently kissed the corners of her lips, her cheeks, her eyes, her lips again. "We're going to that line shack…and for as long as necessary… this is all I'll do… Just kiss you"—another kiss—"and taste these beautiful lips"—light, fluttery touches with his mouth—"and we won't need to do anything else but hold each other for however long you need holding."

Someone tapped at the door. "Pa, it's me. We're all loaded up, and Rodriguez made some biscuits and boiled eggs. Can Mom eat?"

"Come on in."

"The boys are out here. They're real anxious to see Mom. Does she want to see them?"

Randy pulled away. "Yes!" She managed to stand up, clinging to a table.

"Bring them in," Jake told Lloyd.

Lloyd opened the door and motioned for the boys to

come inside. All three of them came bursting inside, their boots covered with snow and their noses and cheeks red. Little Jake started crying over the bruises on her face, and the other two just waited, not sure what to do.

"Grandma, can we hug you?" Stephen asked.

"Just take it easy," Jake warned them. "Don't hug too hard." He took a cigarette from a tin he'd left on the table and lit it while each boy took a turn at hugging their grandmother very carefully.

"We're sorry," Little Jake cried.

"Don't you dare be sorry," Randy told them. "The three of you fought so bravely! I've never been more proud of you."

Lloyd stepped closer and spoke quietly. "She's up and around?"

"For the moment. She's pretending to be strong, but it won't last. One minute she's hysterical, the next minute she's crying, and the next she's laughing. She's all mixed up right now and still full of laudanum. It will do us both good to spend some time alone at that line shack."

"Take all the time you need, Pa."

Jake drew on the cigarette. "For the first time in thirty years, I'm not sure how to handle a woman, and she's the one I've been living with all those years."

"Are you kidding?" Lloyd tried reassuring him. "You can handle a woman as good as you handle a gun. You're Jake Harkner." He lit his own cigarette. "You'll figure it out."

Jake watched Randy reassure the boys she was just fine. He knew better. He knew her every breath, her every movement, every hair on her head...knew when her heart was breaking. He'd damn well mend it.

Forty-two

FOR TWO DAYS THEY TRAVELED IN NEAR SILENCE, A soft snowfall enshrouding them, the snow on the ground muffling all sound except for the swish of the horses' hooves and the gentle clink and squeak of saddles and tack. Jake and Lloyd talked only about the ranch, how in spite of the cold, there at least had not been any new snowstorms, hoping they hadn't lost too many cattle this winter. To relieve the horses, they traded Randy back and forth, both worried about how, after behaving strong and just fine in front of the boys, she'd fallen back into near silence and at times didn't even seem fully aware of all that had happened. She was back to wanting only Jake and once cried so hard when Jake handed her over to Lloyd that Lloyd had to convince her in her confusion that he was Jake and she was safe. Both men ached over how weak and worn and bruised she was. She cried out with pain every time they moved her around, and she constantly shivered from cold no matter how many blankets they wrapped around her. Last night, when they had to sleep on the ground, they wrapped her in her rabbit coat and extra blankets and made her sleep between them.

To Jake's relief, they reached the line shack before dark the second day. Charlie McGee was there waiting. He'd been ordered to bring supplies up to the cabin when Jake and Lloyd left with the others to find Randy.

"Oh my God," he muttered when the two men arrived, a bundle of something in Jake's arms. He knew who it had to be. He was glad they'd found Randy, but the way Jake held her and the way she was silently curled against him didn't look good. He glanced at Lloyd.

"I'll explain when we leave," Lloyd told him. "Did you bring everything?"

"Yes, sir. There's plenty of wood stacked inside, lots of canned goods, pots and pans, a small barrel of water, and even flour and whatever she might need if she wants to make some of that famous bread. We didn't know, but maybe after whatever happened she'd feel better if she could bake or something." He shrugged. "Hell, I don't know. We even brought up a Dutch oven. I waited here to make sure somebody showed up. I'm glad to see you and Jake are okay."

Lloyd dismounted, and Jake handed Randy down to him. "Thanks, Charlie. Did you bring extra clothes? Blankets?"

"Yes, sir. And I've got a good fire goin'. I slept on the floor so's not to mess up the—" He glanced at Jake as Jake dismounted. "Well, I just didn't want to mess things up is all." He hurried up the steps to open the door for Lloyd, who carried his mother inside. Jake paused to light a cigarette. "Take care of my horse, Charlie. Is there feed in that shed over there?"

"Yes, sir. We thought of pretty much everything. There's some ammunition inside, too, both for your rifle and your .44s, just in case you need them. Hell, a storm could come over the mountains and bury you here. You might need to hunt for your food or fend off a bear."

"Yeah, well, you might not see us for a while either way." He took a deep drag on the cigarette. "You ride back with Lloyd. The last thing I need right now is to get home and find out something happened to him on the way home. It's none too early for grizzlies to be out snooping around, and wolves are pretty hungry after a long winter."

"Yes, sir. I hear them howling every night."

Jake thought how he'd heard wolves howling before dark a time or two last fall. It wasn't normal to hear wolves in the daytime, and the sound had seemed so ominous. Now he knew why.

"You okay, Jake? Midnight kicked you pretty hard the night of the fire, and God knows what's happened since. Ain't my business."

"I'm all right...physically." He kept the cigarette between his lips. "They're all dead, in case you're wondering. And they were never here. Understand?"

Charlie nodded, scratching at a several-days'-old stubble on his face. "I kinda figured that."

Jake studied the man. Charlie wasn't all that old. He was of medium build and inconsequential looks—just another ranch hand. "I don't know a damn thing about you, Charlie, and I don't want to know. You could be a damn bank robber, or maybe you ran off with some man's wife. It doesn't matter to me. I read a man pretty good, and I'm glad to know I was right about you being one of the good ones. I know better than anybody that a man's past doesn't mean a damn thing in the present. Thanks for hanging around and making sure of all this."

Charlie grinned a little. "Actually, it's the latter."

"What's that?"

"I *did* run off with another man's wife, but she went back. I kept all the money we stole from him, though. Somewhere out there is a real pissed-off husband who'd like to beat the hell out of me."

Jake grinned. "Well, you're safe on the J&L."

Charlie sobered. "She wasn't nothin' like that woman in there, Jake. Not many women *are* like her. The shape the missus is in, I expect somethin' bad happened, and you gotta know that every man back home is hopin' she'll be okay and wishin' they could have had a hand in dealin' with them that hurt her. It won't never be brought up in front of her, and nobody's gonna say anything about them bein' here. You don't need no more of that kind of trouble."

Lloyd came out onto the porch. He lit his own cigarette. "She's already sleeping again. I laid her on the bed, and she was out like a snuffed lantern." He came down the steps. "Charlie, let's put up Midnight, and you and I can get some riding in yet before it's completely dark. We can be back home by midday tomorrow. Right now, I'm real anxious to see my Katie."

Charlie grinned again. "Sure can't blame you there. You Harkner men sure know how to pick 'em. Are the boys okay?"

"They're good," Lloyd told him. "Still bruised up, but we let them help in their own way, and I think that made them feel better about this whole thing." He came all the way down the steps. "They're in a bit of trouble, though, that's going to take some discipline. Little Jake decided to sneak off with one of Cole's extra six-guns and tried to join in the shoot-out. Brian is pretty upset with him."

"I'll bet! That kid is Jake reborn. He's going to be a handful for poor Brian and Evie."

"Yeah, well, Cole isn't happy he took that gun. I think he put the scare into Little Jake. The kid won't be trying something like that again anytime soon." Lloyd took a drag on his cigarette. "Go ahead and tend to Midnight, will you?"

"Oh, sure!"

Jake took his saddlebags and bedroll from Midnight, along with his rifle. Charlie walked the horse to a nearby shed, and Jake turned to Lloyd. "You be careful going back."

Lloyd nodded. "I'm going to send someone up here every couple of days just to make sure you and Mom are still okay."

"I'm a big boy, Lloyd. We'll be fine."

"Just the same. This can be mean country this time of year. And if something happens to Midnight, you'd be on foot. Besides that, by the time you come home, you'll need an extra horse, so I'll have somebody bring one up, along with more supplies."

"You reassure Evie that your mother will be all right. I hate for her to have to revisit something like this. You tell her that if anybody can make things better for Randy Harkner, it's me. And tell her I'm okay. I'm not going to go crazy or anything."

Lloyd smiled sadly. "You're doing better than I thought you would. This is when you usually leave. You stay with her and be strong for her. You can't leave this time, thinking she's better off—and she can't see any fear or doubt in your eyes. She has to see the man—the *man*. Not the terrified, sorry little boy that shows in your eyes sometimes. She knows you like a book, Pa, and if she thinks for one minute you're blaming yourself for this or you're going into that dark place, she'll be devastated. When you're like that, she's the one who has to be strong, and right now she's *not* strong, so *you* have to be! Do you know what I'm saying?"

Jake smiled a little. "You getting ready to hit me again?"

"I will if I have to beat some sense into you. I know how you think sometimes, but you have to rise above that…for *her*. This is not your fault. It's not my fault. It's not *anyone's* fault. It just…*is*, and you can make it better. You're the *only* one who can bring her around."

Jake took one last drag on the cigarette, then threw it down and stepped it out. "Go home to Katie, Lloyd. Your mother and I will be fine."

Lloyd just stood there a minute. "You're sure?"

"I'm sure."

Lloyd's eyes teared. "You've lived one hell of a tough life, Jake Harkner. Not many men have been as beat up and dragged around their whole goddamn life like you have. Don't think I don't understand how sometimes it's hard as hell to climb out of all the shit and see the good. You think Mom is your rock, but you're the foundation of her strength. She needs you way more than you've ever realized. I've seen it in her eyes and heard it in her voice the times she thought she might lose you. And truth be known…" His voice broke on the words, and he turned away, heading for his horse. "I don't know what I'd do without you either." He mounted up. "You can be such a pain in the ass sometimes, Pa, but I'll be damned if I can ever stay mad at you." He turned his horse. "Tell Charlie he'll have to catch up. You take care of my mother. And you remember that the best revenge is to love her and take her back. They couldn't change that, Pa. Revenge can be sweet, and it doesn't always mean needing a gun."

Lloyd rode off, and Jake watched after him, wondering how in hell he'd produced such a wise and solid son. The last three days he'd so lovingly helped take care of Randy tore at his heart. *One thing is sure*, he thought. *When something does happen to me, Randy Harkner will be in damn good hands.*

He turned and looked at the cabin door. He was alone in this. Randy was in there, and she needed him like never before. He said a rare, quick prayer for the strength he would need. *Just put the right words in my mouth, Lord. I don't pray often, but I'm doing it now. Evie says you even listen to men like me, so I'm counting on that.*

He thought about the last time they were here, how happy they were, how sweet the lovemaking was, how they'd teased each other. *I don't just love you*, he'd told her. *I worship you. I adore you.* She'd loved hearing that. And he'd meant every damn word.

Forty-three

FOR FOUR DAYS, RANDY MOSTLY SLEPT...AND SLEPT.
Jake literally had to wake her up and make her eat and
drink something, but she was unnervingly quiet. She'd
turned to saying almost nothing, and when he pressed
her to talk, she'd turn away and curl into the blankets.
When she had to urinate, he picked her up and carried
her out to the privy, which to his relief he could tell
Charlie had scrubbed. It warmed his heart to think what
the men thought of Randy.

Most of the time, Randy's only words were "Don't let
go of me." So Jake slept with her, holding her close. He
dared to get up only when he was sure she was in a deep
sleep and wouldn't cry out for him. His inner struggle
made his chest hurt. Lloyd was gone, and there was no
one with whom to share this agony. Always before, this
was about himself or someone else, and he could always
turn to Randy for comfort and support.

This time it was about Randy, and there was no one
to lean on. In all his years of ruthless handling of men,
he'd never felt so helpless. It was up to him now to face
this worst hurt and devastation on his own. It was his
turn to be the emotionally strong one, and that was one
area in which he'd never felt strong.

He was alone with his thoughts, alone against the
blackness that tried to destroy his will. There was nothing
to do but stoke the fire, make more coffee, smoke, and,
once in a while, tend to Midnight. The only thing left to
pass the time was to read, and his very clever, conniving,

Christian daughter had made sure the only thing around for that was a Bible. Jake knew it was her way of loving him and trying to show him the only answer was to turn to God and the Good Book.

Reluctantly, he picked it up and thumbed through it, grinning at knowing Evie could be as mischievous and cunning as he could—or Lloyd—or Little Jake—but in a much different way. She was so much stronger than people gave her credit for, and it was this book that gave her that strength. He wondered if it could do the same for him. For years, he'd fought the goodness Evie swore existed in his soul. His father's railings about how worthless he was had never left him and probably never would, but it was nice to think others saw that little bit of worth in him—and no one believed in him more than Evie…and Randy. Now he didn't know what to do with the one woman with whom he'd been so intimate for so many years—this woman who now was shutting him out when she wasn't begging him not to let go of her.

What did that mean? *Don't let go of me.* He was beginning to think she meant more than not letting go of her physically. Maybe she meant that she didn't want him to let go of the Randy she was before all of this…the Randy who gave herself to him so willingly and freely and with such desire and pleasure…and with so much love.

Revenge is sweet, Lloyd had told him, *and it doesn't always mean needing a gun.*

Jake opened the Bible, not even sure why. Damned if Evie didn't get to him even when she wasn't around. The Bible practically fell open to the Book of Ruth. He felt completely inept at this and didn't want Randy to catch him reading it, but when he glanced at her, damned if she wasn't lying there, watching him. She held his gaze.

"Perhaps what I've been through is making me hallucinate," she told him, her voice weak. "I could swear my husband is reading the Bible."

Jake grinned, wondering if he dared think she was getting some of her spunk back.

"Well, all you do is sleep, and it's snowing out, so I'm getting restless and bored. I had to do *something*, and our very devious daughter made sure a Bible was the only book included in the supplies they brought up here. I'd gladly read Hawthorne or Dickens or one of those other fancy books you always talk about."

"Is that so? Why don't you tell me the *real* reason you're reading that book?"

He watched her closely. *God help me say the right things.* He shrugged. "Evie always says that when she has a problem or is feeling down, she prays about it and then picks this thing up and reads the first thing she turns to. It almost always helps her find the answer."

"You *prayed*?"

"Maybe."

Randy smiled a little. "There's no *maybe* to that question, Jake. You *did* pray."

"You think you know everything about me, but you don't know half of it."

"I guess that's one of the secrets you keep that we talked about."

"I guess so."

"And what's the first Bible passage you turned to?"

He struggled not to break down. He wanted to rush over and grab her close and beg her to come back to him in spirit. "Well, I'm not so sure it was a chance thing. I can tell Evie bent this back a little too much so it would fall open to this spot, the Book of Ruth. On top of that, she underlined something." Was she really studying him lovingly? What the hell was he supposed to do?

"Read it, Jake."

He sighed again and ran a hand through his hair. "It's, uh, right in the first chapter, verse sixteen."

Randy knew the verse and spoke it for him. "*And*

Ruth said, Intreat me not to leave thee, or to return from fol-
lowing after thee: for whither thou goest, I will go; and where
thou lodgest, I will lodge: thy people shall be my people, and
thy God my God. Where thou diest, will I die, and there will
be buried: the Lord do so to me, and more also, if ought but
death part thee and me."

Jake closed the Bible and set it aside. He just sat there, leaning forward, saying nothing.

"That's how I've always felt, Jake. All the times you tried to leave, I wanted to go with you. You've never understood that a hard life *with* you meant so much more to me than an easy one without you. I think Evie wanted you to read that because she knows that no matter what happens, we belong together. We have followed each other to hell and back, and here we are…just you and me. Some day when one of us dies, the other will die soon after, because we can't be without each other. And we'll be buried…right up here at this line shack…where we can see the J&L below us." Her voice broke, and she put a shaking hand to her mouth.

"Talk about it, Randy." Jake didn't make a move toward her. "All these years you've told me I shouldn't keep things inside—that I should talk about it. It took me years to finally open up about my father to you—years longer to open up about him to Lloyd and Evie—even longer to tell the grandkids. Don't let this fester and change you from the vibrant, joyful, gracious woman I've lived with for the last thirty years."

She jerked with sobs. "I just…want you to make it… go away."

He still didn't move, petrified he'd break the spell. "Tell me how. I don't want to do one thing you aren't ready for or one thing that will make you retreat back into that shell."

"But you're my Jake. You know how to…make it go away. You always make it beautiful." She pulled a blanket closer around her face. "You never asked me... in all our years together...to do anything...like that. You probably did that with those...other women...but—"

"Randy!" He spoke her name firmly. "There is a big difference between just feeling good and feeling...I don't know...satisfied in so many other ways. I'd *never* use you like that! In all these years, I've never used you just to feel good. It's always been so much more. Even that first time in that wagon, I felt crazy with the want of you—*all* of you—the whole woman. I knew how dangerous it was to feel like that for a woman I didn't deserve. If it was just to feel good, I could have left and done that at any brothel, but it was so much more than that. I didn't want it to be just a good time with a lonely widow woman. That's why I fought it. That's why I tried to make you hate me. I knew that if I gave in to those feelings, I'd be lost forever, and you'd learn what hell is like, and you were too good and sweet for that. Hell was *me*! And once I gave in to that weak moment, I knew the least I could do was always make it special and beautiful and that I would never do anything with you that you wouldn't like or anything that would make you feel used or disgraced or dishonored. Every time I touch you, it's because I honor you and need you and adore you and love you more than my own life."

She didn't answer right away. She just watched him, crying. "Jake, when you first rode away—back in Kansas—I cried and cried," she finally said. "I didn't want you to go. I was so scared, heading west alone. And then that awful...trading post...and that snakebite. And then...there you were!" She wiped at tears as she sat up, moving to the edge of the bed. "When I heard your voice...and I felt you lifting me up...I thought, *It's Jake. It's my Jake.* It didn't matter that we'd never... done anything yet. I wasn't even thinking about that. I just felt so...so incredibly safe. And that first time..."

She covered her face. "I just wanted to be a part of Jake Harkner. I wanted to share your soul, Jake. I wanted us to melt into each other and just be one. It's like you said. It meant so much more than just feeling good. You've always…made it so nice and so…beautiful…and they went and—"

She felt him lifting her, pulling her into his arms so her feet were off the floor. She wrapped her arms around his neck and cried. "Do you know…how much I love you for…never asking for more…than I could give?"

"All I've ever asked for is that you love me, *mi querida*. It's your love that makes me feel good—your love that pleases me."

"Take me back, Jake. I want it to be like it used to be," she sobbed. "You know how. My Jake knows how."

"You're all bruised up. I'll hurt you."

"You would never hurt me. You're always so gentle and kind and—"

"Hush, *mi amor*." He found a corner of her mouth and kissed it lightly.

She turned her face enough that his lips found hers fully.

He kissed her ever so lightly. "I don't want to hurt you," he repeated.

"I'm all right," she wept.

"I don't want you to be afraid."

"I'm with you. Why would I be afraid?"

He carried her to the bed and laid her on it, moving on top of her. He'd spent most of the day inside and wore only long johns with a shirt. He'd kept the fire stoked, and the room was warm and the light growing dim as the sun began to settle behind the mountains. He reached into his shirt pocket and pulled out a short stick of peppermint. "Will this help?"

"Oh, Jake!" She cried more, actually smiling through her tears. "Yes."

Jake put the peppermint into her mouth and came close to take the other end. He rested on his elbows, afraid to put his weight on her. He grasped her hair along with putting his hands on either side of her face, and they each bit off their share of the peppermint and chewed it, holding each other's gaze and smiling in spite of the fact that Randy also couldn't stop crying. Jake kissed her more deeply. "Look at me and tell me who you belong to, Randy."

Tears continued to pour from her eyes and sometimes into her ears. "You."

"Say my name."

"Jake."

"Who do you belong to?"

"Jake Harkner."

"Every beautiful inch of you, including this delicate face." He kissed her bruised cheeks, kissed her wet eyes, licked at her tears. "And including these beautiful lips." He traced a thumb over her lips then reached over to a nightstand and grabbed a clean handkerchief he'd left there, hoping there were enough left to continue soaking up all her tears. "Here. You're a mess of tears, and it's hard to kiss you this way."

Randy actually laughed lightly. She blew her nose and wiped at her eyes.

"I have something else for you," Jake told her. "Stay right here under me. I love having you under me." He reached over and opened the one drawer of the nightstand, taking out a sachet. He sniffed it deeply then held it to her nose.

"Jake! My rose petals!"

"A few weeks ago, I found out where you keep them. Before we left to find you, I told Evie to pack this. I thought it would help comfort you."

She closed her eyes and breathed deeply. "Oh yes, it *is* comforting!" She started crying again. "Oh, Jake, you thought of everything!"

"How well do I know you?"

"Better than I thought." She inhaled deeply again, then kissed the sachet. "You're a man of incredible contrasts, Jake Harkner. Who would ever think a man like you would think of something like this?"

"No one knows how much I love you." He kissed her eyes again. "I'm so sorry, Randy. The other night should never have happened. I'll never leave you unprotected again."

"It wasn't your fault." A hint of terror moved through her eyes, and she laid the sachet aside. "Jake, take back what they did. You know how."

He kissed her lips ever so lightly again.

"Make me yours, Jake. Take it all back." She jerked in a sob. "I can trust you," she whispered.

He kissed her again, licking her lips, running his tongue inside them, moving his tongue ever so carefully into her mouth as the kiss grew deeper. She returned the kiss almost desperately, as though taking his mouth into hers would take away the other...the ugly...the violent and the vile. He let her pull on his mouth in her attempt to let him "take it back," and he knew she meant he should take back her mouth, her lips, the violation. She belonged to Jake Harkner. Even her mouth belonged to Jake Harkner, and only he should touch it.

He lingered at her mouth, kissing, tasting, cleansing it with his tongue, taking back what belonged to Jake Harkner. She wore only a robe, and he pushed it aside... very gently...very cautiously...carefully caressing her breasts, her belly. Finally, he left her mouth and kissed at her bruises—her chin, her neck, her breasts.

Had they touched her here? He would take it back. Had fists landed into her ribs? Her small belly that bore scars from surgeries he feared she'd die from? He would take back her ribs, her belly. Her hip bones. Her thighs. Her legs. The bottoms of her feet. Her legs again. Her thighs again. That little crevice where leg met secret places. He kissed her there. He would take that back, too.

He felt no resistance. No horror. No tense withdrawal from his touch. He kissed her between her thighs then moved back to her breasts, her throat, her mouth.

She returned the kiss, crying at the same time. She hugged his neck. "Make love to me. I want to know it's my Jake making love to me in that nice way you have."

"Randy, you have to be sure," he said gently, kissing the bruises at her throat again. "I don't want to wake up bad memories."

"Not with you," she moaned. "It would never be that way with you."

"But you're so bruised and sore."

"Take me back, Jake."

It was the first time in his life he'd been afraid to make love to a woman, and she was his own wife. "Are you really sure?"

"You're my Jake. I'm really sure."

He tasted her mouth again, gently licking her. He moved a hand down to places that belonged only to him, gauging her reaction when he ran a finger inside of her, wanting to be sure she was ready for this. Slowly and carefully, he used only a little foreplay to be sure she was ready and that nothing would hurt. He watched her eyes as she met his gaze lovingly and with desire. She leaned up and grasped his face in her hands, kissing him almost wantonly. He kept up his touches until he felt the moistness that meant she really did want this. Suddenly, she started crying again. She reached down and grasped that part of him that she considered only hers. "Jake, if you want—"

"No. Never."

"You're a beautiful man. I would do anything—"

"No. You wouldn't, and you *won't*. It's all right, Randy."

"Maybe you need that to feel like you're the only one…"

"I don't need that." He kissed her desperately as he moved inside her, forcing himself to be gentle but wanting to ram hard, wanting to claim her fast and deep but afraid of hurting her. She was so small, so thin, so perfect, so wounded. How sweet of her to offer the one thing that would bring back her awful ordeal. He would not do that to her.

He fought his own weaknesses, wanting to weep himself, wanting to cling to her because he'd almost lost her, wanting to tell her he'd go crazy without her. But he had to stay strong. She *needed* him to be strong.

He buried himself deep, gently grasping her bottom. And there it was—not just the exquisite pleasure, but the sharing of souls, the joy of becoming one body in a way that nothing and no one could ever change. Her heart beat in his chest and his beat in hers. Thirty years. Thirty years, and it was just as good as ever, and he needed no more than this—to be inside this woman and spill his life into her—to claim every inch of her and feel her breath against his lips, feel her heart beating against his own—this little slip of a woman who'd hid his guns and dared him to beat out of her where they were.

She knew he wouldn't. She knew it.

"Tell me you love me," she whispered.

"*Yo te amo, mi querida.*"

"Don't let go of me."

"I'm right here. *Lo nuestro será eterno…esta tierra es eterna…tu y yo estaremos unidos eternamente.*"

Randy recognized the words "always" and "forever."

"Who do you belong to?" he asked again.

She closed her eyes, and Jake was surprised she was finally able to climax. "Jake Harkner," she gasped.

"You bet." Jake continued slow, rhythmic thrusts. "And I'm taking back every inch of you."

She cried out his name, again begging him never to let go of her. Jake couldn't help his own release, and after the tension of the last few days, he felt completely spent as he relaxed beside her. He kept her in his arms, and she nestled into his shoulder as he pulled the blankets over them.

"You won't ever take that job, will you?"

"I told you I wouldn't. Have I ever lied to you, or broken a promise?"

"No."

"I'm not doing one thing that means being away from you for days at a time, Randy. I already told you that."

"Did you kill some of those men?"

"Yes."

"But they were shooting back, right? They took me, and you had a right to go after them."

"That's right."

"Jake, I…I killed Brad Buckley, didn't I?"

He kissed her hair. "Yes. But you had every right. The state you were in, no one could ever blame you for that."

"I did it for you. I was scared the law would come and take you away."

"Randy, I would have had the right to kill him. You didn't need to do that."

"I was scared for you. Are you sure you aren't in trouble?"

"I'm not in trouble, and no one will know. Buckley had no family left, and I doubt anyone will ever miss the drifters with him. No one who was there will ever talk. The men buried their bodies, and I told them I never want to know where. They stayed behind to burn down that cabin, and that will be the end of it. As far as I'm concerned, it never happened." He kissed her gently, over and over. "I just want you to be able to live with this and be my Randy again."

"I will. God knows I had a right to kill that man, doesn't He? He won't blame me, will He?"

"I can't imagine that the loving God our daughter is always talking about would ever blame you for what you did. I'm the one who has to live with the guilt of it. You should have let *me* do it, Randy."

"I couldn't! I don't want to lose my Jake." She snuggled closer. "Tell me we'll come back here more often."

"As often as you want."

"This is our special place, Jake. I'll cry this time when we leave it, because of this beautiful memory, but I know we have to go home. I miss my little girls…and those wonderful boys who fought so hard to help me. They're such good boys, Jake. And they love you so much."

"They've reached an age where they need a lot of talking to."

"They'll be fine. They hang on your every word." Randy sighed deeply. "Don't let any of the men use this place, Jake."

"I won't."

"You can see half the ranch from up here. Our beautiful ranch where our beautiful sons and daughter and our beautiful grandchildren live—the descendants of the magnificent Jake Harkner."

Jake had to laugh lightly. "Please stop saying that."

She smiled through tears. "But you *are* magnificent." She kissed his chest. "Don't let go, Jake."

"I'm right here." He found the sachet under a pillow and gave it to her.

Randy squeezed it into her hand and held it to her nose again, loving him more than she'd ever loved him before for remembering the roses.

≈

Jake carefully eased away from his sleeping wife and pulled on a pair of denim pants. He took down a woolen jacket and put it on over his bare torso, buttoning it up and then grabbing a cigarette from a tin on the table. He glanced at Randy once more to make sure she was still asleep, then stepped into a pair of deerskin slippers and quietly walked outside, leaning against a porch post to light the cigarette. He shivered a little and slowly exhaled, watching the cigarette smoke drift lazily into the endless horizon. The J&L. Maybe at last the family would know true peace. Every last man who'd started all of this was dead now.

Lloyd had been right. He'd taken his revenge in the sweetest, most delicious, most gratifying way a man could enjoy revenge. All those who'd come against him had lost, and he still had his Randy...his beautiful, gentle Randy who loved him in spite of all he'd been, all he'd done, all the running, and all the times he'd tried to leave her.

The quiet almost hurt his ears, though he knew his hearing wasn't quite as good as it used to be. Too much gunfire over too many years had done that. He did hear an owl hoot, though, and something rustled in the nearby underbrush. He came instantly alert and reached for a gun that wasn't there. The guns that had brought him so much fame and so much heartache still hung inside the cabin.

A deer jumped out from the brush.

A deer.

Not an outlaw. Not a lawman. Not a drunk. Not an Indian. Not a cattle rustler. Not a prostitute. Not someone out to claim he'd killed Jake Harkner.

Just a deer.

"Jake? Get in here," Randy called. "You'll catch your death."

Jake grinned, tossing the cigarette into the snow and going back inside.

❧

Amazing grace, how sweet the sound
That saved a wretch like me.
I once was lost, but now I am found,
Was blind, but now I see.

Through many dangers, toils and snares
I have already come.
'Tis grace that brought me safe thus far,
And grace will lead me home...

From the Author

When I finished *Love's Sweet Revenge*, it was obvious to me that I had to write a fourth book about Jake and his family. Not only does the ending to the third book beg for one more sequel, but I am also having trouble leaving Jake and his family behind. I am thoroughly attached to these characters, as I hope you, the readers, are also. Throughout the first three books, Jake has managed to grow and change, but deep inside, he is so deeply scarred by his tortured childhood that a book involving some kind of closure for Jake seemed in order. His every emotion, every decision, every powerful reaction to certain events is based on memories of his brutal father. It's time for him to come face-to-face with those dark memories.

In addition, now that you have finished *Love's Sweet Revenge*, you can see that Randy will need some time to heal. In the fourth book, she will be deeply affected by what she survived, to the point where she becomes very clingy and hates being away from Jake for any length of time. This will present a problem when something vital forces Jake to leave for Mexico to face his childhood. This parting will be a big test of Jake and Randy's marriage, to the point of almost tearing them apart…

Can Randy overcome these challenges and grow strong again? Will Jake finally put his dark past behind him? Will an ever-changing West tear them apart, or will it bring them to an even more solid and everlasting love in their golden years?

Whatever comes for the Harkner family, you will not want to miss *The Last Outlaw*!

Rosanne Bittner

INTRODUCING THE MEN OF TEXAS LEGEND BY *NEW YORK TIMES* BESTSELLING AUTHOR LINDA BRODAY

to LOVE *a* TEXAS RANGER

Men of Legend, Book One, by

LINDA BRODAY

❧

Three brothers. One oath. No compromises. The Ranger

Gravely injured on the trail of a notorious criminal, Texas Ranger Sam Legend boards a train bound for his family ranch to recuperate—only to find himself locked in battle to save a desperate woman on the run. Determined to rescue the beautiful Sierra, Sam recruits an unlikely ally. But can he trust the mysterious gunslinger to fight at his side?

Sam is shocked to discover his new ally is not only an outlaw, but also his half brother. Torn between loyalty to his job and love of his family, Sam goes reeling straight into Sierra's arms. Yet just as the walls around his battered heart begin to crumble, Sierra is stolen away. Sam will risk anything to save her—his life, his badge, his very soul—knowing that some bonds are stronger than the law…and some legends were born to be told.

———— ❧ ————

One

Central Texas
Early Spring 1877

DEEP IN THE TEXAS HILL COUNTRY, WIND SIGHING through the draw whispered against his face, sharpening his senses to a fine edge. A warning skittered along his spine before it settled in his chest.

Texas Ranger Sam Legend had learned to listen to his gut. Right now it said the suffocating sense of danger that crowded him had killing in mind. He brought the spyglass up to his eye and focused on the rustlers below. All fifteen had covered their faces, leaving only their eyes showing.

Every crisp sound swept up the steep incline where he crouched in a stand of cedar to the right of an old gnarled oak. He'd hidden his horse a short distance away and prayed the animal stayed put.

"Hurry up with those beeves! We've gotta get the hell out of here. Rangers are so close I can smell 'em!" a rustler yelled.

Where were the other rangers? They hadn't been separated long and should've caught up by now.

Letting the outlaws escape took everything he had. But there were too many for one man, and this bunch was far more ruthless than most.

He peered closer as they tried to drive the bawling cattle up the draw. But the ornery bovines seemed to be smarter. They broke away from the group, scattering this way and that. Sam allowed a grin. These rustlers were definitely no cattlemen.

A lawman learned to adjust quickly. His mind whirled as he searched for some kind of plan. One shot fired in the air would alert the other rangers to his position if they were near. But would they arrive before the outlaws got to him?

Or…no one would fault Sam for sitting quietly until the lawless group cleared out.

Except Sam. A Legend never ran from a fight. It wasn't in his blood. He would ride straight through hell and come out the other side whenever a situation warranted. As a Texas Ranger, he'd made that ride many times over.

From his hiding place, he could start picking off the rustlers. With luck, Sam might get a handful before they surrounded him. Still, a few beat none. Maybe the rest would bolt. Slowly, he drew his Colt and prepared for the fight.

Though winter had just given way to spring, the hot sun bore down. Sweat trickled into his eyes, making them sting. He wiped away the sweat with an impatient hand.

"Make this count," he whispered. He had only one chance. It was all or nothing.

The first shot ripped into a man's shoulder. As the outlaw screamed, Sam quickly swung to the next target and caught the rider's thigh. A third shot grazed another's head.

Damn! The next man leaned from the saddle just as he'd squeezed the trigger.

Before he could discharge again, cold steel jabbed into his back, and a hand reached for his rifle and Colt. "Turn around real slow, mister."

The order grated along Sam's nerve endings and settled in his clenched stomach. He listened for any sounds to indicate his fellow rangers were nearby. If not, he was dead. He heard nothing except bawling steers and men yelling.

Sam slowly turned his head. Cold, dead eyes glared over the top of the rustler's bandana.

"Well, whaddya know. Got me a bona-fide ranger."

Though Sam couldn't see the outlaw's mouth, the words told him he wore a smile. "I'm not here alone. You won't get away with this."

"I call your bluff. No one's firing at us but you." The gun barrel poked harder into Sam's back. "Down the hill."

Sam could've managed without the shove. The soles of his worn boots provided no traction. Slipping and sliding down the steep embankment, he glanced for anything to suggest help had arrived, but saw nothing.

At the bottom, riders on horseback immediately surrounded him.

"Good job, Smith." The outlaw pushing to the front had to be the ringleader. He dressed all in black, from his hat to his boots. "Let's teach this Texas Ranger not to mess with us. I've got a special treat in mind. One of you, find his horse and get me a rope. Smith, march him back up the hill. The rest of you drive those damn cattle to the makeshift corral."

The spit dried in Sam's mouth as the man holding him bound his hands and pushed him up the steep incline, back toward the gnarled oak high on the ridge.

Any minute, the rangers would swoop in. Just a matter of time. Sam refused to believe that his life was going to end this way. Somehow, he had to stall until help arrived.

"Smith, do you know the punishment for killing a lawman?" Sam asked.

"Stop talkin' and get movin'."

"Are you willing to throw your life away for a man who doesn't give two cents about you?"

"You don't know nothin' about nothin', so shut up. One more word, an' I'll shoot you in the damn knee and drag you the rest of the way."

Sam lapsed into silence. He could see Smith had closed his mind against anything he said. If he ran, he'd be lucky to make two strides before hot lead slammed into him. Even if he made it to the cover of a cedar, what then? He had no gun. No horse.

His best chance was to spin around and take Smith's weapon.

But just as he started to make a move, the ringleader rode up beside on his horse and shouted, "Hurry up. Don't have all day."

Sharp disappointment flared, trapping Sam's breath in his chest. His fate lay at the mercy of these outlaws.

They grew closer and closer to the twisted, bent oak branches that resembled witch's fingers. Those limbs would reach for a man's soul and snatch it at the moment of death.

Thick bitter gall climbed into his throat, choking him. The devil would soon find Sam had lost his soul a long time ago.

The steep angle of the hill made his breathing harsh. The climb hurt as much as his looming fate. He'd always thought a bullet would get him one day, but to die swinging from a tree had never crossed his mind.

As they reached the top, an outlaw appeared with Sam's horse. The buckskin nickered softly, nuzzling Sam as though offering sympathy or maybe a last good-bye. He stroked the face of his faithful friend, murmuring a few quiet words of comfort. He'd raised Trooper from a foal and turned him into a lawman's mount. Would it be too much to pray these rustlers treated Trooper well? The horse deserved kindness.

"Enough," rasped the ringleader with an impatient motion of his .45. "Put him on the horse."

Sam noticed a crude drawing between the man's thumb and wrist—a black widow spider. Not that he could do anything with the information where he was going.

One last time, he scanned the landscape anxiously, hoping to glimpse riders, but saw only the branches of cedar, oak, and cottonwood trees swaying gently in the breeze. He strained against the ropes binding him, but they wouldn't budge.

Panic so thick he could taste it lodged in his throat as they jerked him into the saddle. His heart pounded against his ribs. He sat straight and tall, not allowing so much as an eye twitch. These outlaws who thrived on violence would never earn the right to see the turmoil and fear twisting behind his stone face.

Advice his father had once given him sounded in his ears: *When trouble comes, stand proud. You are a Legend. Inside you beats the heart of a survivor.*

Sam Legend stared into the distance, a muscle working in his jaw.

The ringleader threw the rope up and over one of the gnarled branches.

Bitter regret rose. Sam had never told his father he loved him. The times they'd butted heads seemed trivial now. So did the fights with big brother Houston over things that didn't make a hill of beans.

Yes, he was going to die with a heart full of regret, broken dreams, and empty promises.

The rope scratched, digging into his tender flesh as the outlaw settled the noose around Sam's neck.

"You better find a hole and climb into it, mister," Sam said. "Every ranger and lawman in the state of Texas will be after you."

A chuckle filled the air. "They won't find us."

"That wager's going to cost you." Sam steeled himself, wondering how long it took a man to die this way. He prayed it would be quick. He wondered if his mother would be waiting in heaven to soothe the pain.

"Say hello to the devil, Ranger."

With those words, he slapped the horse's flank. Trooper bolted, leaving Sam dangling in the air. The rope violently yanked his neck back and to the side as his body jerked.

Choking and fighting to breathe, Sam Legend counted his heartbeats until blackness claimed him. As he whirled away into nothingness, only one thing filled his mind—the vivid tattoo of a black widow spider on his killer's hand.

Two

A MONTH AFTER TEXAS RANGER SAM LEGEND ALMOST died, an ear-splitting crash of thunder rattled the windows and each unpainted board of the J. R. Simmons Mercantile. The ominous skies burst open, and rain pelted the ground in great sheets. A handful of people scattered like buckshot along the Waco boardwalk in an effort to escape the thorough drenching of a spring gully washer.

Sam paid the rain no mind. The storm barely registered—few things did, these days. The feeling of the rope around his neck was still overpowering. He reached to see if it was there, thankful not to find it.

The nightmare had him in its grip, refusing to let go. More dead than alive, he moved toward his destination. When he reached the alley separating the two sections of boardwalk, he collided with a woman covered in a hooded cloak.

"Apologies, ma'am." He glanced down by rote, then blinked. All at once, the world and its color came rushing back as Sam stared into blue eyes so vivid they stole his breath.

A pocket of fog drifted between them. Was she just a dream? He could barely see her.

She nodded and gave him a smile for only a brief second. He reached out to touch her, to see if she was real, but only cold damp air met his fingertips.

The man beside her took her arm and jerked her into the alleyway.

"Hey there!" Sam called, startled. He'd been so focused on those blue eyes he hadn't realized anyone else was there. "Ma'am, do you need help?"

He received no answer. Through the dense fog, he watched her companion force her toward a horse at the other end of the alley where a group of mounted riders waited. The hair on the back of his neck rose.

Intent on stopping whatever was happening, Sam lengthened his strides. Before he could reach them, the man threw her onto a horse, then swung up behind her. Within seconds, they disappeared, ghostly riders in the mist.

Sam stood in the driving rain, staring at the empty alley. It had all happened so fast he could hardly believe it.

Hell, maybe he'd imagined the whole thing. Maybe she'd never existed. Maybe the heavy downpour and gray gloom had messed with his mind…again. Ever since the hanging, he'd been seeing things that weren't there. Twice now he'd yanked men around and grabbed for their hands, thinking he saw a black widow spider between their thumbs and forefingers. The last time almost got Sam shot. Folks claimed he was missing the top rung of his ladder and now, his captain was sending him home to find it.

Crippled. The word clanked around in his head, refusing to settle. But even though he had full use of his legs, that's what he was at present. The cold fear washing over him had nothing to do with the air temperature or rain. What if he never recovered? Some never did.

His hand clenched. He'd fight like hell to be the whole man he once was. He had things to do—an outlaw to hunt down, a wrong to right—a promise to keep.

Sam squared his jaw and drew his coat tight against the wet chill, forcing himself to move on down the street toward the face-to-face with Captain O'Reilly. Again. It stuck in his craw that they thought him too crazed to do his job. The captain thought him a liability, a danger to the other rangers. Wanted him to take a break.

His heart couldn't hurt any worse than if someone had stomped on it with a pair of hobnail boots. Maybe the captain was right. If he'd imagined that woman just now—and he really couldn't be certain he hadn't—then maybe he *needed* the break. Sam Legend, who had brought in notorious killers, bank robbers, prison escapees, and the like, had become a liability.

But one thing he knew he hadn't imagined, and that was the blurred figure of Luke Weston standing over him when he'd regained consciousness that fateful day. There had been no mistaking those pale green eyes above the mask. They belonged to the outlaw he'd chased for over a year—he'd have staked his life on it.

When his fellow rangers had ridden up, Weston disappeared into the brush, leaving Sam with questions. Had Weston cut him down from the tree? Was he with the rustlers? And why had the outlaws left Trooper behind? Awful considerate of them.

So what the hell had happened, dammit?

Rangers who'd ridden up told Sam they'd seen no one. He'd laid on the ground with the rope loosened around his neck, drifting in and out of consciousness.

Those questions and others haunted him, and he wouldn't rest until he got answers. Somehow he knew Weston was the key.

At ranger headquarters, he took a deep breath before opening the door. He pushed a mite too hard, banging the knob against the wall. Captain O'Reilly jerked up from his desk. "What the hell, Legend? Trying to wake the dead?"

"Sorry, Cap'n. It got away from me." It seemed a good many things had, recently.

The tall, slender captain waved him to a chair. "I haven't heard this much racket since the shoot-out inside that silo with the Arnie brothers down in Sweetwater."

Sam removed his drenched hat, lowered into the chair, and stretched his long legs out in front of him. "I hope I can talk you out of your decision."

O'Reilly sauntered to the potbellied stove in the corner and lifted the coffeepot. "What's it been? A month?"

"An eternity," Sam said quietly.

"Want a snort of coffee? Might improve your outlook."

"I'll take you up on your offer but doubt it'll improve anything. I need this job, sir. I need to work." Revenge burned hot. He'd not rest until he found the men who'd hung him, and when he did, they'd pay with their blood.

"What you *need* is some time off to get your head on straight. I can't have you seeing things that aren't there." O'Reilly sighed. "You're gonna get yourself or someone else killed. I'm ordering you to go home. Rest up, then come back ready to catch outlaws."

"Finding the rustlers and catching Luke Weston is my first priority."

"That wily outlaw has been taunting you for the last year." O'Reilly's eyes hardened as he handed Sam a tin cup. "It seems personal."

"Hell yeah, it's personal!"

Weston had been there. That much he knew for damn certain. The outlaw could have strung him up himself. Why else would Sam remember those green eyes, so pale they appeared silver?

In addition to that, and though it sounded rather trivial when compared to a hanging, Weston had taken Sam's pocket watch during a stagecoach holdup a year ago. Sam tried to protect a payroll shipment, but Weston did the oddest thing. The outlaw took exactly fifty dollars, a paltry sum compared to what remained in the strongbox, and left the passengers' belongings untouched. He did, however, seem to take particular delight in pocketing Sam's prized timepiece. The way the wily outlaw singled Sam out was downright eerie. Weston knew exactly where to find the treasured keepsake. No rifling his pockets. No fumbling. No uncertainty. Memories of how Weston had flipped it open and stared intently at the inscription for almost a full minute before tucking it away drifted through Sam's mind.

"Makes me mad enough to chew nails." The thought filled Sam's head with so many cuss words he feared it would burst open.

The captain leaned back in his chair and propped his boots on the scarred desk that Noah must've brought over on the ark. To make up for a missing leg, someone had cut a crutch and stuck it under there. "Sometimes we all get cases that sink their teeth into us and won't let go."

"I just about had him the last time." And now the captain was forcing him to take time off. Sam would lose every bit of ground he'd gained.

Luke Weston had led him on a chase this past year from one end of Texas to the other. To this day, other than a vague outline of his figure, Sam had yet to glimpse anything solid except a pair of cold, pale green eyes glaring over the top of a bandana. Eyes that only held contempt and anger. Except for this last time, when they'd seemed to hold concern. But maybe he'd imagined that.

Damn! He really didn't know what was real and what wasn't anymore.

Maybe the captain was right.

Reaching for a poster that lay atop a pile on his desk, Captain O'Reilly passed it to Sam. "Got this yesterday." Bold lettering at the top of the page screamed: *WANTED! $1,000 reward for capture and conviction of notorious outlaw Luke Weston. Sought for robbery and murder. Armed and considered extremely dangerous.*

The murder charge was new since the last poster Sam had seen. The reward had been only two hundred dollars then. He stared at the thick paper and narrowed his eyes, wondering whose fate had intersected with Luke Weston's.

"Who did he kill?"

O'Reilly's face darkened. "Federal judge. Edgar Percival."

"Stands to reason Weston would turn to outright murder eventually. Seems every month he's involved in a gunfight with someone, though folks say they were all men who needed killing."

And yet the new charge did shock Sam. He'd come to know Weston pretty well. A period of four months separated all of the outlaw's robberies, with only fifty dollars taken each time. And in every single instance, Weston had never shot anyone. Maybe he robbed out of boredom…or to taunt Sam.

"A bad seed." The ranger captain's chair squeaked when he leaned forward. "Some men are born killers."

This poster, as with all the others, didn't bear a likeness, not even a crude drawing. There were no physical features to go on. Frustration boiled. The lawman in him itched to be out there tracking Weston. The need to bring him to justice rose so strong that it choked Sam. Weston was *his* outlaw to catch, and instead, he'd been ordered home.

Hell! Spending one week on the huge Lone Star Ranch was barely tolerable. A month would either kill him, or he'd kill big brother Houston. The thought had no more than formed before guilt pricked his conscience. In the final moments before the outlaw had hit his horse and left Sam dangling by his neck, regrets had filled his thoughts. He'd begged God for a second chance so he could make things right.

Now, it looked like he'd get it. He'd make the time count. He'd mend bridges with his father, the tough Stoker Legend.

Family was there in good times and bad.

Despite his better qualities, Stoker had caused problems for him. Sam had driven himself to work harder, be quicker and tougher, to prove to everyone his father hadn't bought his job. Overcoming the big ranch, the money, and the power the Legend name evoked had been a continuing struggle.

Captain O'Reilly opened his desk drawer, uncorked a bottle of whiskey, and gave his coffee a generous dousing. "Want to doctor your coffee, Sam?"

"Don't think it'll help," he replied with a tight smile.

"Suit yourself." The hardened ranger put the bottle away. The white scar on his cheek had never faded, left from a skirmish with the Comanche.

Sam studied that scar, thinking. Although Sam had intended to keep quiet about the woman he may or may not have bumped into on the way over, out of fear of being labeled a lunatic for sure, he felt a duty to say something. He wouldn't voice doubts that he'd imagined it. "Cap'n, I saw something that keeps nagging. I collided with a young woman a few minutes ago. All I said was sorry, but a man grabbed her arm and shoved her into the alley between the mercantile and telegraph office. I saw fear in her eyes. When I followed, they got on a waiting horse and rode off. Can you send someone to check it out?"

Sam winced at how quickly doubts filled O'Reilly's eyes. The captain was wondering if this was one more example of Sam breaking with reality. Hell! If he'd conjured this up, he'd commit himself into one of those places where they locked up crazy people.

O'Reilly twirled his empty cup. "After the bank robbery a few weeks ago, we don't need more trouble. I'll look into it."

"Thanks. I hope it was nothing, but you never know." Relieved, Sam took a sip of coffee, wishing it would warm the cold deep in his bones.

"When's the train due to arrive, Legend?"

"Within the hour." Sam would obey his orders, but the second his forced sabbatical was over, he'd hit the ground running. He'd dog Luke Weston's trail until there wasn't a safe place in all of Texas to even get a slug of whiskey. He'd heard the gunslinging outlaw spent time down around Galveston and San Antone. That, Sam reckoned, would be a good starting point.

O'Reilly removed his boots from the desk and sat up. "I seem to recall your family ranch being northwest of here on the Red River."

"That's right."

"Ever hear of Lost Point?"

Sam nodded. "The town is west of us. Pretty lawless place, by all accounts."

"It's become a no-man's-land. Outlaws moved in, lock, stock, and barrel. Nothing north of it but Indian Territory. Jonathan Doan is requesting a ranger to the area. Seems he's struggling to get a trading post going on the Red River just west of Lost Point, and outlaws are threatening."

"I'll take a ride over there while I'm home. Weston would fit right in."

"No hurry. Give yourself time to relax. Go fishing. Reacquaint yourself with the family, for God's sake. They haven't seen you in a coon's age."

"Sure thing, Cap'n." The clock on the town square chimed the half hour, reminding him he'd best get moving. Relieved that O'Reilly had softened and allowed him to still work a little, Sam set down his cup. "Appears I've got a train to catch."

O'Reilly shook his hand. "Get well, Sam. You're a good lawman. Come back stronger than ever."

"I will, sir."

At the livery, Sam hired a boy to fetch his bags from the hotel and take them to the station. After settling with the owner and collecting his buckskin gelding, Sam rode to meet the train. He shivered in the cold, steady downpour. The gloomy day reflected his mood as he moved toward an uncertain future. He was on his way home.

To bind up his wounds. To heal. To become the ranger he needed to be.

And he would—come hell or high water, mad as a March hare or not.

Right on time, amid plumes of hissing white steam, the Houston and Texas Central Railway train pulled up next to the loading platform.

Sam quickly loaded Trooper into the livestock car and paid the boy for bringing his bags. After making sure the kerchief around his neck hid his scar, he swung aboard. He had his pick of seats since the passengers had just started to file one. He chose one two strides from the door.

Shrugging from his coat, he sat down and got comfortable.

A movement across the narrow aisle a few minutes later drew his attention, as a tall passenger wearing a low-slung gun belt slid into the seat. Sam studied the black leather vest and frock coat. Gunslinger, bounty hunter, or maybe a gambler? Bounty hunter seemed far-fetched—he'd never seen one dressed in anything as fine. Such men wasted no time with fancy clothing. A gunslinger, then. Few others tied their holster down to their leg. No one else required speed when drawing. Likely a gambler too. Usually the two went hand in hand.

His coloring spoke of Mexican descent. Lines around the traveler's mouth and a gray hair or two in his dark hair put him somewhere around the near side of thirty. Though he wore his black Stetson low on his forehead, he tugged it even lower as he settled back against the cushion.

The fine hairs on Sam's arm twitched. He knew this

man. But from where? For the life of him, he couldn't recall. He leaned over. "Pardon me, but have we met?"

Without meeting Sam's gaze, the man allowed a tight smile. "Nope."

Darn the hat that bathed his eyes in dusky shadows. "I'm Sam Legend. Name's not familiar?"

"Nope."

He'd been so certain the man looked familiar. "Guess I made a mistake." Maybe his madness had taken over again. Odd that the man hadn't introduced himself, though.

"Appears so, Ranger."

How did he know Sam was a ranger? He wore no badge. "My apologies," Sam mumbled.

The train engineer blew the whistle and the mighty iron wheels began to slowly turn.

Sam swung his attention back to the gunslinger. A few more words, and he'd be able to place him, surely. "Would you have the time, Mr. . . . ?" Sam asked.

"Andrew. Andrew Evan." The man flipped open his timepiece. "It's ten forty-five."

"Obliged." Finally, a name. Not that it proved helpful. Sam was sure he'd left his real one at the Texas border, as men with something to hide tended to do. By working extra hard trying to make himself invisible, Evan had as much as declared that he had things to conceal.

Worse, the longer Sam sat near Andrew, the stronger the feeling of familiarity grew. And that was something Sam's brain had not conjured up. He glanced out the window at the passing scenery, trying to make sense of the thoughts clunking around in his head. When he next looked over at Andrew Evan, Sam wasn't surprised to find the slouching gunslinger's head against the seat with his hat tilted over his eyes.

The hair on his neck rose. Sam felt Andrew's eyes watching from beneath the brim of the Stetson. Then he saw a muscle twitch in Andrew's jaw and watched his Adam's apple slide slowly up and down.

Tension electrified the air.

As Sam stared at Evan's hands, searching for the tattoo, a woman rushed down the aisle. She came even with them just as the train took a curve and tumbled headlong into his lap. He found himself holding soft, warm curves encased in dark wool.

Stark fear darkened the blue eyes staring up at him, and her bottom lip quivered.

A jolt went through him. Lucinda? But no—it couldn't be her. Yet this girl had Lucinda Howard's black hair and blue eyes framed by thick sooty lashes.

His body responded against his will as he struggled with the memory. Hell! At last, he realized this girl was not the faithless lover he'd once known.

But she *was* the woman he'd collided with on his way to Ranger headquarters.

"Are you all right, miss?"

"I—I'm so sorry," she murmured.

He felt her icy hand splayed against his chest through the fabric of his shirt, where it had landed when she tried to break her fall.

"Are you in trouble? I can help."

"They're—I've got to—" The mystery woman pushed away, extricating herself from his lap. With a strangled sob, she ran toward the door leading into the next car.

Sam looked down. Prickles rose on the back of his neck.

A bloody handprint stained his shirt.

Acknowledgments

Many thanks to the most talented editor on the face of the earth, Mary Altman at Sourcebooks. Her comments and advice have taken my writing up several notches, and all the great reader feedback I have received for my Outlaw books proves that. If you think this book was a wonderful read, you can thank Mary, who had so much to do with making it the best it could be.

And again, a big thank-you to author/reviewer/critique expert Dana Alma for her help with the Spanish used in this book and in *Do Not Forsake Me*.

And I can't leave out my agent, Maura Kye-Casella, who got me back on the bookshelves after a long "hunger spell." Having an agent who understands your writing and believes in it is a wonderful gift.

Some of my depictions of ranch life come from a novel called *Winter Grass*, by Richard S. Wheeler. It's a wonderful, realistic story about real ranch life and the problems that came to old-time ranchers who were hit with new laws and regulations that changed ranching in many ways, and in my opinion—not always for the better.

And thank you, Jon Paul, the most fabulous cover designer to ever strike a paintbrush to a canvas and find the most perfect models to portray historical characters. The Outlaw covers are the most beautiful covers I have ever enjoyed on any of my books. I wish all my covers could be by Jon Paul. Check out his hundreds of other breathless covers online at JonPaul.com.

Thank you to my husband, Larry, for putting up with hours and hours of "alone" time when I am buried in these big sagas that take so much time and take so much out of both of us. We've been married fifty years, and he never once stopped believing in me.

Most of all, thank you to my faithful readers who have followed Jake and Randy from when they were young and in love and standing alone against the world—those readers who read *Outlaw Hearts* back in 1993 when it was first published, those readers who remembered Jake so well and fell in love with him back then and were thrilled to find out I was able to continue his story in *Do Not Forsake Me* and *Love's Sweet Revenge*. This man came so alive for me that I fell madly in love with him. My husband understands that happens sometimes. Finishing this third book was very hard for me, because by the time you have covered thirty years with the same characters, you become very attached, and when a book is done, you feel like you're saying good-bye to dear friends.

I intended that these books end as a trilogy, but I feel there is more to tell about the Harkners, and I'm not quite ready to leave them. I have a fourth book planned called *The Last Outlaw*, so be prepared for one more book that will take you right back into the lives of Jake and Randy Harkner and their growing family... and grandsons who will eventually move into their own stories as (I hope) I can continue the Harkner saga in future books. After all, I want to know what happens to "Little Jake" when he's not so little anymore. I have a feeling my readers will want to know, too. After all, he and his brothers and cousins will inherit the J&L...and, in spirit, Little Jake is a replica of his grandfather. We all know what that means.

About the Author

Award-winning novelist Rosanne Bittner is highly acclaimed for her thrilling love stories and historical authenticity. Her epic romances span the West—from Canada to Mexico, Missouri to California—and are often based on personal visits to each setting. She lives in Michigan with her husband, Larry, and near her two sons, Brock and Brian, and three grandsons, Brennan, Connor, and Blake. You can learn much more about Rosanne and her books through her website at www.rosannebittner.com and her blog at www.rosannebittner.blogspot.com. Be sure to visit Rosanne on Facebook and Twitter!

Last Chance Cowboys: The Lawman

Where the Trail Ends

by Anna Schmidt

— ❧ —

But can she trust him not to break her heart?

Jess Porterfield fled to the big city after his father's sudden death, leaving behind his family ranch—and his childhood sweetheart. Now Jess has returned as the local lawman, determined to prove his worth...and win back the one woman he could never live without.

Young frontier doctor Addie Wilcox was devastated when Jess left her behind. Now he's back and it's difficult to remember why she should keep her distance. But with the town's richest man set to see her hang for a crime she didn't commit, Addie must put her faith in the lawman who broke her heart—and trust that together they'll find their second chance at love.

— ❧ —

Praise for *Last Chance Cowboys: The Drifter*:

"A feisty heroine and a hero eager to make everything right. What more could a reader want?"
—Leigh Greenwood, *USA Today* bestselling author of *To Love and to Cherish*

"Readers wanting a good old-fashioned Western romance need look no further than this one." —*Dear Author*

For more Anna Schmidt, visit:

www.sourcebooks.com

No One but You

by Leigh Greenwood

USA Today bestselling author

———————— ✥ ————————

First Comes Marriage...

Alone in the world and struggling to make ends meet, Texas war widow Sarah Winborne will do anything to keep her two small children safe and her hard-won ranch from going under. She hasn't fought for so long to lose everything... and if that means marrying a stranger to protect her family's future, then so be it.

She never expected anything but a business arrangement, but there's something about Benton Wheeler's broad shoulders and kind eyes. He makes her feel beautiful. He makes her feel desired. And even though their marriage was never intended to be more than a matter of convenience, as Benton stands between her small family and the wild and dangerous West, Sarah may just realize that the cowboy she married is the love she never dreamed she would find...

———————— ✥ ————————

Praise for Leigh Greenwood:

"An emotional, rich, adventurous romance."
—*RT Book Reviews* for *Forever and Always*

"You can't beat a historical Texas romance by Leigh Greenwood. He writes of Texas like no other author."
—*The Good, The Bad, and The Unread* for *Texas Pride*

For more Leigh Greenwood, visit:

www.sourcebooks.com